Rob lives in Northamptonshire, England and is very nearly 30. He's worked in retail ever since leaving school and is still a salesman for a particular electrical store.

He has been writing for the majority of his life with his debut novel "The Black Flame" having been in production for several years, being published in 2007 by Libros International.

More information on Rob can be found at..

www.robmackellar.com

The right of Rob Mackellar to be identified as the Author of this Work has been asserted by him in accordance with the Copyright, Designs and Patents Act 1998.

Copyright © Rob Mackellar 2007

All characters in this publication are fictitious and resemblance to real persons, living or dead, is purely coincidental.

All rights reserved. No part of this publication may be reproduced, stored in a retrieval system, or transmitted, in any form or by any means without the prior written permission of the publisher, nor be otherwise circulated in any form of binding or cover other than that in which it is published and without a similar condition being imposed on the subsequent purchaser. Any person who does so may be liable to criminal prosecution and civil claims for damages.

ISBN 1-905988-05-2 978-1-905988-05-1

Published by Libros International

www.librosinternational.com

Acknowledgements

This story is a journey. As with many journeys it wasn't made alone. I really want to thank…

…Kate Dawidziak for the right amount of prodding and joking. Without you this may never have reached the point it's at now. Bekah Baker for the unconditional support over the years, Will "Lard Teamaker" Mackellar, Mum and Dad for never once telling me I was wasting my time, Ben Smalley, Tim Haines, Katherine Branton, James Barclay for all the advice and inspiration over the last year or so, Lizzy Hill and all the forumites (both my own and those on the Barclay forum) for preserving my sanity when it needed it, Marianne and Allan for the prodding that led me to focus again, Robin Carter for being a tremendous agent and giving me the big push, Sue Clocherty and Ken Douglas at Libros International, thank you both for having faith in the story, Mark, Derek, Erik and Darron for the extra inspiration here and there, and Jess Hill for being an excited reader in waiting.

I sincerely thank you all for the support, advice, inspiration and love I've been blessed with from you.

To my parents, my family and my friends

Thank you for believing

38/50

The Black Flame

Rob Mackellar

[signature]

"QWAN DO WE REALLY
WAKE TO DWNOY A
FALLEN GOD?"

Libros International

Chapter One

Thin shards of bright sunlight cut in between the slats in the heavy, wooden shutters, providing the only light in an otherwise dim room. The air inside the room crackled and vibrated with power. Shadows danced on the walls even though this was impossible since the only light source was the fixed sunlight. They flitted in and out of the dark, fading out one moment only to appear nearby a heartbeat later. The granite walls themselves were bare but for a small collection of yellowed maps, drawn in a quick, sketching style, and an oval mirror. A large, red armchair sat in one corner. The only other furniture in the study was a small desk set into the wall and a tall bookcase, filled to overflowing with tomes. More books were stacked on the table and at various points on the polished oak floor.

Hedrial sat cross-legged, his eyes closed and his head sagging forward slightly as if he were asleep. The only indication that he was not were the quick movements of the fingers on his left hand. A large, yellowing map was unrolled on the floor in front of him, its corners anchored to the floorboards by small rocks. On the opposite side sat a large round compass, arranged so Hedrial was facing north to correspond with the map.

The air began moving, shifting as if a breeze had found its way in. The shadows seemed to whisper, chanting in almost unheard singsong voices. Hedrial's lips moved slightly as he spoke under his breath. Palm facing down, he passed his right hand in an arc over the map. Faint sparks of green energy fell onto it, sinking into the yellowed parchment. For a moment or two the chanting shadows stopped, waiting patiently as Hedrial's hand came back to the floor by his side. His left hand stopped its strange twitching movements and grasped an ornate dagger tightly. His knuckles whitened as he clutched the weapon in his fist. Raising the hand level with his face, he extended his arm fully and passed the blade over the map.

The speckles of green ingrained in it sparkled furiously as his hand passed above them. Again the shadows whispered, growing louder and more urgent. Lines of jade green light formed in the markings of the map, tracing the outlines of mountains and rivers. Seas and oceans were drawn in, followed by the borders between continents and countries. The light cast eerie shadows across Hedrial's face, giving his ageing features a grim appearance. Sparks crackled off his short, grey hair and beard. A beam of green light, a mere pin width, sprang up from the map, connecting to the dagger's blade. The map tried to rise up, as if there was some unseen magnetic force. The air in the room grew suddenly still. The shadows stopped their chattering and faded away to blend in with the darkness again.

Hedrial snapped his eyes open and looked down at the map. For a moment or two the dark blue orbs just held onto the beam, unfocused. Gradually he came round from his trance and recognition filled his eyes. The pinpoint of light held firm to a small area of the map. Committing the location to his memory, Hedrial turned his hand away, breaking the beam. Instantly, the air lost its suffocating feel and returned to normal. Hedrial let out a long sighing breath. He unclenched his grip with a painful expression on his face. The dagger's hilt had left its imprint in his flesh. Placing it down onto the floorboards beside him, he rubbed the painful callouses in his palm. With a piece of chalk, he drew a circle around the noted area of the map.

He winced, trying to ignore the cracking in his knees as he pushed himself up to his feet. As if just getting up from the floor had taken a lot of energy, Hedrial moved over to the window and pushed the heavy, wooden shutters open, allowing the brilliant sunlight to flood into his study. After breathing in a deep lungful of air, he moved across to the armchair. He stared at the map, allowing various thoughts to run their course in his head. The dull ache in his knees seemed to want to battle for domination with the pain in his hand from clutching the dagger. He let out a weary sigh and melted back into the chair. His gaze went to his desk on the other side of the room. The books he wanted to look at were currently sitting in daunting looking piles. He pinched the bridge of his nose, willing the dull ache in his body to fade into memory and sighed, "The sooner I start."

Gripping the soft arms of the chair with a pair of wrinkled hands, he pulled himself up onto his feet again. Picking his way around the map and compass, he first made his way to the window. Gazing out on the scene before him he gave a wry smile. Turning away from the village outside, he was faced again with the books. The first was a large, faded brown tome, sitting on the table. The title, 'Myths, Fables and Legends', was painted in now fading gold on the cover. Carrying it back to his soft armchair, he opened it, seemingly at random. In truth though, Hedrial had looked at the same page so many times in recent months that the book could now fall open at the desired place. Sinking back into the comforting depths of his chair, he scanned the words. He had gone through the passage so many times most of it was fixed firmly in his memory. He screwed up his tired eyes. After a moment or two, his head slumped against the thickly padded chair back. Still holding the book open in front of him, his arms sank forward, letting it come to rest on his knees. The weight of it on his legs made him open his eyes again. A weary sigh tumbled from his lips as Hedrial realised he had allowed himself to fall asleep again. "Of course you are," he muttered to himself reproachfully, "you've been at this search for too long now without any rest."

A barely audible snort was the reply to his words. It was followed by, "Especially at your age."

Hedrial turned his head a little. It was Dionis who had just called him old. He knew exactly what he was getting at, but Hedrial asked anyway, "And what is that supposed to mean?"

Dionis shrugged, a gesture made more impressive by the fact it partially showed off his black leathery wings. The wizard's familiar, a giant bat, swivelled his head round. Then it focused a pair of large brown eyes that blinked uneasily in the presence of the sunlight on Hedrial.

"Sometimes being able to see is a pain, you know."

"I'm sure it's an ability we can take away if it really bothers you that much," Hedrial replied dryly.

"I didn't say I wanted to be as blind as a… well, you know," Dionis answered, "I just wish every now and then you'd let me sleep till a normal nocturnal hour like normal bats, instead of going around opening windows."

Hedrial sighed again, louder this time. "Is there a point to this discussion or are you going to simply explain what you meant?"

"I just meant," he replied, knowing full well that he was probably the only one in the entire world who could get away with talking to the wizard like this, "that neither of us are as young as we were. Time has moved on and you're still here in this search."

Hedrial nodded sadly. His gaze wandered around the room, coming to rest almost magnetically on the window. As the sight of hazy, cloud covered mountains came into his view, his eyes opened wide. All the sadness brought about by Dionis's words evaporated faster than a raindrop over a volcano.

"Except," he muttered, his voice thoughtfully quiet, "I've found it."

"What?" Dionis replied.

The wizard looked at his familiar and, allowing his voice to return to its former deep tone of authority, he said, "I've found him. He really does exist."

The bat almost fell from his perch in shock. After his compelling need for silence had passed, he carefully asked, "Are you sure?"

A thoughtful pause answered the bat's words. Hedrial was staring at the map on the floor, a knuckle pressed against his lips. The fingers of his other hand were flicking absently at the pages of the book still in his lap. He nodded, slowly at first as if he was still checking all the facts in his mind. "The translation has been done badly. It's all very basic."

"But then you've been looking through a book that was created for children," Dionis interrupted.

Hedrial cast a weary glance over at his companion. "Sometimes I regret your being able to talk. You know very well what I mean. Here, listen," he said.

Even though Dionis had heard the various passages read aloud to him so many times he felt he could recite them backwards, he listened patiently as Hedrial read aloud.

The Immortal Ones would send their Chosen One out into the Dark World. But the fallen One would be prepared. He would create a prison for his immortal enemy. He would send out many dark minions and the Warrior would be captured and taken to this place. And this place, once revered even by the Immortal Ones, would become his prison. The greatest Warrior of all would be bound in iron and held there. His guard would be the fearsome Beast itself, keeping even the mightiest of mortals away. The Immortal Ones would be powerless to intervene. For upon reaching this place They would become as weak as mere mortals. Their power would not aid them for the black-hearted Dark Lord of terror would have woven his lifelong spell. But One shall rise above the others. One and only One shall free him. And then He will follow the Warrior to fulfil his destiny and face the Dark Lord.'

"Yes," Dionis replied, "very badly done. I agree."

"I sometimes wonder if you're not missing the point on purpose, Dionis," Hedrial answered. It was not meant as an insult, just an observation. "The original version of this text was written supposedly before the events themselves happened."

"Or were supposed to have happened." Dionis's scepticism remained solid.

"Oh no," Hedrial shook his head defiantly, keen not to have his words doubted, "they happened. Maybe not exactly as these stories tell us they did. But they did happen. The point I'm making is that the original text was written by a prophet."

A flicker of realisation flashed through the bat's mind, reflected in his large eyes. "And everybody knows," Dionis said, "the prophets were at best a cryptic bunch of madmen."

"But were they mad if their visions really came true?" Hedrial asked.

Dionis stared blankly at his companion, "Fair enough, I take your point."

"I checked that passage against the ones in the histories and against a few of the other prophecies and their relevant stories. The prophet responsible referred to the Gods as the Immortal Ones. The fearsome Beast is a name they gave to a dragon." Hedrial said with a growing pride in the results of his extensive work. He looked blankly across the room at Dionis as a slight sound reached his ears. "Dionis, it has taken me a long and very annoying search to learn this. The least you could do is pretend to stay awake."

"Sorry, but it's like the middle of the night for me, remember," Dionis replied. "And I expect you'll want the usual patrols done tonight."

The wizard paused again, "Oh yes. Of course, patrols as usual. We need to be extra vigilant now."

"You still think they know then?" Dionis replied.

Hedrial nodded. "Despite all my efforts to keep the knowledge hidden, they know something."

"It might not be you they know about though. Maybe there's something else. Something we don't know perhaps. Could be the dagger?"

"No. That would be too much of a coincidence." Hedrial went silent again, thinking the possibility over.

"So we...?" Dionis prompted when he had judged the pause to be long enough.

"I'll begin travelling immediately," Hedrial shrugged.

"Why does it have to be you though?" Dionis asked. "You haven't started to believe you're this Chosen One, have you?"

Hedrial stared at him blankly for a moment before replying, "No, I haven't started to believe such nonsense. It's just that now I know where to go so there's nothing to stop me."

A companionable silence fell between the two as they both allowed the full impact of Hedrial's plan to settle in their minds. The sounds of the village at midday floated in through the window. Children at play, adults at work, dogs barking and the faint strains of birdsong seemed to make the blanket of quiet more amiable.

"Actually," Dionis said, "there is something."

The thought seemed to worm its way into Hedrial's mind at the same instant. He let out a long breath, eyes going to the map on the floor. "I hadn't forgotten about him. He can stay here in my absence."

He was referring to his eighteen-year-old apprentice, Uthan Camarr.

"You could always bring him with us," Dionis suggested.

"No, he's far from ready to be going off on this kind of adventure. His powers are still too volatile," Hedrial said. "And you'll be staying here with him. I'll trust you to keep an eye on him. Make sure he doesn't turn someone into a tree or something."

"Sometimes I think you wished you hadn't had to take an apprentice," Dionis remarked. Almost to himself he added, "At times like this I wish it also. I'll be missing all the fun."

The comment about Uthan had made Hedrial's memory spark into action. He remembered the Choosing ceremony with a clarity that made it impossible to believe it had been three years previously. "If it hadn't have been for that damned Council mage, I wouldn't have," Hedrial said quietly. "But then I have to wonder if it wasn't destiny that selected him." He sat back and let the memory of the ceremony flow back through his mind.

It was the day of the Choosing. Hedrial looked over at the window for what could have been the hundredth time. Sitting in near total silence he became aware of the subtle changes outside. The sound of working had died away, replaced by the eager chatter of a large group of men and women congregating somewhere. The smells had changed as well. The thick odour of smoke from the blacksmith's forge only a few doors away had faded. There was now a strong scent of meat being cooked. The villagers had started their own preparations for the Choosing ceremony.

He stood up and went to the window. Peering out, he saw the village square. It was nothing more than a flat area of dark green grass, kept trim on a regular basis by one of the locals. The area was not even a square as such, Hedrial reflected: it was more of a triangle. Already a large crowd of the villagers had gathered on the grass. The local inn, The Griffin's Wings, being one of the buildings on the very edge of the square, had set up a collection of small folding tables. It was now doing some very good business. The innkeeper, clearly knowing exactly where the money would come from, had taken on extra staff in order to keep the food and drink coming.

Hedrial cast a scrutinising eye over the crowd. Almost too quickly for his own personal liking, he found the fathers of three of the boys. They stood together in a small group, tankards firmly in hand, chatting. The wizard could see the pride at their sons being put forward. It was etched in their stances and on their expressions. The old wizard shook his head. He failed to understand how the trio could be so happy on this occasion. After all, this selection could result in the chosen boy's life being put in jeopardy. He had considered how he could always just not pick one, put on a flashy show of lights and say none of the boys had the abilities required. Quickly though that thought was dismissed. He knew it was not really a possibility, more just wishful thinking.

Swinging the great door to his tower-like home open, Hedrial found himself looking out into the sunlit village square. From the small area he had been able to see from his window, he had been expecting only half of the crowd that faced him. Many of them had seen, or maybe felt, the door open and were now looking in his direction. Still shrouded in the shadows of his hallway, Hedrial paused a moment, releasing a long drawn out sigh. Breathing in again deeply, he drew himself up to his full height. Then, he moulded his form into the imposing presence the villagers had come to know and respect and, in many cases, fear. The noise of the crowd died down as he stepped out onto the gravel path. His footsteps sounded heavy and dramatic as the wizard moved, staring directly ahead of him at the village square. People involuntarily held their breath as he strode past, not once looking in anyone's direction. Even the smallest of children and noisiest of pets had fallen into the all-encompassing silence.

Finally coming to a stop in the centre of the grassy square, he spoke, using a loud booming voice, "People of Kora-Tus. We are all gathered here today so that I may choose an apprentice from one of your children. One who has reached the age of fifteen. I believe there are five children of that age here today. Please bring them forward."

Five youths, all dressed as smartly as their parents could afford were ushered to stand in front of Hedrial. Quickly the wizard motioned for them to stand in a line before addressing the villagers once more, "Many of you will be aware that I do not, nor have ever wanted to take an apprentice in these dark times. However, it is the High Council of Magic's ruling that I must. And even I must adhere to some kind of law. I trust the people involved here today will adhere to that law also and remember that the decision is mine alone as to whom I shall choose."

He stood before the boys, one by one, at first just staring at them with emotionless eyes. The ornate staff he had brought with him purely for appearance was touched to the forehead of each boy in turn. For the first three of the five candidates, the clear glass orb on the end of the staff did nothing. When it touched Uthan's forehead, the glass began to vibrate, humming with a resonance that had echoed through the staff and into Hedrial's bones. The clear glass clouded over with inky blue swirls. Hedrial's heart sank. He heard the crowd gasp aloud as if they were one entity. Uthan had been chosen to become his apprentice that day.

It had concerned him greatly that he had not actually chosen Uthan; rather something else had chosen him.

"You're thinking again," Dionis said, cutting into Hedrial's thoughts.

"Yes," Hedrial agreed, "I was remembering the Choosing. I still have my concerns over it."

"Just accept you made a good choice and live with it," Dionis replied. "Whether you chose him or not, he's still your apprentice."

"Indeed, but it's still a worry, more so with these hit-and-run raids going on," Hedrial replied.

Dionis said, "You know full well he can handle himself. Remember that fight at the Griffon's Wings he broke up?"

"I know he can," Hedrial replied, remembering the incident. Uthan had broken the nose of one local man after levitating him into a wall. The drunken fight had stopped almost instantly, the alcohol-fuelled rage evaporating from everyone there. "But I don't think he's ready to be left here to defend Kora-Tus on his own. He still has so much to learn."

"Spoken like a true perfectionist," Dionis said. "He'll always have a lot to learn. You just have to accept that."

"He's not ready to defend against raiders, Dionis. Not here on his own," Hedrial replied.

Dionis shrugged. "But he won't be on his own. I'll be here."

"And that is something I'll be grateful for," Hedrial answered gravely.

"Right then, if you don't mind, I'd like to get some sleep now. I'll leave you to learn to look on the bright side of things," Dionis said. "Remember I still have work to do tonight."

"Yes, well be careful out there. Remember we still don't know for certain the real reason for these attacks," Hedrial cautioned.

Dionis paused in thoughtful silence. Finally he asked, "You don't suppose there's a chance that they know about the boy, do you?"

A deep, stunned silence fell as Hedrial realised that it was a strong possibility. His piercing eyes swung round to focus on Dionis, who returned the fearful gaze. Speaking in a hushed voice, Hedrial answered, "It's a very strong chance. But they obviously don't know his whereabouts exactly. Something," Hedrial continued, "I intend to keep exactly as it is." He paused again, deep in thought, before adding, "You'd better get some sleep. I want you to keep your wits about you tonight."

The sound of deep throated snoring coming from the bat's perch told Hedrial his last words had been unnecessary. Hedrial put his head against the padded chair back and breathed out heavily. He closed his eyes for a few brief moments, resting them while he let his mind run through the new events. After a moment or two of quiet contemplation, he allowed his mind to go blank, letting the thoughts sort themselves out inside his head, an old trick he had learnt early on in his magical career.

There was a loud hammering at the front door. Hedrial exhaled a deep a sigh but stayed where he was, hoping the caller would just go away. After a few minutes of silence, a second, louder knock told the wizard that his peaceful rest was now over. Gripping the arms of the chair hard in his irritation, he opened his eyes. It was no longer the bright light of afternoon. Looking out at the early evening sky,

Hedrial felt an overwhelming sense of unease.

"I was wondering when you'd wake up," Dionis said, in far too cheerful a tone for the wizard's liking.

"I wasn't asleep," Hedrial answered quickly.

The knocking sounded again, reminding the wizard that his visitor was still outside waiting.

"Then what other excuse are you going use to explain why you're keeping whoever it is waiting?" Dionis answered.

"I thought Uthan could at least answer the door," Hedrial grumbled.

"He went out somewhere. He did come to tell you. I think he mistook your snoring for an answer," Dionis replied.

Quickly Hedrial stood up. Suppressing a groan as a dull tired pain drummed in his knees he walked to the front door. He paused briefly to check himself in the large hallway mirror, making sure he was not showing how tired he really was. He felt a telltale crackling of energy in the air. Even before he opened the door he knew who was behind it. He instantly stood up straight again, determined to be seen as bright and alert.

Uthan stood there with a young girl in his arms, no more than fourteen. A long gash lay open on the top of her head. Her long, brown hair was matted with blood, which was already congealing. Breathlessly, he said, "More trouble at the Griffon's Wings."

"Is it dealt with?" Hedrial asked, standing to one side to let Uthan in.

"I think so," Uthan said.

Hedrial could not tell whether he smiled with the answer or just grimaced.

"And who else is lying injured over there this time?" Hedrial asked, raising an eyebrow.

Uthan carried the girl through the wood-panelled corridor to stand before an iron-studded door, that led into a makeshift dispensary. Waiting for Hedrial to unlock it for him, Uthan watched the wizard take the key down from its hook on the wall.

As he held the door open, Hedrial said, "Lay her on the table, I'll take a look at the wound."

"This village needs a healer not a wizard," Uthan muttered, doing as he was told.

"It's true for the moment. All we seem to be doing is patching people up from bar brawls," Hedrial said. "However, young Uthan, don't be so hasty to wish for any more excitement."

"I know," Uthan answered as if he had heard the words many times before, "fate has a way of showing us the error of our wishes."

Hedrial looked up from cleaning the girl's wound. He studied his apprentice for a few moments, thinking about how Uthan's fate may have already been dealt out. He remembered the young boy who had arrived at his home that night, bringing with him a wealth of possibilities and just as many questions.

Uthan was not much different now, merely a few years older. Tawny blonde hair had been combed back from his forehead, a few strands hung across a face untouched by the blemishes of youth. Uthan had not grown much in the past few years; he was still shorter in height and more slightly built than most of the other men in the village. Yet still very few of them troubled him. It was in the eyes, Hedrial had long decided. Uthan's pale blue eyes stared off into space, thoughtfully. Thinking about all those unanswered questions reminded Hedrial of a conversation. The first he had had with Dionis the night Uthan had arrived at his home.

"Did you ever ask your parents about having mages in the family?" Hedrial asked as if simply making conversation.

"Many times," Uthan replied. "Each time I got the same answer. No."

"That'll be from your father I assume," Hedrial replied. He did not like Uthan's father. To Hedrial's mind, the baker was a man with a mind so narrow it could be used as a plank.

Uthan shrugged, "Mother always tells me to ask him instead."

"I will have to look into it myself in the future I think," Hedrial said. "Pity I don't have time before I go."

"Go? Where?" Uthan asked, suddenly looking at his master.

Putting the dampened cloth back into the shallow bowl of water, Hedrial tried redirecting the conversation, "This wound isn't as bad as it looks after all. A couple of stitches should be all she needs."

"Master Hedrial, you're talking about going somewhere," Uthan said.

Hedrial sighed. He had forgotten that Uthan could be stubborn. "You know I've been studying a lot of late myself. Well, I believe I've found what I've been looking for at long last."

"This is to do with that dagger, isn't it," Uthan stated flatly. "I can feel the energy that comes from it."

Hedrial raised an eyebrow at this. Glancing at the unconscious girl laying on the table, he ushered Uthan outside the room and closed the heavy door behind him. "How did you know about the dagger?"

"I can feel the energy it gives off," Uthan said slowly. "Curiosity got the better of me and I looked at it."

"You felt its energy from outside my study?" Hedrial asked, wide-eyed. "But the iron in the walls should stop any energy from seeping out."

Uthan shook his head. "It was when I came to speak with you earlier. The dagger was on the floor. I just assumed you'd worked an enchantment on it and was curious as to what it was. I'm sorry. I shouldn't have pried."

Hedrial waved the apology off. "Forgiven, but don't do it again. Yes, the dagger has a part in my going away but it isn't the reason. I've discovered a way that might put an end to the nonsense of these Black Flame Knights and their raids."

"You're going to attack them?" Uthan asked, wide-eyed.

"Not quite, no. I wish I could gather an army behind me to do that but quite frankly I'm not sure where I'd find an army. I'm travelling a long way away to find something. That's all I can truly say on it at the moment. You'll just have to trust me."

"I do trust you."

"Good, then you'll understand when I say you're not coming with me," Hedrial said.

"But," Uthan gaped, "I can help you better if I travel with you surely."

"And who would watch over Kora-Tus in my absence?" Hedrial asked. The wizard stared straight at his apprentice with that same intense, blue-eyed gaze he had used during the Choosing ceremony. On almost everyone else it had the desired effect of stopping arguments but not on Uthan. The young man's will was never easily dismissed.

"Maybe not having someone to patch them up after fights will be the answer to stopping their petty squabbles," Uthan countered.

"I don't feel you're ready to face the kind of dangers I may have to contend with," Hedrial said.

"Not ready? Yet I'm ready to be left here on my own to protect these people against each other?"

"You won't be on your own, Dionis is staying with you. Now I don't want to hear another word on this. We have a young lady in there in need of stitches. If you can do that for me and then take her home again please, I'll be in my study. There are still things that need to be done."

With those words ringing in his own ears, Hedrial walked back along the corridor and began the climb up the mountain of solid wooden stairs to his study.

"Sounds like he took that well," Dionis said, as Hedrial closed the iron-studded door firmly behind him. One of the benefits of the magical bond between Dionis and Hedrial was the ability for them to tune into the senses of each other. Dionis had clearly been using that ability as he continued, "I can understand how he feels though."

"Dionis please, I'm too tired to argue any more on this. I'm going and you two are to stay here until I return," Hedrial said so firmly that even Dionis felt it was better not to push the subject further. "Isn't it time you were going out anyway?"

"Oh sure, kick me out now. Just to stop me arguing, isn't it?" Dionis said, with his own version of a smirk.

"I thought I'd already stopped the arguing," Hedrial replied.

"And if I actually listened to that then you'd probably complain that I wasn't keeping the old traditions alive," Dionis returned.

"And what old tradition would I be arguing for exactly?"

"The one that had me arguing against every one of your decisions," Dionis replied, smirking again. As the smirk faded, he added, "I don't think I'll be back till very early. There's a lot of ground to cover. Now don't wait up for me."

"Fine, but be careful, Dionis. They're getting too close for us to be anything else," the wizard replied, his tone softening.

The bat dropped from his perch. Then beating his wings with a leathery thumping sound, he circled the room at head height a couple of times before shooting out of the open window.

"And of course he probably won't be careful at all," Hedrial sighed to himself, sitting back amongst his books again.

Chapter Two

Pressing his hands into the middle of his sweat-soaked back, the man stretched, arching over as far backwards as his body would allow. He sighed contentedly as the move helped to unwind his aching muscles. Straightening back up again, he looked up at the cloudless sky above him. From his perspective the sun was only a finger's width from dropping down behind the tall, dense forest that ended the fields surrounding his village. He had been working in these fields all day. The height of the sun now signified his working day had ended. Grasping his loose fitting vest from the handles of the plough and slipping it over his head, he turned and started to walk back to the village. He intended to down a few pints at the inn to rid his throat of the dust of the working day. Something he saw out of the corner of his eye halted him dead in his tracks.

Moving slowly, as if he did not really want to see for certain, he turned round and stared out over the fields. From the direction of the distant, high peaked western border mountains he could only just make out the dark cloud. It hovered above the road running into the village. Shielding his eyes from the glare of the evening sun he watched in silence for a few moments. Suddenly his eyes widened in fear. He spun on his heel and sprinted back towards the collection of stone and wood buildings he called home. His legs stamped hard at the ground, his arms pumped tirelessly as all the weariness from the day's work slipped from him. Even though his lungs heaved with the effort of breathing, he still managed to yell a warning, "The Black Flame Knights are coming!"

At first only a few villagers heard him. Eyes looked from the hurriedly approaching figure to the horizon he signalled at. As if they had been suddenly doused in iced water, the villagers sprang into life. Their voices joined in with the shouted warnings. Moments later the entire village was alive, every man, woman and child aware that an army of invaders was hurtling to their doorstep.

The village blacksmith stepped calmly out of his forge. Sweat still dripped from his broad back and shoulders. Hearing the commotion, he called back inside to his young lad. As the sandy haired boy stepped out of the hellish looking glow of the fires, the blacksmith said, "Better run over to the inn, lad. Tell them trouble's on its way."

The boy did not waste time on arguing. He could see the worried expression on the blacksmith's face. He knew of the man's reputation as far as fighting went. He knew when the smith said the word trouble he did not use it lightly. As he ran, he saw farmers, store owners and other workers gather things that could be used as weapons and hastily prepare something they could consider a defence. He burst through the large double doors of the village's only inn and, watched curiously by the small collection of drinkers, bent forwards to try and catch his breath again.

The innkeeper, a thin wiry man with a sour expression permanently etched on his face, had waited long enough. "Well, what is it, boy?" he prompted.

Struggling between breaths, the boy looked up and said, "It's them. They're coming."

"The Black Flame?" muttered one drinker. "But we're not nearly ready."

"We'd never be truly ready for them," said a voice from the first-floor landing. Everyone looked up at the man leaning confidently against the banister. "But most of you are ready enough to stand up to them."

"We don't want to just stand up to them. We want to beat them once and for all. Our women and children need us to stop them," the innkeeper replied. He brought a pair of short swords from behind the bar, followed by a small, but dangerous, pistol crossbow.

A murmured wave of voices rippled through the drinkers, most of the words echoed the innkeeper's sentiments. The man on the landing reached up behind his head and bunched his long, dark hair back, tying it in a tight ponytail. He then leant back against the banister and folded his arms.

"We'll fight them and we'll beat them. Maybe we'll even give the Black Flame enough of a bloody nose this time that they'll never return to Lessa-Tus again," he said, the faintest flicker of a smile turning the corners of his mouth upwards.

This time a roar of approval went up from the drinkers. They downed the rest of their drinks, punched the air and clapped each other on the back. The only man in the inn not yelling and cheering was the innkeeper. He remained stony faced, staring at his crossbow and swords.

Back outside in the village, the urgent wave of panicked shouts had reached the ears of the local wizard. The middle-aged bald man looked up from the wounded hunter lying on the table in front of him. Ever since the man had been carried into his home muttering things about black clad men attacking him and his party, the wizard had been anticipating an assault.

"I'm afraid I'll have to leave the remainder of your healing for the time being. It appears the village is about to need my help," the wizard said, trying to keep the nerves from his voice.

He had at least managed to stop most of the bleeding. Now all that remained was to seal the long, tearing wound in the man's side. The wizard moved away from the table and hurried to his front door. He opened it just in time to see another of the village children sprinting hard along the road to him. Seeing the wizard in the doorway, the boy skidded to a halt and pointed over his shoulder.

The wizard held up a calming hand and nodded, "The Black Flame are heading this way. I know."

The boy grimaced and turned away, sprinting back off in the direction he had come from.

Looking to the outskirts of the opposite end of Lessa-Tus, the wizard saw the black dust cloud. It was getting closer and then slowly disappeared as the creators of the cloud moved onto different terrain. Just on the edge of his hearing he could pick up the sounds of horses' hooves thundering against the ground. Although he had had no real experience in the situation, he was guessing from the sounds that it was a large force heading towards them; much larger than the one he had heard had been raiding some of the neighbouring villages. Breathing a deep sigh, he turned back around, disappearing back into the dark interior of his house. Closing the door behind him, he suddenly felt a rush of white pain sear through his chest. His vision was too hazy to see at first, but slowly he managed to clear the blurred image. He put a trembling hand to his chest, feeling the warm, sticky wetness of his own blood there.

The wounded hunter stood in front of him. In his gloved hand he held a long, ivory handled knife; the blade dripped with blood. The wizard recognised the blade as one of his own. He had been about to use it to seal the man's wounds. He noticed the hunter holding his right side tightly. The wound was still bothering him. Swiftly the wizard lashed out a hand, catching the hunter's ribcage. The man grunted in pain at the sudden pressure on his side. In answer he swept out his other hand, drawing a line of crimson across the wizard's throat. Blood gushed from both wounds, leaving the wizard to topple backwards. For a few moments his eyes and fingers twitched in spasms, then, releasing a barely audible rush of air, the wizard died.

The hunter stepped forward, looming over the body. He looked down into the lifeless eyes that stared off into the distance as though in a daydream. He unceremoniously prodded the wizard's cheek with the toe of his boot, making sure the old man was dead. From outside he could now hear the screams of the villagers and the thundering of hooves. Satisfied his work with the wizard was finished, he pulled open the door and stepped outside.

Dionis slipped effortlessly though the night sky, his wings beating lazily. The evening air was cooling as it pushed its way through his thick fur to find his skin. The bat savoured every moment of its touch as much as he enjoyed the peace around him. The leathery thump of his wings against the air was the only sound he could hear at this height.

In the distance ahead he caught sight of a flickering orange glow. Then he saw the clouds of black smoke piling into the air. At first the smoke was difficult to see against the darkened sky, but the bat's nose confirmed his suspicions. As the smell got stronger and stronger, burning and itching at the inside of his nostrils and lungs, Dionis found he had to fly lower, hugging the ground where he could. He had also noticed the smell was not simply that of burning wood. Mingled with it was the faint, but still sickening stench of scorched flesh. He pulled back up.

Dionis knew what was happening. Lessa-Tus, the nearest neighbouring village, was being raided. The bat had a pretty clear idea by whom. He angled his wings, forming his body into the shape of an arrowhead and dived at a steep angle towards the ground. In his ears he could hear the rushing of air. It drowned out every other sound except that of his heart racing. He could feel it pumping hard, forcing blood through his arteries. An overwhelming feeling of exhilaration caught him, driving his breath from his lungs. An idea had formed itself in the back of the bat's mind. Dionis was going to try and cause some mayhem. He sped in circles, twisting his way between towers of thick black smoke, gliding on the heated air.

All throughout the village, houses and other buildings had been touched by fire. Some were now nothing more than blackened frames, fire licking at the last remnants of flammable material. On the streets outside lay the twisted bodies of dead men, women and children. More people ran across the streets, trying to find some kind of respite from the massacre around them. Black armoured knights roared by on horseback, trampling the bodies of the dead under hoof while driving their swords down hard into anyone unlucky enough to be nearby. In all the stories of the massacres Dionis had heard, he had never expected to see such carnage. He had never believed that any human, despite how evil their soul, could really stoop to such needless bloodshed. He watched as more knights ran on foot through the streets, carrying flaming torches as well as their swords. They touched the flames to anything that was not already burning, including the clothing of the bodies lining the streets. Unable to do much more than watch the death and destruction, Dionis circled the village, unseen by the raiders.

Flying above the inn, he noticed that it and the majority of the surrounding buildings were untouched by the flames and the fighting. He saw a quintet of knights galloping hard through the streets towards the building. They either hacked down with their swords at anyone in their path or simply allowed their horses to run over them. They drew their horses up into the cleared square and climbed down from the saddles. One of them, Dionis noticed, wore different armour to the others. Where their helmets had short, black crests, he had three thick ponytails. They were made from the same black horsehair but they flowed down the back of his helmet. Where the cloaks of the other knights were heavy, black cloth, his appeared to be thin leather. He had to be an officer, Dionis concluded. A plan unfurled in his mind. If he could cause an officer some damage or distress, maybe even death, then he could score a large victory against the Black Flame Knights.

The officer handed the reins of his horse to one of his men. Quickly the five horses were tied to a long low beam of wood outside another building. All the time, Dionis noticed, the officer had his eyes firmly locked on the door of the inn. Without looking away, he strode confidently across the open area towards it, his fingers twitching by the hilt of the sword at his side.

Once the men were far enough away from their horses, Dionis moved himself into position and soared down towards the beasts.

The five animals stamped and snorted loudly as the bat slipped over their heads, his slipstream ruffling their manes. The sound made the five men spin round. All they could see were their mounts pulling hard against their reins, trying to escape. Dionis flew around the corner of a building, slipping out of view even before the knights had had a chance to see him. Allowing his dark, shadowy shape to blend against the background of a thick smoke cloud, he climbed in a vertical line back up high again. The height gave him a good view of the men as two of them moved back to the horses to try and calm them.

The officer continued his walk to the inn, seeming to radiate pure anger and hatred in every step he took.

Another dive took Dionis on a steep angle, headed right towards the horses once more. This time he soared right over their backs, raking at the saddles with his claws. The horses panicked and fought harder against the rail and the two knights as they felt the leather being torn like parchment. One of the knights was kicked in the face by a horse, throwing him onto his back. The second knight forgot instantly about the horses and drew his sword. He had seen the dark blur cut deep tears in the leather of his saddle. Holding his sword in a double handed grip he flashed his eyes everywhere, trying to find the strange shape again. "Sir," he called in a nervous voice.

The officer stopped dead in his tracks. At first he turned his head a fraction, looking back at the knight through the corner of his eye. He noticed one of his nearby men had his sword drawn too and was looking at the sky above. Following the knight's gaze, he saw Dionis not too far above their heads, banking and wheeling through the air.

"Whatever it is, sir, it's dangerous," said one of the men in a quiet awed voice. He sounded as if he had chosen his words carefully. The officer merely watched the shadow, fiery hatred and anger blazing in his dark eyes.

Dionis surveyed them looking back up at him. Deciding on a more direct approach to the attack, he half closed his wings and dropped from the sky. Once he was no more than five feet above the ground, he levelled out effortlessly and sped right at the officer and his men. The knight closest to the horses ran forward into Dionis's path, bringing his sword up in front of him. As the bat got closer, he brought his sword down, missing Dionis by inches. The bat spun round in the air, folding one wing most of the way to allow a tight left turn. He flew back at the knight again and rushed past his face, tearing into the exposed flesh with his claws. The knight called out in pain, clutching at the torn skin around his eyes.

The officer held out a hand to one of his men and, without taking his eyes from the approaching bat, said, "Crossbow."

The knight unhooked a small crossbow from his belt and pulled back the string. He quickly slid a black shaft into place and handed the bow to his superior. Holding the bow in one outstretched arm, the officer took aim. The bat continued speeding towards him, unperturbed by the sight of the bow. The trigger was pulled, sending the bolt hurtling forwards with a loud twang.

Dionis barrel rolled, letting the bolt slip by his body by a fraction of an inch. A scream of agony behind him suggested the knight had not been as fortunate. Dionis risked a quick glance back, knowing the general would have to waste moments reloading the crossbow. He saw the bolt sticking out of the eye of the knight, who dropped first to his knees then flat onto his face, dead. With a tremor of excitement ripping through him, Dionis turned back to his next targets.

The bolt struck him hard in the shoulder. He could feel its tip, icy against the warmth of his blood and inner flesh. With an audible grunt, he dropped from the air and hit the ground hard, unable to move through the explosions of pain that flared through his body.

The officer, still glaring at Dionis, handed a second bow back to his knight and turned away. Taking one last look at their comrade, killed by their own officer without any remorse, the remaining knights turned and followed. Their leader strode up to the thick doors of the inn and, without making any signal or gesture to his men, hammered his boot into the middle. The doors burst inwards on the kick. They swung hard on their hinges, slamming against the inside walls. Before they could swing back all the way again, the officer took a couple of steps inside, allowing some of the firelight outside to illuminate the gloom within.

Someone had banked the fire in the main, central fireplace. Now only the dull, glowing embers remained where usually a roaring fire would be. Most of the lanterns dotted around the walls and on tables had been doused as well. Only a few remained lit, casting a half light over the room that merely emphasised the darkness.

"General Cornak, I've been waiting. Having problems with your horses?" a voice spoke from the landing.

The general looked up to the gloomy staircase and growled, "Nothing that couldn't be handled."

The owner of the voice stepped slowly down the stairs, his booted footsteps echoing through the inn. The man, who had been so assuring to the drinking crowd in the inn before the attack, had apparently lost none of his confidence. With a broad smile he stepped further into the light, allowing the flickering shadows to play over his handsome face. "So, General, can I buy you a drink for old times?"

General Cornak did not return the smile. Instead he growled, "My spy was right. The outlaw, Medoran, babysitting a bunch of farmers who want to play soldiers. It makes me sick to think about it." When Medoran did not reply, Cornak added, "This collection of village idiots actually has you believing you can lead them in a rebellion, doesn't it?"

"What can I say?" Medoran answered with a shrug. He wandered to the bar and leant on it, watching Cornak and his men carefully. "I guess they just saw real talent."

"Do they realise that when the fight really gets going, you'll turn tail and run away, or, worse for them, maybe even sell them out," Cornak sneered. He paced slowly around a table, kicking one of the chairs away.

Medoran bridled at the comment. His eyes flashed angrily. Setting his jaw, he returned, "You're the only traitor here, Cornak, you and your Black Flame scum. Guess your conscience isn't bothering you. The fact that you personally sold out over a thousand men doesn't even concern you, huh? You've sent so many men to their deaths that none of it registers."

Cornak's eyes flickered in amusement. He could see he was getting to Medoran. With a nonchalant shrug, he said, "Does it matter? I've sent thousands more to their deaths since then. The numbers make no difference to me. Medoran, don't you wish you could be more like me?"

Now Medoran had begun to tremble with rage. A fire had started in the pit of his stomach. As the images of fallen comrades' faces and the faces of men, women and children he had seen butchered by the knights over the years filled his mind's eye, he found the building unbearable.

Indicating the sword hanging from Medoran's belt, Cornak asked, "So, can you still use that thing? Or is it just for show?"

The blade flashed into view with a loud swishing sound. The sword was quickly held ready in Medoran's hand, shards of dull candlelight reflected from the steel. Even though the rest of his body seemed to tremble violently, his sword arm was held steady, like a rock. He knew Cornak was goading him into a fight. But then Medoran's inner voice told him that was what he had been waiting for. From the rear of the common room Medoran heard footsteps. He saw the slight incline of Cornak's head and the movement of his dark eyes.

"Look, Medoran, here's some more of your farmyard rebellion. Are you going to show them how to fight for real, or just how to surrender like a coward?" Cornak jeered. An almost bestial howl of rage bellowed from the pit of Medoran's stomach. The swordsman surged forward, his sword held at throat height. Cornak was ready for him. The general instantly had his own sword free from its scabbard and was holding it in front of him, vertically. The two blades clashed together, the ring of steel upon steel loud in the common room. The general was smiling broadly, knowing he had successfully lured his enemy into the attack. Medoran slipped his sword away from the block and took a swift step back, then spun off to his left. His sword came up, seemingly of its own accord, blocking a return swipe from the general. The black armoured Cornak effectively blocked a sudden flurry of hard slashes and thrusts. With equal skill each attack was returned and blocked. The two men were perfectly matched, each combatant unable to get the first strike in.

At a subtle hand gesture from the general, his knights moved slowly around in a circle, trying to get behind the furious rebel swordsman. With a high-pitched cry of agony, one of them toppled to the floor, clutching at his knee. A long arrow shaft stuck out from between the slender gap in his armour. The tip of the arrowhead was just visible, covered in blood, from the fleshy inside of the knee joint. The other two knights spun round fluidly, crossbows in hand. All in one movement they took aim and fired. There was a loud crashing sound from the rear of the room. Medoran took a few steps back, safely out of the range of Cornak's sword. He risked a glance over his shoulder and saw the bowman, slumped against an overturned table. Two short black shafts were embedded in his chest and throat with lethal precision. The man's eyes stared over at Medoran, pleading with him lifelessly for help.

Medoran turned back quickly, intent on cleaving the grinning General Cornak in two. Bright colours exploded in front of Medoran's eyes as he felt the solid steel hilt of Cornak's sword hit him on the bridge of the nose. A wave of nausea suddenly swept over him and he staggered back, his limbs feeling leaden and useless.

More trembling, this time from the dizziness instead of fury, seized his body. Shaking his head, he desperately tried to clear his field of vision, inwardly knowing it would not be long before Cornak followed up with the deathblow. Blinking away the bright colourful flashes, he was just in time to see Cornak's metal plated gauntlet strike him full under the jaw. The rebel swordsman dropped to the floor unconscious and his sword clattered noisily beside him.

Staring disdainfully down at his fallen opponent, Cornak growled, "Bring him with us. He might yet prove useful."

Without argument, the two knights lifted the unconscious swordsman under their arms and half dragged, half carried him from the inn.

Cornak looked down at the third knight, still writhing around on the floor in agony and clutching at his knee. "Is it bad?"

Through gasping pain filled breaths, the knight answered, "It hurts like hell."

"The knee is a painful place to be attacked," Cornak said with a nod.

His face then twisted into a mask of pure violence as he lashed down with his sword. The knight's head was severed cleanly from his armoured shoulders. The black helmet clanked loudly as it struck the polished, hardwood floor, leaving the body to slump sideways. Cornak turned and left the inn, keeping his bloodstained sword clutched firmly in his hand.

Straight away the wounded hunter came over to him. Fresh bandages had been wrapped tightly around his ribcage, covering his wound completely. Small patches of light red blood were staining through, showing the injury to be still open in places. The hunter flinched as he thought he could see an expression of hunger crossing the general's wolf-like face.

Speaking in a calm voice, the general indicated the wound and asked, "The wound is real?"

The hunter nodded and smiled proudly, "Yes, sir."

With a thoughtful nod, Cornak asked, "Can you ride?"

"I'm not certain to be exact but I should be able to in a few days."

Again Cornak nodded calmly, "And the wizard?"

"He's dead, sir."

"Good," Cornak muttered. "At least your presence here wasn't a total loss."

"I'm sorry sir. I don't understand," the hunter replied,

shaking his head hurriedly.

Cornak spun and backhanded his sword into the hunter's freshly bandaged chest. The edge of the blade was embedded so deep it remained in the man's ribcage as he dropped down onto his knees. Confusion swamped his face as he looked up with disbelieving eyes at his general. Wrenching his sword free with force to inflict maximum pain, Cornak growled, "The wound was a foolish idea. I have no place in my army for fools. Consider yourself discharged."

Choked whimpers of pain escaped the man's lips. Thin trickles of blood flowed from the corners of his mouth, running down his chin to drip onto the ground by his knees. More blood flowed from the deep cut in his chest. Cornak glared at him in disgust before slamming the sole of his booted foot into the man's face. By the time the hunter's head hit the ground he was dead. The general closed his eyes and inhaled deeply. The smell of wood smoke mingled with the now stronger scent of blood filled his nostrils, heightening his senses. His own blood pounded its way through his veins, carrying adrenalin with it along the way. Opening his eyes again, he surveyed the scene around him.

His knights were touching the flames of long handled torches to the roofs of buildings, tossing smaller cloth ones in through doors and windows. The clothing of corpses lining the streets was set alight indiscriminately. The scene of pure destruction as the knights of the Black Flame set about wiping the village of Lessa-Tus from the map brought a fresh triumphant smile to his face. As he scanned the work around him, he saw the dark form of Dionis lying in the square. He noticed his knights were hesitant to approach it. Taking a couple of steps nearer he noticed the heavy rise and fall of its chest. The thing was still alive.

With a curiously evil glint in his eyes, Cornak moved the last few paces across the square and stood, towering above the bat's body. As he watched, he noticed Dionis slowly etching a small symbol in the dirt with the claws of his left wing. Snorting and shaking his head, Cornak struck out with his boot. His armour-clad foot connected with Dionis's already painful ribs. He snorted again, noticing that the rise and fall of the bat's body, although hardly visible, still continued. A slow dark smile crossed Cornak's face for a fleeting moment as he realised the bat was dying after all. With the heel of his boot, he rubbed the half finished etching from the dirt and stalked off.

Sergeant Jarrier sat in his saddle watching the carnage going on around him. His sword blade hung from his belt, it had not been drawn since the attack on Lessa-Tus had started. Instead the sergeant had been content to allow the men under his command to cause the damage. A broad smile crossed his face as he watched a small group of villagers, armed with swords that looked as if they would fall apart before they could be used, being herded into the waiting weapons of more of his men.

The small group were outnumbered and, it seemed, clearly outclassed by the heavily armoured knights. Yet still, they fought on with a determination Jarrier knew he would never see in his men. A small flicker of superiority flashed through his mind as he remembered that only a few years before, he could easily have been amongst them. Then he would have been fighting not only for his home but also his life and those of his family.

One of his knights swiped out viciously with his sword. He caught a villager across the throat, killing him instantly. The blow nearly took the head off his closest comrade. The other knight momentarily turned to him and glared angrily. There would be an exchange of words between those two men later on, Jarrier thought. The moment of distraction was enough for one of the villagers. He drove forward and plunged his sword deep through the knight's exposed face. The knight was dead immediately, depriving Jarrier the opportunity to witness the argument between the knights.

A sharp cry of pain caught Jarrier's ears from somewhere to his left. He pulled a little on his reins and turned his horse so he could look in the direction of the sound. From one of the darkened doorways stumbled another of his knights. The man was not wearing his helmet any more and blood poured from a huge gash above his eyes. The armour around his lower left side was slick, shining in the firelight. He took a few more steps away from the door and collapsed to his knees. Jarrier's curiosity was instantly peaked. He swung down from his saddle and let the reins hang free. With his hand resting on the hilt of his sword, he slowly moved towards the darkened room. From inside he heard another cry of pain, closely followed by an enraged scream. Jarrier smiled again. The voice that had screamed belonged to a girl.

Entering into the dull light of the building, he asked, "What's going on here?"

"This little bitch just attacked us, Sergeant, but we've got her cornered now," grunted one of the knights. He touched two fingers to the flesh under his eyes, wincing as he touched the open wound there.

Jarrier allowed his eyes to become used to the light and took in the scene. There were five of his knights surrounding a young, brown haired girl. In her left hand she held a bloodstained short sword. She ducked suddenly under a horizontal sword swing and broke through a gap between the knights. Before they could grab her again, she ran for a ladder, and then climbed it to the hayloft. One of the knights followed up after her; he reached up for her ankle. The girl slammed her foot down hard into his face, knocking him back down the ladder.

Looking at each of his knights, Jarrier saw that not one of them had escaped without getting a cut, bruise or graze to their head. "Yes, you're doing such a great job at that," replied the sergeant, sarcastically.

"She's not like the others," the knight said defensively.

"Yes, I can see that," Jarrier said.

He looked up at the girl who was now perched above their heads, brandishing her sword in case they tried to get up the ladder. Her brown eyes reminded him of a cornered animal in the way they flicked between his men. Her rounded jaw was set in an expression of pure defiance, the slender lips drawn back in a faint snarl. Her long, brown hair was tied back, it moved like the tail of an angry housecat. Jarrier let his gaze linger on her lithe body instead. A quick flash of an olive-skinned shoulder seen through a tear in her shirt sent his mind racing over various possibilities.

Turning back to his men, Jarrier barked, "General Cornak wants the entire village burned to the ground and there's still more to do."

"But what about this one?" asked one of the knights. His voice had a tone to it that the girl clearly did not like.

The sergeant, just stared at him blankly before saying, "Kill her."

In the streets outside, the small group of villagers continued to fight on as best they could. Half of them had now been killed, the other half only able to watch and hope they could gain some measure of revenge. The knights had formed an arc in front of them, preventing the villagers from advancing. They were like a bladed barricade of steel, effectively holding the small collection of villagers exactly where they wanted them before slowly picking them off.

The villagers were losing badly until the blacksmith, followed by two men who from the heavy axes held tightly in their hands must have been woodsmen, sprang from nowhere. The blacksmith held a large double-headed battleaxe. It appeared far too heavy to actually lift, let alone wield in the furious arcs that the man was swinging. He swept out and took the head from the shoulders of the closest knight. A wave of panic swept over the better trained knights. Seeing a new advantage tossed their way, the villagers' hopeless struggle to stay alive gave way to mob mentality. They surged forwards, bitter madness gleaming in their eyes. Some managed to overcome knights, knocking them from their feet wherever they could and then hacking and stabbing at their vile enemies. Others died instantly as they ran onto the sharp tips of swords. The fray was no longer an organised skirmish. It had given way to sheer madness.

From another street, hoof beats could be heard thundering along the ground. The majority of the mob had either ignored the approaching sound or had not heard it. The only one amongst them to react was the blacksmith. He brought his axe down hard into the shoulder of a fallen knight, cleaving the arm from its socket. The man was unable to scream for long as a nearby teenager thrust a pitchfork into his face, piercing his brain. The blacksmith nodded to the killer and turned to face the sound. He held his axe horizontally in both hands, spinning the shaft in anticipation. As the sound came closer, he rolled his head, stretching his neck muscles.

A huge white charger burst into the small street. Its rider was an exceptionally beautiful woman. Long blonde hair flowed out behind her, bouncing in time with the horse's graceful movements. In one hand she held a broadsword that gleamed in the firelight. Even though she cast a fearsome appearance, dressed in steel-plated armour of black and gold, the blacksmith relaxed a little and smiled. By his feet he felt another knight fall. Without looking around, he swung his axe down, feeling it strike steel then flesh. The cry of pain died within seconds. Watching the oncoming horse he could swear the beast looked ready to breathe flames from its nostrils. "Demien," he called cheerfully, "Welcome to the battle!"

The rider brought her horse to a halt not far from where the mob was decimating the remaining knights from the squad. The beast seemed unhappy at not being allowed to charge into the fray.

"Easy, Kainan," the woman said soothingly into his ear. "There'll be time enough for a fight soon." She slid down from the saddle and left the horse to stand, stamping his hooves like a child throwing a tantrum. Still holding the sword by her side, Demien walked over to the blacksmith and nodded to him. "I see you already have this under control, Hailk."

The smith shrugged, "They're not as lucky over at the inn from what I hear though. Many more knights flooded that area."

Demien's eyebrows shot up and she looked worried, "Medoran?"

"Cornak captured him. A prison cart dragged him away not long ago."

"No one stopped him?" the woman asked. She was trying hard to hold onto her calm.

"Rellus was with him. The bastards shot him though. A small group of men just went over there to try and free Med but they were slaughtered. They ran right into an ambush. Demien, there was honestly nothing that could be done," the blacksmith said. He started to place a hand on the woman's shoulder but stopped when he saw the sudden anger flash over her face. "I'm sorry. The rest of us will either run or die fighting here. There's not much we can do to win this time."

The woman had clenched her jaw tightly. Through gritted teeth, she asked, "Where's Cassmed?"

"Sorry, I haven't seen her since the raid started," the blacksmith now looked extremely sincere in his apologies.

While he knew the relationship between Demien and Medoran was not just to do with the rebellion against the Black Flame, he realised there was a stronger bond between the swordswoman and her younger friend. He appeared to find something a lot more interesting to watch on the shaft of his battleaxe. One of the villagers from close by came over to them. It was the teenager who had joined in the battle armed with a pitchfork. He was breathing hard and sweating from the exertion of the unaccustomed fighting.

"She... attacked a group of them coming this... way. Killed one of them," he said between ragged gasps of breath.

Demien looked over to the corpse he was pointing to. A spark of pride seemed to flash through her. She then glanced back to the boy and repeated, this time more slowly and deliberately, suggesting that a negative answer was not a good idea, "Where's Cassmed?"

The boy stopped for a moment. He looked back at Demien blankly as if he had already given the answer and was surprised she had asked again. His shoulders slumped a little, telling the swordswoman that he did not know. A shout sounded from a nearby stable, followed by the clash of steel on steel.

Snapping her head round to look in the direction of the darkened doorway, Demien realised she recognised the voice. She sprinted towards the door, calling over her shoulder, "Never mind, I've found her."

She ran across to the doorway, ducking to the side as a knight stumbled out. His eyes were wide, mouth gaping open. His left hand was clamped tight around his right forearm from which his right hand was missing completely. With a snarl, Demien slashed her blade across his face, feeling it bite deep into the bone. The knight pitched to the side, his legs kicking out in death throes. Feeling like she was overwhelmed with the fires of righteous fury, Demien stepped through the doorway.

One knight lay dead at the foot of a ladder that went up to what once could have been a hayloft. Cassmed was standing at the top, holding her sword in front of her. Her face was pale, eyes darting from one knight to another as they carefully tried to get up to her. All the time, Sergeant Jarrier was jeering at both the men and the girl. The rungs of the ladder were covered with the blood of her first kill. Catching sight of Demien in the doorway she grinned broadly. "I was wondering when you'd get here!"

The men turned in time to see the warrior woman as she drove her sword deep into the eye socket of the closest knight. Taking advantage of the distraction, another made for the ladder, climbing fast. Cass drove the edge of her blade down onto the top of his helmet, stunning him. He tumbled from the ladder, his armour smashing the lower rungs as he struck them and landed with the sickening sound of his neck breaking. Demien ducked under a wild swing before driving her blade up into the next knight's armpit. She let go of her sword, leaving the man impaled on it, before snatching his weapon from his lifeless fingers. The knight could not defend himself as Demien stabbed him in the throat.

"Two warrior women?" Jarrier sneered as he drew his sword.

"Two warrior women who've slaughtered six of your knights," Demien seethed.

Jarrier shrugged nonchalantly as he said, "They weren't exactly the toughest of men now, were they."

For an answer, Demien brought up her sword and, in one fluid movement, thrust the blade deep into Jarrier's chest. Dragging the blade clear again, she watched the man's corpse topple over backwards. "It's not like you were much better," she muttered disdainfully. Looking at her young friend, she asked, "Are you hurt?"

Cass shook her head, trying to regain her composure. She came down the ladder and sank to her knees, dropping the sword in front of her. She was breathing heavily. With a barely noticeable tremor in her voice, she said, "Thank you for coming. I was having a bit of trouble there."

All the fury seemed to drain from Demien. The disdainful snarl slipped from her face. She became calm again and crouched in front of Cassmed, "We have to leave here, Cass. The village is being destroyed. We can't hold against the knights."

"But this is home," Cassmed said between ragged breaths. "Where else are we to go?"

Demien felt her heart heavy in her chest. The village of Lessa-Tus had been home to both of them for a few years. It had been one of the few places where the two had actually felt welcomed. Somewhere they believed they could belong. Now it was being taken from them, reduced to nothing more than a memory by the raiding party of black armoured marauders. She felt like crying herself but knew she needed to appear strong for her friend's sake. "We'll find somewhere, Cass, we'll have to. Lessa-Tus is going to be wiped from the map," she replied, keeping her voice calm.

"Where's Med? What about the rebellion?" Cassmed asked

"They've taken him. If my guess is right, Cornak will try to get the whereabouts of the other groups from him. And if the stories Med has told us are true, the general is probably going to take a lot of time over it," Demien replied.

She watched through the doorway at the battle going on outside, more to prevent Cassmed from seeing the few tears rolling from her eyes.

Cassmed asked, "Is someone going to try and rescue him then?"

"Yeah."

"Us?"

"Yeah."

Cassmed stood, picked up her sword and wandered over to stand behind her friend. Watching the fighting outside die down until it was more like an execution, she asked, "Is it only us two then?"

Demien just nodded this time. "Same as it ever was," she muttered after a short while.

The pair continued to watch the street outside until all the fighters left, leaving only bloody pools, broken weapons and corpses. Replacing her sword in its sheath, Demien ran outside at a trot, the girl closely following at her heels. Kainan waited with a clearly forced patience as the swordswoman swung back up into the saddle and pulled her friend up to sit behind her.

A pool of sticky crimson coated the ground around Dionis's shoulder. It was matted in the fur around his wound and had already dried in some places. The bolt sticking out of his shoulder had sapped most of the bat's energy. He had noticed that the locals who had arrived in the square to fight for their village had steered clear of him. His breathing, which had already been shallow and painful, had become worse after the savage kick to his ribs from General Cornak.

A hazy black frame had entered his vision, making it impossible for him to see anything unless it was directly in front of him. He was unable to move his head anything more than an inch. The searing, white hot pain of the wound had died away, now only the echoes remained. His breath was leaving his throat in rattling gasps that hurt his chest. Both wings and the lower half of his body felt numb. Dionis knew he was dying. He also knew there was one last thing he had to do.

Summoning up all the energy he could, he managed to get a little blood flowing back into his left wing. Life returned to the limb. Able now to move it, he weakly scraped his claws across the dirt, drawing small symbols. He could feel the last of his strength slipping away, his wing was getting cold again. Finishing the last of the symbols, Dionis allowed his wing and his head to rest on the ground. He closed his eyes, wanting only to sleep and forget about the pain and cold. A moment later, Dionis's weakened heartbeat stopped completely.

Chapter Three

A ball of flickering, blue flame floated in the air above Uthan's head as the apprentice chanted quietly. It spun and rolled, leaving faint blurred images in its wake. Uthan was seated on the floor of Hedrial's study, eyes screwed tightly closed. He was concentrating on the mental images of both the ball above his head and a sheet of parchment that lay in front of him. On it were drawn several small magical symbols. Hedrial sat watching patiently from the comfort of his armchair. His gaze flicked from the ball of flame dancing in the air to the face of his apprentice.

After a while he said, "I don't like the colour. Make it green if you can."

There was a subtle change in Uthan's chants. It would have gone unheard by anyone except Hedrial as his apprentice subtly replaced one of the words with another. The ball above his head flared and became green, getting deeper in colour.

"That's much better. Now you need it to be a little higher. I really don't like the smell of singed hair," Hedrial continued. He settled back into the depths of his armchair even further. "Do you think you can remember how to change the shape?"

In response to the question, Uthan changed his chanting again. The ball above his head seemed to stretch and melt. It twisted and writhed angrily. Small yellow sparks darted back and forth across the shape's surface, occasionally discharging into the air.

"Careful now Uthan, it's breaking..." Hedrial started to warn.

The words became a low moan as Hedrial tried to fight off an overwhelming wave of dizziness. Uthan flicked his hands; mimicking a move he had seen Hedrial do earlier in the lesson. The energy shape above him shifted again and disappeared as if just switched off. Feeling a similar sense of heavy inertia, Uthan opened his eyes, finding the simple move a struggle to accomplish. The air around him seemed to shimmer as if he was watching through a waterfall. The effect made his eyes water. "What did I do?

What's happening?" he called urgently.

The wizard did not answer. He had his eyes screwed shut, trying to stop a savage bout of shaking that wanted to surge through him. His skin was pallid and putty like.

"Something is... I don't know... " Hedrial answered finally. His voice was strained, as if talking was using ten times more energy than he could spare.

Blinking away the tears, Uthan watched through reddened sore eyes as a flickering blue shape tried to gather some form in the air between him and Hedrial. Looking past the shape in surprise, Uthan noticed that Hedrial had managed to open his eyes as well. Although the wizard was still pale, he had stopped shaking and the waves of dizziness and revulsion had left him. Both master and apprentice watched the energy floating in front of them begin to form into a shape.

It became birdlike, two massive, glowing wings stretching out to either side. Then, from the head, two large ears grew up and back. As the energy shape took on its final details, Hedrial gasped in shock. He suddenly sat forward, gripping the arms of his chair with tense white knuckled hands. The shape hanging before him was Dionis. But this was not his companion. This was something formed from what looked like pure energy. Blue in colour with a brilliant white aura and white snake-like energy bolts dancing around the bat's body.

"You already realise it's bad news," the spirit Dionis said. His voice now carried a faint echo and a slight, barely heard distortion that was still enough to raise the hairs on the back of Uthan's neck and arms.

Hedrial's eyes continued to water, although whether it was from the effect of the spirit's appearance or seeing his friend's ghost, Uthan could not tell. The added strain of keeping the crack from his voice was apparent in his features as he replied, "What happened?"

"General Cornak was just that little bit quicker than I'd given him credit for," Dionis replied with a flickering smile. "Listen, Hedrial, I can't hold this form here for long. This ghost stuff isn't all it's supposed to be."

"Who's General Cornak?" Uthan asked suddenly.

Hedrial held up a hand to silence his apprentice before asking, "Who's General Cornak?"

"The kind-hearted and gentle general is a complete bastard really. From his appearance I'd say he's one of the Flame's more important knights. Looks like he's in charge to be honest," Dionis answered.

His image flickered for a moment, growing fuzzy and faint before returning strong again. "They attacked Lessa-Tus."

"I thought I told you to be careful," Hedrial said in disbelief.

There was a pause as the spirit of Dionis just looked back blankly. "I'm sorry, Hedrial, but I'm really finding holding this form difficult."

"Yes of course, I'm sorry," Hedrial replied sincerely.

"They've destroyed most of the village. It was typical barbarian style raiding. The good thing is though, they're not looking for Uthan. They routed some rebels. Some man, I did hear his name, Medoran or something, I think he's the leader. Anyway, Cornak took him away. I think he intends on learning the whereabouts of any other rebels in the area," Dionis continued. His voice grew faint a few times, only to strengthen again after a moment. The overall effect was difficult to listen to as the master and apprentice both strained their ears to catch the faint words.

"There's a rebellion against the Flame?" Hedrial asked incredulously. "How did this slip past us?"

"I doubt many in the village know about it. They'd have to be pretty secretive right now," Dionis said with a shrug.

"What about the Imperial Knights?" Uthan put in quickly. "Why haven't they done anything?"

Hedrial looked to his apprentice, irritated momentarily at the interruption. After realising Uthan did not quite understand the strain that was being put on Dionis's spirit form, he answered, "They are. I'll explain more later on."

"You should alert the village, Hedrial," Dionis said, more faintly than ever. "Lessa-Tus was our closest neighbour. The knights will be coming here next."

"Are you certain?"

"I'm sure of it."

"You shouldn't have done it, you know," Hedrial said, tears rolling down his cheeks.

"Get involved you mean?" Dionis asked. "Yes, I should have. Maybe I didn't help the people as much as I'd hoped to, but I tried."

"Yes, you did. No one can fault you for that," Hedrial said quietly. "I really wish you hadn't though. I'll truly miss you, old friend."

Another violent flicker passed through Dionis's spirit form. He disappeared completely, returning an instant later. This time though he was extremely faint and transparent. "I can't hold this form here any longer, Hedrial. I need to go. If you insist on this plan of yours, make sure you don't do anything too stupid?"

"Like you did, you mean?" Hedrial replied with a sad half smile.

"Exactly," Dionis said, returning the smile. He faded out of sight again.

Hedrial waited, sitting in silent contemplation until the dull blue afterglow had faded completely. Rubbing the tears from his face, he shakily stood up and wandered across to the window. Pushing the shutters open he looked out on the village of Kora-Tus. Like his aching weary body told him he should be doing, the village inhabitants slept. "Well," he said moving across to the door quickly, "better get to waking them all up."

The villagers, as Hedrial had expected, were less than pleased as they answered the dull ringing of the alarm in the centre of Kora-Tus. With no visible sign of attack, many of them were already cursing and casting accusing glares at Hedrial who stood patiently by the bell. Standing dutifully alongside his master, Uthan felt the piercing brunt of many of the stares also.

"OK, Hedrial, you had better make this good," said one of Kora-Tus's many carpenters. He, like so many of the others around him, had dressed hurriedly and held a weapon. In his case, a long knife was clutched tightly in his hands.

"I have just received word that Lessa-Tus has been burned to the ground." Hedrial quickly raised a hand, palm facing outwards to cut off the murmured words from the crowd.

Again the carpenter was the only one to speak openly, "This couldn't have waited till morning?" There were more sounds from the crowd. This time the surprise in the voices was directed at the carpenter. Suddenly aware that everyone's eyes were on him, he shrugged, confidence slipping away, and said, "Well there was no point in calling us out here unless we're being attacked, right?"

All eyes went to Hedrial. "We are Lessa-Tus's closest neighbours. You people do a good trade with them, exchanging your woodwork for their metalwork. The Black Flame Knights will attack us next," Hedrial answered calmly.

"How can you be certain?" asked a voice from the middle of the crowd. The owner stepped forward to reveal himself to be Mallan Camarr, Uthan's father.

Casting his eyes over the expectant people, Hedrial gauged their reactions as he ignored the question and asked one of his own. "How many of you know about the rebellion against the Flame?" When no one answered and there were no telling reactions, Hedrial continued, "The knights were in Lessa-Tus to crush the rebels there before they could get fully organised. Now it stands to reason that if they knew about the rebels there then they would know about the trading between us. If they are looking for more rebels then their next logical target would be here." He gestured around him at the collection of buildings for effect. Then, looking directly at Uthan's father, he said, "That is how I can be certain."

"So we prepare ourselves for a fight, right?" asked the carpenter.

Hedrial's piercing eyes made him shrink back again. "How many here are experienced fighters?" He counted the raised hands. "I see seventeen of you. And there is no time to teach the others to defend Kora-Tus."

"So you're saying we should just run and hide?" Uthan's father asked. His voice reflected his disgust at the idea.

"I'm saying," Hedrial answered, patience wearing thin, "that trying to fight them would be suicide."

"But what about you, and your magic? You can defend us," another voice chimed in.

Shaking his head, Hedrial answered, "I've found a way to put an end to these assaults but I have to leave now."

"You're leaving us to face this attack on our own?" pleaded another voice. "You have to help us!"

The words seemed to wake something up inside Hedrial. An angry glint flickered across his eyes. He clenched his fists and held them behind his back, trying to keep from trembling. Keeping his voice level and calm, he said, "Tonight I have lost a close friend because of this attack. He died fighting the knights. The people of Kora-Tus have relied on my magic for too many things. So much so you now have no defence of your own, other than this bell and seventeen men who can hold a sword the right way up. Now I suggest that if you want a magical defence you pack up your belongings and go north to the town of Ravellin. The few of you who can actually fight would come in more useful there working alongside the Imperial Knights stationed in the town. I'm leaving as soon as I'm ready. I suggest you do the same."

Without allowing the villagers a chance to break the shocked silence that had fallen after his words, Hedrial turned and strode back to his house. Uthan walked alongside him, trying hard to keep up with the wizard's pace.

"Are you still determined not to let me come with you?" he asked.

"Yes" Hedrial stopped walking and turned to look at his apprentice. There was a silence as the wizard was either having difficulty keeping his temper under control or he was thinking about his reply. "You're not ready to come with me. I wish you were, but I am going somewhere that is most likely beyond my abilities. It's regrettable that I haven't trained you enough but there isn't time now for regrets. I'm not leaving you here either though."

"Where are we going?"

"To see an old friend."

"That's all you're going to tell me right now, isn't it?" Uthan said.

Confirming his assumption, Hedrial remained silent, leading Uthan back inside his house.

"Pack your things together quickly," the wizard said moving rapidly up the stairs.

A short while later both master and apprentice had a small collection of belongings packed. Two chestnut horses were saddled and ready to leave. Hedrial turned a large brass key in the door lock. In the fearful silence that hung over the village, the clicks, as the intricate lock workings fell into place, echoed through the air. Uthan turned over his shoulder, setting an image of his childhood home forever in his memory. Silver pools of moonlight highlighted the stone and thatch of the buildings. A gentle night breeze moved along at ground height, sending ripples through the grass like waves. Pangs of sadness and regret stole over him as he realised the sight he was now seeing would probably be his last of Kora-Tus.

Climbing onto the horse next to Uthan, Hedrial took a last glance at the village too. Only a few of the villagers had decided to follow his suggestion. He could see their houses lying empty now, windows darkened like hollow eyes. The vast majority of the locals must have chosen to stay and fight. Shaking his head sadly, Hedrial turned his back on the village again and tapped his heels to his horse's flanks. Almost immediately after leaving the outskirts of the village, Hedrial turned them off the road and in through the tree line.

Plunging into the sudden suffocating darkness, Uthan began to believe he could hear strange noises that seemed to speak of legendary monsters. Trying to expel the thoughts from his head, he asked, "So now will you tell me where we're going?"

"A friend's house," Hedrial replied quietly.

"You told me that earlier."

The wizard cast a sidelong look at his apprentice. "This place is still too dangerous. What I'll be telling you is too important to risk the wrong ears hearing."

The night-time breeze wound its way between the trees, moving branches and rustling the leaves. Uthan could not tell whether it was the wind or if he really was hearing whispered voices from the canopy above him. They seemed angry and shocked. The feeling of tiny pinpricks spread over his neck. Giving in to the impression of being watched, he peered up amongst the thick web of branches above his head.

"Damn sprites think they own the forest," Hedrial muttered. "Ignore them, Uthan. They won't dare do anything more than taunt us."

Consciously ignoring Hedrial, Uthan strained his ears, trying to make out the words. It was not long before he could clearly hear a quiet female voice.

"You shouldn't be here. Go home."

"How do you know they won't try to stop us?" Uthan asked, more out of curiosity than anything else.

With a barely concealed smirk, Hedrial replied, "They remember me from last time they tried."

They continued riding at a slow walk along the unseen path through the darkened forest. All the time the voices from above followed the pair, words echoing threats and curses. Uthan had long switched himself off from them, allowing their words to be nothing more than background noise. If Hedrial was paying any attention to the sprites he did not show it. Instead he peered ahead into the gloom, impossibly guiding his horse between the trees and bushes. It was not much longer before they came within sight of an unusual house.

Surrounded by trees, it sat in a small man-made clearing. Thick tree stumps still littered the ground. The cleared area allowed moonlight to shine down on the dwelling, giving them both a better look at it. It was built from expertly chiselled stone blocks around a dark wood frame. Tiles made from varnished wood covered the roof. They had a silver glow as the moonlight caught them, acting like a beacon for the travellers. Entering the clearing they realised just how dead the house appeared. No lights shone within the windows.

"Don't you think your friend might be asleep?" Uthan asked.

His voice was nothing more than a whisper as they dismounted, tethered their horses and moved forward on foot. A small axe suddenly whistled through the air. The head bit deep into the ground by Hedrial's feet. Uthan was amazed, as the wizard had not even flinched.

Instead he glanced sideways at his apprentice, clearly amused and said, "No."

"Stay right where you are!" barked a voice.

It came from a darkened area beside the house that Uthan had not previously paid any attention to. Both master and apprentice stood perfectly still, attempting to catch the slightest glimpse of the owner of the voice. As Hedrial took a cautious step closer, the voice barked again.

"You don't get a second warning!"

This time it had come from the opposite end of the house. A short stocky figure stepped into the moonlight. In both hands he held a long handled woodsman's axe. His long, greying hair was braided and hung down the middle of his back. His equally grey beard was braided in the same way; only it was a little shorter than his hair. A wide, toothy smile split the dwarf's face as recognition flashed through his eyes.

"See him away, dwarf! He trespasses where he has no business," interrupted the sprites in their shudder-inducing voices.

Another small axe appeared in the dwarf's hand. He drew his arm back and hurled it. For the first time since Uthan had known Hedrial, he saw the wizard flinch as the axe spun through the air past his head. The sharp edge narrowly missed removing the wizard's left ear by a fraction of an inch. Instead it sailed on and embedded itself hard into a large oak tree behind them. Instantly the sprites fell silent.

Ignoring them further, the dwarf continued walking towards the wizard. He leant the larger axe against a tree stump on his way past. "And it's about time you showed up here."

Gesturing towards the axe at his foot, Hedrial said, "And with such a welcome mat, I'm wondering why I took so long."

"Creeping around in the forest at night-time? You could have been Black Flame Knights," the dwarf replied, shrugging.

"Well anyone trying to sneak up on you would have a hard time," muttered Hedrial.

"Those sprites? Yeah, annoying little buggers most of the time but they have their uses. Trying to get you to go home, huh?"

"Amongst other phrases, yes."

"Well," the dwarf continued smiling as he spoke, "they haven't forgotten you in a hurry."

The same quiet voices were heard again, bitter and angry. Their words were once again directed at the wizard and his apprentice.

The dwarf, Gauduin, moved closer to the tree line and bellowed, "Will you just shut up!" The forest fell silent. "Horses?" he asked, turning back to Hedrial. The wizard nodded. Directing his voice into the gloom of the tree line, Gauduin boomed, "Those horses had better not run off or anything."

There was the sound of whispering from the trees. At first it sounded like wind through the leaves. Uthan stood back in amazement as a couple of bushes parted and their horses trotted out into the clearing with a tremendously docile look in their eyes.

"Damn creatures love stealing people's horses. They untie them and just send them running away. Take them into the lean-to at the back of the house, lad," Gauduin said watching the horses make their way over to Uthan. Turning back to Hedrial, he said, "So, what brings you out here in the middle of nowhere at night?"

Hedrial nodded in Uthan's direction as he led the pair of chestnuts away. "This young man is my apprentice. I want you to watch over him for me."

"Giving you trouble, is he?"

"Far from it."

"So why bring him here?"

"I can't leave him in the village now, Gauduin. The knights are on their way there as we speak."

"So you bring him here. Fair enough," the dwarf said, pushing open the front door of his house.

He led Hedrial inside to a decent-sized sitting room. Ushering the wizard into a large armchair by the fireplace, Gauduin knelt down at the hearth and fiddled around with a tinderbox. After a series of muttered curses, he stood up, indicated the pile of logs and twigs and looked questioningly at Hedrial.

"Seeing as you're here?"

Walking as if he expected to have to stoop, Uthan entered the sitting room.

Hedrial pointed to the fire and said, "Light that, will you?"

As Uthan busied himself with lighting the fire, Gauduin sat in the other armchair.

"So where are you off to that you can't take the lad with you?"

Uthan looked up at Hedrial sharply. Ignoring the look from his apprentice, Hedrial replied, "There wasn't enough time to teach Uthan all he'd need to know to come with me. I'm going to look for something in the Demonic Realm. I can't risk his life there."

"The Demonic Realm? At your age?" Gauduin asked incredulously. "Why?"

Hedrial chose to ignore the age comment, glaring his displeasure instead. "I'm going to put an end to this Black Flame invasion once and for all."

"The Imperial army can't stop the knights fully. How are you going to?"

Forming a steeple with his fingers and touching his nose to their tips, Hedrial replied, "I'm going to the heart of the problem."

"The heart?" the dwarf asked. After a few moments his confusion faded as he realised what Hedrial meant. "No. You can't be seriously thinking about attacking the Flame itself."

"Not in so many words, no."

"Then I think you'd better explain things a little more clearly. What exactly are you planning?"

A wide smile of triumph filled Hedrial's face. "I've found the location at last."

Gauduin's expression darkened. "What in the seven hells are you babbling about, wizard?"

"The Forged One exists, Gauduin. I know where it is."

"Senility has set in at last, huh?" the dwarf suggested. "The Forged One is a piece of legend. A bedtime story told to get children to go to sleep."

"No. I've been searching every book and map and whatever else I can find for months now. A few days ago I came into possession of a dagger," Hedrial said.

Watching his friend with a careful eye, Gauduin said, "Go on"

"It's made of dragon steel." Hedrial produced the dagger from his pack and handed it to the dwarf.

He watched with pride as Gauduin turned the dagger over, scrutinising every inch from the ornate scrollwork on the hilt to the barely visible etchings on the blade. Gauduin gasped in disbelief, "Dragon steel? You're sure?"

"Yes, Gauduin. It really is dragon steel. There's the bluish tint. It never tarnishes or even gathers dust. Trust me, I've tried burning and staining it. As you can see, it's as good as the day it was forged," Hedrial said before continuing to explain. "It lends a lot more weight to the existence of the Forged One. I performed a few search spells this morning. They all point me to the right place. It's there, Gauduin. All these years and it's been there."

"It's been where, Hedrial? And stop looking at me like that. You're making me nervous," Gauduin returned.

"Mount Drakkar."

"The middle of the Demonic Realm! Hedrial, we're no longer who we used to be. We're old men now, Qwansien has disappeared, off playing outlaw somewhere and Suman is dead," Gauduin replied. His eyes had dulled with his sadness at saying the words.

"We may be old but we're not helpless, Gauduin. Are you seriously trying to make me believe you couldn't chop down one of those redwood trees with that rusty axe of yours?" the wizard sighed.

"My axe is not rusty," Gauduin replied, "but it's not a battle axe either."

"The way you were prepared to use it out there it didn't look that way." Hedrial shrugged then asked, "If I don't go, who will?"

The three were silent as Hedrial waited to hear Gauduin's answer.

Finally the dwarf asked, "What if it is there? It couldn't do what it was supposed to have been forged to do all those years ago. What makes you think it can do it now?"

"Do you have another suggestion?" Hedrial asked in response.

"Get a group of soldiers to go with you. Take the steel and forge weapons and armour out of it. You then get more soldiers to find the Flame and destroy it," the dwarf answered.

Shaking his head, Hedrial said, "That would take more time than we have. The knights are attacking villages every day. They're whittling away at the Imperial armies and any rebellions down to nothing. Soon there won't be anything left to fight for. Every soldier has to remain here to defend. And just imagine how difficult it'd be to convince them what I'm doing is right, let alone convince them to actually travel there."

"Doesn't that last thought tell you something, Hedrial?" Gauduin asked. "We'll talk about this properly in the morning. It's late, I'm going to bed; I suggest you two do the same. If you are going to go through with this madness then you'll need to sleep in a proper bed for one last time. I'll show you to your rooms."

He led them both up a short staircase and along a corridor. Their footsteps echoed off the polished floorboards, giving the impression that there was more than three of them. Stopping in front of two facing doors, Gauduin pushed on both of them, letting them swing open into two, tidily made-up spare bedrooms.

"Everything you'll need for the night should be there."

He wandered off back down the corridor before either master or apprentice could say anything. Uthan yawned loudly, surprised at not noticing how tired he was until now. Stepping inside one of the rooms, he said goodnight. Hedrial waited in the corridor a moment, reflecting on the conversation with his old friend as he heard Uthan's door close. Dionis's death had made him more determined to put an end to the reign of terror posed by the knights. He walked inside the bedroom that was to be his for the night and closed the door behind him.

A large bed with dark red sheets dominated the room. On the floor at the foot of the bed lay a large round rug. A pattern of two dragons tangled round each other had been woven in the centre of it but the bed hid half of their bodies. A chair, table and wardrobe of dark stained wood made up the only other furniture in the room. Hedrial wandered over to the table and tapped the sides of the bowl that sat on it. Circular ripples formed in the surface, disappearing in the centre. With a halfhearted sigh, the wizard drew the chair up to the table and sat down. Rolling up his sleeves he placed his hands in the water and drew a couple of symbols on the bottom of the bowl. More ripples formed in the surface as he spoke a few muttered words. Milky blue light began to emanate from the water itself. It slowly clouded over; the bottom of the bowl disappeared from sight completely. Hedrial muttered a few more words under his breath and the clouds began to roll back to the sides of the bowl.

Instead of the white base he could see Kora-Tus. By now the village was empty and deathly silent. Muttering under his breath, Hedrial moved the image to get a better look at the village. At the north end of the village, Hedrial noticed a small group of shadows moving in the dim light. At first the wizard dismissed it as the movement of the livestock in their night corrals. Then he noticed a pair of slumped shapes lying by the gates. Another muttered word caused the image to close in on the shapes, revealing them to be a pair of the livestock's guard dogs. Both had been slashed open. Another shadow detached itself from the darkness of the corral fencing. His black armour betrayed his identity to Hedrial. The Black

Flame Knights were now at Kora-Tus. Although the water image offered no sound, Hedrial almost imagined he could hear the thundering of horses' hooves as a large unit of the knights rode into the village. Hedrial watched the remaining villagers emerge from their homes only to be ridden down or run through. The massacre was over all too quickly. Hedrial pulled his hands from the bowl, sending cascades of water down from his open fingers to break the surface. The image disappeared amongst the ripples immediately. Drying his hands on the small green towel behind the bowl, he moved round on the chair and looked out of the window at the moonlit sky.

Shadows cast by the wavering branches danced on the floor. Hedrial sat and watched them for a moment or two, considering what would happen to the village. He wondered if the knights would just leave after searching the houses for locals. Somehow he doubted there would be anything other than burned out rubble for him and Uthan to go back to. One thought led to another and Hedrial soon found himself wondering how long it would be until the knights made their way through the forest and stumbled upon Gauduin's house.

He got up and paced the floor. Finding himself in front of the large window, he stared out into the gloom. He was aware of faint movements amongst the trees. He thought they could just as easily have been the sprites going about their nocturnal lives as much as the wind rustling leaves. He realised that should the knights attempt to make their way through the forest, the sprites would be able and more than willing to keep them back for some time. The woodland spirits kept intruders out, and the forest predators in, as much as possible. There was very little need for the packs of guard dogs that many of the villages employed to keep both predators and people away from the livestock at night. It was a shame, he thought, that the villagers did not realise it.

Lying back on the bed he became aware of his weariness. The endless amounts of energy he had felt he had while leaving his home had been depleted. His eyelids grew heavier and it had become increasingly impossible to keep them open. Dismissing thoughts that perhaps Gauduin and Dionis had been right and he was too old, Hedrial gave in to the warm embrace of sleep.

Loud chirping and warbling from birds directly outside his window caused Uthan to wake up the following morning. Bright sunlight filtered in through the branches to make flickering, dancing shadows on the floor. He rubbed the sleep from his eyes then sat up. The brilliance of the sunlight, although still partially hidden by the trees, made him blink. He looked around him at the room. It did not look as bare in the daylight.

He ran the previous day's events through his mind again. He wondered if the Black Flame Knights had reached Kora-Tus and, if so, what had become of his family and friends. Making a conscious decision to go back and take a look if Hedrial was still resolved to leave him here, Uthan climbed out of bed, dressed and washed. The smell of bacon frying found its way into his nostrils. Suddenly feeling exceptionally hungry, Uthan went downstairs.

"I don't quite understand it myself either, Gauduin. He was chosen for me. I didn't want an apprentice. I was ready to trick them all into thinking no one was to be chosen," Hedrial explained. He watched the dwarf sitting opposite him tucking into a heaving plate of bacon and eggs. Indicating the large amount of food, he asked sarcastically, "Are you certain you won't starve later?"

"Sarcasm never was your strong point, Hedrial," Gauduin replied, not looking up from his food. "So you want me to do what with the lad exactly?"

"Make sure he doesn't go back to Kora-Tus and try and keep him as far from the Black Flame Knights as possible. I'm still not absolutely certain they haven't been looking for him," Hedrial said.

"How could they know about his great power if you didn't and he was right under your nose all this time?"

"That's one of my concerns," the wizard replied.

"And isn't it also possible that they may be able to find him here?" Gauduin asked.

"That's my other concern."

"You're thinking that the sprites wouldn't be able to keep them out for long, right?" Gauduin asked, pointing a fork with a piece of bacon stabbed on the end at his old friend. Hedrial nodded and sat back in his chair. "Then don't worry. Those sprites may be as annoying as itching powder in your underpants but they'd be able to keep a bunch of humans away for some time."

"Nice analogy, annoying as itching powder in your underpants," Hedrial said with a smile.

"What I'm worried about, Hedrial, is if they know of the boy's existence and they can't get in here," Gauduin stated.

"What do you mean?"

"I mean, if they realise a human can't get into this forest, how long will it be before they decide to send something that isn't human or dwarf, elf or goblin for that matter? Or worse, decide the forest really doesn't need to be standing anyway."

"Gauduin, you're the only one I can trust to look after the boy. I can't find Qwansien and Suman isn't going to be much use."

"On account of being dead," Gauduin added. "Even if he was still with us he'd probably do something stupid. He'd have the boy carry all his weapons while he took him off gallivanting all over the place. No, I'll do it. I just need to understand what I'm doing."

They heard footsteps coming from above them. Hedrial looked directly at Gauduin, leant closer, and said, "I'd rather he didn't know what I've just told you either." The dwarf's mouth opened in surprise. "And close your mouth, something will fly in," the wizard added.

"You mean you haven't told him?"

"No, I haven't. He's still young. And someone young with that kind of power is potentially bad enough, but one who knows he has that kind of power is much worse."

"Good morning," said Uthan as he entered the kitchen.

Gauduin indicated the food on his plate and said, "There's more on the stove if you want it."

Uthan helped himself to breakfast, then sat at the table with Hedrial and Gauduin. Looking to each of them, he asked, "Are you still determined that I'm not to go with you, Master Hedrial?"

The wizard shook his head and said, "The Demonic Realm is a far more dangerous a place than bedtime stories would have you believe. I can't risk your life there."

"Then I'd like to go back to Kora-Tus later."

"I'd rather you didn't," Hedrial said slowly. A feeling of dread started in the pit of his stomach.

"Why not?" Uthan asked calmly.

A sigh escaped from Hedrial's lips. "The knights attacked last night. Only a few people stayed behind to put up any kind of a fight. They were killed."

"If the knights continued doing what they have been for months now, Kora-Tus has been burned to the ground," Gauduin continued.

Uthan was silent, staring at them both, "Who stayed behind?

Was it my parents?"

"No, that I am sure of," Hedrial answered.

"Then who?"

"I couldn't see their faces. I'm sorry," Hedrial apologised.

"If you couldn't see their faces then it could have been my father," Uthan said quietly.

"No, that I am sure of," Hedrial replied.

"We spoke to the sprites earlier, Uthan. They confirmed that your parents left Kora-Tus last night. They travelled amongst a caravan of people heading north," Gauduin explained.

Uthan played idly with his food, apparently no longer hungry. "Why hasn't the Emperor stopped them?"

"The knights have been hitting towns and villages at random. For months now they've been whittling away at the Imperial reserves. No one is left to tell anyone where they came from, so the Emperor doesn't know where their bases are," Gauduin answered. "Every scouting party he sends out is returned to him dead. What we want you to understand here, Uthan, is these knights are dangerous."

"And they are only the beginning of the Black Flame's army," Hedrial added.

Gauduin looked across at his friend, eyebrows raised in query causing the wizard to explain. "These knights, as dangerous as they are, are simply in place to make sure the real invasion goes through without a problem."

"Invasion?" Uthan asked. His fork clattered down onto the plate noisily.

"If you know something for sure, shouldn't you have told the Emperor about it?" Gauduin asked calmly.

"I would think he already knows. Despite his youth, Emperor Paracis is an intelligent young man. He'll have scouts and spies everywhere, including the Demonic Realm," Hedrial answered.

"How do you know there'll be an invasion?" Uthan asked.

"Little over a year ago a fruit trader came to Kora-Tus. He dealt in the trading of information as well as fruit. I'd had him gathering what knowledge he could on the Forged One. It was he who had that dagger sent to me, along with some very disturbing news. A large army has gathered in the plains north of Skull Gate. The message spoke of many species joined together to fight under one warrior. That warrior is Meligonn," explained the wizard carefully.

Gauduin sat back in his chair. He pushed his plate away, no

longer hungry. "Meligonn," he repeated.

"Who's Meligonn?" Uthan asked.

The dwarf glanced up from his plate, "Meligonn is the General of the Black Flame's demon horde or whatever he calls them." Uthan appeared stunned. Turning back to Hedrial, the dwarf continued, "So all the pieces have slotted into place."

"And the Empire will be lain to waste if I can't stop the Flame itself," Hedrial surmised.

"My question stays the same however," Gauduin said. "Why does it have to be you?"

"Those who will can't. Those that can won't," the wizard said with a shrug. "I'm the only one. If something goes wrong and Meligonn's army gets through the Barrier Mountains, I want you to take Uthan to Dacenheim as quickly as possible."

"How are we supposed to know they've broken through?" asked Uthan. He was growing annoyed at apparently not having any say in what happened to him.

Gauduin glanced quickly at him and said, "You'll know."

"Why," Uthan asked carefully, as if he felt he should already know the answer, "doesn't the Emperor ask the Wizard's council for help?"

"Because they're arrogant bastards who want nothing to do with this realm unless it has something they want or fear," Gauduin answered.

Nodding in agreement, Hedrial added, "Which is something you'll come to realise if you continue your magical studies." He leaned back further in the chair, thinking quietly to himself. "I think," he said finally, "I should be going."

Without a word, Gauduin and Uthan followed Hedrial through the house and outside. Uthan was mildly surprised to see the wizard's horse tethered at the front, waiting patiently for him. Climbing up into the saddle, he looked down at Gauduin.

"Thanks for watching over Uthan while I'm gone, Gauduin."

"Just pray your trust hasn't been misplaced," the dwarf replied.

"And if I don't return..." Hedrial started to say.

"Get into Dacenheim quickly. I know," Gauduin replied before adding, "But you're going to return. You always do no matter how hard we try to get rid of you!"

Hedrial grinned, "And you, Uthan, if I don't return, you are free from your apprenticeship." His grin disappeared as he looked at Gauduin again. "Goodbye, Gauduin. If worst comes to worst, I'll see you on the other side."

Watching Hedrial's horse turn and walk off, Gauduin laughed loudly and said, "You mean even in the afterlife I won't get any peace?"

The wizard disappeared around a corner in the overgrown road, vanishing from view completely.

Uthan watched the dwarf for a while, trying to figure out what the dwarf was thinking. Finally he asked, "You don't think he is coming back, do you?"

Gauduin looked at the boy in silence for a few moments. Realising he could only tell the truth, he sadly said, "No. I believe that's the last time I'll have seen him in this life."

Chapter Four

Medoran sat in a small cage that hung nearly ten feet off the ground. His shirtless, bruised back rested against the cold iron bars. The chill of the metal helped to ease the dull ache in his muscles. A throbbing pain filled his head. He felt as if something wanted to burst free from inside his skull. His left eye was useless, the flesh around the socket stung as sweat and dirt mingled with the blood from the numerous cuts. Large bruises covered his exposed torso, colouring his flesh with an ugly purple. He drew in a deep breath, shuddering and wincing as more pain lanced through his ribcage. The quartet of knights who had been ordered to beat him senseless had done their job a little too well for his liking.

A blurred frame hung around the vision in his good eye. It made him feel nauseous as he looked around at his surroundings once more. His cage had been hung in the main yard of a large fortress. The walls around him were solid, grey stone blocks, each one easily double his body weight. Thick, green moss covered a large portion of the walls. Tufts of grass and small weeds sprouted up between the cracked stonework of the yard floor. Ivy and some other vine plant that Medoran did not recognise clung stubbornly to the walls of the buildings. Black Flame Knights littered the fortress. They reminded Medoran of ants in their nest. He noticed he was the only prisoner in the cages that hung from the framework. That meant he was on his own in his escape. Good, he thought to himself, less to worry about.

The huge gates, blackened wood studded with shining steel spikes, were pulled open. General Cornak rode in through the archway, followed by twelve more knights. Almost as if Medoran's hateful glare had yelled at Cornak, the general looked up. The jailer and prisoner locked eyes, their wills battling each other silently. No one around them took much notice as Cornak climbed down from his saddle and made his way over to stand beneath the cage.

"Your rebellion is finished."

"Go and choke on something, Cornak," Medoran growled.

"With the exception of yourself and less than a handful of survivors, they are all dead. Nobody is coming to help you, Medoran. How does that feel? To know you're truly alone at the end."

"This is far from over, Cornak."

A sneer spread across Cornak's face as he countered, "Really? So who's coming to rescue the great rebel leader? Another bunch of farmers? Or maybe this time it'll be bakers and stable hands."

"And I bet you feel really secure now, huh?" Medoran replied.

"They were just another conquest. As were you, Medoran."

Medoran hawked and spat a large globule of blood, which splattered on Cornak's left boot. "Add that to your list of conquests."

The general glared down at the blood then back up to Medoran, catching the hate in his eyes. His face suddenly contorted into a mask of rage as he yelled to the nearest guards, "Get him down now! Beat some respect into this miserable dog!"

As the cage was lowered to the ground, Medoran allowed himself a smile. He had managed to get to the general again. As Cornak turned and stalked off across the courtyard, Medoran called after him. "What's wrong, Cornak? Can't you even beat up an unarmed prisoner on your own anymore? Oh, how the times have changed!"

Stopping only a few paces from the doorway to one of the buildings, Cornak turned to watch as the cage door was thrown open. Two guards stepped forward, each holding a long pole, six or seven feet in length with a thick rope hoop at one end. They slipped the hoops over Medoran's head and pulled back on them tightening the rope around his neck. Watching the rebel struggle between the two guards brought a sadistic gleam to the general's eye. Two more guards moved in, brandishing clubs. While Medoran strained against the poles, he was clubbed repeatedly over his head and torso until he finally dropped to his knees. Gritting his teeth to keep from crying out in pain, he continued to stare at Cornak long after the general had turned his back once more and moved into the darkened doorway.

The men gathered in the room all stood up sharply as Cornak entered. All but one of them wore the black plate armour of high ranking knights. Cornak cast a look of disgust over them. Nothing about them suggested they had seen real battle. This was clear to him from their lazy posture to their completely untarnished armour, but mostly he could see it in their eyes. Eyes that showed they had never truly looked death in the face. Meligonn gets a legion of demons while I get a legion of cretins, Cornak thought to himself. He pulled his helm from his head, letting the remnants of a ponytail tumble down his back. His black hair was soaked in sweat, sticking uncomfortably to his scalp. He indicated for the briefing to proceed.

"General," one of the men started.

Cornak flashed him a look that suggested his report had better be good. The man fought with himself, trying hard to hold Cornak's gaze. He gave up after only the briefest of moments, choosing the corner of the table as his focus point instead. The slight hesitation had been too long for Cornak's patience.

"Continue," he growled threateningly.

"Several of the more organised rebellions and local magic users have been..." the man stalled, looking for the right word, "...eradicated."

"How many are left?" Cornak asked.

"It would appear the only real magical force in the Empire would be the Wizard's council, but it's widely known they don't bother themselves with the goings on of the Empire," the speaker answered.

Cornak shook his head. He paced across the floor and pulled a chair from under the table. He settled into it with a sigh and, keeping his voice steady and his gaze fixed on the now sweating man, said, "The council will bother when the Black Flame asserts his presence here."

"But, General, what could they do in comparison to his Almighty Power?" asked another of the knights.

The general flashed his stare onto the new speaker, making the man instantly wish he had stayed silent. "The original council formed part of the crusade before. They could easily bring others to join another crusade. What of the physical armies?"

The first speaker nodded, "The force of any real worth now is the Emperor's own. All rebellion forces have been routed further west and south. The only ones to remain here are mere handfuls of outlaws and villagers."

"This was the very same report you gave me last week, was it not?" Cornak asked. The man nodded, by now trembling. As if he could smell the man's fear, Cornak pressed on. "Only a day ago I uncovered a nest of the vermin. Only a day ago I had three hundred rebels put to the blade. Their leader is currently outside in my courtyard being tortured for the hell of it. You're aware of this?"

Again the man nodded, this time a little more hurriedly.

"Why did you try to feed me a report about no real opposition when

I discovered this rebellion for myself? I know you're not stupid."

"It was as I was informed by our spies, General."

"I am not stupid either," Cornak cut in quickly, his voice rising. "I ride out again in a few days when my own spies get back to me. You had better hope I do not hear of anymore talk concerning uprisings."

He turned to look at another man seated in a chair in the corner. This one wore the dusty cloak and lightweight armour of a scout. Calm once more, Cornak asked, "What of the outlaws?"

The scout shook his head and shrugged, "It looks as if they raided the camp and just vanished into thin air."

"Vanished? Men do not just vanish," Cornak replied.

"Two soldiers were alive when my party arrived. Both men said the same thing. The raiders came from nowhere and went back to nowhere. I've had my men scouting the area for the past week. We've found nothing. They'd even removed their arrows from the bodies of the dead," the scout concluded.

"So you confirm the soldiers' story then?" The scout nodded. "Are they alive now?"

"No, General. One died from his wounds soon after questioning. The other was unable to travel."

As the scout spoke, Cornak's eye took in the sight of the scout's hunting knife sheathed on his thigh. "What are your conclusions regarding the attackers then?"

The scout was silent for a few moments, thinking on his words. "I'd say they have Elves amongst them. It's the only reason I can give to the 'from nowhere to nowhere' thing."

"Mages?"

"There was nothing to suggest any."

"Could they pose a real problem?" Cornak asked.

The very first speaker turned to look at the scout. As the scout returned the gaze briefly, he noticed a look of warning flash across the knight's face.

Coolly, the scout replied, "In the not too distant future they could, sir. Right now, I don't believe so. They've only been attacking small camps and outposts. From that I'd say, although they're dangerous, there aren't enough of them."

"You will ride back out tonight and continue your search for them," Cornak said.

The scout stood up and saluted sharply. Cornak merely nodded, dismissing the man. Waiting for the scout to leave, the general looked back to the first speaker. "Does that not sound like a potential uprising to you?"

"Surely you don't take this handful of outlaws seriously, General?" the knight asked. From the tone of his voice he had clearly hoped to back the general into some kind of metaphorical corner.

Cornak glared at the knight, instantly reducing any such hope. "This handful of outlaws took apart a camp of supposedly well trained soldiers. Almost two hundred knights in fact. Out of that two hundred only two lived long enough to talk about it. No traces of these outlaws have yet been found. I don't find that even remotely amusing, do you?"

"No, General."

The general flashed his glare over the assembly and each individual felt unable to look at the wrath-filled face. Looking directly into the eyes of the speaker again, Cornak said, "Yes. I take this handful of outlaws seriously." He waved a hand, irritably dismissing the group. As he watched the collection of so called warriors meekly leaving the room, Cornak was once more filled with disgust. Sighing loudly, he muttered, "I have to promote some better people."

Medoran had been put back in his prison again. Angry red welts covered his torso and arms. Blood ran freely from a gash under his eye and from his lip. Each breath drawn caused him to wince in pain. He had broken another rib, he thought to himself, trying to breathe as easily as possible.

Looking out across the courtyard, he noticed an old man wandering around. Although his path seemed winding and aimless, he was trying to look busy. Gradually the man made his way over to the water barrels kept only a few feet from Medoran's cage. The knights either completely ignored the old man's passing or made some joke at him. The man himself just kept his gaze on the ground in front of him. There was something familiar in his walk as well, Medoran noted to himself, although through the haze of his mind he could not place what it was.

"Hey," he called, waiting for the man to reach the barrels and begin to drink. The man did not seem to hear him. A little louder he called, "Hey you! I'm talking to you."

Without turning the old man said quietly, "They'll kill us both if I talk to you."

"They'll kill me anyway," Medoran muttered.

"True," the man agreed softly.

"You're a prisoner too?" Medoran asked as if to make conversation.

For the first time, the man turned to look at Medoran. His eyes were as wild as his hair. He appeared to be trembling a little. "I am the caretaker here," he said.

"Oh, right." Medoran answered. He was second-guessing at his attempt to get information out of the old man. Deciding there was no other choice after all, he continued, "And where is here?"

"You are now sitting in the courtyard of Caslodor, one of the last remaining fortresses of the Royal Knights," the man answered. As he spoke, he straightened up, bursting with pride.

Now Medoran recognised the place all too well. He had only ever been to the fortress once before and then he had only been a new recruit. Flatly he replied, "Doesn't look like the Caslodor I knew."

"That's because it has been polluted by Black Flame vermin," was the disgusted reply.

Medoran had the feeling the old man would have spat at that moment. "So why are they here?"

The old man merely shrugged and took another drink from the ladle. "Even General Cornak himself has to admit the fortresses built by the Royal Knights are still the best in the realm."

"Wonder why that could be," Medoran muttered sarcastically. He knew exactly why. Turning his head a little he asked, "Could I have a drink?"

The old man turned and looked at him. He looked around, eyes darting everywhere to make sure he was not being watched. Quickly he dipped the ladle into the barrel again and moved over to Medoran. Before the water could reach the prisoner's lips, a black-gloved hand batted it away. The owner of the hand, a heavy-set knight with a large brow and thick black moustache waved a fist at the old man. To his credit, Medoran noticed the older man did not give way but continued to stare defiantly back. It seemed as though a battle of wills was going on. Then, quite suddenly, the old man backed down. His shoulders slumped in defeat.

"Now get away from here before I have you hanged," the knight growled.

Watching the old man turn and move off, almost like a scolded cat, the knight turned back to stare Medoran down. The prisoner returned his captor's gaze evenly.

"Don't tempt me to kill you," sneered the knight.

Without breaking eye contact, Medoran answered, "How about you let me out of here and we'll see?"

Suddenly, as if unable to hold the prisoner's stare any longer, the knight began to move away. "You'll keep for later."

Medoran settled himself back against the cold comforting steel bars. "Yeah," he said quietly, "that's what I thought."

The rebel swordsman closed his eyes. He now knew why the fortress had looked so familiar. From outside, he heard the thunder of horses reminding him of a previous time. Trying hard to relax he let the memories from his youth flood back, hoping something in them would lead him to a possible escape route.

A younger Medoran lay on his bunk bed back in the barracks staring at the darkened ceiling above. He could hear the baying of the hounds in the distance outside. A shudder passed through him as he remembered images of the dogs tearing at the flesh of his former comrades from earlier in the day. It was no way for a man to die, he thought. Screwing his eyes tight closed, he tried to think of something else to shut out the baying of those accursed hounds. A song, a story from his childhood, an image of the girls from the town he grew up in, anything. But nothing would come. Sighing, he rolled over and, eventually, managed to drift off to sleep.

It seemed no time at all had passed when he became aware of frantic shouting from outside. For a few moments he remained absolutely still, listening and trying to make some sense of the noise. The shouting was soon joined by the sound of hoof-beats, then the clashing of steel on steel. The screams followed soon after. Medoran sat bolt upright in bed. An attack had started. Looking around him at the large room that had been full of sleeping soldiers, he saw several of them were already on their feet. Armour and weapons were hurriedly put on as soldiers called across the room to their comrades to wake up. Medoran wasted no more time. He rolled over to his left and dropped from his bed, narrowly missing the feet of the man who used the bed beneath. While mumbling something in the way of an apology, which went unheard, he grabbed his sword from its peg on the bedpost. Jogging across to the doorway he realised he had slept in his armour.

Outside the barracks, men were running back and forth. The fortress was in a state of panic and Medoran realised, with a chill passing through his blood, the sounds of fighting. As if to confirm this, a quartet of the heavily armoured riders raced past the barracks. They swept out with long curved swords, hacking out at unfortunate soldiers who were still half asleep. A trio of soldiers came to stand behind Medoran.

"They've broken in!" one of them exclaimed.

Another muttered from further inside the room, "But how? All the defences were impregnable, Cornak said so himself."

"We should find the captain," piped up another soldier, "he'll know what to do alright."

Medoran glanced over his shoulder into the dull room behind him. As he was making a quick count of the soldiers left, a man fell at his feet from outside. Startled, he jumped back, staring down. The man was bleeding badly from a cut to his chest but was still alive. "Quick, pull him in here," Medoran hissed to the two nearest soldiers.

They grabbed the man under the shoulders and dragged him inside. Two more comrades picked his legs up and between the four of them they placed him on the nearest bed. Medoran indicated for three of the guards to stand by the doors and keep watch while he set to, desperately trying to save the man. As he worked, helped closely by another soldier, he ordered the others who had carried the wounded man onto the bed to check outside for further casualties. Such was the confusion of the attack they did not object to a man of equal rank giving them orders. It was not long before he had several injured men to deal with. As he worked, Medoran was aware of a heated conversation going on between some of the soldiers. However he was finding it difficult to comprehend.

The soldier, telling the story, had been sitting on the catwalk, huddled in the shadows of a merlon. He told of how he had watched Captain Cornak stride confidently across the yard right between the pair of huge trebuchet catapults. He had walked right up to the gatehouse and had stood talking with the pair of guards there for a few moments. The soldier had not been able to hear the conversation properly and, wishing to hear something that might ease his mind, he had crept over to a better vantage point. From there he had witnessed Cornak draw his blade and behead the first guard. Before the second could do anything, the captain had run him through. Then, to the soldier's horror, Cornak had moved over to the gate opening mechanism and had hauled the gates open. He had then stood there signalling to the waiting attackers with a blazing torch before mounting his horse and leaving the fortress. Moments later the attack had begun.

Medoran sank back, sitting on the next bed along as he heard of the betrayal. From behind him the two guards were still talking.

"No. It couldn't have been Cornak," said one.

"Why not? You saw him earlier. He did nothing to help those poor bastards out there. And then when young Darph asked about the defences he looked like he was going to kill him. The man has betrayed us," the other soldier answered.

The first soldier came up to stand next to Medoran and asked, "How are they?"

"I've stopped the bleeding. Providing we can repel this attack and they rest then they'll make it," Medoran said. He felt well pleased at being able to keep them alive.

Another guard came running into the room. Instantly four swords were drawn and held ready. Two bowmen stood a little way back, arrows held against taut strings. The soldier held up his hands and stepped closer into the dull torchlight to reveal he was one of them.

Pacing down the line of beds he asked, "Who's in charge here?"

Everyone slowly glanced at Medoran.

The newcomer then looked at Medoran and said, "I expect you've heard the news about Cornak?" Medoran nodded. Behind him someone spat in disgust on the wooden floor. The soldier continued, "We're holding one section of the fortress. But it's weakening. We have barricades and bowmen everywhere holding the bastards back. From the stables to the southernmost barracks are ours. I came to scout out for survivors here."

"You want us to come with you?" Medoran asked. The soldier nodded. "What about the wounded? We can't move them properly yet, we only have one stretcher."

"Bring one of them along with us on that. We'll come back with more stretchers for the others. Bar the doors and leave two men to watch over them till we can return. For the next hour they should be safe enough," the soldier answered. "We have quite a few wounded ourselves. It's been a vicious fight."

Moments later, Medoran was running across the ground outside, heading for the safe zone. They ducked around the corner of a squat stone building and stopped for a moment. Harsh voices could be heard behind them. Two of the soldiers unsheathed their swords and moved to stand by the corner and wait. The rest of the soldiers started off again, moving down a narrow alleyway between two long barracks.

Suddenly from behind them they heard the sounds of clashing weapons. Two screams rose up into the night. The soldiers stopped in their tracks. Medoran spun round to look in the direction they had just come from. The hulking figure of a huge Nierhoth, clad entirely in dirty fur pelts, stumbled into the alley.

The Nierhoth had once been nomadic tribesmen. Despite their long fangs, jutting both up and down from huge, gaping jaws that pushed out from dark, hairy faces, they had once been peaceful. Now they made up a large and very violent part of an already massive army led by an unknown master. Stories of violent ritual magic and ceremonial killings added more fuel to the fear instilled by their appearance.

Without thinking about it, Medoran removed his sword from its scabbard and sprinted forward to meet the Nierhoth. It was clear the tribesman had not even noticed the group of soldiers as Medoran crashed into him. The young warrior brought his sword blade up into the Nierhoth's chest, piercing the thick breastbone so deeply his sword was stuck fast. He stepped to one side as the huge figure stumbled forward. He risked a quick glance around the corner of the building to check if more were nearby. The sight that greeted him made his blood freeze.

The barracks that he had left the wounded in was only just in sight through a small gap between some buildings. He could see a small group of Nierhoth disappearing inside. Medoran's eyes flashed wide open. Those Nierhoth were inside with the wounded he had only just saved. Reaching down he picked up the huge serrated sword of the dead tribesman by his feet. His eyes took on a distant look. Grasping the heavy sword handle in both shaking hands, he started forward, moving with defiance in his stride.

Behind him he could hear the murmured voices of the soldiers who had been with him. They sounded as if he was listening to them through water. He could only think about the Nierhoth ahead of him. The sound of his own blood pulsed in his ears, his heartbeat pounding a steady rhythm in his mind. A fiery heat boiled up from deep in his guts. A split second later he was consumed by an uncontrollable desire to do nothing but kill. Raising the weapon high above his head, he let out a loud yell. There were no words, only a furious noise. It was as if the sound had unleashed some other personality deep within Medoran, then he surged forward. Charging into the room he stopped in his tracks, taking in the sight around him. The soldiers he had saved from bleeding to death had been hacked apart. A few still lay in their beds, in the same positions they had been when he had left. The two soldiers who had been on guard lay on the floor, both cut to pieces. Three tribesmen stood over them, bringing their weapons down hard into the bloodied corpses again and again.

The wave of fury washed across Medoran once more. He propelled himself forward, sword held out in front of him. One of the tribesmen turned around to meet him in combat. Quickly Medoran slammed the edge of his weapon into the jaw of the Nierhoth. The sheer weight of the sword forced it to cleave through the tribesman's skull completely. As the lifeless body pitched sideways, Medoran hacked his sword down into its chest. The second blow sheared through the heavy ribcage completely. Blood was flung up from the body, splattering his young face. For the briefest of moments he closed his eyes, trying to keep the blood from blinding him.

When he next opened them, the remaining two Nierhoth tried to rush at him. As they ran up, Medoran sidestepped into a gap between two of the beds and lashed out with his blade. It caught the nearest one at stomach height. Pushing the weapon further in and downwards, Medoran completely opened the tribesman's belly, spilling his guts to the wooden floor. Before the other Nierhoth could react, the berserk soldier leapt at him. His weight slammed into the tribesman who caught him in a bear hug. As two powerful arms started to squeeze down on Medoran's rib cage, he plunged his sword into the Nierhoth's lower back. Howling in pain, the Nierhoth let Medoran go. As he dropped to the floor, Medoran grabbed another of the huge serrated swords. Yelling his angry defiance at the top of his lungs he hacked away at the tribesmen, sending fountains of crimson across the beds and floor.

With his own heart thundering in his ears, Medoran stopped and took a step back. He let go of the weapons in his hands; barely hearing them clatter to the wood floor. Breathing in harsh ragged gasps he looked around at the carnage of the room. On the beds and floor lay men, who despite only knowing them for a short while, he had come to like. He had stood alongside many of them earlier that day. He had shared their fear and their revulsion. Now they were dead, their bodies mutilated. And one man was solely to blame for it all.

Cornak.

Opening his eyes again, Medoran found his gaze fixed on the darkened doorway Cornak had entered. He had not worked out an escape route from the Royal fortress. But he had remembered, however, just why he hated his captor so much. In all the hate, the swordsman had nearly forgotten. The face of every corpse in that fortress flashed through his mind's eye once more. A sudden calm feeling passed over him. The initial anger subsided quickly. All it left behind was a cold feeling of hate and an almost suffocating desire to kill.

Chapter Five

"Are you sure he said here?" Cass asked. She could not see over Demien's shoulder and therefore was unable to see what her friend was studying.

What Demien had in view was the large fortress of Caslodor, squatting on the open empty field. In the dawn sunlight, her keen eyesight picked out the black flags flapping against the purple and pink streaked sky. This highlighted the figures, clad in black armour, pacing along the battlements.

"Yeah Cass, I'm sure."

Turning Kainan into a grove thick with trees, Demien swung from the saddle. Getting her first real look at the fortress, Cassmed's eyes widened. Her eyesight was not quite as good as her more experienced friend's, however she could still see Caslodor was occupied after a decade of standing empty.

"You're not going in there alone?"

"I'm going to have to, Cass. I can't afford the time to go and round up an army."

"Let me come with you. I can help."

"No," Demien returned quickly, "I want you away from trouble here. I can't watch over you."

"You won't have to," Cass answered.

"You're not coming with me," Demien said with a tone that commanded the end of the argument.

"But there has to be hundreds in there. It's suicide. At least wait until night," Cassmed pressed on. She was vaguely aware her voice had a pleading edge to it.

"We've just missed one night. Besides, you know they can't kill me," was Demien's reassuring reply. She grinned as she said it.

"Maybe not," the younger girl muttered, "but they'd certainly try hard."

Demien did not appear to hear the comment. She was watching the fortress intently, deep in thought. Quietly, she said, "I'm not going in to fight them anyway."

"I'm sure they'll take that into consideration during the whole second it takes them to draw swords."

The swordswoman turned back to her young friend. She paced back over to Kainan. Grasping the sides of the large white head, she whispered, "If I don't come back, you take care of her."

The horse snorted and bared his teeth. From up in the saddle Cassmed saw the response.

"See? Even Kainan thinks it's a bad idea."

"He's just annoyed I'm not taking him," Demien replied. "I'm serious, Cass. If I'm not back by midday you leave without me."

She took a miniature oiled leather pack from the saddle, then knelt down close to a tree and began pulling handfuls of grass up by its roots. A small bottle and some cloth, sewn into what resembled a badly made tunic were deposited on the ground. The thick contents of the bottle were poured over the joints in her armour, bathing them in an oily film that would make them silent as she moved. Demien then slipped the cloth over her armour and began stuffing grass inside.

"And round up some kind of army?" Cass asked, clearly unsure of herself.

"If I get caught I'll take as many with me as I can. And you know that's going to be a lot of them," Demien smiled again, standing back up. She handed the half empty pack to her friend.

Cass did not smile as she took the pack. "That doesn't make me feel any better about this, Demy."

"Relax, Cass. They're only men. Besides, there are not enough of them in there."

Before Cassmed could comment any further, Demien turned and moved off through the grove of trees. The girl strained her ears, listening for her friend but Demien was moving like a ghost, impossibly silent over the earth littered with twigs and leaves. All that the girl could hear was the subtle breeze playing with the very top branches above her.

Demien slipped through the woods, far more stealthily than she would have normally considered worthy. She crouched behind the trunk of a beech tree, watching a knight lazily leaning against a merlon. His back was turned to her and she was fairly certain there were no others with him. Her eyes went to the open field between her and the fortress. There was roughly five hundred yards of empty grassland, with a slowly rising sun shedding its growing light on her.

She shifted her position, putting all of her weight onto the balls of her feet. The muscles in her thighs were pulled tight, waiting for her brain to send the command. Drawing in a deep breath, Demien sprang forward and sprinted across the grass. Her breathing had only just started to become laboured as she slapped her body flat against the crumbling stonewall. For a moment she offered a silent prayer. Thanking whoever would listen that she had had the foresight to muffle the metal in her armour, preventing it from clanking against the stone. A few feet above her head thick vines had begun to burrow their way through the ancient mortar. They clung stubbornly to the stone and moss giving Demien a makeshift ladder. She kept flat against the wall, letting the vines hide her from the eyes of the guard above while she slowed her breathing again. The smell of moss and mould invaded her nostrils. They were the only odours in the decaying fortress.

Turning to begin the steady climb up the vines she stopped suddenly. Cassmed's words sounded again in her mind. Demien hesitated, realising exactly what she was ready to do. Sneaking into the heart of the enemy was crazy, Cass was right about that. It is only crazy if you do it for no reason, Demien thought to herself. She did not really need reminding that Medoran was in there. He was her reason. Testing her weight on the vines, Demien began her ascent of the fortress walls.

Two guards, not one, stood on the battlements only a few feet to her left as she slipped over the top. Engaged deep in conversation, neither man saw her. She crouched low, allowing the shadow of the wall to hide her while she looked over her surroundings. The pair of guards nearby was the only immediate danger. Silently she drew two, curved bladed knives from her boots. Giving one last check behind her, Demien shot to her feet and came up behind the guards. Drawing the blades across their throats with the precision of a surgeon, Demien killed them both before they could make a sound. Catching the bodies before they could fall and clatter noisily to the floor of the fortress, she pushed them over the side. Without waiting to hear the corpses thud against the ground Demien darted across the walkway. Coming into clear view of the courtyard, Demien froze. Black Flame Knights could be seen everywhere. She counted them under her breath even though she knew there were too many to fight. Lowering herself onto her haunches she paused to think.

Almost as if the gods themselves had decided to help, Demien saw many of the knights were mounting horses and forming a column. She watched patiently as nearly three quarters of the force waited to leave. There was a series of orders barked from the man at the head of the column. She could just hear the reply before the huge gates ground open. More orders were shouted from the column leader before he moved his horse on, racing out of the fortress. If these men had not been her enemy, she felt she would have been impressed with how quickly the yard had emptied. She watched the column as it moved across the fields, gradually resembling a black snake, until it disappeared from view.

Her gaze went involuntarily to the cage in which Medoran sat. She could not see the figure clearly but she just knew it was him. He was slumped back against the bars, head leaning to one side. One arm was held across his stomach. Seeing the condition of her lover, Demien felt a furious heat begin to flow through her veins. Looking down at her hands, she noticed the fingers trembling. Her heart pounded hard in her chest. Unable to control the wave of anger, Demien stood up and paced right back to the wall before taking a running leap off the walkway.

Landing lightly on the flat stone roof of a barracks, Demien flattened out. Pressed motionless against the stone, she waited, listening for the telltale signs that someone had seen her. After a few moments had passed she crawled quickly across the roof to the edge. Peering over she saw a guard below. He sat in a doorway, idly tossing his knife into the doorframe opposite. Believing he had not heard her, she moved across the flat rooftops, keeping as low as possible to avoid being seen. With only guesswork to guide her towards Medoran, Demien found her way onto the last building before the yard. She turned her head slowly, taking in the placements of every visible knight below her and on the walls. She counted only three on the wall and they were too far away to see her clearly, hidden on the shadowy roof. Sighing in relief, she turned back to look down at the yard.

There were four knights standing guard over Medoran. Their idle stance told Demien that they were not paying any attention to the prisoner. Clearly they believed there was no threat. A few feet from the cage there was a stack of barrels. An old man who looked incredibly out of place around the thuggish knights, skulked close by them. From the distance, Demien could not see him clearly enough to be certain but she thought the old man was muttering to himself. He could have been talking to the prisoner but there was no sign that Medoran was listening.

Then, one of the guards glanced over and saw the old man. He stalked over and grabbed him by the collar before marching him past his laughing comrades and away. Two of his comrades followed behind, mocking the old man as he struggled in the knight's grasp. It left only one to guard Medoran.

Demien allowed herself a smile. One would be easy.

She slipped from the roof, dropping into a half crouch before sprinting to the shadows of the wall. The lone guard remained where he was, facing the opposite direction. Treading carefully, she skirted along the wall, concerned that at any moment the guard would turn and see her. Constantly searching the rest of the yard, she noticed there were no other knights to be seen. She ducked behind the stack of large barrels, working her way closer to the guard's exposed back. Finally getting within reach, she snatched a dagger from its sheath on her thigh and drove it deep into the side of his neck. As the guard thrashed wildly, Demien caught him and pulled him back behind the barrels. Another dagger thrust silenced him for good.

Medoran was crouched in his cage now. He watched the yard, expecting to see more knights. Demien slid her dagger free from the corpse and moved across to him. "Miss me?" she asked, offering him a quick smile.

"The other guards will be back soon," Medoran answered quickly.

Slamming her dagger down against the lock of the cage, Demien broke it open. "We're leaving before they do, I hope."

"Unless they heard that," Medoran answered.

He pushed the door open and climbed out. Straightening up to his full height, he stretched his back and neck. Demien only barely noticed the half hidden wince of pain that crossed his face. She grinned and stepped up to kiss him lightly on the lips.

"How did you get in?" he asked calmly, helping her place the dead knight in his cage after first stripping it of the black armour.

"I came over the wall," she replied. With a grin she added, "I thought about just knocking on the front door but I didn't think they'd let me in."

"And how are we leaving?"

"I thought this time we'll go through the front door. The place seems deserted enough."

"Most of them left on a raid not long ago. But if we're lucky, there'll still be a few horses left," Medoran said.

Demien nodded, "Get to the gates and hide there. I'll be back soon with a horse."

Medoran snatched up the dead knight's sword and made his way to the gates. Demien watched him limping, feeling a pang of concern. Instantly she steeled herself again, trying to remain cool and composed so she could get the two of them out of the fortress alive. Using the wall as cover again, she made her way round, searching for the stables.

Medoran reached the gatehouse quickly. There was a single knight there who had not even seen him as Medoran ran the sword through his neck. Leaving the blade where it was, Medoran pulled the knight's own sword from its scabbard instead. He pushed the corpse further into the shadows of the darkened hut and waited there for Demien.

The stables had been even easier to find than she had dared to hope. And luckily, there were still horses left. A pair of knights stood at one end of the long building, talking. Demien slipped into one of the stalls, easing her way past the horse. The beast snorted loudly and stamped its feet, uncertain about sharing its space. The noise attracted the attentions of the knights. She could hear their boots on the cobblestones as they approached. Carefully she ducked into the next stall along and reached for the bolt on the top half of the stable door. She drew the bolt quickly and slammed her fist into it. The wood swung out wildly, catching one of the knights hard in the face. He fell to the floor, blood streaming from his nostrils, shouting in puzzlement. The horse charged out of the stall, alarmed at the movements around it. The other horses stamped and snorted.

The unharmed knight reached out a hand, trying to stop the escaped horse. It reared suddenly, causing him to back up. He kept his eyes on the huge flailing hooves, dodging away from what could be a fatal blow. Hearing the cry from his comrade, he turned just in time to see Demien as she slit his throat. The knight with the broken nose had got back to his feet. Blood streamed down his face and into his open mouth. Demien rolled past the horse, coming to her feet again immediately in front of him. Her dagger blade pierced his chest. He made a small whimpering noise before dropping to his knees, clutching at the wound.

Without giving him a second glance, Demien swung up onto the back of the horse, and spoke soothingly into its ear, trying to calm it down. From outside now she could already hear shouts. Knights were coming to the stables, demanding to know what the noise was. She could not wait any longer. Kicking her heels to the horse's flanks, Demien burst out of the stable and raced across the yard, knocking knights from their feet as she passed. Making for the gates, she saw Medoran already pulling one side open. Through the gap she could see the lush green grass beyond, promising their escape.

"The gates! They're going for the gates!" yelled one knight

Four other knights had turned to look and were now running at Medoran. Demien got there first though. Her dagger was hurled at them hard. The hilt struck the breastplate of one, driving him onto his rear, winded. Sliding her sword free from its sheath on her back, she swung out wildly, trying to keep the others away while Medoran had pulled the gates open enough. One of the knights got too close. The tip of Demien's sword opened a deep cut on his forehead. He stumbled back, clutching his head. It was enough of a warning to the others to be more cautious.

"Close those damn gates or I'll have all of your heads!" roared a voice from a doorway.

Medoran turned from his work to see Cornak emerging from the shadows. He met the general's stony-eyed stare with his one good eye and smirked. Holding his sword up in a mock salute to Cornak, he moved to Demien. The swordswoman snatched at his hand hurriedly, pulling him up behind her. Her horse kicked up dust as it was guided towards the gates.

"Nice rescue," Medoran called over the pounding of the hooves on the ground as they raced out from the fortress. He cast one quick look behind him to see Cornak running for the stables.

Cass had sat patiently against a tree, waiting for Demien to return. Hearing the shouts, she sprang to her feet. From her vantage point she could see a single horse with two riders racing towards her. She could also see the group of riders coming up quickly behind them. "Kainan, I think it's time we were going," she muttered to the horse. As quick as she could she pulled herself into the saddle. The horse remained still, patiently waiting for Demien to return. His ears twitched as he listened to the oncoming riders. Cass heard him snort twice. "Kainan, we don't have time. They're coming now, let's go!" Cass said, pleading with the horse to move.

There was still no movement from Kainan. Then suddenly he leapt into a tight turn and raced off through the woods with Cass clutching the reins tightly. Demien looked up to see the white blur slipping through the trees up ahead.

"You have that horse too well trained," Medoran yelled over her shoulder. "Do you think we can catch him?"

"He's taking his time to let us," Demien answered. She smiled to herself. Few things in her life had been as dependable as Kainan. Medoran started as a tree, the first of many, whipped past them. Demien leant her head back to him and called, "A bit jumpy, aren't you?"

"I didn't expect you to be aiming for the trees."

The sun above them shone through the canopy, dazzling them with flashes of bright light. Behind them they heard the loud crashes as the Black Flame horsemen entered the woodland too. Demien turned to check the distance when something caught her eye. Looking back to where she thought she had seen the shape there was nothing. Leaning back again she nodded at the trees.

"There's someone else in here."

Even before she had got the words out, another figure stepped out from the shadows, longbow firmly in hand. She saw the bowstring pull taut, an arrowhead pointing in their direction.

"I noticed them too," Medoran yelled back.

The archer suddenly let his arrow fly. It whistled through the air, racing past their horse. Behind them they heard a cry of pain and a crashing in the undergrowth. One of their pursuers had taken the arrow in his unprotected face. His body had toppled back sharply, pulling hard on the reins. The horse in response had reared, moving up and back at such a steep angle it fell backwards as well. The next horse had leapt its fallen brother easily and continued the pursuit.

"There're three more to the right," Demien said loudly as a two figures stepped from behind bushes and a third dropped from the branches of a tree. Again, all three held longbows drawn ready to fire. She called again, "Friends of yours?"

"I was about to ask you the same thing."

Two more arrows flew, one taking their pursuer's horse in the neck, the other high on its head. The rider leapt from his mount before it fell and stepped back to allow his comrades to ride past. The third archer released his bowstring; his arrow slipping past the riders and taking the lone knight through an impossibly small gap between his belt and his breastplate. The remaining riders suddenly pulled to a halt, confused. Quickly their leader signalled to five to follow the archers while the others were to continue the pursuit of the escaped prisoner.

"They've split the pack," Demien called over her shoulder.

The moment of indecision from the Black Knights had given them a few extra moments. The woodland around them was thickening. Gaps between the trees were getting narrower with every racing moment. Obstacles such as thorn-covered bushes and fallen branches littered the forest floor in front of them. The ground had begun to dip and rise sharply, making each step a hazard. Ahead of them they could see the white form of Kainan winding easily between the trees and bushes with Cassmed clinging tightly to his back. His path was angling towards them.

"As soon as he's close enough, I'll jump on. I know he can carry Cass and me easily," Demien shouted, indicating her horse. She heard the sharp intake of breath from Medoran as their horse leapt a large fallen branch. "Do you think you can make it?"

Medoran nodded quickly, clenching his jaw and replacing the pained expression with a mask of focused determination. Demien allowed herself a smile. Even in his current state of health he still felt he had to appear to be indestructible.

Kainan suddenly burst through a bush and landed gracefully beside them. He raised his head and snorted loudly. On his back Cassmed clung to the pommel of the saddle as both horses took another jump. No sooner had they landed than Demien reached over and tapped her young friend on the shoulder. Cassmed turned around ready to drive an elbow into whoever had touched her. Seeing Demien, she lowered her arm again and called, "Are we dead yet?"

"Not yet but we're working on it!" Demien called back.

Cassmed leant back in the saddle allowing Demien to climb from horse to horse. Crashing through a gap in the trees obscured by branches, they emerged into a clearing. The relatively flat ground gave their horses a sure footing, in turn granting them the extra speed needed. Medoran, gripping a fistful of the horse's mane in one hand, pointed to two different exit spots in the opposite tree line.

"We'll split up. Break the pack down further."

Demien nodded and tugged on the reins slightly. "Be careful," she said, as Kainan took the new direction.

"Make for the river. I'll find you there," Medoran answered.

He watched Demien nod again.

Behind them the Black Flame horsemen crashed through the woods. With open ground between them and their prey, they split into two groups. Medoran risked a quick glance back. His pursuers were gaining ground. He knew they were just the few who had had the presence of mind to get to their horses quickly. Not far behind them could be a larger hunting party, probably headed by Cornak himself. His horse plunged into the woods again, momentarily slipping on a shallow dip. Through the trees and bushes to his left he could see Kainan, taking the harsh terrain of the forest easily. He spurred his mount on, putting its skittishness down to the terrain and the near fall. A sudden shout behind made him risk another look. One of the Black Flame horses had fallen on the same dip. Its rider pitched forward to the ground. The horse had then rolled back up and was now standing and snorting loudly.

Medoran smirked. His horse leapt a thick tree trunk, felled years ago by the wind. The rebel had not expected the jump and was thrown from the horse's back. Landing hard, he felt a sharp stabbing pain in his shoulder. Behind the log he could hear the Black Flame riders drawing nearer. Pushing with his leg muscles, Medoran scrambled closer to the tree, hoping the riders had not seen him fall. As the horses leapt one by one overhead and continued after his horse, he knew they had not. Another smirk crossed his face. He had managed to lose them. He fought against the pain in his shoulder to stand. The queasiness spreading through him suddenly became too intense. His vision spinning, he grasped the fallen tree and tried to breathe in deeply. To his right he could hear hooves pounding the forest floor but he was too disorientated to tell if they were coming towards him or not. Coughing violently, he was forced down to his knees again. Each cough brought more pain to his ribs and shoulder. There was a shout to his left. They had found his horse riderless and were returning. Using the tree, he pulled himself upright again and started walking.

"There he is!" yelled a voice not too far away.

"Remember the general wants him alive," replied another.

Medoran tried to break into a run. He had taken only a few steps before he stumbled and fell to his knees. His whole body cried out in pain. Unable to take it any longer, Medoran lapsed into unconsciousness.

Wary of a trap, the Black Flame riders slowed their mounts. Two held crossbows trained on the prone form of Medoran while the remaining two dismounted. An arrow flashed through the trees. One of the crossbow men fell from his saddle, the shaft protruding from his eye. The remaining three knights spun round, searching the forest around them for the bowman.

"Get him on a horse and let's get out of here," suggested the remaining crossbow man.

A lone rider vaulted the fallen tree sending the horses into panic. Another arrow took the other crossbow man in the throat as he tried to take aim at the newcomer. The other knights quickly climbed into their saddles again and drew their swords.

"I don't know who you are but you've just ridden into more trouble than you can handle," said one of the two slowly.

From beneath the thick brown and green cloak, the rider produced a slender bladed sword. The knights charged both with swords ready to cut down the cloaked rider. Pulling hard on his reins, he caused his horse to rear up, kicking with its front legs. In reply, one of the enemy's horses tried changing direction too quickly. It lost its footing on the forest floor, pitching sideways. The knight was caught underneath the heavy warhorse, falling at such an angle that his neck was snapped.

The last knight managed to keep his horse under control and got around beside the rider. He lashed out with his sword as hard as he could. The slender blade came up to block his attack easily. He tried four more times with heavy slashing arcs, each time the cloaked rider blocked. On the next attempt, the rider ducked instead and thrust out with his weapon. The tip skewered the knight through his throat, tearing it open. As he fell, choking on his own blood, the rider walked his horse over to the prone form of Medoran. From the bushes around them, three more cloaked figures emerged. One made its way across to the fallen knight, still alive and in tremendous pain. With an elegant looking short sword, it decapitated the knight. The other two figures had picked Medoran up and placed him as carefully as possible across the saddle in front of the rider.

"Make sure no more follow," said the rider in a calm quiet voice.

The figures all nodded once then disappeared into the forest again. The rider spurred his horse on, heading in the direction that Medoran had originally been travelling in.

Kainan burst through the tree line with a powerful leap. Coming to land on solid even ground again, he galloped off faster than before.

He had added an extra twenty yards of distance between him and their pursuers before they too left the woodland. With very little control from Demien, he wound his way around the thinning trees; giving them much needed extra cover. Behind them, the Black Flame horses gradually fell behind. They were unable to keep up with the furious pace of the huge white warhorse, Kainan.

"The river's ahead, just beyond those trees," Demien said. She nodded to a thick stand of pine ahead of them. "We'll have to lose them there."

In her ear she heard Cassmed gasp. The girl's fingers gripped hard into Demien's shoulder, cutting her words off. Demien winced a little at the sudden pressure. Cass's knuckles were white.

"Cass, what's wrong?"

The trees around them grew thicker again. Plunging back in amongst woodland, they lost sight of the Black Flame Knights. Over the thundering of Kainan's hooves and Cassmed's hard breathing in her ear, Demien heard the river. Its dull rushing sound acted like a beacon. Kainan leapt a shallow dip and steadily climbed the hill opposite it. Racing over the top, Demien saw the river ahead of them and angled Kainan down the slope towards the bridge. It was narrow, wide enough for one horse at a time. Its old moss-covered support beams did not look strong enough to hold even one horse. Demien slowed Kainan to a trot, eager for him not to lose his footing on the damp planks. Halfway across, she stopped, watching the opposite bank. A lone, cloaked rider emerged from the trees. It reined its horse in, waiting for Demien to cross. Another figure was draped over the saddle in front of it. Demien recognised the unconscious figure immediately. Before she could call out, a crossbow bolt hammered into the upright support next to her. Kainan spurred into action, ignoring the pressure on his reins that called for his caution in crossing. Four arrows flew from the opposite bank in answer to the knights. Two struck home, killing their targets before they knew what was happening. The remaining pair, believing they were outnumbered, turned and spurred their horses away. The cloaked rider signalled to the trees. Another figure, wearing an identical green and brown cloak jumped from the branches and jogged over. The rider leant down and said something. Nodding once, the figure darted past Kainan and across the bridge.

"Is he alive?" Demien asked the figure, gesturing to Medoran.

"He lives for now. But he will need medical attention quickly to stay alive," the figure replied. The voice was male and had a strange accent to it. "It looks like your friend needs attention too."

Demien turned in the saddle quickly. Cassmed's face was pale. A film of sweat covered her forehead and cheeks. Then Demien saw the shaft, it sat at an ugly angle, piercing the flesh of the girl's right shoulder. Her voice rising a little in panic, Demien said, "Cass, speak to me!"

"Can we get this out first please? I really don't feel like talking right now," replied the girl as jovially as she could.

"There is a village twenty miles over there," the rider said. He inclined his head to the direction he meant. "We need to get them both there quickly. Soon this forest will be swarming with Black Flame. My men can merely distract them. We can't fight an army."

Demien nodded and followed him as he spurred his horse off toward the village.

Chapter Six

The spike of rock that was Mount Drakkar loomed ahead of Hedrial. Its peak rose sharply into a cloudless sky, reaching up to the heavens. Clearly considered unassailable centuries ago, someone had gone to the trouble of carving steps out of a natural shelf that wound its way up and around the mountain. The claustrophobic humidity of the jungle had eased as the trees and bushes had thinned out into open grassland; a mile of exposed land lay between Hedrial and the mountain.

The word exposed stuck in his mind and vibrated along every nerve. His hands twisted on his staff nervously as he contemplated the final stage of his quest. With an eye constantly on the sky above him, Hedrial wandered forward. He kept one hand on his long staff and the other clasped the hilt of the sword that hung from his belt. Beneath his dark green robe, worn purely to make him as invisible as possible without using his magical stamina, Hedrial wore chain mail armour. It was the first time he had done so in nearly thirty years. It felt uncomfortable and awkward but the old wizard was leaving nothing to chance.

Around the base of the mountain, the ground became broken. Chunks of rock stabbed up through the soil. A narrow trench, no more than a couple of feet at its deepest point, wound a path around the mountain. It was as if Mount Drakkar had shot up through the ground, and grown higher and higher. And as it had emerged it had pushed rock and earth aside, forming the small hills on which Hedrial was now standing.

Taking care to make as little noise as possible, Hedrial trailed between the foothills until he found the foot of the stairs. Whoever had painstakingly carved them all that time ago had taken extra pride in crafting a gateway from the very same rock. It consisted of two thick pillars, joined by an arch of carved stone. Atop the pillars sat a pair of stone dragons, their unseeing eyes watching whoever might enter the gate. Just beyond, the stairs were partially sheltered by a high wall, presumably left in place so climbers would not tumble over the edge. Counting the steps under his breath, Hedrial began the long climb.

After the sixtieth he had been forced to conserve his breath and count in his mind. The nervous, excited wave that had built up inside him with every footstep had proved too much to be able to count aloud. On counting one hundred and seven steps, Hedrial stopped breathless again. Ignoring the wind that bellowed in his ears and tried to pull him closer to the edge of the steps, he sat down heavily and looked out over the plain to the trees. Listening to the sounds of the jungle in the distance, the wizard tried to calm his heart, which pounded in his chest. With his staff propped up against the mountain wall and his pack lying on the step below his feet, Hedrial allowed himself to rest and read from the small scroll he had brought with him. Under his breath he muttered words, consigning them to memory.

The sky was streaked with purple, orange and red as the sun began to disappear. Hedrial looked over into the darkening twilight jungle. Night was falling fast and the wizard did not relish the idea of freeing something else that might enjoy the darkness. A small sigh escaped his lips as he got to his feet once again. The chance to relax for even a few moments had been gratefully accepted by his legs.

Holding a scroll up to compare a drawing on it with the mountain itself, Hedrial placed a hand on the rock, palm flat. Taking one last look at the scroll, Hedrial closed it and put it firmly inside his pocket. Sighing again, this time with more depth he pressed his right hand against the solid wall and began to form an outline. He drew his hand across the rock, a foot to the right then a few inches down and to the left, tracing an invisible pattern. Leaning forward, he placed his forehead on the mountain, feeling the rough surface against his skin. "Shou-oo-arkch-da'tett," he said quietly. Then he pressed harder against the rock and, speaking in a loud voice that appeared to echo around the mountain, he commanded, "Open!"

The pressure on his arms was released a little. The rock moved. Hedrial lifted his head and looked from hand to hand. Pushing again and repeating the command, he was awash with excitement as a section of rock wall was pushed slowly inward. The sound of stone grinding against stone was loud in his ears. It competed against the heavy drumming of his heart. Pushing the wall in a little further, Hedrial noticed the long winding passageway to his left. Stairs, once carved smooth but now carpeted with a thick layer of dust, ran down into darkness. He took a step back from the moving wall and smiled. All that remained now was to walk down the stairs and find the end of his journey.

"Another Imperial squad has been slaughtered," Gauduin said calmly.

He walked up behind Uthan quietly, careful not to break the apprentice's concentration. The object in question was a woodsman's axe. It sliced and chopped at logs as Uthan guided it through the air, one lapse by the apprentice and the axe could be thrown anywhere.

Watching the axe with a mixture of awe and nerves, Gauduin muttered, "I wish you'd do that the normal way."

About to speak, Uthan instead winced. His hands went to his head, fingertips pressing against the sides of his skull in pain. With a groan he toppled sideways, falling from the tree stump, which he had been sitting on. The axe suddenly spun high into the air. As Gauduin watched, it reached the top of its ascent before beginning its fall again, towards the prone body of Uthan. No more than a foot above his head, the axe bounced away, as if it had hit a shield. The ricochet sent it gathering speed until the head slammed hard into a tree branch.

As Gauduin ran over to check on Uthan, a voice around him echoed, "Get him inside."

The dwarf did not waste time on looking for the owner of the voice. He knew whom it belonged to and where they were. "What are you doing here?"

"I need to speak to you."

"Well it can wait," Gauduin answered, picking Uthan up carefully.

As the dwarf carried Uthan in through his front door he saw the blue-tinted shimmering ghost of Dionis hanging from one of the doorframes. "Put Uthan to bed. We have to talk."

"And what can we possibly have to talk about?" Gauduin snorted. He carefully placed Uthan on his bed and took a step back. "Besides, who are you to order me around in my own home?"

Dionis interrupted, "There's something wrong, I can't feel the link with Hedrial anymore."

Dionis's words stunned Gauduin into silence. Feeling suddenly ashamed for his bickering, he then tried to make sense of the news. Unable to keep his weight upright, he sat heavily in the one single chair in the room. "He can't be dead. He's…"

"Indestructible? Immortal?" Dionis cut in again. This time there was more than a hint of irritation in his voice. "They weren't quite the words you used to describe him before, were they? Old man, wasn't it?"

"How?" Gauduin asked.

"You're thinking the worst. I've not found him on the other side yet. All I do know is the link has been severed."

Gauduin nodded. He disliked Hedrial's familiar but realised the bat understood these things far better than he could. "Did he reach it?"

"I don't think so. Nothing seems to have changed." Again Gauduin nodded.

On the bed Uthan groaned. Dionis looked over, seeing the apprentice clutching his head. "Has he had headaches like this a lot?"

"This is the worst so far. It's never caused him to screw up a spell like that before," Gauduin answered. "He owes you thanks for that shield."

The ghostly bat looked directly at Gauduin, "I didn't put up a shield. I can no longer cast." The dwarf looked stunned. "There's something about this lad that Hedrial didn't know," Dionis continued. "I'm going to have to learn more."

"What happens with Uthan in the meantime?" Gauduin asked, raising one eyebrow at the ghost.

"Do just what you have been doing the past few months. Hide him from the Black Flame. Keep him safe," Dionis answered.

Before Gauduin could say another word on the subject the ghost of Dionis faded, letting the room grow dimmer again. He turned to look at Uthan, who was no longer moaning and holding his head. Although the pain was echoed in his expression, Uthan was asleep.

Behind Hedrial as he placed his right foot on the first step, the setting sun was suddenly blacked out. Simply out of curiosity, he turned to look.

Two enormous, yellow eyes watched him, full of baleful intent. A pair of nostrils, only slightly smaller than the eyes, flared as huge lungs drew in breath. The exhaled breath was heavy with the stench of sulphur and made the wizard cough. He felt his excitement turn to a fear that threatened to loosen his bowels. The dragon then drew in a deeper breath while drawing back its head.

Quickly Hedrial formed symbols in the air with both hands, trying desperately to cast a shield to protect himself. His fingers felt unresponsive and trembled visibly. He sidestepped, making for the stairwell and, he hoped, cover. The burst of flame was just a moment faster than he could move and he was engulfed instantly. The oxygen in his lungs was aflame, killing his dying scream of agony.

Uthan woke with a start, it was as if he had been there with Hedrial.

No, not with him. Inside him.

He had seen the events through Hedrial's eyes, felt his excitement of finding the doorway. He had experienced the moment when excitement became dread, as the wizard knew he was facing death. Realising he too had then felt the pain of fire across his flesh, Uthan hurriedly rolled up his sleeves. His arms were normal, no blisters or burns.

"How are you feeling?" Gauduin asked. He stood in the doorway, a look of concern on his face.

Uthan shrugged, "Okay I think."

"You're going to feel worse when I tell you that.." Gauduin replied gravely.

"It's about Hedrial isn't it?" Uthan said with a finality that startled Gauduin, "He's dead."

"You heard what Dionis said then?"

Uthan looked up at the dwarf, "No. I just... knew."

"Well, the bat was here. As far as he knows the link with Hedrial has gone," Gauduin said uncomfortably. He fell into silence again upon seeing Uthan's face so pale.

Uthan was only half paying attention to him however. The young man was staring, bleary eyed at a corpse. The apparition was a burned up human. Hedrial. His flesh was blackened, tinted here and there with the dark crimson of dried blood. Blackened rags hung from his body, fused into place by the searing heat where they had been in contact with his skin. Despite there being no eyes in the sockets, Uthan felt a shiver to realise the ghost was staring at him. It took a step forward, limbs crackling as the cooked flesh moved. The stench was sickly sweet, making Uthan's stomach turn violently.

"Free me Uthan. Please."

The words seemed to rattle from the throat of Hedrial's ghost and entered Uthan's head without using his ears. The ghost took another couple of steps toward Uthan and extended a hand in a plea for mercy.

"Please."

"So what do we do now?" Gauduin asked.

As if the dwarf's words had broken through into his mind and cast the illusion aside, the apparition disappeared. A feeling of intense sickness swam through Uthan. His mouth watered unpleasantly. In different circumstances, Gauduin might have been amused that the young man answered his question by suddenly throwing up on the floor by his bed.

"Did you see him?" Uthan asked. His voice was weak.

"Dionis? Yes he was here."

"No," Uthan shook his head, "Hedrial. He was right there." He pointed to where the ghost had been. The hairs on the back of Gauduin's arms and neck rose on end. A shiver ran through his flesh. Uthan continued, "He asked me to free him, Gauduin. He pleaded with me."

"Free him?"

With a nod, Uthan said, "His exact words."

Gauduin was quiet a moment, "Dionis said the link was gone. He couldn't find him. Maybe Hedrial isn't on the other side yet."

"I have to help him, Gauduin," Uthan replied.

The dwarf looked at him gravely, "I was wondering how long it'd be until you said that. Well, lad, Hedrial himself would call us stupid, I'm sure of it. But we owe it to him, so we're going."

"Good to hear, Gauduin," said a new voice inside the room. It was Dionis, his spirit hung from the window, watching the dwarf.

"Have you brought us more bad news?" Gauduin asked gruffly.

"Hedrial's spirit is not on the other side. He's trapped somewhere," Dionis said before going on, "I heard Uthan telling you about seeing his corpse here."

"So we're going to go and free him," Gauduin shrugged.

Dionis looked hard at him, "I can only hope it'll be that simple."

Gauduin looked at Uthan, "Get the horses ready. We'll be leaving immediately."

He waited for Uthan to go before moving closer to Dionis, "Did you learn anything else?"

The bat shook his head, "Nothing, but usually around a mage of any kind there's a sort of magic aura, like an outline around them."

"Yes, I know about that," Gauduin said, impatiently.

"Well, not around Uthan. Somehow he's managing to hide it."

"Or maybe you're not looking hard enough."

"If you think you can do better, why are you asking me?" Dionis replied. His tone had taken on a harder, irritated edge to it.

The dwarf fell silent a moment before he continued, "I'm concerned about him. He has headaches when a mage is killed, someone cast a shield spell to protect him from that axe and now you tell me he has no magical signature. It doesn't smell right, Dionis."

"Nothing about this does," the spirit replied. "If I learn anything more I'll find you. Until then, take care of him and yourself."

Gauduin nodded as the pale blue light that surrounded Dionis faded. Then he went into his hallway. A large cabinet stood there, set into an alcove in the wall itself. A heavy looking lock was set in the centre of the doors. Getting down onto his knees, Gauduin reached his stubby fingers into a dark gap under the cabinet. Retrieving the key, he sighed and stood up again. Pulling the doors open, he felt a surge of excitement and pride rush through his veins. Sitting on a wire mannequin was his armour. Despite being unused for years, he had kept it in perfect condition. In its polished breastplate he saw himself reflected in the shining bronze. There was a glimmer in his eyes he had neither seen nor felt in years. Breastplate, then greaves and bronze plated boots were all put on and fastened together. A pair of leather gauntlets was tucked into his broad leather belt, ready to be used when needed. Throwing a thick, green cloak over his shoulders and fastening it, Gauduin stopped to look at himself in a mirror.

He raised an eyebrow disapprovingly at his reflection. He ran a comb through his long grey beard then braided it. His hair, as long as his beard, was combed and braided as well. He reached back into the cabinet for his bronze helmet then went back to the mirror before placing it squarely on his head.

"Once more the warrior," he muttered to himself, smiling.

On the inside of the cabinet door was a heavy looking, wide-bladed sword, an equally heavy looking battle axe and a curved bladed scimitar. Each of the three weapons had been well crafted and looked after. A few small chips taken out of the axe head was the only sign it had ever been used. He strapped a scabbard onto his back and slid the sword blade into it, savouring the sound of steel on leather.

Stepping out of his front door, he saw Uthan leading two horses around. One of them, a small grey mare, was saddled ready for Gauduin. The stirrups were higher to allow for his shorter dwarf legs. Uthan stood next to his own horse, a chestnut stallion, equally as eager to go as his rider was.

"In a chest in the hallway you'll find weapons. Pick something simple to use as I won't have much time to teach you," Gauduin said. His grey mare whinnied and stamped the ground happily at his approach. "Yes, Marlery. I'm here."

The sight of Gauduin in his armour, although mostly hidden by the green cloak stunned Uthan into silence. A sudden look from the dwarf made him run into the house to fetch a weapon. Saddlebags had already been filled with food, water and a few other necessities. As he emerged from the front door, breathless, looped onto his belt was a short sword. Having taken a last look at his home, Guaduin led Uthan into the forest.

"It'll soon be time to camp for the night," Gauduin said breaking the silence.

His voice cut through Uthan's thoughtful silence, making the young man raise his head. The sun was sinking into the horizon, painting the sky with broad strokes of orange, red and purple. Taking Uthan's silence to be reluctance, Gauduin said, "I'm not comfortable spending another night in a forest that could easily be crawling with Black Flame Knights either. But I'm even less comfortable with walking into them in the dark."

"Sorry, I was thinking about something else," Uthan said, coming to reality.

"About the journey?"

"Kind of, but more about what we're going to do when we set the Forged One free. If the Black Flame is as powerful as the stories say then we'll have trouble getting to him."

Gauduin nodded, "However, Uthan, we're not going that far. We'll set the thing free and it will find the Flame as it was made to do. Killing the Flame is its job, not ours. We have Hedrial's soul to save." He swung out of his saddle and started to lead his horse off the road. "If I'm not mistaken, there should be a fairly good place to camp around here."

They walked their horses into the forest itself. Around them the deep fiery orange of the sunset bathed the trees in an almost magical light. It was not long before they reached a semi-clear area. Huge tree trunks lay on the ground, leaning against trees that were still standing, offering their support to fallen brethren. Broad stumps stuck up through the ground and thick, green moss clung to the fallen trees, giving them a furry appearance. Leading his horse around a particularly large trunk, Uthan found himself standing on the top of a high hill. On the slope below him other trees had been cut away, thinning out the forest. From his vantage point he could see the top half of the dropping sun.

"Savour it now. You'll never know when you'll get to see another one," Gauduin said.

Pulling his eyes away from the sunset, Uthan saw the dwarf sitting on a tree stump, watching the same thing.

"It's unbelievable, isn't it," Gauduin continued. "Years ago some woodsman started to clear this place, hoping to build a town. They could only fell the trees you see before you. The sprites wouldn't let them take anymore. I used to come up here at times and just watch the sun setting."

Uthan could only nod, only half listening before asking, "Won't we be exposed here?"

"I doubt it. So much littering the ground here that we could light a fire and it wouldn't be seen from the road." Gauduin said. The tone of his voice suggested to Uthan that he was still immersed in the sunset.

"What about down there?" Uthan indicated the hillside sloping down in front of them.

"Only the slope itself is exposed you notice. The sprites wouldn't let the men take anything further. We'd know about anyone coming up from there right away."

As the last rays of sunlight finally faded into the dull hazy grey of twilight, Gauduin pulled himself away from his seat and set to work making a small fire. Uthan tethered the horses to a broken down tree and set about making them comfortable for the night. Getting the first flickering flames going at last, Gauduin gently heaped more and more twigs around them. Contented to leave the fire to feed itself for a short while, the dwarf sat back. The barest movement to his right side caught his attention suddenly, "Uthan?"

"Over here," came the reply from the horses.

"I thought so." Gauduin carefully moved to one knee, making the pretence of going back to building the fire. From the corner of his eye he saw another half seen movement. His hand inched its way to the sword hidden under his cloak.

"By the time you reached it you'd be dead already," said a quiet voice.

Gauduin pushed himself to his feet and turned round. The figure stood on the top of a tree, fallen but left leaning against another. The long, grey green cloak it wore hid everything except for the longbow. Seeing the arrow notched and aimed at him, Gauduin moved his hand away from the hilt of his sword. Uthan moved around the horses, muttering something under his breath. He had seen the cloaked archer and, believing the archer had not seen him, he was preparing a spell. Suddenly an arrow was pressed against the back of his neck.

"You cast and I let this arrow go. Understand?" said another voice. Uthan nodded. "Good. Now go and stand beside your friend."

Uthan did as he was told, moving around the horses and over to stand next to Gauduin.

"There are more of them in the bushes to my left," the dwarf said softly.

"We didn't hear them coming, did we," Uthan said sarcastically.

The first figure jumped down, landing lightly on the ground. Its movements were fluid as it picked a way nearer to them. The bowman who had stopped Uthan casting emerged from his place in the shadows as well, taking up a position to the right. Two more figures came from the left, both brandishing bows.

"Well you're not clumsy enough to be Black Flame. That's a good thing for you," Gauduin said suddenly.

"And you're too short to be Black Flame. Which is better for you," replied the first figure. Its head inclined slightly to the two to the right. Slowly it lowered its bow, releasing the tension on the string.

Quickly Gauduin's hand went to his sword. The faint sound of steel on leather was audible. A whistling stopped the dwarf from removing it further. Both of the figures on his right side had arrows aimed at him. Pushing the sword back in place, he muttered, "Can't blame me for trying."

"Good to see you still on form after all this time," the first figure replied casually. With one hand, he drew his hood back, revealing elfish features. His dark hair was cut short showing off the pointed ears. Two dark eyes glimmered in amusement, watching the features on Gauduin's face undergo a series of expressions, confusion, recognition, then anger.

"What the hell are you doing here, Qwansien?" the dwarf said nearly exploding.

A half smile twitched at the corner of the elf's mouth, "I was on my way to see Hedrial. My scout saw you two leave the road and I couldn't resist this little play as soon as I knew it was you. So what brings you out here into the great wide world you abandoned?"

"What did you need with Hedrial this time?" Gauduin asked carefully avoiding the elf's question.

Qwansien shrugged, "Just a little information. Why?"

"Hedrial's not up to giving out information anymore."

Concerned, Qwansien asked, "What's wrong? Is he ill?"

"He's dead," Uthan answered slowly.

As if seeing the young man for the first time, Qwansien looked at Uthan, then back at Gauduin for confirmation. "Dead?" The dwarf nodded. "That's... it's... well," Qwansien started to speak. He rubbed the back of his head and looked at the ground instead. "How?"

"I think it was a dragon," Uthan said quietly. "But I'm not sure."

Nodding absently, Qwansien moved to sit on a tree stump. He glanced up and remembering his three comrades still had their bows drawn ready, signalled. The three lowered their weapons and stood motionless. "It's okay, you can head back to camp now."

Without Gauduin or Uthan noticing they had gone, the three figures faded back into the shadowy woodland and disappeared. Qwansien looked up at Gauduin again. In the few passing moments all traces of amusement had left his elfish features. "Is there a dragon in the Empire then?"

"No. Hedrial didn't die in Kora-Tus."

"Oh. Is that why you're on the road again? To avenge him?"

Gauduin shrugged, "He was at Mount Drakkar."

"What was he doing there? Alone I take it?"

A faint look of shame crossed Gauduin's face, "Yeah, he was alone. He'd found out the Forged One really does exist."

"And he'd gone to set it free or whatever. Sounds like Hedrial," Qwansien said. He dropped his face into his hands.

"We're travelling there ourselves with the plan to set it free," Gauduin continued.

Qwansien nodded, letting silence fall over the trio instead. For a long time neither dwarf or elf said a thing.

Finally feeling overpowered by the quiet, Uthan added, "Hedrial's soul is held somewhere around there. We're going to free him as well."

The elf got his feet. Slowly he wandered over to stand in front of Uthan. He extended a hand to him. "I don't know who you are and I apologise for my ignorance. My name is Qwansien Tiomie."

"Uthan Camarr," Uthan answered, taking the offered hand.

Gauduin said, "Uthan was Hedrial's apprentice. He's a very talented boy. Very talented."

Picking up on the emphasis Gauduin put into the words, Qwansien nodded. "Come back with me to the camp. Tomorrow we can leave."

"We?" Gauduin asked carefully.

Nodding, the elf answered, "Yeah. I'm coming too."

Chapter Seven

"Not very well guarded, is it?" Gauduin said as they entered the camp.

Qwansien answered with a shrug. "Don't tell the archers up there. They might get annoyed."

Both Gauduin and Uthan looked up to where Qwansien nodded. Four archers sat amongst the treetops. Their thick, green brown cloaks were pulled around them, making them even more difficult to see properly in the twilight. Winding his way between what seemed like a maze of trees and bushes, Qwansien led them away. Uthan felt he could see the eyes of the four archers firmly fixed on him. His skin prickled at the thought.

Ahead of them, something growled menacingly. More growls joined in the chorus. As Qwansien stepped to one side, Uthan and Gauduin saw a pack of wolves lying in front of them, guarding what appeared to be a dense thicket.

"And you really shouldn't mention that whole guarding thing to them either. They do take it very personally," Qwansien said with a half smile.

"Wolves?" Uthan asked.

The elf nodded, "Only a fool would consider trying to get past them."

Gauduin nodded in agreement. "And you expect me to just walk by them? Why don't you just have dogs, Qwan?"

"Dogs bark, wolves don't, Gauduin. People are usually more terrified of wolves. They hear the howling and the growling and they keep away from them," the elf replied. He crouched down by a large white wolf, which had sat up at his approach, and held its jaw in his hand. The wolf sniffed the air between itself and Qwansien. The wolf yawned and looked to two of the others. The whole time, Uthan had noticed, the other wolves had been watching expectantly. The large white had to be the pack leader. It whined and snorted and looked over at Uthan. Almost instantly the pack settled down again, ignoring the dwarf and young man as Qwansien signalled them over.

"Good wolf, stay," Gauduin muttered, more to himself, as he walked past.

"They really won't bite you now. The big white has been with me for nearly seven years. I watched him assemble that pack from strays. They're devoted to him. He tells them you're a friend, then you're a friend," Qwansien said.

"Well at least I know we're safe from Black Flame for tonight," Gauduin replied.

"Oh, the knights have found ways into our camp before," Qwansien said. He was a little too happy about that fact for Gauduin's liking. Seeing the scowl on the dwarf's face, he continued, "But we kicked seven shades of shit out of them. Their scouting parties never return."

"So this is what you do now?" the dwarf asked.

"What?"

"Act as a pain in the arse to the Black Flame Knights."

"And the Emperor still."

Gauduin shook his head and, with a rueful smile, answered, "Some things never change."

The camp consisted of a circle of green tents with a large campfire burning in the centre. A large section of netting had been strung high above the fire. Leafy branches had been woven into the netting, making the camp invisible to eyes from above. More of the same camouflage covered the large tents, making them appear to be nothing more than bushes to a casual onlooker. A collection of men and women sat around the fire, some no older than teenagers. A hushed word from one young girl made them stop talking and turn to look as Qwansien approached.

"Recruiting again?" asked a loud, cheerful voice from the nearest tent.

Qwansien stopped and turned. With a wide grin on his face, he answered, "Yeah, Boron, I'm replacing you."

A hearty laugh followed, then Uthan found himself taking a step back as the owner of the laughter emerged from the tent. He was a large, muscular man standing nearly seven feet tall. His long, black hair was tied back in a thick ponytail, running down to the small of his back. He strode over to Qwansien and grasped the elf in a massive bear hug, lifting him off the ground, until the elf tapped him on the shoulder, indicating that breathing was becoming a problem.

"So what's the news?" Qwansien asked quickly.

"Let me get changed first at least, man. Gods, have you no concern for the comfort of your friends?" Boron laughed, indicating the black and green plate mail armour he wore. At his side were two swords, while a heavy looking axe was strapped to his back. "And you could at least introduce me to your friends here."

Qwansien nodded. "Yeah. Sorry, Boron. I've just received some bad news about an old friend of mine. Comforts and introductions have slipped my mind."

"Dead?" Boron asked carefully. The toothy grin which had only moments ago split his bearded face was now gone. The elf nodded. "Anyone I know?"

"No, I don't think you did. His name was Hedrial."

"The wizard you've told me about?" Boron asked. As Qwansien nodded, his friend laid a huge hand on the elf's shoulder, "My condolences. By the stories you've told me he was a great man." Again the giant Boron looked over at Uthan and Gauduin. As his eyes rested on the dwarf, a faint glimmer of recognition filled them. "Then this must be Gauduin?"

"Gauduin, meet Boron," Qwansien said as Boron strode over, hand extended.

"Maybe sometime you can tell me if the elf was lying about some of his exploits," Boron said. The grin was back in place.

"He's probably been exaggerating it a bit," Gauduin replied. He smiled as he took the offered hand in an iron gripped handshake.

Boron turned to Uthan, offering his hand again. "Forgive me, young man, but I don't have a clue who you are."

"Uthan Camarr," Uthan replied, awe struck by the size of Boron. "I was Hedrial's apprentice."

"Ahhhh," Boron said as if a thought had suddenly occurred to him, "this is a business visit, right?"

"Pretty much, Boron. I'm going to have to ask you for a favour. A big one," Qwansien asked.

The giant turned back to Qwansien and nodded. "Just name it, Qwan. If I can, I will."

"I need you to take the lead here for a while."

If Boron was surprised, he did a good job of not showing it. He scanned the elf quickly, silently checking his expression. "I can't say I'm not honoured. You're going to avenge your friend's death?"

Qwansien nodded. With a small shrug, he added, "Maybe we will be able to put an end to this Black Flame thing while we're at it."

"Hedrial was killed by the Flame?" Boron asked, looking from Qwansien to Gauduin to Uthan and back again.

"No. But the whole situation does involve the Black Flame," Gauduin answered quickly.

Boron nodded, "I see."

"I'll be leaving with them in the morning. Do you think you'll be fine with things?" Qwansien asked.

Again with the large grin, Boron added, "I think I can manage it. Want them to keep up as before?"

The elf nodded, "Now go and change and get something to eat. I need to know your news before I even attempt to sleep."

As Boron wandered away, Qwansien led Uthan and Gauduin away. Speaking as quietly as he could, Gauduin asked, "What have you been doing here all this time?"

"Taking the fight to the Black Flame Knights as best we could," the elf replied.

Gauduin looked around him at the collection of people. Many of them looked like refugees rather than fighters. "And how are you doing that, Qwan?"

"Hit and run tactics. Attack their raiding and scouting parties," Qwansien replied with a shrug. He wandered over to the fire and chose a quiet spot. Sitting down on the grass he caught Gauduin looking at the other outlaws. "Most of them aren't fighters."

"I wasn't going to say it, Qwan," Gauduin acknowledged, choosing a spot next to the elf.

"Some of them are here by choice, they want to fight the Flame's soldiers. The others feel they have no other option. Everyone here has had something dear to them taken away by the knights. All they have left is each other." Qwansien kept his voice low, hiding his words under the crackling of the fire from everyone but Gauduin and Uthan.

"What about the Imperial forces?" Uthan asked carefully.

"Hunting parties are sent out to search for Black Flame outposts. Most of the parties are killed however," Gauduin answered.

"Why isn't he doing something more? Like using his armies?" Uthan asked.

Qwansien stared into the flames. The mention of Imperial forces had sent him into a stony silence. He opened his mouth to answer when Boron came up behind them.

"The main bulk of the Imperial force is in the far north."

"But why?" Uthan pressed.

Boron sat down on Qwansien's other side. The absence of his armour had not made him look any smaller. Dressed in brown trousers and a shirt, he did however look much friendlier. He crossed his legs in front of him and balanced a plate on his knee. Large slabs of roast beef rested on the plate, their aroma surrounding the small group. "Reports had come in of a massive invasion being planned on Dacenheim."

"And so the Emperor sent out his armies to meet them at the western borders," Qwansien continued. "Three ships had appeared carrying warriors. That was the big invasion force. Once the ships had been burned and all the invaders killed it was discovered they were Nierhoth. The Emperor ordered his armies into the far north to intercept what he was assured would be a full Nierhoth invasion."

As Qwansien fell into silence again so Boron finished the explanation, "He left a small force behind to act as guard and to try and combat what was a minor problem at the time."

"But this small force isn't enough," Uthan said, more to himself now.

"While the Emperor is out trying to gallantly prevent a second coming of the beast wars he's letting the Black Flame rape, pillage and destroy," Qwansien almost spat the words. He looked at Boron and asked, "So what's the news?"

Boron tore into some of the beef and chewed thoughtfully. "Four Black Flame outposts have been constructed along the southern range. Nothing too well fortified which makes me think they're only temporary."

"Cornak?"

"He splits his time between Caslodor and Dessendor. Mostly Dessendor though."

"So Dessendor has to be the heart?" Qwansien asked.

Boron just nodded, continuing to eat before saying, "There's something else."

"Oh?"

"Yeah, I made five different knights talk. One of them was an officer. He spoke about an invasion." Boron stared into the fire as he spoke.

"Nierhoth?" Qwansien asked. The elf finally turned his gaze from the fire, looking straight at the giant Boron next to him.

"He didn't say. All I know is, the knights themselves are scared, with the exception of Cornak himself. So it makes me believe it's something big. I doubt Nierhoth are enough to do that."

"Have you sent word to the Emperor?" Qwansien asked carefully.

Boron nodded, "Although whether he believes it after that ruse will be something else entirely. But the main bulk of his legionaries are turning back for Dacenheim now."

"At least you people should have some help fighting here then," Gauduin suggested. The look that Qwansien cast him, made the dwarf think he had said something completely stupid. "Maybe, maybe not. The Black Flame Knights are good at what they do."

"Those legionaries would have to be trained to fight like we've had to. Hit and run. The pride of the Empire rests on them. I don't think they'd be able to run," Boron continued. Gauduin nodded, conceding the point. "Although, Qwan," Boron said, "they could definitely storm Dessendor. Maybe even take it."

The elf shrugged, "They could try but they'd probably have themselves slaughtered doing it though."

Boron sighed and then, leaning forward, he put his face into his hands.

"I'll be honest with you, Gauduin," Qwansien said, the defeat in his voice was as visible as that in Boron's slumped shoulders, "we're fighting a losing war here."

"Many said that of the beast wars," Gauduin said quietly.

"Every war is a loss really," Boron voiced his opinion.

Qwansien, Gauduin and Uthan all looked at the giant. Qwansien raised an eyebrow inquisitively, "That's a little philosophical for you, isn't it?"

With a wide grin, Boron replied, "Yeah, and I can't even be bothered getting drunk yet." Qwansien fired him an amused questioning look. Catching this, Boron added, "Okay, so I can't be bothered going to the nearest inn."

"There isn't one for miles anyway," Qwan answered flatly.

Boron gasped in mock horror. "No inn for miles? How are we going to last?"

"Well, I'll last by not getting drunk," Qwan replied. "I really don't want to start out on a journey with a hangover tomorrow."

Tutting loudly, Boron replied, "Well you're no fun anymore."

The giant rose to his feet and wandered off in the direction of a large tent. Watching him go, Gauduin said, "He reminds me of Suman a little."

The elf nodded, "Yeah, that's what I thought."

"Where'd he come from? He's clearly not like most of these others here," Gauduin asked, quietly indicating the large group sitting on the other side of the fire.

"Boron? He was a mercenary. Three men he served with joined the Flame. He did too." Qwansien paused, watching their reactions. Gauduin scowled a little. Uthan remained blank and unfocused. "They were assigned to a raiding party which was to attack a small legionary fortress. For once the Emperor had done something right. The defenders outnumbered the Flame knights three to one. Cornak wasn't happy and killed three of his own men. One of those three was one of Boron's friends. Boron himself flew into a rage and made to attack Cornak."

"But Cornak got to him first and imprisoned or tortured him?" Gauduin guessed.

"Not by a long shot," Qwansien replied. A wry smile broke out across his lips. "Boron killed four of the knights around him without hesitation. The man is that good, Gauduin. He'd started towards Cornak when he heard the bow, he has a scar on his right shoulder from the bolt, then he got on his horse and fled the area."

"He was Black Flame though," Gauduin said in a deliberate tone.

"For a month," said the elf, shrugging. "He's been here fighting alongside me for a year and a half now."

Gauduin shrugged in reply, clearly not happy, "Do you trust him?" Qwan nodded. "Then that's good enough, I guess. You're stupid, arrogant, and most of the time, a complete ass but I will say you're a good judge of character, Qwan," Gauduin said. His eyes went to the tent that Boron had gone inside, "Would there be beer in there?"

"Remember what I said about hangovers," the elf answered. Gauduin got to his feet and began to walk over to the tent. Qwan called after him, "And don't listen to a word he says."

Watching the dwarf disappear out of view, Qwansien look sidelong at Uthan, "So you think it was a dragon then?" Uthan nodded. "Have you ever seen one before? I mean a real dragon. Not the little flying lizards they call dragons in Dacenheim," Qwansien asked.

"Only in pictures," Uthan said with a shrug.

Qwan was silent for a while. Slowly he said, "Hedrial used to do this spell where he could show us things in a bowl of water. Things that have happened or were happening."

"The Seer spell?" Uthan asked.

The elf nodded. "I think so. Can you do it?"

Uthan only shrugged in reply at first, then said, "I think I might be able to try. You want to see something?"

"The dragon that got Hedrial. I want to see the beast I have to kill," Qwan replied. "It's always a good idea to check the enemy out. Especially if it has the ability to turn you to ash or something."

"I'll give it a try," Uthan nodded.

He brought his pack around in front of him and reached into it for a small, leather-bound book, while Qwan signalled to someone nearby. A small girl no older than twelve came over; the elf asked her to fetch him a bowl of water.

"As big as you can carry," he said, calling after her as she ran off to find one. He looked back at Uthan and asked, "Anything else you need?"

Uthan snapped the book closed and shook his head, "Just the water please."

A large pottery bowl was set down on the ground in front of him. The light from the fire rippled on the surface of the water as it sloshed around. Eager to see what she had helped with, the little girl sat down next to the bowl and watched, wide-eyed. Uthan waited for the water to settle before he slid the tips of his thumbs into the bowl. Under his breath he muttered three words, chanting them over and over again.

The little girl beside him gasped. The bottom of the bowl became cloudy and dark. Tendrils of what looked like smoke curled up to touch the surface, creating ripples. Slowly the tendrils came together and the water became a milky white. As Uthan concentrated harder on the image of Hedrial and Mount Drakkar, a picture began to take shape.

"Who is that?" the girl asked.

"An old friend of mine," Qwan replied.

The words filtered into Uthan's mind, as if coming to him from a long way away through a fog. From somewhere else in his mind, he heard the weary crunching footfalls as Hedrial climbed the steps at Drakkar. Again the girl gasped. Uthan heard the distant sound of growling, then the sound of the searing inferno that had engulfed Hedrial. It served as a reminder of his dream, breaking his concentration. He sat back, pulling his hands from the water. Looking around him he saw the girl sitting forward, eyes wide in terror and excitement.

She looked up at Uthan in wonder and asked, "Was that a dragon?"

"Yeah, a nasty one too," Qwansien replied. "Baymothesis."

"What?" Uthan asked. The Seer spell had disorientated him and his head swam with images and sounds from several realities.

"The dragon, it looks like Baymothesis," the elf replied. "There are stories about him throughout the Empire. He led a brood of dragons that attacked Dacenheim two hundred years ago. Then he burned the great Monastery of the Ashkraa and finally he slaughtered an army of two thousand men three days after."

"Wow," Uthan was stunned.

Qwansien shrugged and said, "They're only really stories. No one knows how much truth is in them."

Uthan looked into the water in the bowl, reflecting on the dragon in silence. Finally he said, "You believe the stories?"

The elf nodded, "The monastery was burned to the ground. I guess it is possible. I've never killed a legend before so this could be interesting. Although dragons really aren't as difficult to fight as people believe. They can't keep breathing fire all over the place for a start. With the smaller ones, it's not always much more powerful than normal fire anyway. Most of the time they'll try and get in with their teeth and claws. And flying, well that's tricky. They have to fill themselves up with air and heat it up as quickly as possible to take off."

He stood up, sighing at the sounds of roaring laughter from inside the tent Gauduin and Boron were in. Gesturing to a darkened one behind them, he said, "And that puts an end to our lesson. You should sleep; we're leaving early in the morning."

Chapter Eight

Despite sleeping on what he considered to be very uncomfortable ground, Uthan awoke feeling completely refreshed. His sleep had been dreamless. After the previous day's events he was grateful for that fact. Before he had managed to drift into sleep however, images of Hedrial's charred face and the malevolent eyes of the dragon had filled his mind.

Qwansien and Gauduin sat on the grass outside the tent. They both looked up from the bustle of the camp as Uthan emerged into the early morning sunlight. The first thing the young man noticed was the shards of golden white light falling through the treetops.

"I hope you slept well," Qwan said. "We've got a long ride ahead of us today."

"When are we leaving?" Uthan asked, rubbing the sleep from his eyes.

The elf shrugged and replied, "Whenever Boron gets back here."

"Where's he gone?"

"Scouting," Gauduin replied slowly.

"For Black Flame Knights?"

Both Qwan and Gauduin nodded before the elf continued, "He's checking we have a good clear head start through the forest to Dacenheim."

Uthan shook his head, "Why Dacenheim? Doesn't that take us miles away from the gates to the Demonic Realm?"

Qwan looked at Gauduin who merely shrugged. Finally the elf answered, "Until yesterday I believed Baymothesis was merely a story. That beast you showed me looks just like the descriptions in all the tales, down to the very last scale. If I am going to be fighting a legend I want to be properly equipped. Both physically and mentally."

"Dacenheim is the place to go in this case, Uthan," Gauduin added. "If you can't get it in Dacenheim, you can't get it at all."

"And maybe," Boron said, marching up to them, "you'll be able to skin the beast when you're done. Dragon scale armour is worth a lot. But if I was going to hunt a dragon I'd look into getting a good slaying beast."

Qwan looked at Gauduin and shrugged, saying, "It's a good idea in theory."

"Yeah, but something else in practice," Gauduin replied. "Gryphons are difficult to control at the best of times. It'd cost more than we have to spare and finding one is nearly impossible."

"I notice you put the control part in first there," said Qwansien wryly. The dwarf fired him a dark glance.

Oblivious to the comment and glance between the elf and the dwarf, Boron continued, "I know of a merchant who came into some gryphon young a few years ago. Assuming he still has them they should be of fighting age."

"What are the chances he'd have kept them?" asked Qwansien, interested now.

The giant warrior shrugged, "He knows the potential payoffs with hiring them out to guard vaults and suchlike so I would imagine quite high. If you mention my name he should give you a discount too."

"He owes you?" Qwan asked.

"Many times over," Boron replied. "I used to ride with some of his caravans into the north and west."

"Can we trust him?"

One of Boron's characteristic grins split his face as he replied, "He's a merchant of his word. Of course you can't."

"It'd be worth looking into at any rate," Qwansien said, more to Gauduin.

"His name is Varion Doo'ar Cherre. Last I heard he had some house in the south east precincts of Dacenheim," Boron concluded.

Qwansien rose to his feet and walked over to the giant. Extending his hand to the man, he said, "Thanks again, Boron."

"No problem. Just get back here as quickly as you can. I don't want to be leading this bunch of misfits for too long," Boron replied, grinning as widely as ever.

The elf nodded silently then without saying another word he walked past Boron and over to a trio of saddled horses. Gauduin and Uthan quickly followed, shaking Boron's hand as they passed.

"You don't trust him, do you?" Qwan asked Gauduin. They had been riding for a few miles in near complete silence since leaving the camp.

"I don't know him," replied the dwarf slowly. "For all I know he could be a good man."

"He is," the elfish outlaw said.

"In which case he has the chance to prove me wrong."

Qwansien pulled his horse to a halt. For the last mile they had left the thick woodland and now rode across open grassland. The sun was almost at its midday peak and the temperature had risen dramatically. The elf unfastened his thick green and brown cloak from around his shoulders and rolled it up. Beneath it he wore a dark brown leather vest with dyed chain mail covering the back. His arms were surprisingly muscular, the biceps well carved under the pale skin. Despite the heat though, Uthan noted the dark leather glove on his left hand remained.

"It's an old war wound I don't like to show," the elf stated flatly, catching Uthan staring at the glove.

Uthan reddened a little and looked away.

"Yeah," Gauduin added sarcastically, "he probably got a thorn in his thumb."

A dark look from the elf quickly stopped Gauduin from making any more comments.

Strapped to Qwansien's back was a slender sword. The black and silver hilt pointed down so as to allow the weapon to be unsheathed from beneath the thick camouflage cloak.

"You still have it then," Gauduin observed, nodding at the weapon as Qwan looked at him.

At first the elf just nodded. Then, after a short pause, he added, "It's the only thing I have left to remind me of home." To himself, he muttered, "Only good thing anyway."

"You were an Honour Guard?" Uthan asked.

Qwan reined his horse in. "You know your weapons. I'm impressed."

"My brother told me about them."

"He travels?"

Uthan shrugged, "He's a lieutenant in the Emperor's guard."

Qwan nodded, "Then he's bound to have had many dealings with the Honour Guard."

"He told me you never leave though," Uthan said.

The elf smiled and rode on in silence for a few moments. "He was right, but probably for the wrong reasons. It's a belief that the Honour Guard is exactly that. It's as if the elfish Empire is favouring you. They don't like people announcing they're leaving. The only way you leave the Honour Guard is to die."

"Or to kill your commanding officer," Gauduin said quietly.

Qwan flashed him another look. "You know damn well that was self-defence."

"I didn't say otherwise," Gauduin answered.

Uthan looked wide eyed at the elf. "You killed another guard?"

"It was self-defence!" Qwan replied again, this time a little louder. Realising how loud his voice was he quickly lowered it again. "I couldn't walk away."

"What happened?" Uthan asked carefully, not wanting to have the elf raise his voice again.

"Maybe another time I'll tell you about it," Qwan replied. He touched his heels to his horse's flanks, sending it into a trot.

Gauduin leaned closer to Uthan and muttered, "All you need to know for now is that he was betrayed by a woman. He was denounced as a traitor and a spy."

The two of them then spurred their horses on, catching up to the elf. Over the hammering hoof beats, Qwan called, "There's a village about twenty miles away. We'll stop there and rest."

"With Black Flame Knights so close by, do you think that's a good idea?" Gauduin called back.

The elf shrugged, "The people there have no love for the knights so I would think it'd be fine."

"Rebels?" Gauduin asked.

"No, which is why Cornak has largely left them alone. He's more concerned with the small uprisings to the north. Around Lessa and Kora-Tus."

At the mention of Uthan's home, Gauduin glanced at the young mage. His jaw had clenched, eyes focused directly forward, intent on keeping his attention on the land ahead.

Bringing the horses finally to a walk, the trio reached the slope of a hill by early evening. Below them at the base of the grassy hillside lay a thick stand of trees beyond which the village sat. A wispy blanket of white smoke hung above the rooftops, hiding many of them from view. There was still some activity to be seen in the village: children were playing next to a large communal well; a small group of young women were sitting away from the well, talking and watching a trio of young men who, in turn, were watching the girls. Birdsong filled the air, joined by the barking of a few unseen dogs. The scene looked like the very image of peace to the travelling companions.

Again Uthan felt pangs of grief, his own home having been so similar but now empty and ruined. "Why would Cornak destroy it?"

Both Gauduin and Qwansien looked at him thoughtfully. The question had been spoken so quietly they were unsure if Uthan was talking to himself or not.

Even so, Qwan answered, "He wants to make sure the spirit of the realm is broken."

They noticed the apprentice clench his jaw again. Some unspoken thoughts passed through his mind as he watched the village below. "I'm going to put an end to it," he said finally.

"Uthan, what are you thinking about?" Gauduin asked, clearly worried about the answer.

Uthan tapped his horse into motion. "I'm going to make sure the Black Flame and General Cornak pay for all they have done."

Both elf and dwarf watched him guide his horse down the slope. Turning in his saddle, Qwan asked, "He's serious, isn't he?"

With a nod and a grunt, the dwarf set his horse off to follow Uthan down to the village.

No one cast a second glance at Uthan as his horse emerged from the trees and walked into the village. At first they would have taken him for a young refugee, escaping the Black Flame destruction had he not been so clean. Gauduin and Qwansien followed, riding side by side. Both dwarves and elves were common in the Empire. The villagers would have seen enough not to give the two a second glance either but the armour and weapons changed that. Ahead of the trio, the group of young men moved into a position where they could watch the travellers. One of them gestured quickly to a child who promptly ran off behind a building.

"Nice to be noticed," Qwan muttered, taking in the staring eyes of the villagers as he rode by.

"Will there be trouble?" asked the dwarf, shifting uncomfortably in his saddle.

"Just keep riding, we're going to the inn," Qwan advised. He spoke from the corner of his mouth, keeping his voice just quiet enough so he could still be heard over the horse's hooves. "It's up ahead."

They reined their horses in at the front of a large building. The sign above the wide double doors had a picture of a large sea serpent painted in bright, almost gaudy colours. From the outside the place was quiet, almost as if it was closed for business.

Qwan wrapped his horse's reins around a tethering post and walked up the steps. Stopping on the wooden porch he turned to look back along the way they had travelled. He breathed in deeply, savouring the scent of wood smoke and cooking meat, then said, "They're still watching. You'd think they'd never had travellers here before."

"They probably haven't recently. And more likely than not, not ones wearing armour and carrying weapons," Gauduin answered.

"I'm not wearing armour," Uthan stated.

The dwarf nodded, "And they weren't paying attention to you." He looked back up to Qwan on the stairs and continued, "They're watching us, just in case."

The elf nodded, turned and walked inside the inn. The noise was little more than a murmur as he entered. The child who had been sent ahead by the group at the well sat on the bar, legs dangling down the side. Qwan met the gaze of the man at the bar and nodded. The bartender nodded back casually. Then he helped the boy to the ground and patted him on the head before turning and leaving through another door.

Gauduin and Uthan came in to find Qwan sitting at a table next to the wall. He had rested his chin against his hands, fingers steepled in front of his nose and lips, watching the room around him. All eyes were focused on the three companions. The conversation had either stopped or was nothing more than muttered words.

"We're going to be the talk of this place for days," Qwan said calmly.

"Where's the innkeeper?" Gauduin asked, looking round. "I'm thirsty."

One of Qwansien's fingers gestured to the door, "He went through there just after I came in. He's gone to tell someone about us."

"That's not good," replied the dwarf.

The innkeeper emerged from the back room a moment later, casting a nervous look at the three outsiders, followed closely by a girl. Grabbing an apron from behind the bar, she wandered over to the table, all the time tying the apron behind her back.

"Can I help you?" she asked.

Uthan looked up, noticing her for the first time, then looked down again quickly. He could not have imagined a face more lovely.

"Beer," Gauduin ordered quickly, ignoring the raised eyebrow from his elf companion. "And something without alcohol for these two."

She smiled and nodded at Guaduin.

As the girl walked away, Qwan muttered, "I think we should be extremely careful here. She signalled to the innkeeper behind her back when she walked over."

"I saw him reach below the bar for something," Gauduin said nodding.

"Loaded crossbow is my bet," Qwan continued. "And yet there's something about that girl."

Uthan nodded and said, "She's beautiful."

"She's familiar, I know the face," the elf replied, before turning to Uthan. "And I'm surprised you could see with watching the table. What was so interesting in that wood there anyway?"

"What do you mean she's familiar?" Gauduin asked, suddenly realising what Qwansien had said.

With a shrug, the elf replied, "I mean I know her face but I just can't think where from."

"Could she be Flame then?" the dwarf asked carefully.

Qwansien just shrugged and sat back in his chair.

"Do you think they'll be a problem, Cass?" the innkeeper said as Cassmed returned to the bar.

"Both elf and dwarf look like they can handle themselves in a fight. The third, I doubt it. But there's something else about him," Cass replied. "They're drinking by the way. Two apple juices and one beer."

The innkeeper smiled broadly, "At least there's that."

"I'll go and tell Demy and Med," she said, slipping behind the bar and over to the back room again.

"Well, is it trouble?" Demien asked before Cassmed could enter the room properly.

Cass shrugged, sat down and reported, "It's hard to say. An elf, a dwarf and a man barely out of his teens, but they're armed for a fight. There's something about the elf though. His sword seems familiar." Both Demien and Medoran appeared puzzled as the girl shrugged and continued, "I've seen it before. It looks like an Elfish Honour Guard sword."

Medoran went over to the door, opened it a tiny crack and peered through the gap with his one good eye. His other eye, having been disfigured months previously, was now hidden beneath a black eyepatch. Two jagged scars ran down his cheek from the lost eye, forever changing his face and causing him to lose his vanity. He whispered, "He doesn't look like Honour Guard though." He gestured to Demien, holding the door steady so it could not open any more. "Take a look."

Demien pushed her long blond hair around her neck and over her right shoulder as she stood up. She wore leggings and a shirt, both dark brown. Taking hold of the door, she looked through, "I can only see the hilt of the sword, Cass."

"That's all I could," the girl answered.

"It does look like an Honour Guard weapon but he doesn't look like a member of the Honour Guard."

"Then how would he have got the weapon?" Medoran asked.

Demien shook her head slowly, "Honour Guards are passionate about those swords. They'd never get rid of one. He'd have to have killed a guard to get it."

"So maybe he's a killer?" Cass continued.

"Maybe," agreed the woman. Turning her attention to the dwarf, she continued, "I like his armour."

"The dwarf's? It wouldn't fit you," Med replied playfully, a sharp elbow to his breastbone from Demien shut him up.

"I mean it's been well crafted, well looked after and probably well worn too."

"What about the other one? He doesn't look like trouble to me," Cass said.

"Looks aren't everything," Demien replied with a shrug, "but I agree he doesn't look like trouble. They could be hunters; they've got that mercenary look about them. But that doesn't explain the lad." She moved away from the door and sat down.

"We need to find out for certain," Medoran replied.

"I guess I have to go play serving wench and make conversation," Cassmed sighed.

"Play dumb though," Demien advised. "And be careful."

"We don't want to have to kill them," Medoran replied quietly.

"You know, Gauduin, I really don't think we'll be staying here tonight after all," Qwan said slowly.

The dwarf cracked a wide smile, "The place isn't too friendly, is it."

"We need to keep moving anyway, don't we?" Uthan asked. The

young apprentice had been feeling impatient about them stopping the night in the village. He wanted to continue moving.

"We're older now, Uthan, we need to rest," Gauduin answered.

The elf chuckled, "Speak for yourself. I'm not decrepit yet. Even so, Uthan, we do need to rest while we can."

"We'll eat and have a few drinks here and then move on," the dwarf finished.

Qwan half put a hand up to stop them talking further as the girl came over with their drinks.

"Sorry about the wait, I have food cooking in the kitchen as well," she said smiling. Uthan looked up at her and found he was staring. Suddenly she returned his gaze, her eyes softening as they met his. Uthan reddened and looked away quickly, finding something interesting in the table again. Noticing the flushing in his cheeks and neck, Qwan smiled a little.

"Food?" Gauduin looked up, oblivious to Uthan's blushing, the girl's staring and Qwan's amusement.

"There's a steak pie in the oven. It'll be ready soon if you'd like some."

The dwarf cracked another large toothy smile and rubbed his hands together excitedly. "A large piece please."

Qwan nodded, "Make it three pieces, unless young Uthan here is more interested in the table than eating."

Uthan looked up and met the girl's eyes again. "Yes please," he said meekly.

Cassmed smiled again, "I'll get them to you as soon as I can then." She half turned to leave, then turned back and asked, "Will you be staying here tonight?"

"I think we'll let our stomachs decide. If this pie is any good, we'll stay the night," Gauduin said. By now he had noticed the flustered Uthan and he too could not resist grinning like an idiot.

"You should stay, we don't get many warriors in town these days," Cass replied.

"We guessed," answered the elf.

He flashed a quick look to Gauduin who, from his careful smile, was thinking the same thing. The girl was fishing for information. Gauduin drained his beer mug in one long gulp. Offering it to the girl, he asked, "Damned fine brew that. Would you fetch me another please?"

Cassmed smiled and took the mug before walking back to the bar, leaving the three of them on their own again.

"Do you still think she could be a spy then?" Gauduin asked carefully.

Qwan nodded, "I'm almost certain of it. We'll eat, then leave."

"She can't be a spy, can she?" Uthan asked slowly. "She's too..."

Gauduin put a consoling hand on Uthan's shoulder. "They make the best ones, Uthan. Sorry, lad."

Another mug was placed on the table in front of Gauduin. With a flashed smile, Cassmed said, "I'll go and see about that pie for you."

She walked into the back room again and over to the table. Three slices had been cut from a large pie on the stovetop. Picking up the plates she said, "They're planning on leaving after they've eaten."

"Did you learn anything else? Where do they plan on staying the night?" Medoran asked.

The girl shook her head, "I don't know, the dwarf cut me off before I found out anything."

"Okay," Demien began, "if they leave then we don't have to worry about them. We've stayed hidden all this time so they don't know we're here."

"It would help matters if everyone in the town hadn't just stopped life to stand and stare. It's made them wary," Cass continued. She took three plates, each with a slice of pie, and left the room.

Nearly an hour had passed since finishing their food before Qwan, Uthan and Gauduin entered another thick stand of woodland. Under the cover of the trees, Qwan called a halt, climbed from his saddle and set about clearing a small area. Gauduin tethered the horses to a nearby tree, instructing Uthan to rub them down and get them settled for the night. He then moved off in the direction they had come from to make sure no one was following.

"It'll be a cold camp tonight. I'm not willing to risk a fire being seen," Qwan said.

Uthan nodded, realising that both elf and dwarf had been extremely cautious upon leaving the village. "How soon will we reach Dacenheim?" the lad asked.

"Day after tomorrow, or the day after that, I think," Gauduin replied, wandering back to the small man-made clearing.

Settling down on the cold ground, the three waited for the darkness of night to descend. Gauduin sat facing the direction they had come from, occasionally looking up on the chance of seeing intruders in the camp. But it was nearly midnight when the sounds of Gauduin and Qwan moving had awoken Uthan. Sleepily, he sat up and blinked, trying to focus in the dark. Gauduin's face appeared close by, pale grey in the gloom.

"Stay silent. We have trouble," the dwarf whispered.

Uthan was about to do exactly the opposite and ask what was going on when he heard the thunderous hoof beats, echoing in the forest. Through gaps in the trees he saw a line of orange dots moving closer. The dots writhed and flickered, becoming flaming torches as the riders were nearly upon them. He glanced to his right and saw Qwan holding his crossbow ready, the bolt aimed for the chest of the first rider. Gauduin was on the left, his fist curled tightly around the hilt of his sword, blade half drawn in anticipation. But the riders rode past, oblivious to the three friends lying in wait. As the head of the line burst out from the trees, Qwan looked to Gauduin.

"They're going to attack the village," he said quietly.

Gauduin moved carefully and made his way closer to the edge of the camp, peering through the trees at the wave of black garbed riders. "They won't stand a chance. They can't know they're coming."

"We should help them," Uthan whispered slowly.

Qwan nodded, "I agree with the boy."

"But what about Hedrial? We can't help him if we're already dead," Gauduin said.

"Then we don't die," Qwan answered.

Demien lay in bed, lost in thought, the sheet half draped over her body. A soft calm breeze moved the curtains a little and blew across her naked chest. Through the open window she could see the half moon, blurred behind the thin clouds. Cass had been right about the elf from earlier, he had seemed familiar. It was the sword, she told herself, and she had seen the sword before. An elfish Honour Guard sword but customised. Beside her, Medoran stirred. He rolled over in his sleep, laying an arm along her thigh. A faint mischievous smile played across her lips as she carefully lifted his arm by the wrist and slid it under the sheet to touch her naked flesh.

From outside there was a barely heard rumble. Thinking it was thunder; she rolled her head back to the window again to watch for the lightning. Suddenly a brilliant flash of white light lit up the room.

Medoran sat bolt upright, suddenly very awake. His hand moved away from Demien's inner thigh without him noticing where it had been.

"What was that?" he asked, shocked.

Demien rolled out of bed and moved across to the window. "I thought it was a storm after hearing the thunder. But... oh hell."

"What?" Med asked, looking over to her.

She backed away from the window a few paces, then quickly snapped into action, pulling on her leggings and shirt. Sitting down heavily on the bed, she started pulling on her boots. "We've got company. Lots of it."

Medoran jumped out of bed and went to the window. Out on the fields between the village and the forest rode a horde of riders. He could see their black armour clearly in the brilliant flashes in the sky. Several of the knights had turned in their saddles, straining to see the lights shooting up from the trees to explode in the sky above them.

"Where is that light coming from?" he muttered.

Demien shrugged, slipping her sword sheath over her shoulder, and said, "Someone wants to warn us, obviously."

Moving back to the window to look, she kissed Med on the cheek. "I'll go and rouse them all. See you outside."

Leaving Med to hurriedly get dressed and armed, Demien slipped out of the room and threw Cass's door open. The girl lay in bed next to a young blond man. Cass sat upright and looked at Demien, her face flushed a little.

Ignoring the boy who stared, mouth opening and closing, Demien said, "There's trouble on its way. Get your things and get outside." Cass nodded quickly and slipped out of bed while the boy hesitated a few moments. "You," Demien said, staring almost straight through him, "you'd better get a sword and get ready to fight. If you survive tonight, we'll be talking about this incident later."

Clumsily he got up and looked around for his clothes as Cass, throwing her shirt over her head, left the room with Demien.

"Black Flame?" Cass asked as they strode along the corridor. Demien was pushing doors open and calling inside, announcing the imminent attack.

"Yeah, quite a few by the look of things," Demien replied.

They reached the stairs, leaping down them two and three at a time. Demien's long legs carried her across the floor of the inn's main room quickly. On the porch outside, she rang the large bronze bell.

Its loud metallic peal echoed in the night air.

Men, armed with whatever weapons they could lay their hands on, were already emerging from their homes. The lights must have awoken many. They gathered at the inn, eyes on the approaching riders who were getting steadily closer.

"Look at them all," muttered one man in the crowd. A general murmuring was the reply as people took in the numbers.

"And they will slaughter you all without thinking about it. It is time to fight, if you don't want to or can't, then run away now," Demien called out.

Cass tapped her on the elbow and whispered in her ear, "Rousing words but shouldn't you have waited for Med to do it?"

"There's no time," she replied. She started forward, jogging away from the inn to meet the front line of knights. Over her shoulder she called to Cass, "Get the horses. We'll meet them on equal terms."

Behind her, many of the villagers stood waiting, weapons held ready as they began to feel the soft vibrations from the charging horses.

"How many are there?" asked one man to her left.

"I don't know."

"Did those travellers tell them?" asked another.

Again, Demien shrugged and replied, "I don't know."

"Can we win this battle, Demien?" a third voice asked.

From the back of the group, Medoran answered, "Of course we can."

The group turned to see him standing waiting, both swords drawn and ready. He was dressed in dark crimson pants and a white cotton shirt. His usual black eye patch was in place.

"Have you seen how many there are?" Demien asked, eyebrows raised at his arrogance.

The swordsman shrugged, "There's a few of them, I know." He walked forward, men moving back to let him through, until he stood immediately behind Demien. Placing a hand on her shoulder he leant around and kissed her neck before whispering in her ear, "I think we might die here tonight. I just don't want them to know that."

She nodded and replied, "I love you too."

He turned to the rest of the villagers and called, "Let them come in between the buildings. They can't charge you down then. As soon as we get rid of them, I want everyone getting water buckets ready. There'll be a lot of fires to put out."

"Cass has gone to get the horses," Demien said quietly.

Med nodded, "Good idea. We'll meet them on horseback."

They looked at each other again and kissed. Pulling away, Demien muttered, "For luck. I love you."

"I love you too," he replied, bringing his sword up into a salute to her.

Riding on a large black horse, Cass returned, the reins of Kainan and another chestnut gelding held firmly in her hand. Demien quickly swept herself up into her saddle and patted Kainan's neck. The warhorse snorted loudly and pounded the ground with his front hooves. The other two horses snorted and whinnied. Looking over her shoulder, Demien saw a group of four men, armed with longbows, scrambling up onto the stone roof of the inn.

"Make sure I'm covered, okay?" she called to them.

As they waved in response, Cass asked, "Why? What are you going to do?"

Kainan sprang forward suddenly, racing to meet the oncoming knights with Demien in the saddle.

Medoran watched her go as he climbed into the saddle of his chestnut mount. Shaking his head and smiling, he said, "She is going to get herself killed one day."

"No, she won't," Cass whispered.

The swordsman chuckled, "No, you're right. She won't." He looked up to the archers and called, "Once they're within bow range start shooting. Take as many out as you can and stay up there unless it goes really bad."

The ringing of steel on steel, the snorting, the hooves pounding against earth and shouting was all Demien could hear. Kainan had shouldered past three of the enemy's horses, knocking two of them to the ground. Then she had slashed her blade across the throat of one of the riders, killing him outright. Another of them had fallen under his horse, crushed inside his armour by the weight of the beast. A third rider got too close and found the point of Demien's sword piercing his right eye and sinking into his brain.

More riders swarmed by, leaving the challenge of fighting her to those few nearby. A sword blade flashed by her face, mere inches from removing her nose. Demien leant back in the saddle quickly, switching her sword to a dagger grip and thrust the blade back under her arm. There was a gasp from behind her as the sword pushed into flesh. Giving it a sharp twist, she pulled again, removing the blade.

Changing grip again, she swung out wide. The sword tip opened a shallow cut on the cheek of another knight. Then she was nearly thrown from the saddle as Kainan bucked and kicked out suddenly. His back hooves thudded into the chest of yet another knight, throwing him from his saddle.

Three more knights rode over, slowing their horses after seeing the ferocity of Demien and Kainan. The first thrust out with his sword. As Demien twisted to avoid the blade, the second knight brought his weapon down. She raised her sword to block a vicious mid section cut from the third and backhanded the blade away. In the same sweep, she swung her sword arm out and slashed a deep cut across the eyes and nose of the first knight. He instantly dropped his sword, clutching at his eyes and screaming in agony, blood gushing between his fingers. Demien twisted again in the saddle, narrowly avoiding another sword blow that would have cleaved her shoulders, before slashing out again. The edge of her sword cut through the blinded man's neck and hands, severing them from his body. As the head hit the ground, Demien caught a glimpse of the face. The eye sockets had been destroyed, the eyeballs themselves reduced to a bloodied mass.

Another sword swipe from one of the remaining knights swept down, inches from her shoulder so she retaliated with a vicious backhand. The back of her fist struck the knight under the jaw, stunning him while she thrust her sword deep into the semi-exposed throat of the other knight. The last knight regained his senses and attacked again. Demien ducked under his arm before bringing her sword up hard, sinking the tip into the soft fleshy area of his armpit. He toppled from his horse, bubbles of blood erupting from his mouth and nostrils. Seeing the rest of the raiding party enter the village, Demien spurred Kainan back.

The first of the knights charged into the village, torches held high. A sudden volley of arrows cut into the first group, striking both men and horses. For only a moment there was a sense of panic in the knight's ranks.

"Cornak isn't with them," Medoran noted. "They weren't expecting resistance."

He sat on his horse, watching the knights. His sword was held high in one steady hand, the blade catching the moonlight. From above, another volley of arrows flew down. Three more knights and one horse dropped to the ground, screaming. All eyes however had now turned to the steady sword of Medoran. The blade slashed down, as he tapped his horse's flanks, driving the beast out into the wide street to meet the knights. All around him, villagers swarmed out from the buildings, an angry mob ready to tear the foe apart.

Some of the knights tore away from their party, charging forward. An arrow whistled down, taking the rearmost in the face. His scream went unheard above the rage-fuelled roar of the villagers who swarmed around him, hacking his body to pieces. Medoran pulled hard on his reins and his horse reared violently, nearly throwing him from the saddle. It kicked out with its front hooves sending the nearest knight's mount into a blind panic. He patted the smooth neck, talking soothingly, until the horse was on all four hooves again, as calm as was possible with a battle raging around them.

"Easy boy, it's all right," Med reassured his steed.

Without looking round, Medoran swiped out his sword arm again. A dark bladed sword shot up to block the blow. Steel clashed loud against steel as both Medoran and the knight attacked and blocked. He reached back with his sword arm, ready to lash out hard again when suddenly the knight was pulled back. A large heavyset man dumped him hard on the ground as if he was nothing more than a toy. The knight struggled to get up but was sent sprawling by a violent kick to the face. A long scythe was swung down, finding its way into the knight's stomach through a gap in the armour plates. The villager raised a blood splattered face then smiled toothlessly at Medoran who nodded before kicking his heels and spurring his horse into battle again.

Qwansien and Gauduin had ridden on into the village, leaving Uthan behind in the relative safety of the woods. He had spent his time sending up flares of pure energy that exploded in the sky like lightning. Uthan could now feel himself tiring; using energy flares was not something he was accustomed to. Beads of sweat covered his forehead and neck. His hands shook with the effort of sending one last flare of brilliant blue light up into the night sky. He sat down heavily on the ground; looking heavenwards, he could see a faint afterglow of purple. If he had not alerted the villagers by now then they were already lost. The thought suddenly weighed heavily on his mind.

The first knights to attack the elf and dwarf fell to bolts fired from

Qwansien's crossbow. Each shot had accurately taken its target through the eye socket causing instant death. Standing up in his stirrups, Qwansien had then replaced the crossbow in its holster at his side and removed his sword from the sheath on his back.

Gauduin was first to meet the knights in hand-to-hand combat, his dwarfish blade striking against the armoured chest of one man. The blow was enough to stun the knight, almost knocking him from his horse. As Gauduin charged on to meet another, Qwansien skewered the knight through the throat. The dwarf cast a quick glance over his shoulder to see the elf slide his blade free from the corpse and follow. Two more knights were killed in a similar way. Gauduin was continuing to hammer out with his sword, striking it against the heavy plate armour and Qwan slashing their throats or stabbing in through a gap in the plates finished them off.

"Just like old times, huh?" Qwansien called.

The dwarf merely grunted a reply and nodded since he knew Qwan would have had trouble hearing above the sounds of fighting. He pulled hard on his reins to stop his horse suddenly as a knight charged towards him, leaning out with his sword, ready to take Gauduin's head from his shoulders. Instinctively, the dwarf brought his sword up in front of his chest and the knight's blade clashed loudly against it. The force of the block jarred the weapon from the hands of the knight. Sparing only a heartbeat's hesitation, Gauduin backhanded his sword. The blade smashed hard against the back plate, denting it in against the man's spine. He fell from his horse, landing motionless on the ground. His screams of agony from a broken back went unheard as Qwansien rode in and, leaning down, plunged his sword point through the bridge of the knight's nose.

Thick, greasy black smoke had begun to drift up into the sky as Gauduin pointed to the inn where bright orange flames licked out from the windows.

"They're going to burn the place to the ground," the dwarf shouted.

Qwan nodded, his earlier smile had vanished from his face as he watched a pair of knights on horseback chasing a girl towards them. Speaking in a soft voice, he said, "This has to stop now."

He spurred his horse on quickly, racing towards the black clad predators. His sword was held parallel to the ground, ready to lance through whatever stood in his path. The girl looked up suddenly, her eyes widened in terror as she saw the oncoming rider. She dropped onto her knees, whimpering to the ground. Then the knights were on her. Qwan's horse leapt the girl, hooves sailing through the air mere inches above her cowering head, and landed between the startled knights. His sword clashed against their weapons furiously as he fought both of them, blocking a blow from one, then the other. The girl risked a glance at the fight and saw the elf battling for his life. She remained on her knees, unable to move until Gauduin rode up next to her.

"You should get to safety, girl," he said, trying to keep his voice gentle. She merely looked at him, nodding dumbly in reply. Quickly, the dwarf turned his attention to the fight. "Hold on, Qwan," he roared, "I'm coming."

His voice had been enough to distract the knights. Both men, believing the other was still paying attention to the elf, glanced to the oncoming dwarf. The moment was all Qwansien needed. Both of them fell from their horses, the elfish blade having slashed across their semi-exposed throats.

"Is she okay?" Qwan asked, nodding at the girl.

She was still cowering on her knees, watching the elf and dwarf.

Gauduin shrugged, "She's too young to have been witness to this."

"Gauduin, we need to stop this from happening again. You, me and Uthan," Qwan said. He was unable to take his eyes away from the helpless girl.

His friend nodded and said, "We will."

"Good." Qwan urged his horse to walk slowly to the girl. He could see her bottom lip trembling violently as though she was fighting hard not to cry. Carefully, he reached down a hand to her. "It's okay," he said soothingly, "we're going to get you to safety."

"Qwan! Watch your back!" Gauduin yelled suddenly.

The elf looked round in time to see another group of knights galloping towards them. They all carried long barbed lances, held ready to impale the pair. They were within a few feet when a sudden blast of energy struck the ground. The horses reared in panic, striking at each other in a desperate attempt to flee. The riders clung on to the reins, fighting hard against their mounts to keep control.

Gauduin looked over his shoulder to see Uthan's horse carrying the mage towards them. Uthan was slumped forward in the saddle, head bowed and shoulders leaning forward. He raised an arm wearily and pointed at the knights, tendrils of blinding, yellow white light burst from his palm, striking two of the knights in the chest. The dwarf charged in, sweeping his sword out in wide arcs. The blade hammered against the breastplate of one knight, breaking the steel shell in two. Blood gushed from the stomach wound as the rider fell from his horse. Qwansien reached for his crossbow and hurriedly slid a bolt into place. He raised the weapon and fired in one fluid motion. Another knight died immediately, a black bolt piercing his forehead.

Gauduin killed the remaining men as they fought against their horses for control. One was beheaded cleanly whereas the second received the point of Gauduin's blade through his less armoured armpit. His feet caught in the stirrups as he fell. His horse galloped off away from the village in blind panic, dragging the dying knight along behind it.

"Is that all of them?" Gauduin called, looking around for more.

The elf nodded, "Looks like it."

The dwarf sighed in relief before turning to Uthan. "You were told to stay in the forest," he said disapprovingly.

Uthan could not answer; he was slumped forward against the neck of his horse. His hair was damp against his head with sweat.

"Although," Qwan added, cutting Gauduin off before he could say anything else, "you did good. We could well have been finished off there." He looked down at the girl who had remained frozen during the entire fight. Her eyes stared unseeing at the bodies strewn in front of her; in particular those Uthan had killed. "You have to get up," the elf said gently.

She looked up at him as if seeing him for the first time. Slowly she reached up, taking the hand offered by the elf, and allowed herself to be pulled up onto the back of his horse. Seeing her properly for the first real time, Qwan guessed she was in her early teens, a few years younger than Uthan. Her long blonde hair, streaked with fiery red in places, was fixed in a loose braid down her back. Eyes that were blue grey in colour, just stared at the world around her. The ordeal had caused her to retreat into the safety of her own mind.

"So, where to?" Qwan asked brightly, looking from Gauduin to Uthan.

"We need to get this youngster to safety," Gauduin said concernedly, looking around him for any kind of safe haven.

Uthan raised his head, "There are still others here. They have to be slain."

"Well, I'm with you on that one," Qwan replied. "We can't let them leave here, Gauduin. You know what will happen to these people."

Gauduin shrugged, "We can't protect them forever."

"No, granted, but we can make tonight count," replied the elf.

"You have too much of a troublemaker in you for an elf, Qwan, has anybody ever told you that?"

Qwan smiled, "Many times, but it's usually been you."

Turning in the direction of the burning inn, Qwan shouted to his horse. It sprang into action, charging off amongst the buildings, leaving Gauduin and Uthan to try and keep up.

Demien sidestepped a two-handed attack, hammering out her boot in reply. The kick struck her attacker on the shin hard; had it not been for his steel guard his leg would have been snapped. As it was, the kick, added to his own momentum, caught him off balance. As he fell, Demien lanced her sword blade into the back of his neck, finding the gap where his helm met the shoulder plates. His corpse added to the growing collection Demien was accumulating.

Knights were still approaching but more cautiously after witnessing the warrior woman slaying their comrades with relative ease. Kicking a limb from her foot, she widened her stance and switched hands with her sword. She had been fighting near to the blazing inferno that had engulfed the inn. Sweat coated her body in a thick, greasy, wet skin, causing her clothing to stick to her. To her left she could see Medoran and Cassmed fighting alongside some of the villagers. They were forcing a group of knights back against a wall. Medoran's wild sword swings were complemented by Cass's accuracy with her long bow.

An armour clad knight ran at Medoran, sword ready to slash down. Before the swordsman could turn to face his attacker, Cass let a pair of arrows fly. The first whistled past the knight's exposed face, tearing a shallow cut into his nose and left cheek and, as he spun, the second arrow drove into his forehead. Another knight appeared from the shadows of a nearby building, creeping to Cass's back. Medoran, turning as his attacker was slain by Cass's arrows, saw the next knight approaching. He moved his foot under the blade of a sword lying on the ground in front of him. In one fluid movement, he kicked the sword into the air, caught it by the blade before hurling it over Cass's shoulder. She twisted out of the way as the sword flew past, flipping end over end. The pommel struck the knight's breastplate, stunning him. Cass deftly caught the sword by the hilt as it bounced away before driving it into the enemy's face. As he fell back, blood spraying into the air, Cass notched another arrow, ready to find a new target.

The next of Demien's adversaries was now within range. Batting his sword aside easily, she twirled on one foot, her sword arm sweeping out to remove his head. Even before the headless body had fallen fully to the ground, Demien dropped to one knee, holding her sword up to block a heavy overarm blow. The clash sent a jarring pain through her left arm, nearly causing her to lose her grip. Gritting her teeth against the numbing in the muscles, Demien dropped back and thrust out a boot. The knight took the foot to his stomach. It forced the steel plating hard against his midriff, doubling him over. A quick but equally hard right fist connected with his nose, flattening it against his face and causing him to reel backwards into one of his companions. The one whose nose had been broken was fumbling around, blinded temporarily. His movements were hampering the other knight who tried hard to get out of his way and face the woman. But her blade flashed through the air, opening a large gash, from chin to temple on the exposed face of one knight. While he was stunned from the attack, she followed up with a hard kick then backhanded her sword hilt into his face. He fell unconscious to the ground. Seeing the ferocity in her attack, the other knight just threw down his weapon, turned and fled.

From behind her, Demien heard the twang of a bowstring. An arrow whistled overhead, finding its target in the fleeing knight. He dropped to his knees, reached up and clutched at the arrow that had penetrated his supposedly well protected kidneys, before pitching face first to the ground.

The broken-nosed knight, blood streaming down his face, began to back away carefully. Hearing movement to his right side he spun suddenly, slicing out with his sword arm. The blade swept harmlessly over the top of a dwarfish head. In reply, the dwarf thrust his own heavy looking sword up into the armpit, the blades tip pierced through the knight's opposite shoulder plate. He convulsed once then went limp.

Medoran, seeing what he believed to be a new enemy, ran at the dwarf, sword raised and ready to cleave him in two. Gauduin swiftly rolled to one side and kicked the swordsman hard in the back as he passed by. The blow was enough to send Medoran to the ground. Quickly, Gauduin leapt on his back and pulled his head back by the hair. In a second the wide sword blade was against his throat. But instantly Gauduin felt the tip of a blade pushing into the back of his own neck. Demien stood behind him, her sword in one hand, pressed beneath his helm.

"Turn the sword arm around," said Qwansien deliberately. From the corner of his eye, Gauduin saw the elf holding his crossbow levelled at the woman's head. "We're not your enemies here."

Chapter Nine

"Take that bow away from my head now or your short friend will have to learn to breathe through the back of his neck," Demien said through gritted teeth, meaning every word. She did not look away from Gauduin and the point of her sword.

Keeping his voice at an equally level tone, Qwansien countered, "If he dies, you die. It's that simple."

"And I'll have opened your friend's throat as well, girl," Gauduin added.

Ignoring the dwarf, Demien cocked her head, looking right down the crossbow at Qwan. "Think you can do it? Let your friend die and kill me?"

The elf met her gaze and froze. His brow furrowed, "Gauduin, lift his head."

"What?" The dwarf asked puzzled.

"I want to see his face."

The sight of Medoran's eye patch made him lower his crossbow. Almost whispering, he said, "I thought I recognised the girl."

"What are you babbling about, elf?" Gauduin asked. He could feel the sword tip pricking into his flesh.

Qwansien answered, "A few months ago, my men came across some people being chased through the forests near Caslodor. One man and two women, the man's horse threw him from the saddle in the middle of the chase. He was already injured beyond belief and just passed out. My men took care of the knights around him and put him on my horse. I got away from there only to find two girls on the back of a white charger. I brought them here and left them."

"I told you I'd seen that sword somewhere," Cassmed exclaimed. She had emerged from behind the elf; longbow in hand with an arrow notched. The tip of the arrowhead had been only inches from the base of Qwan's skull. Since hearing Qwan recount his story, she had lowered the bow but kept it ready to fire.

"This true, Demy?" Medoran grunted, trying to shift his weight into a more comfortable position.

Gauduin held him down tighter, putting more force against the blade. "Stop moving, we're not finished yet."

Demien nodded, then realising Medoran could not see her, she said, "Yeah, that's how it all happened."

"Like I said," Qwansien still held a tight grip on his crossbow, ready to use it if necessary, "we are not your enemies".

With a grunt, Medoran said, "Put up your sword, Demy."

Not once taking her eyes off the crossbow, Demien brought her sword away from Gauduin's neck. In turn, the dwarf let go of Medoran's head and moved the blade from his throat. Very carefully, he got up, stepping away from the swordsman.

"So what are you doing here?" Demien asked slowly. "It's a little coincidental you're here and the place gets attacked."

"We're passing through on business," Gauduin answered. He noticed that both Qwansien and the swordswoman were glaring at each other; both had their weapons at the ready.

"So were the Black Flame," she answered flatly.

"We came back because we thought you might need help. Obviously we were mistaken," Qwansien countered.

"I'd say you were." Demien brought her sword up, pointing it at Qwansien's face, a half smile turning the corners of her mouth up.

Suddenly blue energy snaked out in front of her, swatting her sword away. It sizzled loudly in the air as it passed, leaving behind a smell of greasy burnt tin. Every pair of eyes darted to where it had come from. Uthan sat in his saddle, hand outstretched. Tiny tendrils of the same blue energy flickered around his fingers, making the air above them seem hazy. Behind him stood the other two horses, looking around nervously.

It was Qwansien's turn to smile. Keeping Demien and Medoran in front of him, he moved around to Uthan. "We'll be moving on now."

Gauduin sheathed his sword and walked past the swordswoman who was now holding her wrist, massaging the flesh with her fingertips. He climbed into his saddle and started to turn his horse away when the girl they had rescued came over leading a large elderly man by the hand.

"Medoran, the knights are all finished. Brenus told me to tell you," the man called to Med. He waited for the swordsman to nod in reply before looking to Gauduin, Qwan and Uthan. "My granddaughter tells me you saved her from knights. Thank you."

"The first thanks I've heard for helping them here," Gauduin grunted.

The old man looked puzzled, his brows creased as he asked, "I'm sorry?"

"A little misunderstanding, that's all, Jerel," Medoran replied.

Gauduin turned in his saddle and replied, "A little? I had a sword pressed into my neck."

The swordsman shrugged and grinned, "You did have your own blade pressed into mine as well."

"Only because you attacked me!"

"Like I said," Qwansien interrupted, raising a hand to Gauduin to stop him continuing, "we'll be going now. We have a long day in front of us and the night isn't over yet."

"I guess you're camping in the woods? Well, after saving little Shemy here I'll have a roof over your head for the rest of the night," the old man said. He ignored the look Demien fired at him and continued, "I expect it was the boy here who put all those lights in the sky to warn us too."

Uthan found himself reddening as all eyes fell on him, "It was nothing really. Just a small spell."

"A small spell that helped us all out, lad," Jerel beamed.

"You really did that?" Demien asked slowly.

Uthan nodded.

She looked down at her sword, lying a few feet away then back to her hand again, and to Cassmed and Medoran she said, "Mage."

The three of them watched as the old man led the elf, boy and dwarf away. Demien looked at her hand again before reaching down for her sword. She shot a glare at Cassmed as the girl muttered, "We didn't thank them."

"We really shouldn't stop too long here, Qwan," Gauduin muttered. The three of them were now walking, being led away by the old man and his granddaughter.

Qwan nodded, "While we're being offered the hospitality though, we'd be fools to decline it."

Gauduin shrugged, "I just don't like the odds of us leaving here without any more trouble."

The old man turned to them, "Don't worry about Med and Demy. They're fine. Just a little wary of strangers, that's all."

"I can understand that - after all we live in troubled times," Qwan replied.

As the old man turned back to the direction ahead, Gauduin muttered, "I actually meant Black Flame trouble."

"I think all those in the raiding party were killed, Gauduin. I don't think we'll be seeing more of them tonight," Qwan replied.

"I wish I could be as certain," the dwarf countered.

Qwan glanced sidelong at his companion, "What makes you certain we'll have more trouble?"

"Gut instinct."

"You're just hungry."

"I'm serious, Qwan. With a few possible exceptions, these people are not fighters. They couldn't have slaughtered the entire raiding party," Gauduin replied.

"If that's true then there'll be hell to pay here soon enough," agreed the elf.

Gauduin nodded, "I hope in that case you're right."

"Whatever happens, we won't be around to change things," Qwan answered. "When first light comes we're moving on again."

Jell Sharan crawled out from the village under the cover of darkness. He had taken a large cut to his thigh and the blood was warm and sticky, caking his trousers to his flesh. A woodsman's axe, wielded with such ferocity by one of the villagers, had cleaved through his gauntlet, taking the third and little fingers from his right hand. More blood seeped from a shallow cut running along the side of his nose up to his forehead.

The sense of failure hurt more than his wounds however. His party had charged right in amongst the villagers, believing the task of murder and destruction to be an easy one. And so it should have been, he told himself. His comrades within the Black Flame raiding party had not known about the fighters there. One half blind swordsman, a girl and a woman. Their ability to band the pathetic villagers together into some kind of militia would have given them a real fight. But the arrival of the elf and dwarf was another matter.

Then there was the mage. They had not been prepared for any kind of magic. The scouts had all come back telling Cornak there was no mage within the village. Jell's train of thought led him to believe the elf, dwarf and mage were just travelling through. Eventually he found a horse standing calmly alone, grazing idly, away from the burning buildings and corpses. It merely looked over at him and snorted as Jell pushed himself to his feet. The pain from his wounds brought him to the edge of blacking out. With his good hand, Jell grasped the reins and pulled himself into the saddle. Casting one dark glance back at the village, Jell urged his horse into a gallop, away from the failed raid.

"So what brought you here?" Jerel asked, ushering Qwan, Gauduin and Uthan into chairs. He made his granddaughter sit in a big comfortable-looking armchair while he himself went about arranging them all a meal.

"It's probably safer for you to not know," Gauduin said slowly.

The old man watched them for a moment, obviously coming to conclusions in his own mind. With a shrug, he answered, "Well, judging from the fight tonight I'd be betting you weren't with the Black Flame. That's all I really need to know."

"It's safer for us as well," Qwan said, "so you'll understand that we really don't want to be telling anyone."

"When you put it that way, I understand even more. It must be something really important then," Jerel replied. He brought a large iron pot over to the table. Its contents bubbled, filling the room with meat-scented steam. Scooping five, large helpings into dark, pottery bowls, he said, "It's not much I'm afraid, but it is filling. I guess you can call it a very late supper or an early breakfast!"

Gauduin laughed and looked at Qwan, "Cold camp, huh?"

A knock at the door had both Gauduin and Qwan reaching for their weapons, the elf's sword was half out of its sheath. Noticing their unease, Jerel went carefully to the door. He opened it a crack and peered through the gap, before grinning broadly. Opening the door fully, he said, "Come in, girl."

Cassmed entered the room, nodding her thanks to Jerel. She stopped in her tracks, seeing the elf with his hand on the hilt of his weapon.

Slowly, Qwan slotted the sword back in place, "Call it a precaution."

"I came to apologise," she said.

Qwan shrugged and went back to eating the stew in front of him. "There's no need, it was a skirmish and you didn't know who we were."

She sat at the table next to them and smiled, "I still don't know who you are."

"That's because we've not told you," Qwan countered.

"Well, I'd like to know the name of the man who saved the lives of my friends and myself."

"I'm not a man and I'm not here for thanks," Qwan replied coolly.

"Why are you here? It's a big coincidence you three come through here the day a raiding party attacks," Cass asked.

Qwan sat back in his chair and levelled his gaze at her. "And that is all it is, a coincidence."

"What I said to you in the inn earlier was true, you know. We don't get many travellers through here. It's pretty obvious your business includes the Black Flame since you camped outside the village and still came back to help," she continued.

The elf nodded, considering her words for a few moments. Slowly and deliberately he said, "Maybe we are actually with the Black Flame." His words caused Uthan to look up, shocked. Ignoring his stare, Qwan continued, "Maybe those raiders were just sacrificial lambs. All this time I could be here trying to gain your trust."

She shook her head, "I'm young, elf, but I'm not stupid. You're not fighting on the same side as the Flame. And even if you were, it'd take more to gain my trust than tonight."

"Good," he said, leaning forward to eat again. "In that case, you'll understand when I say I don't trust you enough to tell you what our business is."

"Now maybe you should go back to your friends and tell them that," Gauduin said quickly.

"Maybe I'll go back and tell them you're here on business with the Black Flame. I'm sure the rest of the village would be interested in hearing about it," Cass countered slowly.

A wide grin split Qwan's face. He laughed loudly, "And how long do you think it would take for us to fight our way out of here?"

"And kill so many innocent villagers? Would you really?" Cass asked, raising her eyebrows, shocked.

"They wouldn't be innocent if they were trying to kill us, girl," Gauduin countered quickly. He shot a glance at Qwan and said, "We don't need any trouble here. It's obvious they have no love for the Flame, even less after tonight."

Qwan leant forward, beckoning the girl closer.

Jerel sat down with them, leaning closer to hear too. Catching the look from the elf, he raised his hands and said, "Remember this is my house. And your secret is safe with me."

"I hope so. I thank you for your hospitality tonight and I would rather have not ruined it by having to make this promise," Qwan said, quietly.

"If we spill the beans, you spill our guts, right?" Cass asked carefully.

"He wouldn't have been as poetic about it, but that's pretty much it, yes," Gauduin confirmed before he continued. "You should both be aware that this knowledge puts you all in danger."

"We're travelling to the Demonic Realm to destroy the Black Flame itself," Uthan explained.

Both Qwansien and Gauduin looked at the young mage. He shifted uncomfortably under their gaze, unsure whether they were angry with him or not. Jerel sat back in his chair and breathed out heavily. Cass sat where she was, eyes fixed on Uthan.

Very slowly she asked, "Is this some kind of joke?"

"No girl, it's the truth. It's more of it than I'd intended on telling you. But that's why we're passing through," Qwan answered. "An old friend of ours went out there after making a discovery a few months ago. He's trapped in the Demonic Realm. We're going to free him."

"And what does that have to do with the Flame?" she pressed.

"He'd found the Forged One," Gauduin answered slowly.

Jerel sat forward suddenly, nearly falling from his chair. "But... but..." he spluttered.

"But it's only legend, right? I told him the same thing. But he swore on it," Gauduin replied.

"And Hedrial has rarely been known to be wrong about these things," Qwan added.

"How do you know he's trapped there?" Cass continued. The tone of her voice suggested she only half believed.

"I've seen him," Uthan replied calmly. He stared fixedly on the table in front of him. "I'm his apprentice."

The girl nodded. "I see. I know how that bond works."

She stood up and walked to the door, "Demien and Med are going to want to know what we have been talking about. What should I tell them?"

"The truth if you have to," Gauduin replied with a sigh.

Cass just nodded and left, closing the door behind her.

"You think that was a wise move?" Gauduin asked quietly.

137

Qwan simply shrugged, "It's done now. I don't see any point in worrying. Besides, I'm tired and need to sleep now."

Jell's horse wandered into the Black Flame encampment a few hours later. The knight was slumped forward in the saddle. The pain from his wounds had sapped all his remaining strength. Seeing him on the verge of collapse, the sentries had run over and helped him from his saddle. One took the horse while the other two carried his semiconscious form into the camp, yelling for assistance.

The calls reached the ears of Captain Darshan. He rubbed sleep from his eyes and wandered to the entrance of his tent to see the sentries approach. Another knight was running towards him.

"What is going on here, Corporal?"

"The raiding party sent out to Karaka-Tus, sir."

"What about it?" Darshan asked suspiciously.

The sentry shrugged, unsure what to say. Finally he said, "They're all dead."

"What!" Darshan boomed. He stalked forward, still only half dressed, until he stood before the sentries holding Jell on his feet. He grabbed Jell's jaw roughly, tilting his head so he could look the captain in the eye. "What in the hell happened?"

In the dull light, Jell was pale and his cheeks and eyes had both become sunken. He opened his cracked lips and muttered, "Ambushed. The rebel leader, Medoran."

Darshan's eyes softened for a moment. There was a flicker of triumph in his growing smile. He turned away from Jell and boomed at another sentry, "I want a rider and horse here now!"

"Something else," Jell continued.

Inclining his head back to Jell, Darshan said, "Go on."

"There was a dwarf and an elf there. They had a lad with them, a mage," Jell said. Every drawn breath brought a wince to his face. Speaking the last words, his eyes screwed closed in agony.

The words stopped Darshan dead in his tracks, "A mage?"

Jell nodded, "Powerful."

Darshan's eyes widened. He turned away from Jell again as a rider on a graceful looking black horse trotted over. Ignoring the messenger's salute, Darshan said, "Ride to Dessendor. We've located the rebel leader. He's in Karaka-Tus. Tell General Cornak I'll have scouts watching the village immediately. And tell him there's a mage there who assisted. The entire raiding party is dead."

"What about him?" the rider said, nodding to Jell.

The captain cast a quick glance at the dying man. He gestured with his eyes to one of the sentries. Immediately the man removed his sword and thrust it deep into Jell's heart. The knight writhed in death spasms for a few moments, then went stiff.

Darshan looked back to the rider and said sadly, "He wouldn't have survived the night."

The rider saluted one more time and rode towards the edge of the camp. The captain watched him go before barking orders to the sentries, "Get me four more riders. I want them to take compass points surrounding the village and keep a look out."

Chapter Ten

Uthan opened his eyes. Rays of golden orange sunlight filtered in through the gap between the curtains. Outside the window he could hear the innocent twittering of birds. He tried sitting up, wincing a little at the stiffness in his arms and legs. There was a steady pounding in his head, like a distant drumbeat. Every nerve in his body trembled as if he had been running all night in his sleep. Rising to his feet brought a sudden bout of nausea. He sat down hurriedly and closed his eyes, screwing them closed to block the dizzy sensation. He gulped down deep breaths of air, fighting against the need to vomit. His ears were filled with a dull roaring sound, almost like the sea.

"Uthan," whispered a voice.

His eyes snapped open. He looked around the room, searching for the owner. Gauduin and Qwan both still slept soundly. There was no one else. He closed his eyes again, listening hard. Again the voice called his name. It was quiet, heard from a distance almost.

"Who are you?" Uthan said, speaking with the voice in his mind.

"A friend."

"And I'm supposed to trust that?" Uthan asked carefully.

The voice was definitely in his head, echoing inside his skull, it said, *"You've been taught wisely."*

Uthan shrugged, "It's helped me stay alive."

"It will, Uthan. But what I have to give you will aid you further," the voice replied. *"You must come to me soon."*

"Where are you?" Uthan asked.

The voice did not answer. Instead Uthan found his eyes drifting closed once again, the lids becoming heavier. He slumped back down on his bed.

A moment later, Uthan opened his eyes. The scene before him was no longer the room he had slept in. He floated in the middle of a harsh desert. Scorched red sand sprawled around him for miles in every direction. A few skeletal trees and bushes, long dead from lack of water were dotted around. In the distance behind him a range of mountains rose, black against the sky. Ahead, Uthan could see a slender pillar of rock. As he concentrated on it, the ground far below him began to rumble. The ground around the pillar vibrated and cracks began to form around the base. With a deafening grinding noise, the pillar began to move up, growing out from the ground like a stone flower. The base widened, growing to more than six or seven times the size of the tip.

As Uthan watched the thing grow, he could see stone gargoyles on the walls, writhing and clawing at the air. Stone wings flapped, beating against the dark, grey walls and twisted pillars covered the tower, looking more like ivy than stone. The ground below continued to shake and the cracks in the ground widened as the tower became wider. Uthan noticed there was not a single window that he could see. The effect was chilling, freezing his blood even in the blazing desert sunlight.

Then finally it stopped. The tower stood statuesque in the middle of the sand, waiting. The gargoyles, seemingly growing out of the stone itself, writhed violently, thrashing at the air around them. Many were focused on the now floating form of Uthan, reaching out with taloned hands for him. At the base of the tower a large set of dark wooden doors could be seen. They slowly swung inwards. The darkness of the corridor beyond was totally devoid of light. Then the voice resonated from deep inside the dark.

"I am here."

Uthan's eyes flashed open again and he groaned, putting a hand to his head. The headache had gone, leaving only the dull after feeling. He sat up, conscious of the strain his body was under.

"You're awake," Gauduin said, handing him a mug. He watched the young mage sniff the contents warily. "It's only apple juice." Uthan nodded, his face pale. "Another headache?" the dwarf asked casually.

"Yeah. It's gone now but..."

"But your head feels like someone took your brain out and filled it with sawdust instead?" Gauduin replied with a grin.

"I'd say it was a hangover if I didn't know for a fact you

hadn't been drinking," Qwan said.

"It is," Gauduin answered slowly. Catching the puzzled looks from both Uthan and Qwan, he continued, "You pretty much overdid the magic last night."

"A magic hangover? Gauduin, you do talk some crap at times," Qwan answered.

The dwarf shrugged and sat down opposite Uthan, scrutinising his pale and tired face. "Hedrial told me about it. He said he'd only ever heard of it once or twice. Mages aren't usually powerful enough to use more magic than their body can handle."

"But he is?" Qwan asked.

"Uthan," Gauduin asked quietly. As the boy looked up, he continued, "For the time being, try to not use as much, okay? You need to let yourself build up to that level."

"But..." Uthan began

Gauduin put a hand up, interrupting him. "...but nothing."

Qwan moved across the room and sat on his haunches beside Uthan. Looking up at Gauduin, he said, "If it is a hangover as such, I think I may know a good cure."

"Will it taste bad?" Uthan asked carefully.

Qwan nodded, "But we need to be moving and you won't be able to ride for long like that."

"I'll try it then," Uthan said slowly. "But if I end up on a healer's table it's your fault."

Gauduin and Qwan both grinned as the elf said, "He's even talking like someone with a hangover." Qwan chuckled.

He stood up and left the room. Once the door had closed behind him, Uthan looked up at Gauduin.

"I had another dream. I think."

"Oh?"

"A voice started talking to me."

Gauduin shrugged, "Voices do that I've found."

"I'm serious, Gauduin. I'm sure I was awake when it started," Uthan replied.

The comment brought a raised eyebrow from the dwarf. "I think you'd better tell me about this."

Uthan told him of the voice, then the dream about the desert and the tower that had grown from the ground. Gauduin moved to sit down in a chair. He was about to say something when the door opened.

Qwan half entered, looking serious. He looked down at Gauduin and said, "I think you need to come out here."

The dwarf stood up again and moved to the door, Uthan following as quickly as he dared. In the room beyond, Medoran, Demien and Cassmed sat around the table. They looked up as Qwan led his companions into the room. At the sight of Uthan's pale skin, looks of concern passed over their faces. Jerel walked over to him, raised his chin and looked in his eyes. He nodded and muttered something, going back over to the kitchen benches.

Beckoning them to sit down, Med said, "Last night you took us completely by surprise."

"The feeling was mutual," Gauduin replied stiffly.

Qwan raised a hand to silence the dwarf. "Let him finish."

"Jerel's granddaughter has told us about your side of the fight. Or the side she saw anyway and I don't doubt her for a moment," Medoran continued. "The rest of the village know you're not the enemy. They don't know why you are here though, and I think, after hearing the truth, it would be better they don't know."

"I'll agree with that," the dwarf returned, with a nod.

There was silence for a moment as a mug of pale white liquid was placed in front of Uthan. He could only stare at the contents. The very sight of them filled him with a nameless dread.

"You have to drink it, Uthan. Looking at it won't help," Jerel said, his experience as a father and grandfather showing.

"Remember what I said about the healers," Uthan said. He lifted the mug to his lips and took long gulps, trying to down the liquid in one. Placing the empty mug back down on the table in front of him, he shuddered, feeling hot shivers run down his spine. A bitter taste coated his tongue, making him desperate for water. The air around the empty mug smelled like eggs and milk and something else that Uthan did not want to think about.

"It'll calm your stomach," Jerel said patiently.

"Strange," Uthan replied, "because I feel like I want to be sick even more."

"Bad tasting medicine always works better. Did your father never tell you that?" the old man responded, clearly amused.

"Yeah, and I never believed him either," Uthan responded. The group broke out in laughter. "How long will this take to work?"

Jerel sat down at the head of the table and shrugged, "It usually works almost immediately."

"So we can leave now?" Uthan asked, looking at Gauduin.

"Do you feel fit enough to ride?" Qwan asked.

With a nod, Uthan said, "I'll get better."

The dwarf sat forward in his chair and looked directly at Medoran. "So is there any point to this meeting? Or did you just drop by to say hello?"

A half smile crossed the swordsman's face, "We came to ask you if you needed some help?"

"We're offering to come with you. If what you told Cass is true, then we think you could use the extra numbers," Demien added. "The Demonic Realm isn't easily travelled."

"We've been there often enough," Gauduin answered stiffly.

Medoran shrugged, "Seems to me that we're on the same side. We may as well help you out."

Looking over the tops of his steepled fingers, Qwan said, "Gauduin? Uthan? What do you think?"

Uthan leant forward, dropping his head into his hands. His voice was muffled, coming from between his fingers when he spoke, "Extra swords sound like a good idea to me."

"And what about these people? The knights will come back here. You realise that. What are they going to do without you three here?" Gauduin asked.

Medoran shrugged a little, "They'll take care of themselves like they did before we came. Wouldn't you say, Jerel?"

The old man replied, "Those who can't fight will hide."

"Going with you to destroy the Flame gives us the better option. We attack the heart rather than the limbs," Demien said.

"Poetically put," Qwan said. "Hope you're as good when it comes to killing."

Demien suddenly stood, pushing the chair away. She began moving towards the door. Cass was right behind, grabbing her arm to prevent her from leaving. Demien turned her head to look at the elf, "We're not here auditioning to be dancers in an Imperial performance, elf."

A wry half smile crossed Qwan's face, "Spirited. Good. You'll need it where we're going."

Cass shot him a wary look, "Then you'll let us come along?"

"I don't really see we have a choice," Qwan replied. "Besides... it's safer for us if you're with us."

Gauduin stood up and wandered back to the room he had slept

in. "You'd better get your things together. We're leaving very soon."

The gates to Dessendor closed behind the messenger. The courtyard was empty except for a small group of guards who stood lazily against the wall of a building. An old man rushed over and took the rider's reins. The messenger looked down at him with disdain. Shaking his head, he swung out of the saddle and straightened his breastplate. As the strange old man lead his horse away, all the time babbling to himself, the messenger strode over to where he believed General Cornak to be.

"What is it?" the general said. He sat at a table, staring at a map. His helmet sat on the table beside him allowing his black hair to flow down from the back of his head, like a cloak.

"I've been sent by Captain Darshan, sir," the messenger said, saluting stiffly.

The general looked up from his map, staring hard at the messenger. Gesturing with his hand, he signalled for the man to enter the room.

"The rebel leader, Medoran, and his friends have been found in the village of Karaka-Tus," the messenger continued.

"And what is the captain doing about it?"

"He's ordered men to watch the village borders to make sure they don't leave."

Cornak nodded, "Did I not order a raiding party to destroy Karaka-Tus only yesterday?"

"You did, sir," the messenger replied carefully. "They attacked but were decimated. All but one man was slain."

"By the rebels?" Cornak glowered at the messenger over the top of clasped hands. The effect was demonic.

"Yes, sir, we believe so."

The general got to his feet and reached for his helmet. "So Darshan is expecting me to ride over there now and do what his men couldn't achieve?"

"Not entirely, sir. He wanted me to tell you about the mage."

Cornak stopped in his tracks, "I was told there was no mage at Karaka-Tus."

"There wasn't," the messenger continued.

"A traveller?"

Nodding, the messenger answered, "Captain Darshan thinks it could be the one you've been looking for."

"A travelling mage. A boy?" Cornak perched himself on the edge of the table, mulling the thought over. "And Darshan has the borders watched now?"

"Yes, sir."

"Good. Go and rest for an hour. You will ride back with me shortly," Cornak said.

"Thank you, sir," the messenger replied. He saluted again and left the room. The very moment he exited back into the morning sunlight, he felt he could breathe again. Wiping his forehead in relief, he set off to find somewhere to rest.

"Why go to Dacenheim? Wouldn't you be better off going to Skull Gate right away?" Medoran asked.

The six of them had been riding in near silence for an hour since killing the guard. A couple of the village boys had been out rounding up the livestock earlier that morning and had discovered the Black Flame Knight sleeping against a tree. Medoran had acted as a distraction while Qwan had sent an arrow into the man's throat. Leaving a warning to the villagers to watch for other guards, the group had raced away, disappearing into the forest. Qwan rode at the front of the group with Medoran. The two were talking over the journey.

Patiently, Qwan answered, "Skull Gate will be crawling with Black Flame Knights if I'm not mistaken. And anyway we need a gryphon."

"And why do we need a gryphon?" Demien asked. She and Cassmed rode just behind, listening carefully the whole time.

"There's a dragon we may need to kill," Qwan answered.

"A dragon?"

The elf turned in his saddle, looking irritated. "I didn't stutter, yes, a dragon."

Demien, looking equally irritated, asked, "You couldn't have told us about this sooner?"

Qwan reined his horse in and glared at her. Gesturing back in the direction they had come from, he said, "If you're uncomfortable with it then feel free to stay home. We don't have time for indecision now."

"Is there anything else we should know before we go on any further?" she demanded.

"Yes," answered Uthan. His head pitched forward suddenly and his eyes glazed over. His voice deepened, resonating in the air around him as he said, *"Bring Uthan to Barache."*

He screwed his eyes closed and quickly put his hands to the sides of his head, pressing against it as if it was about to split. A long moan escaped his lips. He leant back in the saddle and moaned again. His eyes rolled back in his head and a split second later he tumbled from the saddle to the ground.

"Uthan!" Gauduin shouted in panic. He leapt from his saddle and pulled Uthan's semiconscious form away from his horse's hooves.

Qwan grabbed hold of the horse's reins and pulled it away, where it could not trample over the two of them. He handed them to Cass before climbing from his saddle to join Gauduin. "Is he okay?" he asked, concerned.

The dwarf shrugged, "He's breathing, but feel his head. He's boiling."

"What can we do for him?" Medoran asked, appearing at the other side.

"Nothing," Dionis said suddenly.

The sight of his glowing blue form hanging in the air startled them all. The horses began whinnying, fighting against the reins. Kainan was the only one to remain calm.

"What the hell?" Medoran said, instinctively reaching for his sword.

"Oh yeah, that'll do a lot of good," Gauduin said gruffly. The dwarf looked over at Dionis and said, "He'll come out of it?"

"Yes," the spirit answered.

"Who or what is this?" Medoran asked Gauduin, nodding to the bat.

"An old friend," Qwan answered.

The dwarf shrugged. Ignoring them all, he asked Dionis, "What was all that bring him to Barache stuff about?"

Dionis replied, "There's an Oracle there."

"So that's the funny voice and the dream about the tower?"

"I would say so, Gauduin. You know about as much of this as I do right now," the spirit answered. "If the Oracle wants him to go there then there has to be a good reason. I say go."

"You can be sure it is this Oracle doing it and not some Black Flame trickery?" Gauduin replied.

"No, but then I doubt the Flame would be able to locate him like this right now. I do know that Hedrial once contacted the Oracle about his quest. I think the bond might have travelled over to Uthan," Dionis replied.

From her saddle, Demien said, "I've heard of such a thing happening before."

The group looked at her, Gauduin was the first to ask, "But is it likely?"

The warrior woman shrugged, "I don't see why not."

A long groan came from Uthan's mouth. The young mage blinked, putting a hand to his head again. With a painful sigh he sat up, helped by Gauduin.

"Uthan? Are you okay?" Qwan asked, full of concern.

"We have to go to Barache," he answered, slowly.

"Barache is a big place. Do you know where exactly?" Qwan asked.

Uthan shook his head.

"As soon as you reach Barache you'll know, Uthan. He'll call you to him," Dionis said.

Seeing Dionis for the first time, Uthan muttered a feeble greeting. Pushing against Gauduin's shoulder, he forced himself to his feet. "We'd better get going," he said quietly.

"Barache first, then Dacenheim?" Qwan asked the young apprentice.

"Yes, I want this thing out of my head as soon as possible," Uthan replied. His skin was pale and sweat-soaked still. Unsteadily, he climbed back into the saddle again, swaying slightly. Talking to himself, he muttered, "I really am starting to hate this."

"Are you sure you can ride?" Demien asked. She reached out a hand to hold Uthan steady, while Gauduin climbed onto his own horse.

"The pain should pass soon," Dionis said.

"And then start again when this thing contacts him next time," Cass said.

"He won't need to now. He'll know Uthan is on his way there. He should be safe," Dionis replied.

"From headaches at least," Uthan sighed. "But there's still an army of men who would probably like to do me some serious injury."

"And if we don't get moving again, they stand a good chance of finding us," Medoran warned.

"He's right, Dionis, we have to get going," Gauduin said.

The spirit nodded, "Take care, Gauduin. This has all become a lot more than just rescuing Hedrial now. It won't be long before the

149

Flame knows about Uthan, if he doesn't already."

"And when that happens, there'll be more than just men with swords coming after us, I know," Gauduin said.

Keeping Uthan in the middle of them, the group rode off. Behind them, Dionis faded from sight.

It was only hours later when one hundred black armoured knights emerged from the wooded road and into open view of Karaka-Tus. Riding at the head of the column, Cornak reined his horse in and watched the collection of buildings. The village inhabitants were going through not only their daily routines but also a major clean-up after the night before. All of them were unaware that a small army was upon them. He raised a hand, gesturing to the man riding behind him. The man walked his horse off to the right, taking a third of the men with him. Pointing again to another man, Cornak waited as he did the same in the opposite direction. With the remaining men in tow, Cornak kicked his heels to his mount. The large black horse cantered down towards the village.

Chapter Eleven

After a full day's ride from the village they called a halt, preparing a camp for the night. Uthan's headache had left him totally. He had regained his normal colour and was now listening attentively as Qwan outlined the journey.

"So for the next few days our biggest problem is keeping away from Black Flame Knights," he said finally. The elf nodded. "And then what?"

Qwan sucked in between his teeth, making a hushed whistling sound. "Then it gets trickier."

"How so?" Demien was the first to ask, noticing the elf had tensed slightly.

"There are two ways through the mountains. One is just a maze of open pathways. That way is apparently littered with broken bodies of travellers who have got lost or been attacked."

"Attacked by what?" Medoran asked. The swordsman had been thoughtfully quiet since seeing Dionis earlier in the day.

"Some stories tell of strange deformed creatures attacking a city near the mountains. The brave men and women of Cetorheim drove the beasts back into the tunnels. Spells were cast on the pathways there so the creatures couldn't escape to plague them again," Qwan said.

"Where did these things come from in the first place?" Uthan asked. His curiosity was growing.

"A maniac named Arrhn Kesharn had a tower built amongst the mountains. Some say the isolation drove him insane, others claim he was on the Wizard's council until they exiled him for experimenting with Shadow and Death magic. The story goes he abducted one hundred and seventeen women," Demien started to explain.

Qwan looked directly across at her, obviously impressed. "You know your history well. Have you studied much?"

She shrugged as she replied, "I guess you could put it that way, yeah. Kesharn forced himself upon all the women. He created

Summoning magic, spells created to bring forth demonic warriors, planting their essences in the children he'd conceived."

"What happened to the women?" Uthan asked.

"They died during childbirth. Kesharn never even bothered to bury the corpses. Instead he only had them placed in one long chamber at the base of his tower. The Tomb of the Mothers," Demien continued. Breathing out a long sigh, she said, "Kesharn was discovered. There was a group, three swordsmen and a mage, who hunted him for seventeen days until he wandered through Cetorheim, searching for a new victim. The mage read his mind by accident and saw the deeds. However one of the swordsmen was forced to kill Kesharn before he could locate the mothers. The monsters he'd spawned stayed where they were in the mountains for nearly a century as Kesharn had commanded them. But Binding magic can only last for a short time after the mage's death unless someone maintains it."

"Basic magical theory," Uthan agreed, happy to be able to add something constructive.

"Well no one knew about them, so no one kept the spell going." Demien finished, nodding to Uthan.

"But they knew about these things as soon as they flooded out and attacked the city," Qwan added. "Anyway, Kesharn's offspring are supposedly still there. So are the mothers and countless other lost souls that we don't know for sure aren't wandering around up there."

"Okay, I for one am voting against any path that leads near there," Cassmed said adamantly.

"I agree," Uthan nodded.

"I thought you'd all say that," Qwan said with a smirk.

"So why tell us about it? Why not just take the other path you mentioned?" Medoran asked.

Qwan shook his head, shrugging and smiling, "That path is only a little better."

"What?" Demien asked clearly not liking the tone.

"The other path is inhabited."

"Inhabited by who?" Med asked, leaning forward.

"I remember hearing stories about Orc tribes there but it was never proven," Demien replied.

"That's because they were driven out of there," Qwan replied slowly.

Cass whispered, "Something drove the Orcs away? What could do that?"

Demien leant back on the ground, laying her head on the grass. She put her hands over her face and moaned, "Please don't tell me you're talking about what I think you are."

Cass looked around the campfire. Gauduin and Medoran had both gone completely silent. Qwan stared into the flames and sighed. Uthan was the only one beside herself who did not know what they were talking about.

"What is in there?" she almost whispered.

"Daiharlons," Qwan said slowly, Demien had said the same word at the same time under her breath.

"Daiharlons?" Cass asked slowly, her voice sinking.

Uthan sat up, suddenly bright and alert, "Daiharlons?"

Hearing the tone of his voice, Demien sat up again and glared at him, "Yes, Daiharlons. Big, nasty, bestial savages!"

Uthan smiled, "I've never seen a Daiharlon before."

"You won't have, they rarely leave the mountains now," Qwan replied.

"I'm really not sure about this choice, Qwan," Gauduin said slowly. "On one hand we have monsters and semi-dead things. On the other, we're walking into a possible open fight with Daiharlons. It's really not a choice, is it?"

"They shouldn't be too bothered with us actually," Qwan replied.

Demien sighed. She leant forward again, letting her head sink into her hands. From between her fingers, her voice was only barely heard, "How can you be so sure?"

"The last I heard there was a large tribe of Gorren there as well," Qwan said. He acted a little too casually for everyone's liking.

"Gorren?" Uthan asked. "What are Gorren?"

"Savage creatures, they're beastmen like Daiharlons. They worship dark entities that should never be spoken of and have a tendency to kill anything that doesn't look like them," Gauduin answered. "Which of course is everything."

"You really expect to lead us through the home of those creatures?" Demien asked icily.

The elf put up his hands defensively, "It'll take us about four to five hours. We'll be in and out before they know it."

"You hope," she added acidly.

"We still have three days ride between us and the mountains though," Gauduin said brightly. "So there'll be time enough for you two to bicker about it."

"Demy, the Daiharlon pass will be much easier to cross," Medoran said gently, reaching out and stroking her arm.

Qwan nodded, "Kesharn's path is really not a good option. We could be stuck in there for years."

Demien nodded wearily. "I know. It's just... I would prefer another route."

Uthan looked at the elf, asking, "Is there another?"

Shaking his head, Qwan answered, "Nothing's ever been mapped."

Gauduin looked up at the few patches of sky visible between the treetops. Against the orange fire glow, the sky was black. He stretched his neck muscles, twisting his head to the sides. "Who's taking the first watch?"

Demien stretched, extending her hands to the fire, soaking up the warmth. "I will. I don't feel like sleeping at the moment."

"Are you okay?" Medoran asked in a concerned voice.

She only nodded and kissed him on the lips. "Sleep. You'll need it."

Uthan yawned, lying down amongst the folds of his blanket. Within moments he was asleep. It was not long before the others were too, leaving Demien alone with her thoughts. She settled down onto her side, staring into the flames. A sudden image of a maddened red eye flashed through her mind.

Jumping at the image she looked around frantically. There was no sign of the eye's owner. Feeling her heart pounding in her chest, she tried to settle back down again. The flames danced on the campfire, casting a hypnotic pattern before her eyes. Gradually Demien could feel her eyelids growing heavier.

Sparks flashed as a long bloodstained horn grated against bloodied grey stone.

Again Demien was brought back to reality. She sat up hurriedly, looking around her. The rest were asleep. Nothing other than the fire moved. High in the treetops above her, she could hear the chattering of night dwelling birds and the chirping of a multitude of insects. Their presence put the woman at ease once more. She could feel her pulse racing and her heart thumping loudly in her chest again. Beside her she felt movement.

"Okay, I can't sleep either," said Gauduin gruffly. "I'm too used to comfortable beds."

Feeling all her strength had drained from her, she smiled weakly,

"Do you mind if I get some sleep then?"

The dwarf settled himself into a sitting position, his blanket covering his shoulders. He just stared into the flames and muttered, "Be my guest."

"Thanks," she replied, lying down next to Medoran. Pulling her blanket up over her head, she welcomed the leaden feeling of her eyelids. Letting them close on their own, Demien felt the world slipping away from her.

Almost immediately she heard the child's scream in the distance. Her eyes sprang open to see two maddened, red orbs glaring at her. There was a deep snorting sound and warm breath brushed her face. Somewhere behind her, the child screamed again, this time more urgently. A growing sense of panic welled up deep inside her. Unable to do anything else, she cried out.

Cassmed sat bolt upright and looked around hurriedly. Medoran and Qwan were on their feet, swords drawn and ready. Uthan was at Demien's side with Gauduin.

"What's happening?" Cassmed asked anxiously.

"I'm fine," Demien said, trying to push Gauduin and Uthan away. "It was just a bad dream."

"That dream again?" Cass asked slowly.

Demien shook her head, "No, a completely different one this time."

"It's still really early yet. We should all try and get some more sleep," Medoran said, settling back down to the ground again. He put his sword back in its sheath, but held it close beside him.

"I'm going to just sit here and try to keep a watch, make sure no one else heard me," Demien said rather embarrassed.

With the exception of Uthan, the others all settled back down again, getting the last few hours of sleep while they could. He waited for them to be asleep again before saying, "I get bad dreams all the time now."

"The magic?" she asked, eyebrow raised.

Uthan nodded, "What was yours about?"

"A bad memory."

"To do with Daiharlons?"

Demien nodded and said, "Yeah, something that happened a long time ago."

"Maybe this is your chance to get over the fear of them," Uthan replied. "My father tried telling me once that the best way of conquering a fear was to face it head-on."

"I'm not scared of them! It's just something happened when I was younger. Since then I don't like being around them. I've seen what they're capable of."

Chapter Twelve

The mountains marking the border between the Empire and the northern country of Barache loomed in front of the six riders. They had been moving steadily for three days and there had been no sign of Black Flame Knights since leaving Karaka-Tus.

"The entrance to Kesharn's path is amongst the foothills," Qwan called over his shoulder. "It'll be decision time soon."

"Well, whatever the rest of you choose, I'm going the other way," Gauduin said gruffly. "I'm not tangling with things that are already dead if I can help it."

"Daiharlons and Gorren are that way though," Cass said quietly.

"Yeah, and they're alive. Meaning I can kill them if I have to," Gauduin replied.

"He has a point there, Demy," Cass said to her quieter companion.

"I'm not saying you all have to come the same way. Just letting you know now that's the way I'm going," Gauduin continued.

"One Daiharlon is bad enough," Demien said slowly, "I can't imagine the carnage that a whole tribe of them could cause." Her eyes took on a faraway look as she stared fixedly at the back of Kainan's ears.

"I'm still taking my chances with them over the dead," Gauduin answered.

"I would rather not be fighting the semi-dead for days whilst lost myself when I come to think about it," Qwan added.

Sitting in his saddle alongside Demien, Uthan said quietly, "We should only be a couple of days there. If you don't want to come with us through the mountains you can wait here."

Demien turned her head. She searched his face looking for even a hint of mockery. There was none, he was being sincere and did not doubt her courage. "The city of Cetorheim is the closest. But even then it's too far in the opposite direction to where we want to go. No, I'm coming too."

"Are you sure?" he asked.

She nodded in response before flashing him a weak half smile, "Didn't your father ever tell you the best way to conquer a fear is to meet it head-on?"

It was about four hours later when they reached the first of the foothills; boulders of all sizes littered the ground.

"At least we have cover if need be," Qwan muttered, noting some of the gullies between the hills.

"They can also be used as hiding places though," Demien pointed out.

Cass tapped her friend on the shoulder lightly and whispered, "I really did not need to hear that."

Ravens circled in the sky ahead. The wind brought their cries closer. "Remember what I said about carnage?" Demien said, pointing to the birds. "I think we may get to see it up close."

"Everyone stay tight. It's only a few birds so it doesn't mean a thing," Qwan said quickly.

They had just crested a hill and stood at the mouth of the pass. Spread out in front of them was a scene that Demien had described so accurately. Carnage. A collection of brutally dismembered corpses was hanging from gallows, impaled on spikes or staked out on the ground. Carrion birds hung in the air, viewing the scene as a large feast. The riders got closer then Qwan dismounted and jogged over to the nearest of the bodies. The birds around him waddled away, finding another corpse to feast on. He returned to the group moments later, paler than normal.

"What is it?" Medoran asked, uncertain.

"We have to get far away from here," replied the elf, hurrying back into his saddle again. "They're fresh."

"Do you think they'll be back?" came Gauduin's question.

"Oh yes, and I'm certain there'll be trouble as well," Qwan answered. "Those corpses are all Daiharlons."

"What?" Demien was wide-eyed. Her hand found its own way to her sword hilt, opening and closing involuntarily around it.

"We're standing in a Gorren killing field. And I don't want to be here when the Daiharlons notice the carrion birds in the sky and come to investigate," Qwan replied. He pushed his horse on into a trot.

"They'll come through the pass though, won't they?" Cassmed asked, watching the path ahead.

"Just be looking for places to hide," Qwan muttered. "We may need them."

The frenzied sound of wings beating echoed around them as crows and ravens flew away while they rode past.

From his saddle, Uthan tried taking in as much of the corpses as he could, even though he knew it was morbid. He reasoned that he might never see a Daiharlon otherwise. The sightless eye sockets staring back at him did not fill him with the same dread that the others were obviously feeling. Moments later and with the killing field behind them, walls of rock loomed on either side. High above them, they could see boulders, perched, ready to rain down on them at any moment. The horses' hooves echoed down the pass and to the ears of the travellers, the sound seemed to bounce off everywhere as nosily as it could.

"Those bodies? Left by Gorren?" Uthan asked.

Qwan cringed at the sound of Uthan's voice bouncing from the mountains. He replied, "Yes, that's why we're hurrying."

"Uthan, Rule One never piss off a Daiharlon," Gauduin called over his shoulder. "Rule Number Two, never, ever piss off a hundred Daiharlons."

"In other words, lad, when the beasts find that killing field, they'll tear this pass apart. This trip will be over really quickly if we're here then," Medoran continued.

"That much I didn't doubt," Uthan answered. He had to increase the volume of his voice in order to be heard over the beating hooves. "What I did wonder was would they add humans to that field?"

Qwan turned in his saddle and looked at the young man. "Yeah, they would."

"Then we need to ride faster," Uthan called back as he pointed behind him.

The elf followed where he was pointing and cursed, "Faster! We've got trouble!"

Behind them a large dust cloud was filling the mouth of the pass. Riders could be seen in front of the cloud. There was a small group of them, all riding large horses. The wide curling horns that sprouted from the Gorren's heads could be seen clearly.

Demien risked a glance over her shoulder at them, and then looked back ahead. A few hundred feet away, the pass started to narrow. They would have to ride three abreast for a short while. Above them the mountain walls tapered in places with clusters of rocks that had piled together, making a very unstable looking ceiling. She looked back over her shoulder. Thanks to the impressive size of their mounts, the riders had already gained a short distance on them. The animal skins they wore as cloaks could now be seen, flying at their backs. She reined Kainan in to a halt. The others stopped their horses too, just inside the narrowed section of the pass.

"What are you doing, Demy?" Cass asked, her voice raised in panic.

The warrior woman shook her head sadly, "They've been gaining on us all the time. We can't outrun them."

Uthan sat in his saddle calmly watching the oncoming riders. Slowly he extended his left hand, fingers outstretched. Tendrils of brilliant blue light snaked around his fingertips. He wove them together, forming a small ball of flickering energy. Muttering one single word under his breath, he tossed the ball away, before turning to the others.

"Run!" he shouted at the top of his voice.

Without hesitating, the companions spurred their horses on quickly, making for the narrow pass. The pathway took a series of bends and angles, making it impossible to keep riding at speed. Close beside him, Uthan heard Cassmed say that the Gorren would catch them.

Then came an explosion that shook the mountains violently. Tremors rippled through the ground, sending the horses into panic. They reared, thrashing out with their front hooves as the riders tried desperately to gain control. The only horse to remain calm was Kainan, the charger stood as still as a statue, only whinnying a little.

In the direction they had come from, they could hear the panicked shouts. Harsh guttural voices were cursing and yelling.

Uthan turned to the others, "It won't last long. We should keep riding while the tremors have them occupied."

"Won't last long, huh?" Demien asked, watching the bend behind them in case a Gorren rider should appear.

The young mage nodded and said with a grin, "I got the feeling that bringing a mountain down on us all would put an end to our trip."

They all looked at him. Demien was the first to speak, saying, "Good thinking."

The tremors faded after a few minutes and mere heartbeats after, they could hear the harsh voices of the Gorren again as they echoed from the rock walls. They took two longer, sweeping curves before the pass narrowed again. From here on they could only ride in single file.

"We travel on for another few hundred feet then it gets wider again from what I know," Qwan called over his shoulder.

They turned another sharp bend and, as Qwan had said, the pass opened out. The mid afternoon sunlight lit it up more as the mountains became less sheer. At the other end of the section, boulders had been strewn across the ground, seemingly haphazardly.

"It's a perfect spot for an ambush," Medoran muttered, noting the boulders.

Riding past the first few, they had to rein in their horses suddenly. A collection of loud angry snorts and whinnying came from the horses as they were forced to an abrupt halt. Blocking the path ahead was a group of Gorren warriors.

They stood waiting, growling or sneering as much as they could with their strange doglike faces. Each warrior stood over seven feet tall, dwarfing the travellers in both height and build. Four curling horns swept back from each head, many were stained with a dark rusty colour. Black eyes focused on the travellers, balefully revealing their murderous intent. The Gorren wore furs and the occasional piece of studded leather or chain mail that barely concealed hairy bodies. Behind them, large horses were tethered to a long dead tree. The beasts pawed the ground anxiously. Two of the Gorren held lengths of chain that rattled faintly. Both chains ran up into metal loops, fixed to a steel archway.

Uthan gasped; he was the first to see the lone Daiharlon warrior hanging from the steel archway by his ankles. The Daiharlon had a horselike head on a heavy-set human body that must have stood just over seven feet. Two long horns branched out from the back of his skull, curling towards the front slightly. A thick black mane ran from the top of his forehead and down to his neck. His dark eyes showed nothing other than pure rage. Thin black fur covered his upper torso and shoulders. The chain links were pulled tightly around his ankles, biting in, uncomfortably, through his brown boots. The beastman lashed out with his arms, trying vainly to grasp at one of those holding the chains. A third Gorren lashed out hard with a cruel barbed whip. The leather cracked across the back of the beastman, the barbs tearing at his flesh. Then the whip holder drawled at his companions, "You'll get your turn."

The Daiharlon replied with something but the group could not hear;

they all suspected it was not flattering.

"Kill them first!" the whip holder bellowed suddenly, pointing at the group as the thundering of hooves sounded from behind them.

"Well, I'm not going without a fight," Medoran growled as he reached to his side and removed his sword.

Qwan already had his crossbow loaded. He took aim at one of the advancing beastmen. Pulling the string, he sent a bolt whistling through the air to take the closest Gorren between the eyes. The warrior fell from the saddle, only to be trampled into the ground as his comrades rode over him. The elf unsheathed his sword and waited patiently.

Gauduin patted Uthan on the arm, "Take the girl and move to the side, boy. No sense you getting in on this yet."

"But I could help," Uthan protested.

"Yeah, and you could get yourself killed too. Protect the girl," the dwarf returned hotly.

Cassmed glared at the dwarf and yelled, "I don't need protecting!"

"Do as he says, Cass! There's no time!" Demien yelled back. "Use your bow if you have to!"

Uthan reached over, grasping hold of the reins to Cass's horse. He urged his own to a gap between two boulders, placing the two of them out of sight and, he hoped, out of danger. Behind him, the girl had unslung her longbow and was taking aim with the first arrow. Dressed entirely in furs, one Gorren strayed too close to the pair and Cass's reactions were quicker than Uthan's. As he focused his mind, trying to concentrate on a magical blast, the girl released her arrow. The sharp pointed tip buried itself in the Gorren's large barrel-like chest, causing him to roar in pain. As his mouth opened, Cass struck with another arrow which disappeared into the open orifice and out through the back of the large head. He toppled back, sending a small dust cloud up over his corpse. As the two groups of Gorren surrounded the travellers, Uthan looked over to the Daiharlon.

Only two warriors had been left to guard him. Both of them stood watching the attack with gleeful expressions. They smiled, showing the rotten fangs in their open mouths.

"I have an idea," Uthan whispered to Cass. As the girl looked at him, eyebrows raised, he added, "Stay here."

"I'm not your dog," she retorted.

"I'll apologise later. Right now I have to try and save us," Uthan replied.

He slid down from his saddle and slipped out of sight behind the boulder. As Cass watched, he moved carefully across to the other side of the pass, winding his way around boulders and rocks. He crept silently over to the hanging Daiharlon, keeping his eyes on the guards. The beast's eyes were closed and his arms hung down limply.

"If I let you down, will you help us?" Uthan whispered to him.

The Daiharlon snapped his eyes open. He focused on Uthan, letting the full rage in his brown eyes subside once he saw a human rather than a Gorren. "Who are you?"

"I'm Uthan Camarr."

"And why would I help you, Uthan?" the Daiharlon replied, as quietly as possible.

Uthan looked to the two guards, they had moved a few paces further away from them, watching as the remainder of his friends clashed with the Gorren. Turning his attention back to the beastman, Uthan replied, "My friends are over there fighting with Gorren. They're your enemies too unless this is some game."

The Daiharlon snorted loudly, his large nostrils flaring, "This is no game, boy. Let me down."

"I have your promise then?" Uthan asked quickly.

"I don't see any other choice. They'll slaughter your friends, then you, then me. I die on my terms," the Daiharlon growled in reply.

Uthan pointed at the manacles. They flipped open, letting go of the Daiharlon's ankles. He dropped to the ground with a grunt and instantly the two guards swung round. Seeing their prisoner suddenly free, they bellowed and surged forward.

The Daiharlon was on his feet in a heartbeat. He caught the first Gorren by the wrist as he went for an overhead slash. A sickening snap could be heard as he twisted the arm in an impossible fashion. The Gorren backed away, crying out in pain. He dropped his cleaver, only to have it picked up by the Daiharlon. The second warrior thrust forward, intent on driving his weapon deep into his hated enemy's stomach. Slashing down to block, the beastman slammed an elbow in hard against the Gorren's neck. Another snapping sound could be heard as the Gorren dropped to the ground with a broken neck. Without waiting to see the body drop, the beastman charged forward to the fight itself.

Several of the Gorren had already been slain. Even as the Daiharlon joined the fight, drawing the attentions of some of the enemy, Qwan drove his blade deep into the chest of another. Behind him, Demien pulled on her reins causing Kainan to rear suddenly. His front hooves kicked out, striking another of the foe in the head. The horse smashed the skull further as he dropped down again, hooves driving down hard through the bone. Gauduin and Medoran were engaged with a trio of the Gorren. Their swords clashed against the heavy cleavers wielded by the beastmen. As Medoran slid his blade off one cleaver, he slipped past the guard of another warrior to plunge the tip into his forehead.

The dwarf backhanded his blade into the face of his nearest opponent; the edge opened a shallow line of red across his nose. With his enemy stunned temporarily, Gauduin was able to drive his blade into the stomach, all the way to the hilt. He jerked back on the sword again, pulling it clear as the Gorren warrior tumbled backward. Swinging the weapon above his head, Gauduin opened wounds in two more of the creatures. They both stumbled away, stunned after having their blood tasted by a dwarfish weapon. Then the Daiharlon was amongst them.

He burst into the fight like a demon, swinging the stolen cleaver this way and that. Fire burned in his eyes, steam erupted from his nostrils. The travellers tried hard to keep control of their mounts in the face of the solitary Daiharlon berserker. Putting as much of his strength as he could behind every attack, the Daiharlon opened deep gaping wounds into five more Gorren. Another of them backed away from the berserk Daiharlon right into the waiting arms of Demien. She wrapped one arm around the warrior, pulling his head back as far as she could before opening his throat.

Gauduin leant from his saddle towards the back of yet another and quickly switched grips on his sword. Holding it in his hand like a dagger, he drove it deep in between the Gorren's shoulder blades. Before the warrior could fall, the Daiharlon swept out his weapon, taking the Gorren's head from his shoulders. Demien, Qwan and Medoran had continued to fight from horseback and the remaining foe fell before their shield of hacking, slashing and thrusting, until soon all the Gorren were slain.

Except one.

He lay on his back, with a terrible wound running from shoulder to groin Snarling all the time, he rolled to his feet, reaching for the serrated edged sword on the ground next to him. While the eyes of the group were on the fallen Gorren, he stalked forward, weapon raised, ready to tear the flesh off the Daiharlon.

Uthan was the first to see him. The Gorren was suddenly thrown up into the air by an unseen hand. Bouncing from the rocks like a rag doll, the beastman was hurled against the rock face. As the broken corpse tumbled back to the ground again, everyone turned to the mage.

"I told you I could help," he said with a shrug. " None of you would listen though."

"I for one thank you for your help," the Daiharlon said.

The travellers turned and gasped. Despite seeing him fighting alongside them, they had only just registered the beastman was free. He stood, breathing hard and soaked in his own sweat and blood. For the first time, Uthan saw the harsh whip welts on his torso and the gashes on his head and arms. He looked down at the Gorren cleaver in his hand. With a disgusted snort he threw the blade to the ground and stepped away from it.

"You helped save my friends," Uthan replied carefully.

"Uthan set him free?" Demien whispered to Gauduin.

The dwarf shrugged.

"Yes," the Daiharlon replied, "he set me free so I could help you."

"But why?" was all she could ask.

"You looked like you were having problems," answered the beastman.

Medoran snorted loudly, "And you being their prisoner was the perfect solution to helping us."

The Daiharlon's eyes blazed with anger momentarily, "I was waylaid by seven of the scum. I only saw fourteen chasing six of you. What excuse do you have?"

"Do we have to bicker about this?" Cassmed said loudly. The girl had been growing impatient whilst watching the group fight.

"No," the Daiharlon responded. He turned back to Uthan and extended his hand. "My name is Diarus. I never expected to extend my gratitude to a human but here, you have it."

Uthan grinned broadly. His face flushed red with pride as he said, "I never expected to see a Daiharlon, never mind have one owe me for saving him."

"I didn't say I owed you. Only that I was grateful," Diarus retorted quickly.

"Well," Uthan pressed, "you do kind of owe me."

"And how do you work that out, human?" the Daiharlon responded. He folded his arms across his huge chest, looking down at the young man.

Uthan shrugged and sat down on a rock. "I set you free from those chains, right?"

"But I helped your friends here with the fight."

"Yeah, but then they might not have needed your help really. If it had got to the point where they looked as if they might lose I would have in all probability been able to cast and kill all those things," Uthan explained, then he grinned again.

Diarus nodded and went over to sit on the rock beside him, "You have a point there."

"I thought so."

"So what do you want from me? Safe passage through the mountains?" Diarus asked.

"We'll require it coming back also," Uthan pointed out.

"Coming back I can't promise anything, but I can ride with you this way."

"Then that'll do us."

Diarus was quiet for a few moments, staring off into space. Finally breaking the eerie silence that fell over them, he asked, "Why did you come here?"

The group held their breath as every pair of eyes focused on Uthan. Slowly he answered with, "I have business in the Barache plains."

"Well, little man, we should be going. The Barache plains are no place to be going into at night," Diarus said getting up.

He wandered over to the framework he had been chained to and on the ground nearby was a pile of packs belonging to the Gorren. Pushing the fur-covered bags to one side, he retrieved a belt with two falchions sheathed on it. With a sigh, he buckled the belt around his waist and turned to lead the way.

Gauduin gestured to Uthan, beckoning him over, "What are you doing?"

"You were all worried about the path through here. We've just been given safe passage. Isn't that what you wanted?" Uthan responded somewhat indignant.

"And you trust him to just lead us through?" Demien whispered harshly.

The mage nodded.

"Then you're a fool."

"Actually no," Cass retaliated, "Uthan's right."

"What? Cass, you can't be serious about this too?" Demien responded.

The girl shrugged and continued, "It makes perfect sense to me. Uthan saved his life. If he has any honour then he'll lead us through without any problems."

"That's if he has honour, Cass," Medoran joined in, "As far as we know, he's just a savage."

"I know he turned the tide of battle when I let him go," Uthan said. "And that alone tells me what I need to know. I'm going with him."

"We're all going," Qwan cut in quickly. As Demien, Medoran and Gauduin all looked at him, he added, "We're going in that direction anyway so it's not like we can really avoid him now, is it."

Uthan did not wait to hear anymore. Ignoring the hissed words from Gauduin and Demien, he walked away to join Diarus. The two walked on in front, not bothering to see if the others were following or not. After several minutes without a word being spoken between them, Diarus turned to Uthan.

"Your friends aren't happy about this one little bit, are they?"

"They'll survive it."

"From the looks I was getting I don't know if they intend me to survive it though," Diarus continued, clearly amused.

"They won't harm you," Uthan replied.

"Oh, I know they won't. I really doubt they could right now," the Daiharlon said with a grin.

"So," Uthan started, wanting to change the subject. Being called a fool had stung. In his head he heard the words over and over again. "How did they catch you?"

"I wasn't paying attention," Diarus said. "How about you? Travelling in Daiharlon country I'd have thought you would have been paying too much attention."

"We were. We rode through a killing field and they appeared once we were past."

"Killing field?"

"Yeah," Uthan started, and then stopped, realising he should have kept quiet. The Daiharlon looked down at him, silently warning him to continue. "At the entrance to the pass. Qwan said it was a Gorren killing field."

"Daiharlons?" Uthan answered with a nod. Before Diarus swore, "Damn them."

"This was why we were hurrying through here and why my friends aren't keen on you being with us," Uthan said quickly.

"Why? Were you with the slaughtering party?"

"No, but there are rules."

The Daiharlon looked down again. He raised an eyebrow.

Taking it as a sign to explain, Uthan said, "Rule One is never piss off a Daiharlon. Rule Two..."

Diarus interrupted with a low chuckle, saying, "Never, ever piss off a hundred Daiharlons." He went quiet for a few moments then becoming serious again, he said, "I must tell my Chieftain about this. The Gorren race has taken things too far when they're abducting our people to use as trophies."

"I understand."

"Would you come with me, boy?"

Uthan stopped in his tracks and looked at Diarus. "Me? Why?"

"You have seen the slaughter. I want you to give the Chieftain the details of what you saw."

Uthan's mouth opened and closed as he tried to form words.

"You have my word no harm will come to you or your companions. You'll all be free to leave as soon as my Chieftain knows," Diarus said, almost pleading.

"What's wrong, Uthan?" Gauduin asked, catching up.

"I'm going with Diarus to see his Chieftain," Uthan said slowly.

The group nearly burst out in unison with horror. This time though it was Gauduin who was first to speak. "What?"

"The killing field, Gauduin. Those were Diarus's people lying there. They could have families. These people need to know," Uthan explained, a little more sure of himself.

"Thank you, Uthan," Diarus said with a nod. He turned to the group. "I promise you all no harm will come to you but I understand if you don't want to follow."

"You can guarantee us safe passage afterwards?" Qwan asked, his eyebrow raised in question.

"I have already promised you safe passage."

"I mean, after we meet your people and the whole Daiharlon population knows about us being here," the elf continued.

Diarus held the elf's stare and answered, "I promised you safe passage."

Sitting back in his saddle, Qwan shrugged and said, "Good enough for me."

"Good. Then let's not make this last any longer than we need to,"

Diarus concluded, making it clear that his patience was nearly at an end with the travellers. He then stalked off along the path again with Uthan following close behind.

Chapter Thirteen

"Is that your home?" Uthan asked, awestruck.

Ahead of them sat a huge pyramid-like structure with large blocks of yellow white stone that formed steps up the sides. Perched on the top was an impressively carved statue of a Daiharlon holding two falchions in outstretched hands. The head was thrown back, bellowing a silent roar of victory over the mountains. Behind him, Uthan could hear the mutters of approval from his companions, and the most vocal was Cass.

"Who is he?" she asked.

Diarus stopped and gazed upon the statue with pride. Speaking in an awestruck voice he whispered, "He is Salmul Huhrn, a great warrior, the greatest of the ancestors to our Chieftain, Dansule Huhrn."

"Salmul Huhrn?" Qwan asked slowly. "I've heard of that name."

Diarus turned to look at the elf, "And so you should have. He alone turned the tide against Orcan forces led by Kazuul the Gorefang."

"He saved the Empire from Kazuul," Qwan's voice was barely above a whisper. "I didn't know he was a..."

"A Daiharlon?" Diarus answered bitterly. "No, you wouldn't have. Your history books tell the tales a little differently. To your historians we have done nothing but slaughter."

"That's because there are those amongst you who have done nothing but slaughter," Demien answered curtly. Her words were laced with her own bitterness and venom.

To her surprise the Daiharlon nodded sadly, "You speak the truth. There were those like Tarna."

At the name Tarna, Demien froze visibly.

Diarus saw the effect and asked, "You knew of him?"

"We've crossed paths, yes." She fell silent as if realising she had said something she should not have done.

Diarus watched her intently for a moment or two. He said nothing about the Daiharlon, instead adding, "Still, it isn't like innocence is in abundance amongst mankind now, is it?"

"Can we continue the moral debate another time please?" Qwan asked irritably. "We have a long ride ahead of us and my arse is getting sore."

Rising up to tower amongst the mountains, the pyramid was overpowering. High above the travellers, the statue of Salmul Huhrn seemed to possess powers beyond the norm. The sun, which shone off the white stone he had been crafted from, gave him a god-like appearance. Diarus lead them around the base of the building. To either side, the mountain faces soared in a perfectly vertical line where the rock had been manually carved away and then used to build the stronghold. In the side of the building was a large iron gate, set back into the walls. Through the bars, the travellers could see a corridor, at the other end of which was another set of gates, this time made of black studded wood. The corridor itself had a foreboding look about it.

"We really have to go in there?" Demien muttered, almost to herself.

The Daiharlon turned and looked at her. For the first time since they had met him, he made no show of his disdain towards them. Noting her obvious concern, he said, "You don't have to, but it would be safer as I was attacked not far from here. The Gorren warriors could still have raiding parties in the area."

The gates were pushed open, making a barely heard squeal of steel on stone. Diarus led the way into the shadows, the travellers following closely behind. As soon as they had stepped into view, they heard the sharp intakes of breath from above them.

Two long ledges ran along the tops of the walls. Standing on either ledge was a tall Daiharlon guard. Each one held a long spear, pointed down at the travellers. Diarus held a hand up to them. "It's okay, they come in peace."

"They're humans," growled one of the guards.

Diarus nodded, "I'd noticed that too, but still they come in peace."

"What do they want?"

"Not now, Gazan, please. I have grave news that the Chieftain must hear," Diarus continued.

The other guard pulled his spear away, "It must be grave indeed for humans to come here."

Diarus looked at the second guard and nodded, "I must tell the Chieftain first, you understand."

The guard answered with a nod. He walked along his ledge to disappear through an archway. Moments later a harsh grating sound could be heard from the ceiling. The huge wooden gates were pulled back and behind them were another four guards. All of them stood motionless in shock as they laid eyes on the travellers.

From high up on the ledge they could hear the voice of the first guard say, "See, I told you."

They moved aside in a mixture of respect and confusion as Diarus led them through. The confusion was heightened as Uthan walked past them, nodding and cheerfully greeting them. Diarus beckoned one of the guards over to him and, speaking in low hushed tones, gave the Daiharlon some orders. "Ask the Chieftain if he would come to my rooms. Tell him I'm back and have urgent news he must hear of. I think given the identity of my guests it would be a wise move to keep them a secret for now."

The guard nodded dumbly before running off.

"My rooms are this way. I'll take you through the hidden passages under the circumstances. You can rest there while we wait," Diarus told the companions. He beckoned to another guard and signalled the horses. "Take them to the stables. Make sure they are rubbed down and fed."

The reins of the mounts were handed over to the other guard who also nodded, quite unsure of what to make of it all. Without saying a word he led the horses away.

Demien took one last look at Kainan, then the gate swung closed again. As the light from the doorway disappeared her heart sunk. It felt like someone had filled the pit of her stomach with lead and the sight of the gates grinding shut was as if the doors to her tomb had been closed.

A small, previously unseen door was opened in the roughly hewn stone wall to their left. Diarus led them through into a corridor built from perfectly smooth yet plain, grey stone. The floor was tiled with polished, dark marble that reflected the bright, orange torchlight. Their footsteps echoed along the corridor. Demien, in particular, turned to peer over her shoulder with increasing frequency. Her expression was akin to that of a hunted animal who knew its final moments had come. At the far end of the corridor was another door; this one was of solid oak. It swung open with only the barest swishing sound but the Daiharlon still looked at the hinges critically as he passed through.

Beyond the door was a wider chamber. Sun spilled in through high windows, bathing the grey and brown stone in an almost ethereal light. Along one wall was the foot of a staircase, easily wide enough for four to walk side by side. It disappeared inside the wall at its first turn. Higher up, they could see arched windows carved into the stone, showing the stairwell winding its way up. Shards of sunlight cut through, illuminating tiny dust particles that flickered and danced in the air.

"Where are we?" Uthan asked. His voice was full of awe, quiet in fear of breaking the peaceful atmosphere of the chamber.

Diarus simply answered, "I'm taking you through a part of the fortress that few are allowed to walk through."

"So already we're breaking your rules?" Cass asked with a glimmer of a smile.

"I think it's better for this one to be broken. The Chieftain should meet with you before the rest of my people do," Diarus replied.

"Why is no one allowed here?" Uthan asked, walking beside the great Daiharlon as they began the long climb.

"It is merely a place of peace and serenity. Salmul himself had it built here to reach the top of the city without having to move through the city itself," explained Diarus. Uthan noticed that every time the Daiharlon mentioned the name of Salmul, he swelled a little with pride.

Getting higher up the staircase, they saw more windows carved into the walls. Fiery, orange torchlight filtered into the stairwell mingling with fainter sunlight. For a few moments, the travellers stopped by the closest windows. Demien stepped back, paling at the sight.

Beyond was a huge sprawling edifice. On the stone floor between them and the building was empty ground. Wandering here and there, they could see Daiharlon, who appeared tiny from their perspective. Rings of blazing torches ran around the crafted rock walls. Sunlight cut through in beams from the few windows. The building itself was expertly built from great blocks of grey, yellow and brown stone. It seemed to grow from the furthest wall. Vast towers soared upwards from the lower part of the building, joined together by a network of bridges. Steps rose from the ground to meet the front gates that sat open, like the gaping maw of some legendary beast. More figures could be seen coming and going from the gates, like insects in comparison to the building.

"Is that your city?" Uthan asked, wide-eyed. He gripped the stone window ledge in amazement, trying to lean out to see more.

"Yes, all the city contained in one great fortress," Diarus replied with a proud look on his face. He shot the travellers a quick glance, remembering himself, and said, "Come. We still have to get there."

By the top of the sinuous staircase, the travellers were ready to collapse from exhaustion. They all fought to ignore their protesting limbs and not appear weak before Diarus as he strode onto a great landing. One of the walls opened out, revealing the fortress city in its full glory. A couple of steps built into the rock sides led down onto a partially hidden walkway that clung to the inside of the wall. Without waiting for them, Diarus moved across the ledge. They quickly followed and, despite the low railings on the inside that prevented them from falling, they all had the same urgent need to be as close to the wall as possible. The Daiharlon led them from the walkway to one of the closest towers, built into the wall itself. Checking to see no one was around to explain anything to, Diarus ushered them through a wide door then up yet another staircase that spiralled up even higher and into a large room.

Three tall windows looked out onto the mountains and over the pass they had come through. Looking out over the peaks, the travellers were stunned to realise they had climbed nearly to the top of the pyramid itself. The room was clearly designed with comfort in mind. Plush, brightly coloured cushions covered chairs and couches of polished wood. The wall hangings were bright red, yellow and blue. In the centre of the room was a low table, the seating arranged around it. A large glass bowl sat empty on the dark wood of the tabletop.

"Make yourselves at home, I'll have someone come quickly with food and drink for you," Diarus said hurriedly. He left the room, leaving only his echoing footsteps on the stone floor.

Qwan flopped down on a long couch, scattering purple cushions in his wake. "Oh, this feels good," he sighed.

"How can you relax in here?" Demien demanded. Her gaze went back to the windows and she wandered over and looked out. Although they were high up, the stepped structure of the building would not have been too difficult to escape from.

Medoran dropped his weight into a large padded chair. The hissing sound of escaping air was loud as he sank down. "Demien, we need to rest. Here is as good a place as any."

"If they wanted to harm us, surely we wouldn't be here now. We'd be in some arena or dungeon," Gauduin said as he wandered around the room. He looked at the various carvings on the walls, testing them to see if they moved. He carefully lifted the edge of one of the wall hangings, peering underneath.

The elf glanced over at his old friend. Furrowing his brow, he asked, "What are you doing?"

Gauduin replied, "Just testing things. You know my dwarfish curiosity."

"You're looking for more secret passages, aren't you?" Qwan demanded, sitting up.

"Well, yeah! It doesn't hurt to make sure we're not surprised, does it," Gauduin answered, continuing his search.

"You're being paranoid," the elf responded, sinking down onto the couch again.

"How can you be so sure?" Demien replied. She took a few steps away from the window, advancing on Qwan. "You saw the way the rest of them looked at us. They're just as shocked to see us, as we are to be here. How can we know this Diarus has the power to grant us safe passage through the pass? Do you trust him?"

"No," Qwan answered. He let an arm flop out to the side, pointing a finger at Uthan and added, "But I trust him. I've come to trust his judgement."

A moment later the door opened. Diarus strode in, a young Daiharlon servant behind him carrying a tray laden with fruit and bread. A large polished jug sat on one side of the tray, steam coming from the contents. The servant set the tray down on a small table behind the couch and quickly left the room. All the time, he had tried to look as normal as he possibly could, concealing his shock at the nature of the visitors.

Diarus took a chunk of bread from the tray and sat down in a chair in the corner, watching the doorway. He chewed thoughtfully on the bread, until finally the sound of footsteps in the corridor outside reached them.

A Daiharlon, with a grey mane into which gold and silver beads had been woven, strode into the room. He was just as tall and broad as Diarus. He wrinkled his nose and snorted as he saw the travellers. Ignoring them further, he strode across the room and opened his arms. "I heard you'd brought humans with you."

"There wasn't really an alternative, father," Diarus replied. He got up and embraced the Chieftain.

Uthan watched the exchange, thinking about the words. Slowly he asked, "Diarus, you're the Chieftain's son?"

Diarus turned to the young mage and nodded. "Great, goodness knows how many times, grandson of Salmul Huhrn."

"So what is this grave news you told my guards about?" the Chieftain asked.

Ushering his father into another chair, Diarus sat down again. "The Gorren have erected a killing field at the mouth of the pass. Our people are being used as trophies."

The Chieftain fell silent and his dark ageing eyes went to the floor at his feet. Solemnly he asked, "How do you know of this?"

Diarus gestured a hand to the travellers, "They rode past it coming through the pass."

"Ahh yes. Your new friends," the Chieftain nodded, his voice was thick with disdain. "Tell me, Diarus, what is the heir to my throne doing keeping the company of humans?"

"I was waylaid by a Gorren hunting party. I would guess now that I was to be the new trophy. These humans..." Diarus started.

Qwan sat up suddenly, startling everyone in the room as he interrupted, "Can I just quickly point something out? It's been annoying me for a while now. Notice the ears and the eyes? I'm not human. I'm an elf."

Both Diarus and his father watched Qwan blankly. The Chieftain sat forward, looking Qwan straight in the eyes. Speaking in a slow level voice, he said, "I don't care about your eyes or your ears."

"Father, please. They saved my life," Diarus said, putting up a hand to stop the Chieftain continuing further. "These people were hunted by the same party. They helped me so I helped them."

"And so now you're the very best of friends?" the Chieftain snorted.

"Far from it," Demien answered quickly. "We don't want to be here anymore than you want us here."

"Sir," Uthan began, the Chieftain swivelled his large horse head round, focusing on the young apprentice. Uthan felt himself shrink slightly under the Daiharlon leader's gaze. "Your enemy's enemy is your ally right?"

The Chieftain nodded begrudgingly, "Yes, in theory."

"Then can we be allies for a short while at least?" Uthan asked.

Again the Chieftain nodded, "So then, allies, will you assist us in removing the Gorren threat?"

There was a dreadful silence in the room as everyone looked at Uthan. He shrugged and said, "Maybe, but not just now."

"You have more pressing matters to deal with than helping your newfound allies?" the Chieftain pressed on, voice dripping with cold sarcasm.

"Actually, yes," Uthan replied. His cheeks and neck had flushed red, angry at being baited. His companions all held their breath.

"So? What is this important thing? What brings you through this pass? You had to know who lived here and that if we caught you, you stood little chance of surviving," the Chieftain continued, narrowing his eyes.

"We knew and didn't care, I actually wanted to meet a Daiharlon," Uthan replied.

A broad smile passed over the Chieftain's face. A deep rumbling laughter erupted from his mouth, "I like you, boy."

He stood up, strode across the room and extended his hand to Uthan. The boy took it carefully at first, feeling the steel-like grasp that could possibly crush his own considerably smaller hand at any given moment. Sitting down again, the Chieftain asked, "So, in reality what brings you through my homeland? You didn't come here just to see a Daiharlon surely?"

"We travel to Barache. To see the Oracle," Uthan answered with a shrug.

"The Oracle?"

"I don't know really. I just had a voice in my head telling me to go to Barache and had a strange dream about a tower," Uthan explained.

"Really tall tower? With lots of gargoyles?" the Chieftain asked. As Uthan nodded, the Chieftain continued, "Yes, that's him, an annoying demon-like thing. He helped the great Salmul in his crusade. So why is he seeking you out?"

Uthan sighed, "I doubt you'd believe me."

"Try us, Uthan," Diarus said encouragingly.

The apprentice looked around at his companions. Each of them was watching him, holding their own breath in anticipation of him saying the wrong thing. With a shrug that told them they had nothing to lose, he said, "A friend of ours went to the Demonic Realm to put a stop to the Black Flame. His soul is trapped there. We're going to set him free."

The Chieftain was silent. He sat back in his chair to think over Uthan's words. "And finish the job he started, I'd guess."

To the sound of five people breathing out sharply, Uthan nodded. "My home has been all but destroyed by his knights. I have to do something."

"You really think you can do this?" Diarus asked intently.

"Hedrial seemed to think he could, so I don't see why we can't," Uthan continued.

"And this is why you're being summoned by the Oracle, no doubt," the Chieftain said.

Diarus got up and moved to the door, "Father, I need to speak with you a moment."

The Chieftain, seeing the serious look in his son's eyes, nodded. Turning to the travellers he said, "Excuse us a moment."

"You want to go with them?" he said as he and Diarus stood in the corridor outside.

Diarus nodded gravely, "I know it would take me away from things here but..."

"Of course you want to go. This is your chance to achieve something we've all wanted down our line. If you succeed, your name will be there in the histories alongside the great Salmul Huhrn. How could I refuse you that chance," the Chieftain said.

"I'm sure they could use the extra help," Diarus said slowly, gesturing to the travellers.

The Chieftain glanced over his son's shoulder, looking in at them as they stood together in a huddle. "You can expect them not to like your request though. With the exception of the younger one, they clearly don't trust our kind."

"With good reason," Diarus said carefully.

His father nodded again. "Keep an eye on them, son. I doubt they'll betray you. But keep an eye on them all the same."

"I will."

"There will be a feast tonight in your honour, my boy. I'll go and make the preparations now. And make sure your newfound allies attend, our people should know about this," the Chieftain said. He clamped a hand on Diarus's shoulder, before turning and leaving.

"I don't like this," Demien hissed as the two Daiharlons left the room.

Holding a grape up to the light for inspection, Qwan answered, "We'd picked up on that."

"I have to agree with her on this," Cass said. "What if they side with the Black Flame?"

"You shouldn't have told them the whole thing, Uthan," Gauduin was annoyed.

Demien was back at the windows, looking out at the mountain face when Diarus strode back into the room.

"My father and I have spoken. You have free passage through the mountains while the pass is under Daiharlon control."

"Bad feelings, huh?" Qwan muttered, casting a sidelong glance at the girls.

"I have a request to make however," Diarus added quickly. They all turned to look at the beastman. He stood, back to the windows, casting his seven-foot tall muscular form into silhouette. Arms folded and back perfectly straight, he set himself into a pose that suggested there was no chance they could deny his request. Looking at each of them in turn, he said, "You allow me to come with you."

Medoran sat forward in his chair, "You want to come with us? That's your request?"

"You could use the extra swords," Diarus said.

"True, we could," Gauduin answered.

"What's in it for you?" Demien asked full of suspicion.

"I get to follow in the footsteps of Salmul Huhrn which is the greatest honour I could ever have," Diarus answered proudly.

"So," Medoran said intrigued, "this is a matter of pride for you?"

"When the Black Flame has finished with the Empire, his eyes will turn elsewhere. My people cannot hold these mountains forever. And we won't be able to look to the Gorren for help. If anything, they would side with the Flame," Diarus explained.

"We could use the extra muscle," Gauduin said, studiously ignoring the dark looks he knew would be cast his way from Demien.

"He has a load of that alright," Medoran answered.

Demien looked at Diarus, studying his arms and chest critically. Speaking in a distracted voice, she stated, "You're not really going to let us say no, are you?"

"Oh, you can say no," Diarus replied, "you had just better not mean it."

"Why are we even having this discussion?" Qwan asked suddenly. "He wants to come with us and kill our enemies. He's proven he's capable of doing it and we do need the extra help.

I don't see a problem."

"Congratulations, Diarus Huhrn, you're in," Gauduin said finally. He wandered over, reached up and patted the Daiharlon on the arm, "Now is there any chance of some real food before we set out?"

The Daiharlon strode to the door, "Actually," he said, "there's to be a feast shortly in our honour."

"A feast!" Gauduin exclaimed as his eyes widened at the thought.

"Oh great," Qwan muttered, sinking back onto the couch. "We'll be here forever."

An hour later, Diarus lead them down to the long hall where the celebrations were to take place. They stood in a small chamber, furnished with only a few chairs and a table. A large blue and red curtain covered a doorway on one wall. Beyond the curtain the travellers could hear the murmuring of many deep voices. Clearly the hall was full.

"We will wait here until the Chieftain has spoken. To have you go out now would surely cause a riot amongst them," Diarus said gravely.

As he peered through the curtain a hushed silence fell. Diarus did not look away from the hall but told them that his father had entered. The Chieftain's voice sounded muffled through the curtain as he addressed his people. He explained why they were having the feast. There were more murmurs from the crowds.

"Yes, by now many of you have heard there are humans here. This came as quite a surprise to me too. Yet, their reason for being here is highly understandable."

"He's going to tell them all, isn't he? About the Flame!" Medoran said, freezing in his chair.

Diarus held up a hand to quiet the swordsman.

Out in the long hall, the Chieftain continued telling of his pride in his son and how he would be joining the strangers on their quest.

He finished by saying, "He will follow in the footsteps of the great Salmul Huhrn." At this the hall erupted in cheers and applause. "We Daiharlons have had a long and stormy history with humans. In the past they have enslaved many of our kind, subjecting them to torturous ordeals such as they did to the once great Tarna. Yet we also have not made life easy for them. This pass had remained a place of death to any human who has walked it for nearly a hundred years. Yet now I am asking you to cast aside your feelings towards humans. We live in a dark time. One day your sons, grandsons or descendants may be in need of human help," the last comment brought a series of snorts from the crowd. The Chieftain ignored them, continuing, "or we ourselves may be needed. I have invited the humans to join us. Tonight we shall see if Daiharlon and human can truly co-exist."

In the chamber outside, Qwan shifted in his seat. "Can you remind him I'm an elf please?"

Diarus pushed aside the curtain and strode through into the great long hall. Riotous applause and cheers went up from the crowd, then he turned and beckoned to Uthan. The young mage wandered out into the hall, to face a sudden oppressive silence, the others followed him closely. From the far end of the room someone started clapping, then two more joined in. Within moments, the entire room was applauding the travellers. The Chieftain indicated a row of seven empty chairs to his right.

"Still got your bad feeling?" Medoran asked, glancing at Demien.

The warrior woman shrugged. Nodding in greeting to a few Daiharlons standing close by, she said, "It isn't quite what I expected."

"It's preferable to being gored though, I hope," Diarus said, standing behind her.

The tables were arranged in a large rectangle, everyone being seated on the outside. In the centre of the hall was a raised platform, about two feet in height. After asking Diarus, Uthan was told that it was the stage on which the entertainers would perform. The Chieftain had arranged jugglers, musicians and a trio of acrobats.

Three young female Daiharlons came around to the tables. They were slightly shorter and less muscular than their male counterparts. Their heads bore no horns and their manes were longer, flowing down their backs. In comparison to the thick leather and rough cloth that the males were dressed in, the women wore smooth linen robes in bright colours. They flitted nimbly around bringing jugs of wine and trays of roasted meats that filled the air with their spicy aromas. The very smell itself made mouths water in anticipation of the taste.

The entertainers emerged from the far room. Two jugglers, with burning clubs, wandered around the outside of the stage, next to the tables. The trio of acrobats jumped onto the stage, flipping and throwing each other, demonstrating a balance that looked impossible for the otherwise burly Daiharlons. From the far end of the hall, standing on a balcony, was a small orchestra, playing soothing pipe music. The effect of the juggler's torches, the flipping acrobats and the soft music was comforting to the travellers. Even Demien was beginning to lose her anxieties after only a few minutes.

"You know," Gauduin said after several hours of downing mug after mug of strong wine. "I'm glad I came here now."

Diarus looked at the drunken dwarf through an equally drunken haze. "Oh yeah?" he said finally, slurring his words a little, "why would that be?"

"Erm, I'm not sure I can remember," Gauduin answered. He began giggling uncontrollably and put his head down, burying his face in his arm on the table. Suddenly he lifted his head again and said, "Oh yeah, I remember now."

"Well?" Diarus prompted. The Daiharlon's head waved around drunkenly as he tried to focus. It was as if the mighty horns were too heavy for his neck to support.

"Best wine I've tasted in years," Gauduin said with a big nod. He threw his head back and downed the mug's contents in one long gulp.

A large thump suddenly sounded to his left. Everyone at the table looked round to see Diarus still seated in his chair. The chair however was lying on the floor on its back. Gauduin looking down at the Daiharlon, roared with laughter. The dwarf reached down a hand, offering to help Diarus to his feet again but the Daiharlon was unconscious. The Chieftain looked down at the sleeping form of his son and shook his head. He gestured to his guards and two large Daiharlons wandered over, hefted Diarus onto their shoulders and carried him away.

"Good fellow, your son," Gauduin said, patting the Chieftain on the shoulder with drunken familiarity. The dwarf suddenly belched loudly. "I think I should probably go to sleep now."

The Chieftain nodded and smiled, clearly amused by the dwarf's drunken behaviour. "I think that could well be a good idea. I'll have a guard help you to your room."

"We have rooms here?" Gauduin asked, furrowing his brow. "I don't remember that part."

Another large guard was called over. He stood patiently behind the dwarf as Gauduin tried to untangle himself from his chair. Slowly the dwarf was led away from the long hall, leaving through the same doorway that Diarus had.

"Actually I could use some sleep myself," Demien said to the Chieftain.

The Daiharlon nodded in understanding. "It has been more of a trying day for you than your friends, has it not?"

"You could put it that way, yes," Demien answered.

"My son tells me you have crossed paths with Tarna," he said slowly. "I'd like to hear about that sometime."

"It wasn't a good time for me," the warrior woman started.

The Chieftain nodded and said, "I understand. There were many atrocities carried out by him, but it's a story for another time, I think."

"If we survive our journey then maybe I'll come back and tell it."

"I'd appreciate hearing it," the Chieftain said with feeling.

The guards who had carried Diarus away returned. The Chieftain called them over and asked them to show Demien to her room. Cassmed and Uthan made their excuses and followed quickly after her. Eventually, Medoran and Qwan left their growing audience to join their comrades, realising that tomorrow held more time in the saddle and the searing heat of the Barache plains.

Chapter Fourteen

The sound of Orcan tribal drums echoed from far away over the Barache plains. The travellers had left the mountains and the Daiharlon people behind, letting Diarus lead them out of the pass and through the more open foothills. The sun was slowly sinking behind a distant range of mountains to the west, streaking the sky in fiery reds and purples. What small wisps of cloud there were, were bathed in a soft pink glow. Away from the shelter of the mountains, a gentle breeze blew in their faces, softening the heat from the ground. Ahead of them they could see the vast expanse of open land that was the Barache plains.

Here and there, dark shapes loomed up into the falling dusk; towering rocks, huge boulders and small hills could be made out. Save for a few skeletal trees dotted around in the visible distance, there was no plant life.

"We should make camp soon," Medoran said.

"Where?" Gauduin asked. He indicated the flat desolate land before them. "If we have a fire it'll be seen for miles."

Cass looked around them, taking in the plains, "What's the problem with it being seen?"

Gauduin, Qwan and Demien all looked at her as if she was stupid. "Cass," Demien said finally, "the Barache plains are not hospitable. Nothing friendly lives here."

"You stand a bigger, much bigger chance of the wrong people seeing the fire," Diarus said calmly. "Desert bandits and Orcs. They're all out here somewhere."

"Not to mention Kayloks," Gauduin continued. Seeing the blank looks on the faces of Cassmed and Uthan, he continued, "Huge shaggy things. They burst out of the ground. Very few people survive a Kaylok attack, let alone manage to kill one."

"Okay," said Cass, riding off a little, "I didn't need to hear that."

"Uthan can cloak us though. Couldn't you, Uthan?" Medoran asked slowly. The sunlight had faded totally, plunging them into near complete darkness. The blackness was overtaking the purple streaks in the sky.

Uthan was watching something on the northern horizon and, distantly, he said, "No, I'm riding on."

"When did you go crazy, Uthan?" Qwan burst out. "Didn't you hear what we said about this place?"

"Yes, but I need to go on. He's calling me," Uthan said, without looking back.

"You know where he is, the Oracle?" Cass asked.

Uthan pointed to the northern horizon, "I can see the tower."

Everyone else looked at Qwan who scanned the horizon, squinting, trying to see it. Finally he shook his head, "There's a small shape there, but it's too difficult to make out clearly to even my naked eye."

"But then he's not using just his eyes, is he," Gauduin answered gravely as he started riding after Uthan.

The mage stopped his horse suddenly and turned in the saddle. His eyes glowed brilliant blue in the darkness, radiating magical energy. He extended an arm, holding up a hand to halt them all in their tracks. Speaking in the deep resonating voice that they had heard when the Oracle contacted him before, Uthan said, *"Stay. I'll return soon."*

"So we just stay here and hope you get back to us before something else does?" Cass demanded.

"You will be safe here," Uthan replied.

"And you?" Gauduin returned.

Uthan answered, *"I will return."*

The air around him crackled as he turned back and rode off into the night. Diarus began riding after him but the air in front of the Daiharlon fizzled and cracked suddenly. His massive chestnut horse reared, kicking against the sparks.

"We're not invited to the party," Qwan said as he climbed off his horse and began unsaddling it.

"You're just going to stop here?" Medoran asked him.

The elf pointed in the direction of the invisible barrier, "It's not like we can go much further."

"It wouldn't matter if we could," Demien said. She too had started to make Kainan comfortable for the night. "There's nothing but flat ground for miles."

Uthan's horse stood motionless in the middle of the plains as the mage held his hand up in the air. From his fingertips a brilliant white light illuminated the area around him. Just like in his dream, the great tower stood in front of him. Eyes crackling with power, he looked up as a thousand gargoyles screeched down at him. His eyesight was enhanced incredibly by the magic, showing him the creatures straining against the rock at their backs and clawing the air around them.

Two large stone lions guarded the doors, one sitting on either side. In contrast to the deformity of the gargoyles high above, the lions were perfect stone statues that watched sightlessly as Uthan approached. The doors slowly swung open, revealing a darkened corridor beyond. A dull blue light could be seen from somewhere far down the corridor. It picked out the details of faces, arms and bodies carved out of the stone walls themselves.

Climbing from his saddle, Uthan whispered to his horse, "Stay here."

The horse obediently stood still as Uthan walked up to and through the doorway. The carvings looked as though they had once been real, living creatures encased in stone. They appeared now to be trying to escape, to break free of their solid granite bindings. Uthan wandered straight by them, trying to not look at the outstretched hands that loomed out of the dark. The twisted, deformed faces snarled and leered with open mouths. The thought of the creatures watching him, waiting for him, filled Uthan's mind with dread and the hairs on the back of his neck stood on end.

At the end of the corridor was a stone staircase from which the eerie blue glow filtered down. In the light, the stairs looked like they would crumble the second Uthan put a foot on them. He climbed dozens of steps, only to find another corridor, identical to the first one. More stone figures tried to reach out for him as he wandered past, heading toward another flight of steps with an identical blue glow. After moving up three more flights and along three more corridors, Uthan had begun to feel the energy increase around him. As he walked, sparks fizzled from his clothing and hair and the air smelled and tasted like greasy metal.

On the very edge of his hearing, Uthan caught the sound of stone grating on stone. He turned on his heel and ducked quickly, summoning a power blast to his left hand, just as one of the wall creatures soared towards him. Something inside his head took over. Uthan punched the air in front of him, sending a blast of raw energy hurtling towards the creature. The power ball smashed into its chest, shattering it into small pieces of rock that were sent showering everywhere.

Buzzing with power, Uthan stood up and began backing towards the stairs. Another energy blast formed around his hand on the chance of a second attack. He could hear the grating of stone on stone again but this time it was louder. His right foot brushed against the first step. Almost jumping out of his skin, Uthan spun round, ready to unleash the power ball but seeing only the stairs, he turned back.

More of the creatures pulled themselves out from the walls, charging towards him so Uthan threw the energy ball at the closest. It smashed into splinters. Ignoring the shards of rock that cascaded around them, the remaining creatures surged forwards. He punched his hand in their direction again, sending another blast of energy their way. More shards of rock littered the ground as another of the creatures was blasted into fragments. As the others continued to come towards him, Uthan turned and fled up the stairs. Turning the bend in the stairwell he heard the grating stop. Cautiously, he peered back around the corner.

The creatures were waiting at the foot of the stairs, glaring up at him angrily.

"You can't follow me up here, can you," Uthan muttered to himself.

There were more grating sounds from the corridor above. Summoning more energy to his hands, Uthan crept slowly up the next stairs.

Waiting patiently for him in the middle of the corridor was a large gargoyle. Seemingly carved out of white marble, it stood with its huge arms folded. As Uthan came into sight, the gargoyle turned a stone head, looking right at him. Large bat-like wings unfolded from its shoulders. The creature opened its jaw and screamed at him. The sound was like nails scraping down slate, setting Uthan's skin crawling and his teeth on edge.

Quickly, he launched the power bolts forward. The energy rippled through the air, causing a heat haze as it passed. Both of them impacted off the gargoyle's chest but this time they had no effect. Uthan watched, wide-eyed as the creature just paused a second, shaking its head as if it had merely been stunned. He thought to himself, "This is not good."

He called more energy to his hands, trying to build a more powerful blast. Shaking with the effort, he unleashed it at the gargoyle. The impact sounded like a loud thump as the gargoyle was thrown from its feet. Uthan dashed forward, intent on running right past the fallen creature before it could get up again. There was no time though because Uthan was only a few feet from the gargoyle when it sat up suddenly, glaring at him. Almost without thinking, Uthan sent another blast of energy to strike the gargoyle. Swatting the ball away as if it was no more than a fly, the gargoyle got to its feet. The creature towered over Uthan, standing nearly nine feet tall. Great stone horns adorned its massive head. Glowering eyes of brilliant green balls of energy in otherwise empty sockets glared down at the mage.

It opened its beak-like mouth and in a lifeless monotone said, "Follow me."

Uthan had not been expecting that. He had waited for the gargoyle to crush him beneath hands that were twice the size of his head. The creature then turned and walked off along the corridor, not waiting to see if the mage was following. The walls along this corridor were blank. No more of the hideous carved creatures that Uthan was no longer sure had attacked him, or were just there to escort him.

"This way," the gargoyle droned as they reached the base of a huge spiral staircase. Its large stone feet thudded nosily on the steps as it began walking up. They seemed to climb forever. When Uthan looked at the stairs below him, he could not see the foot of the stairwell anymore. Finally the gargoyle led him up into a round chamber.

The room was empty except for a pedestal in the centre. Stone arms were entwined together in a grotesque fashion. One large outstretched hand protruded from the centre of the pillar, holding a large obsidian bowl. The same eerie blue glow filtered down from cracks in the ceiling, casting dramatic shadows across the floor. The gargoyle waited by the stairwell, arms folded patiently as Uthan started toward the pedestal.

"Where do I go from here?" Uthan asked, half turning back to the gargoyle.

The creature stood, motionless, watching him in return.

"That is up to you to decide, Uthan Camarr," said an all too familiar voice from behind.

Uthan whipped round quickly. The voice belonged to a large eyeball sitting in the bowl on the pedestal, the Oracle. Slender pink and purple veins pulsed across the dull white surface. A solid, black pupil surrounded by a soft, blue iris focused on Uthan.

"Why did you bring me here?" Uthan asked slowly. Deep inside him his fear was giving him the urge to unleash an energy blast at the Oracle.

"You travel to the Demonic Realm to slay a god," the Oracle said.

"No, I travel to the Demonic Realm to find my friend," Uthan countered. "I'll set the Forged One free while I'm there and let it do the rest."

"And if it fails?" the Oracle asked. If it had had an eyebrow, Uthan felt it would have raised it at that moment.

"I don't have the kind of powers it takes to kill the Black Flame. I wish I did," Uthan said hurriedly.

"You are the One who can. The One who will."

Uthan smiled, "If you were human, I'd say you were drunk."

"You do not believe me?" the Oracle questioned.

"I'm an apprentice mage. My master is dead," countered Uthan again. He had begun to tremble.

"You are no longer an apprentice. You do not need a master."

"You're wrong, I do need him," Uthan said.

"You have come this far without him."

"I've come this far because of him!" Uthan's voice was raised.

"I see what is in your heart, Uthan, and I have seen your future."

"And I suppose I'm going to grow up to be an all powerful mage or something?" Uthan countered sarcastically.

There was no hint of sarcasm in the Oracle's voice as it replied, "Yes. The most powerful ever."

"But... but..." Uthan tried talking but could not find the words to express himself.

"Inside you, you must realise it is true. Look how far you've come, Uthan. You assisted in the destruction of a Black Flame hunting party. You have befriended Daiharlons. That in itself was not something easily accomplished," the Oracle continued. "Magic itself seeks to protect you."

Uthan stood perfectly still apart from a slight trembling as his knees now felt weak. His stomach was knotted as he asked, "I'm really supposed to destroy the Black Flame?"

"Yes," the Oracle said, "which is why I've called others here."

From the ceiling, four cloaked figures suddenly dropped to the floor, surrounding Uthan. They each stood nearly seven feet tall and as they drew their weapons, Uthan saw they were not swords but blades of energy and flame.

"So that's why you brought me here," he said, quickly summoning energy to his fingertips, "to kill me."

The Oracle said nothing in reply. It merely watched as the creatures threw off their cloaks. Beneath them, they wore suits of red and black plate armour. The visors on their helmets were grilled, allowing Uthan to see their faces.

The first was pure orange flame. The others in turn were water, then what looked like a miniature tornado inside the helmet. The last was a collection of dirt, dead leaves, twigs and small stones. Uthan had heard tales of Elemental warriors many times; they had become legends, associated with magical battles.

All four held up their swords, blades in front of their faces, saluting Uthan. A flash of blinding white light filled the chamber suddenly. The spirit warriors leapt forward at Uthan before he could unleash his energy blasts. The light faded away, leaving only purple and green flashes in front of his eyes. Then he felt a strange rippling sensation through his whole body. New feelings of raw power surged through his veins as if he was being given new life.

"Consider them a gift, Uthan," the Oracle said slowly.

Uthan spun around, searching for the warriors but they were nowhere to be seen. A little shaken, he asked, "Where are they?"

"Inside you. They will lend you their strengths for the time being. Soon you will need their assistance," the Oracle answered. "You don't have the time now but you will learn all you need to know about them on your journey," the Oracle continued.

"Don't have time?" Uthan asked carefully.

"The General of the Black Flame Knights knows of your presence. He has sent word to the Flame himself. The Black Flame has answered by sending General Meligonn," the Oracle answered. "It won't be long before the demon hordes are in your homeland."

The news sent a chill down Uthan's spine. He remembered hearing Hedrial and Gauduin talk about General Meligonn and the demon army. In his mind's eye he had a picture of thousands of armour clad demonic warriors.

Slowly Uthan muttered, "They'll destroy everything."

"Unless you stop them," the Oracle answered.

Uthan looked at him expectantly, asking, "How do I stop an army?"

"Destroy the Black Flame," the Oracle answered.

"And his armies will stop?"

"The defeat of their leader will leave a void. They will strive harder to fill it instead. You will defeat them easier without their leader," the Oracle answered.

"Where are they now?"

"They are moving through the Demonic Realm. Cornak has been instructed to find you before they arrive."

"The people of the Empire won't stand a chance if they arrive, will they?"

The eyeball was silent, pulsing and watching. Finally it said, "No."

"Can I really stop them?" Uthan asked, unsure of the answer.

"It is in one of many futures that you will."

Uthan thought about the comment and, to himself more than the Oracle, muttered, "All I have to do is make it this future."

"There is something else," the Oracle said. "Your master carried a precious artefact with him. It was stolen from his corpse and has fallen into the hands of the Black Flame Knights. General Cornak carries it himself, unaware of its power. You must retrieve Hedrial's dagger from General Cornak."

Uthan arrived back at the camp only a few hours later. Clearly his friends had known about the Cloak spell the Oracle had cast over them. They were all asleep around the last dying flames of a small campfire. He rode in quietly and settled his horse down. Sitting in front of the fire, he carefully began rebuilding it by adding small twigs around the last few precious flames then blowing gently on them. The air around him suddenly felt chilled against his skin. The horses whinnied, stamping their hooves nervously. Uthan peered into the gloom, distracted from his thoughts. He could see nothing but impenetrable darkness. Then he magically altered his vision.

A Kaylok crouched off to the side glaring at him. Baleful green eyes stood out against the thick coat of greasy black fur. The animal was hunched over, its powerful arms pawing the dirt in front of it. Two curved horns grew from the sides of a wolf-like face framed with long, shaggy fur. Its nostrils twitched on the end of its muzzle as the beast sniffed at the air. A low growl escaped its throat, threatening Uthan. As the young mage just looked directly back, the Kaylok touched the air in front of it, as if testing. There was a shimmer and a spark. The magical barrier the Oracle had set in place was still around them.

Without thinking about it, Uthan tossed a handful of tiny energy sparks at the beast. They sailed past its outstretched hand, to hit its large body. The beast yelped, jumping and twisting in the air. The stomach churning smell of singed, greasy fur was awful and smoke rose from the Kaylok in slender wisps. Uthan waved his hand again. The sizzling sound ceased as suddenly as it had started. The Kaylok stopped jumping and leaping around, coming to sit on its haunches and watch Uthan again. This time there was fear and pain in the stare, as well as the malevolent killing intent.

"Go away," Uthan commanded.

The beast turned and fled, disappearing into the gloom again.

Getting the fire going again, Uthan sat back and just watched the flames. He could only think of what would happen if the demon army did arrive in his homeland. Pictures of the demon horde burning, killing and leaving everything behind in an apocalyptic state filled his head. He knew he had to stop them, he could feel that what the Oracle said was true, even if it did seem a little impossible that he was the One who could stop it all. He just could not even begin to comprehend the idea of how he was going to do it.

He yawned suddenly, feeling all his strength drained. He shook his head and blinked rapidly, trying to wake himself up a little, not realising how tired he had become. He looked around him at the others as they all slept soundly, secure in the fact there was a magical barrier around them that prevented an attack. Sleep became more inviting. Settling down on the ground, he lay back and closed his eyes.

The smell of sizzling bacon filled his nostrils and woke him up. Bright morning sunlight dazzled him, forcing him to close his eyes again hurriedly.

"Nope, it's no good, we know you're awake," Gauduin muttered close by.

"I only fell asleep for a minute," Uthan replied quickly, feeling guilty.

"We didn't bother with keeping a watch last night. This barrier you put up was good enough to keep anything away," Gauduin said.

Uthan sat up, rubbing the back of his head. Cass rushed over and hugged him, causing him to flush bright red as he felt the warmth of her body pressed against him.

Equally red faced, she moved back and said, "I was worried about you disappearing like that."

"I was fine really," Uthan mumbled, feeling his heart ready to punch a hole through his chest with the excitement.

"Why did the Oracle send for you then?" Gauduin asked, sternly. "What exactly happened?"

Qwan came over, handing Uthan a plate holding some bacon and a piece of bread. "Eat up quickly because we have to get going."

Uthan explained his meeting with the Oracle while he ate. His companions sat in silence and listened to him. Even the thought of Meligonn caused Uthan to shudder. He could not bring himself to share the image of the general's rampaging hoard with his friends.

"Where are we headed?" Medoran asked when Uthan had finished. He put the fire out, scattering the ashes to try and disguise the recently used camp.

"Dacenheim," Qwan answered.

Diarus looked up quickly, "A Daiharlon in a human city?"

"Don't worry," Qwan answered, "we'll think of something."

"They won't be happy to see a beastman amongst them," Diarus said, shaking his head slowly.

"It might not be that bad actually," Demien said. She had saddled Kainan and was looking at the other horses. "There'll be the initial looks and comments, but I expect people there will forget soon enough."

Qwan looked from Demien to Gauduin. He raised an eyebrow questioningly.

The dwarf shrugged. "It's been a while since I was there, but I would think she could be right."

"Of course I'm right. Think about it, Dacenheim is a big city. They have humans, elves, dwarves, goblins, and orcs, even the occasional centaur. It's the capital city of the Empire," Demien explained. "A place where you can buy dragons and gryphons isn't really going to pay too much attention to one Daiharlon."

There was a subtle, barely felt, shift in the air. A gentle breeze blew around them for a moment then was gone. Qwan reached down at his feet for a stone. He tossed it to one side, watching it bounce harmlessly to the ground several feet away.

"The spell's broken then?" Cass asked, looking at Uthan.

The mage looked around and shrugged, "The Oracle cast it. I didn't."

"Time for us to be leaving," Qwan said, saddling his horse. The others quickly broke camp, packed up their bedrolls and were saddled and ready to go.

Uthan had turned his horse back in the direction of the mountains again before asking, "How long will it take to ride to Dacenheim?"

Bringing his horse alongside the mage as they all began the journey, Qwan said, "About five or six days riding."

"Six days," Uthan repeated, feeling despondent.

They rode hard through the mountain pass, easily travelling the distance in a few hours. The only sign of Gorren was a collection of corpses, hanging from gallows in what had recently been a killing field full of Daiharlon. The carrion birds had already gone to work on the Gorren warriors, removing pieces of flesh from gaping wounds, opened for the soul purpose of attracting the scavengers. The stench of death hung in the air, making the travellers gag.

"Your people did this?" Cass asked, paling at the smell.

Diarus nodded, then with his voice heavy with sarcasm, he answered, "My people are savages, remember."

"That's not what I meant," Cass retorted.

"This was the revenge my father desired," Diarus said quietly, "the justice my people deserved."

They rode through the foothills, coming to the border of the Empire. Qwan looked out across the horizon of forests and fields. He inhaled deeply and sighed, "Home. Never thought I'd appreciate seeing the place so much."

Diarus looked out at the scenery before him, eyes filled with amazement. "Not one Daiharlon since the great Salmul has stepped foot in these lands."

Medoran patted him on the shoulder as he rode by, saying, "Congratulations. You've made history."

Chapter Fifteen

The group had been riding hard across the Empire for three days at Uthan's insistence. At first they had been reluctant to push the horses as hard needlessly but, as Uthan had continued to urge them on faster, they had agreed. He had not told them his reasons why, keeping the thoughts of the demonic invasion to himself. Only the sight of the magnificent city, sprawled out a mile in front of them, seemed to lift his spirits. The road ahead meandered out of the trees and onto large open grasslands. From further inside the forest, the travellers could already see part of the long stone wall that protected the city of Dacenheim from invaders. The light grey stone reflected the noon sunlight, making it almost seem white. The eyes of both Uthan and Diarus were filled with awe as they caught their first glimpses of the city.

On a hill in the centre of the city was the Imperial Palace. Built entirely from white marble and blocks of smoothly polished granite, the building stood out in the midday sun. Around it, dwarfed by its presence, were hundreds upon thousands of rooftops. They conjured an image of people crowded around some magnificent deity.

"We'll stop and rest once we're inside the walls. I know of a good inn," Gauduin proclaimed, moving his horse off to the front of the group.

Muttering to himself, Qwan replied, "Why does that not surprise me."

Eight men guarded the main gates wearing chain and plate armour, over which was a crimson surcoat. Horsehair, dyed crimson, hung from the top of the polished helmets in a long braid that came down to their shoulders. The faceguards on their helmets were made from chain mail, allowing the guards to see who was who. They stood just inside the walls, four on each side of the gate. As the group got closer to the city, they saw another four guards armed with large crossbows, standing on the wall itself.

Diarus shifted in his saddle uneasily. "This might have gone a little better if there were other travellers on the roads," he muttered.

Riding at his left side, Medoran responded, "Yes, but we live in difficult times so the chances of seeing another traveller on the roads is slim."

"Which means they'll be paying more attention to us, a lot more," Diarus answered.

"We'll be fine," Demien said reassuringly as she moved her horse around to ride in front of Diarus. "Just keep riding, if they stop us then we'll explain."

"Just don't tell them the truth," Qwan said quickly. "too many people know already."

The guards on the wall did not move as the group rode up. Those at the gate moved into position while watching the travellers. Riding through the gates, Demien nodded to those on her left in greeting, the guards nodded in reply. Cass smiled at the four on her right, causing one of them to blush a little. The guards paid no attention to the rest of the party until Diarus rode calmly through, then one guard stepped back in disbelief. The Daiharlon could see the puzzled looks on the faces of the others as he rode into the city. He shook his head and shrugged, relieved at having got into Dacenheim without question.

Demien had caught the puzzled looks on the faces of the guards too. She glanced over at the Daiharlon and, seeing his expression, said, "Now you know how we felt in your home."

Diarus merely nodded.

Laid out before them was a long wide street. The buildings lining either side of the pavement were shops. Here and there were brightly painted signs or large displays of goods, almost spilling out onto the road. A collection of humans, dwarves, and elves and, in some cases, orcan tribesmen wandered up and down the street, going about their own business. Again, Uthan and Diarus stared in wonder at the scene set out before them.

"Dacenheim," Gauduin stated, beaming with pride. "If you can't find what you need here, then it doesn't exist."

"Glad you think that way, Gauduin," Qwan beamed in response to his friend. "We need a gryphon."

The dwarf shrugged and then grinned, "Then you know where to go."

"Cass and I have to go and see someone while we're here," Demien said.

Medoran looked at her and nodded, "May as well while you're here, right?"

Qwan looked from Medoran to Demien. With a raised questioning eyebrow, he asked, "Family visit?"

The warrior woman smiled uneasily, "You could put it that way."

She leant over and kissed Medoran on the lips. Then, with a fond look, she said, "Be back soon, I hope."

With Cass riding alongside, she moved her horse off down the street.

Gauduin turned and, gesturing to the elf, said, "Qwan, you know where to find this merchant so you and Medoran go and see if you can get one of those beasts."

"And what are you going to be doing with the time it takes?" Qwan replied.

"I'm going to get us more supplies and see what I can learn about the general's movements. I'll also keep these two out of trouble," Gauduin answered slowly.

"And no mention of finding that inn you were talking about?" Qwan asked.

The dwarf smiled, "Well, we are in Dacenheim after all."

"I guess it's better you don't meet up with this merchant though. From what Boron has told me he'll have problems enough with me being elfish. We don't need him to shit himself and die when he sees tiny here," Qwan gestured to Diarus. To the Daiharlon himself, Qwan added, "No offence meant but you can be pretty scary looking."

With the mere hint of a smile, Diarus answered, "None taken. I know you wouldn't want to hurt my feelings."

"Can you feel it?" Demien asked Cass. The horses could only walk slowly through the busy Dacenheim streets, the crowds parting a little to let them pass, only to close up again behind them. Surrounded by a constant flow of people, Cass's horse snorted nervously, causing the girl to constantly be whispering soothing words in its ear.

The street in front of them opened out into a square. In the centre was a large, round, stone pool with a fountain reaching the height of nearly ten feet. Statues of lions, unicorns and dragons were perched on the edge of the pool, watching the crowds with their unseeing eyes. Small children played noisily in and around the water, jumping in and out from between the statues while their parents looked on.

Beyond the busy square, a building rose up, towering above the others nearby. On the roof a tall, stone-carved warrior stood looking out over the city, holding his sword above his head.

Cass looked up, seeing the statue for the first time. From her place in the entrance to the square, she could feel the eyes, seemingly staring right back at her. From somewhere in her chest she had felt a thumping. At first she had ignored it, then as she had ridden on she realised it was not just her heart pounding after all. The thumping felt like a drum, beating from somewhere else only to echo inside her.

"I feel something," she said slowly, unable to take her eyes off the statue. "It feels like..."

"Like a drum beat?" Demien enquired before she smiled, shining with pride as she said, "It'll gradually get faster."

The girl nodded, "It already has." She felt energy surging through her veins and her fingers tapped lightly on the pommel of her saddle. It was as if they were in need of something to do with the sudden newfound energy.

Noticing the tapping, Demien laughed, "We'd better get you in there before you drive your horse crazy."

They walked their horses through the square and up to a set of steps. This led the way up between more statues of warriors to a wide, open doorway. They slid down from their saddles, leading the horses closer. Cass started shrugging and rolling her head around, loosening her muscles.

"Is it always like this?" she asked in almost a whisper.

Demien chuckled lightly, "You'll get used to it over time."

"It's about time you came back to us, Demien," boomed a voice from the doorway. It belonged to a short, overweight man. He was dressed in black and yellow robes and his grey hair was cropped close to his scalp. Beside him walked a young man, barely out of his teens, who wandered down and took the reins from both Demien and Cass before leading the horses away.

The large man called after him, "Be careful with that white one, lad. Demien would kill you if he comes to any harm."

"Getting them trained, I see," Demien said, starting up the stairs.

"It's not often we have one of you returning who actually has a real horse! The stable hands have been getting into bad habits," the man replied. He opened his arms as Demien walked up and embraced him. "It's good to see you again, Demien."

"I was starting to think I'd never be back here, Master Dasiel,"

Demien replied with a smile.

"And this must be your Raanshi," Dasiel said, seeing Cass a few steps behind them. The girl nodded at him in greeting. Turning back to Demien, he asked, "Making progress?"

"It'll soon be time," Demien answered.

"So soon?"

"She's come a long way," Demien said with a nod.

Dasiel extended an arm to Cass and put the other around Demien's shoulders. "Come inside. You can tell me exactly where you are with the training and exactly why you're here, Demien."

The house and offices of the merchant, Varion Doo'ar Cherre, were lavish. A walled off garden lay between the house and the road. Small trees blossomed with a variety of colours from pale pink to a soft blue. A white gravel path wound its way through the centre of the garden, coming to a stop in front of the great house. Another wider path, presumably for horses and carts, followed the wall around the garden coming to a halt behind the house. Four thick pillars, carved from a yellow stone that gleamed under the sun, held a large balcony in place against the front of the house. Beneath it, was a small set of stone steps leading into a porch. The front door was a huge, black scorched wood rectangle, studded with brass. Everything about the mansion seemed to be an attempt to flaunt the merchant's wealth.

Qwan and Medoran rode slowly through the iron gates and into the garden. Taking their time, they followed the path up to the front of the house. A man was seated in a white chair on the balcony. He looked out over his garden at the two riders as they approached.

The front door of the house opened and a short man with dark tanned skin emerged. He was smartly dressed in a white shirt and trousers with black boots and a thick black leather belt. Qwan and Medoran rode up alongside him and dismounted. With a broad welcoming smile, the man asked, "How can we be of assistance?"

"We have business with Doo'ar Cherre," Qwan replied.

"Is he expecting you?"

"No, but we were sent by Boron," the elf replied quickly.

"I see," the man said, never once losing his smile. He bowed to them and gestured to the open door. "If you like to wait inside I will go and speak with my master on your behalf."

He led them into a lavishly furnished room. The walls had been covered with brightly coloured drapes and paintings. Along one wall was a great fireplace; logs had been laid in the hearth ready to light. Two long semi-circular couches took up the centre of the floor, facing each other in a rough circle. The scent of lavender and rose petals permeated the air. The servant indicated for the two travellers to be seated while he left through another dark wooden door.

After only a short time, the door opened again. The man they had seen seated on the balcony outside entered the room. He wore a long robe of crimson silk and a pair of black velvet slippers. When he smiled he showed a set of gleaming white teeth. "My servant tells me Boron sent you," he announced as they both stood to greet him.

"Yes," Qwan answered. He noticed the subtle change in the merchant's eyes as he had noticed Qwan was an elf. The smile stayed professionally fixed in place however. With a faint smile of his own, Qwan continued, "He told me you could help us."

Gesturing for them both to be seated again, Varion sat opposite them, leaning back into the soft cushions. Stroking his short forked beard with one hand, he asked, "So how can I do that?"

"We need a gryphon," the elf answered, staring right at the merchant.

There was a flicker of amusement in Varion's eyes, "A gryphon? Are you going to kill a dragon?"

"Actually, yes," Medoran replied. "A very large dragon that should supply us with a lot of dragon skin."

Varion nodded, understanding the unspoken proposition. "And why are you going to kill this dragon then? It can't just be for the skin now, can it?"

"That's half of the reason," Qwan replied cautiously.

Medoran sat forward and added, "We've been paid to kill this dragon."

"By whom?" Varion asked.

"Unfortunately we're not allowed to say. That's part of the contract," Medoran answered slowly.

"And you plan on selling the skin when you're done for a bigger profit?" Varion pressed, his curiosity peaking.

Medoran nodded. Calmly he sat back against the soft cushioned couch, draping one arm over the back. "If we can find the right buyer, we will."

"So you want a gryphon. It must be a big dragon," the merchant continued.

Medoran nodded and glanced to Qwan. The elf shrugged in reply.

"Draconis Majestic, we think."

"What about the bone? Do you plan on selling that too? There's a high demand for dragon bone these days, you know," Varion said.

Medoran smiled a little, "I'm sure we can come to an arrangement. All we need is the skull for proof of the kill."

Varion nodded. "In which case," he said with a broad scheming grin, "you'll definitely need a gryphon."

"Can you supply us with one?" Medoran asked.

The merchant smiled broadly. "I think I could manage that but I will need to look at the flock. I might even be able to give you a substantial discount in return for a share in the skin and bone, so to speak."

Varion stood up and strode across the room, his robes flowing out behind him. Without looking over his shoulder, he said, "If you'll excuse me, I'll change into some more appropriate clothing and then we'll go to the pens. I'll see what I have for you there."

As he disappeared through the door, closing it firmly behind him, Qwan muttered, "That was good thinking."

"Well we don't need him to know anything else, right?" Medoran replied, his voice equally as quiet.

Outside the room, in a small corridor, Varion stood with his servant. He scribbled something on a small piece of parchment and rolled it up before handing it to the smaller man. "I want you to take this to Searth. Tell him to meet me at the pens as I think I have the people he's looking for."

"The dragon hunters?"

"Yes, the supposed dragon hunters," Varion replied. "I think he'll be interested to hear about them."

"Why?" the servant asked, clearly slow in making the connection.

Varion, showing the kind of patience someone does when talking to a child, explained, "The dragon they claim to be hunting is Draconis Majestic. They are all supposedly extinct except for one."

"I still don't understand," said his servant.

"That one is Baymothesis."

The servant's eyes widened as he recognised the name. "The destroyer?"

"The one and the same," Varion answered. "It's all a little coincidental. From nowhere we have some hunters after Baymothesis just when Searth is watching for people heading to the Demonic Realm."

This time his servant nodded.

"Tell him to come to the pens as quickly as he can. I'll take these hunters there and help them to pick out a gryphon in the meantime," Varion continued.

"But, sir, you only have the young gryphon left," the servant said quickly.

"We both know that but they don't. So it'll help me keep them there a little longer while you bring Searth to us."

"Yes, he's a Daiharlon," Gauduin said, with a forced flat tone. He stood at the counter in an armourer's store looking directly at the dwarf behind it. The dwarfish shopkeeper was in turn staring wide-eyed and open-mouthed at the seven-foot frame of Diarus. Meanwhile the Daiharlon was scrutinising the craftsmanship of a double bladed axe.

"Is he dangerous?" the dwarf whispered to Gauduin, only taking his eyes from Diarus for a second.

"Yes I am," Diarus answered quickly, "very dangerous."

Gauduin snapped his fingers in front of the dwarf's face, impatiently. As if just remembering he was there, the dwarf looked back at Gauduin again.

"Now, I understand my large friend here is an unusual sight in these parts but, believe it or not, I didn't come in here to show him off," Gauduin said, his words laced with sarcasm.

"Oh, er, yes. Right. I see," the dwarf started then looked at his feet sheepishly. "I'm sorry. It's just I've never... er... seen one before. You see."

"Yes, I understand that. Neither has the other few hundred people who've stopped to stare at him," Gauduin replied. "Now, we're here wishing to buy something." The dwarf was still staring at his feet. Unsure if he was listening or not, Gauduin added, "That is unless your feet are much more interesting."

"Er.. No.. Sorry," the dwarf started.

Gauduin held up a hand, cutting him off, "Please, I'm looking for a lance."

"A lance?" the dwarf asked. His brow furrowed, knitting the thick red eyebrows into one.

"Yes, a lance for killing dragons. I was told you'd have one," Gauduin said, patiently.

"I do. Are you going to kill a dragon then?"

Gauduin nodded with enforced patience.

"Well, of course you are," the dwarf continued. "Why else would you want a lance to kill one with."

He moved around the counter and into the clutter of armour and weapons that was his shop. Winding his way between several large suits of shining armour plates, he took them to a stand on the wall. Fixed into a long rack was a collection of lances. Some were flat bladed, while others came to a clean sharp point, more were barbed but all of them looked deadly. The dwarf beamed with pride as he gestured to them. "Any of these take your fancy, gentlemen?"

Gauduin walked along the length of the rack, looking at every lance. He occasionally reached out a hand, testing a blade edge or a spike. Then, rattling a handle against a lance shaft, he conceded slowly, "They're all good."

"What kind of dragon are you hunting?" the dwarf asked. He stood with his hands clasped in front of him, rocking back and forth on his heels. His wild blue eyes shone excitedly.

"A very large one," Gauduin answered. He was busily scrutinising the furrows carved into one particular lance. "Draconis Majestic, I think."

The shopkeeper bobbed up and down excitedly. He grinned so much that his face appeared to have been split, "A tough one then. You need a tough strong lance."

"That was our thought too," Diarus said. He stepped around the shopkeeper to look more closely at the lances.

"The last one on the left there," the shopkeeper started. He beamed yet again as Diarus lifted the weapon clear from the rack and held it against his ribcage with one arm. "That would be the best one for the job, I think."

The Daiharlon nodded and said, "It's pretty light though."

"Yes, but tough with it. Those ridges give it extra strength and the notches will help reduce friction when it plunges into the scaly hide," the dwarf replied. To add emphasis to his words, he smacked his fist in his open hand. Brightly, he added, "And it unlocks, so you can fold it up. It makes it easier to travel with that way."

"We'll take it," Gauduin said.

"You'll find you've made the best possible choice!" the shopkeeper beamed. He was nearly bouncing by the time he reached his counter again. As Gauduin handed over the money, the shopkeeper said, "Perhaps when you kill the beast you would come back sometime and tell me how the lance worked? I always like to hear how my work has helped people. It helps me create new ideas, you see."

"If we survive the encounter we will," Diarus grunted. He folded the lance into its three sections and carried it out of the shop under his arm.

"She lacks aggression, despite what she thinks," Demien said, ignoring the black look Cass shot at her. The three sat around a small round table. Half full glasses of bright yellow fruit juice sat in front of each of them. "The confidence is there, to the point of being over confident if I'm brutally honest."

"Aggression will come in time," Dasiel said. "While the confidence issue might be dealt with better through more experience."

"I know," Demien admitted with a long drawn out sigh. "She's one of the best I've ever seen with a longbow."

"And so you make use of this skill as it helps keep her back from actual combat. Then you don't have to worry about her," Dasiel said.

"You are too clever for your own good, master," Demien said, offering a wry smile.

The robed man leant forward in his chair. "If she is as good as you say then you have no need to worry."

"But I do worry. Khanis told me of his raanshi before he found me. That story still haunts my dreams," Demien reasoned.

"I understand your fears," Dasiel said, not unkindly, "but have faith in the girl's abilities. Khanis was a good teacher; you're proof of that. His previous student was too rash however."

Demien fell into a reflective silence. They were sitting in the shade in a rectangular courtyard. At one end, a man in black clothing was teaching five others to fight with a staff. Cass, feeling detached from the conversation about her, watched the staff whirling around in arcs as the teacher fought an invisible opponent.

"And what of her skill with a sword?" Dasiel asked.

Demien answered, smiling, "She's nearly as good as me."

Dasiel's eyes brightened greatly. "This," he said enthusiastically, "I must see."

He turned to Cass and asked, "Would you mind?"

"No, but what do I have to do?" Cass answered, still watching the staff spinning.

Dasiel stood up and called to the teacher. The man stopped,

bringing the staff under his arm, and looked over to them. "Master Chial. I wonder if you would be so kind as to help us with a demonstration."

Master Chial nodded once. He turned back to his pupils and bowed his head, before walking across to the sitting area. He took long confident steps, coming to stand before them, he asked, "What kind of demonstration?"

"Chial, this is Demien and her raanshi, Cassmed," Dasiel replied. His own soft tones at first appeared a complete opposite to the hard sounding confidence in Chial's voice.

"I have heard much about you," Chial said to Demien. The woman nodded in reply.

"Chial. Demien tells me her raanshi is nearly ready. I've asked her for a demonstration. I want you to fight her," Dasiel said.

Cass looked the man up and down, before flashing a nervous glance to Demien. Her friend picked it up and nodded to her.

"It'll be okay, Cass, you can handle it."

"You've not thought so in the past," Cassmed protested.

Demien said, "As Master Dasiel has said, I worry too much. Have faith in yourself. You're more than good enough."

"That," Chial responded, "remains to be seen."

Cass got to her feet and wandered a little bit away from Demien and Dasiel. Chial watched her, until she stopped a short distance away.

"Swords?" he asked gruffly, indicating the blade sheathed at the girl's side.

Drawing her weapon, Cass replied, "Why not?"

Chial looked over to his students, who were now standing ready to watch the demonstration. Picking one out, he sent the boy for his sword. Moments later the student appeared again, carrying the weapon with two red cords draped from its handle.

Cass found herself focusing on the cords as the boy handed the weapon to Chial.

The teacher called over his shoulder, "How is this to be done?"

"To the death?" Dasiel asked, looking at Demien.

Demien paled noticeably, staring at Cass. Dasiel patted her arm gently, causing her to look at his gentle features. Slowly she nodded.

Cass started forward, "Hang on just a moment, Demy."

"Cass, you can do it. Trust me," Demien replied as confidently as she could.

"Trust in yourself," Dasiel added.

"I do trust myself," Cass replied slowly. She pointed a thumb to Chial and said, "The problem is over there."

"Cass, you can do it," Demien repeated.

Chial smirked a little, "So much confidence."

The girl turned back to face him, passing her sword from hand to hand, she took a few steps closer. Chial instantly went into a fighting stance, standing side on. He spun in, circling his sword arm over his head to bring the blade down in a quick downward sweep. Cass easily sidestepped the move, bringing her own weapon up to guard her left side against a second sweep. He spun again, leaping high into the air. His sword arm stiffened, the blade spinning with him. It cut through the air, making loud whooshing noises. Cass brought her sword up again, blocking his attack. As blade clashed against blade, she struck out suddenly with her foot. The kick connected with Chial's ribs, forcing him to back off a little.

Chial paused a moment to catch his breath. Glaring at Cass, he began swinging his sword arm again in wide, cutting strokes that prevented her from getting too close. He advanced on her, continuing the long sweeps. The girl backed off two steps, scanning his attack pattern. Then suddenly, she darted forwards. Leaping high, she narrowly missed a sword swipe that would have taken her legs from under her. Landing on the ground behind Chial, she went into a handstand and thrust both feet into the small of his back. While he blindly stumbled forward, Cass flipped back onto her feet and ran at him, with her sword arm at full stretch. She swung out, sending her weapon in a side thrust that would have cleaved his head from his shoulders had he not ducked in time. Dropping to one knee, he attempted to thrust his blade up into her chest. The girl jumped back quickly, bringing her sword down to drive his blade away. Dasiel and Demien sat watching, as the two combatants raged back and forth, neither giving any ground.

Chial rolled to one side and attempted to cut into Cass's legs. The girl bunched her muscles quickly, pushing herself easily into the air. Before she landed, she thrust her left leg out, striking the teacher under his chin. The blow sent him reeling to floor. Cass quickly kicked his sword away, sending it skidding harmlessly across the flagstones. She touched the tip of her blade to Chial's throat. The man was too groggy to be able to fight any further.

Dasiel stood up and clapped heartily, "Bravo! An

excellent display, my girl!"

"Do I have to kill him?" Cass asked.

"I would rather you didn't. Good teachers are hard to find," Dasiel replied with a wide, beaming smile as he patted her on the shoulder. "Demien was right. You are nearly as good as her. Master Chial is a fine swordsman. Very few have beaten him in exhibition fights."

"He's an exhibition fighter?" Demien asked.

"He used to be," Dasiel nodded, "he often fought in the arenas at Kullmerin. Very highly respected there, you know. Anyway, my dear, you have beaten him. I'd have to say that Demien was right about you." He looked back to Demien as the three of them sat down again. "Now, Demien, you didn't come here just to show off the girl's skills to me, did you?" The warrior woman shook her head as he continued, "So what really brings you to Dacenheim?"

"Is there somewhere else we can talk? Somewhere more private?" Demien asked in a low voice.

"No, but I can send everyone away," Dasiel replied. He gestured to Chial's students to remove him. Within moments the courtyard was empty. "We're alone now."

"We're riding with a party heading out to the Demonic Realm," she started explaining. Dasiel leaned a little closer, folding his arms on the table. "You know I've been involved with a small uprising against the Black Flame Knights? Well this seems to be our best chance at putting an end to the whole thing." Dasiel nodded in understanding. "One of the group we're travelling with is no more than a boy, a wizard's apprentice. His master went to the Demonic Realm a while ago. They claim to be going to free the wizard's soul. However there's often been talk of setting the Forged One free too. Two of our party have gone to get a gryphon because they feel a dragon may stand in their way." Demien explained.

"I'm most interested in the boy, Demien. How old is he?" Dasiel said.

"Eighteen," Cass answered.

"Is he powerful?"

Demien snorted and smiled, "It seems like it. He's been in contact with the Oracle in Barache as well as some spirit creature."

"And this brings you here because?" Dasiel prompted.

"I don't know. Maybe I'm looking for someone to tell me I'm crazy. Everyone in the group is so wrapped up in this that no one seems to see how suicidal it really is," Demien said.

"It is not suicide for you," Dasiel pointed out.

"No, but it could be for Cass here. I can't let my raanshi die foolishly, can I?" Demien asked.

"Then you protect her."

"I don't need protecting," Cass interrupted.

Dasiel turned to the girl and replied, "Oh, but you do, Cassmed. The time ahead is crucial for you, so it's important for us all that you stay safe and well."

"I can't stay safe and well while those around me are being slaughtered though," Cass returned hotly as she flushed angrily.

"Cass, try and remain calm," Demien warned slowly. She looked to Dasiel and apologised, "She still feels the power of the calling."

"You misunderstand me," Dasiel said to Cass. His voice was, as ever, calm and soothing. "I am in no way insinuating that you should hide or stand by and watch as the Black Flame Knights run riot over your homeland, far from it, in fact. I'm just pointing out that it is important that you stay alive."

"Are you saying I'm right in going? Even if it is suicide for the others?" Demien asked carefully.

Dasiel looked back to the warrior woman and smiled warmly. "Demien. In all the legends and myths concerning the Black Flame and the Forged One there is one consistency. The arrival of a Spirit Mage."

"A Spirit Mage?" Cass asked looking at Dasiel. "What's that?"

"A very powerful mage. Usually a wizard has magic in his own soul and can also draw on the magic from the soul of a familiar or some such. A Spirit Mage has many souls to draw on. I think this youngster you travel with could be the Spirit Mage. If this is the case then you must help him. It's written in the legends that he will give us all freedom."

"And in return take only death," Demien finished.

"Ahh yes, you have read it then. But that is nothing that you can change, I'm afraid. Although, you should understand that it doesn't mean it would be his death or the death of anyone but his enemies, in fact," Dasiel said.

He sat back in his chair again and drank from his glass. For a few more moments he regarded Demien as the warrior woman shifted slightly in her seat. He took in the steel plate armour she wore. With a wave of his hand, he said, "I still don't understand why you feel the need to wear all that."

Demien looked down at her armour, "Habit, I guess."

"It's Khanis's old armour if memory serves me," Dasiel mused.

"He gave me it when he took me as his raanshi," Demien answered, suddenly feeling clumsy in the plate.

"Maybe there lies an answer to one of your problems. You don't need the armour. Your talent and your calling is enough to protect you. Maybe you should pass it on." As he said the last few words, he inclined his head towards Cass.

The inn was named 'The Hall' and Gauduin had told them all it was the best inn in Dacenheim. Everyone in the city drank there at one time or another. It stood three storeys high. Its grey slate roof towered above the nearby buildings. The walls were made from blocks of yellow sandstone, smoothed and polished by the wind and rain, and bordered by beams of stained oak. Above the door a long sign was hung, depicting a vast long table around which warriors were feasting.

Inside, the huge common room was crowded with drinkers. Through the haze of pipe smoke a gallery could be seen, surrounding the room. There were more tables up there and more drinkers engaged in conversation. The buzz of voices all talking at the same time faded a little as Diarus entered.

Gauduin indicated an empty table by a large window. He wandered off to the bar while Diarus and Uthan took seats. The Daiharlon merely had to stare back and the curious drinkers were suddenly no longer curious and went back to their own business.

"So what do we do now?" Uthan asked quietly as Gauduin returned.

"We wait for the others to return, then leave," the dwarf answered.

There were more nervous glances shot towards the dim corner and, in particular, towards Diarus, as a group of five men casually wandered in. The innkeeper, who was a short balding man with a strange hawk-like face, called over to them. "I don't want anymore trouble from you lads today, alright?"

The first one that entered waved at the innkeeper with mock annoyance. A pair of elderly drinkers got up from a table and left, leaving it clear for the men to sit down. A serving girl, barely out of her teens, wandered over to them, with a nervous look on her face.

"I'd guess they're the local rabble," Gauduin said, looking over at them.

"Should we be ready for trouble?" Uthan asked. In his mind, he began preparing a Fireball spell. A faint flicker of firelight danced across Uthan's eyes, unseen by everyone except Gauduin.

The dwarf grinned and shook his head. "I don't think there's any need to be burning the place down just yet, Uthan."

One of the men grabbed the girl, pulling her closer. His large hand squeezed her buttocks. She pulled away, flushing angrily and walked back to the bar, leaving the men alone to laugh loudly amongst themselves.

The door opened again and a man, somewhere in his late sixties half staggered in. He was dressed in the chain and plate armour of the disbanded Royal Knights. He made his way to the bar, trying to uphold an air of pride and dignity, while drawing the attention of the five troublemakers at the table.

"Well good day, Sir Serriman," one of them blurted out loudly.

The old man looked at them through red rimmed eyes. As if he had not acknowledged the mockery in the greeting, he nodded and waved before continuing on his way to the bar. At the mention of the name, Uthan looked up. He had paid no attention to the man as he had entered, watching the other table instead. There was a sparkle of recognition in his eyes as he watched the old man reach the bar and lean on it for support.

The murmur of conversation had dropped to a barely audible whisper. One of the men inclined his head, looking at the old man with a smirk fully fixed in place. "So, good Sir knight," he started, his voice thick with mockery, "you look weary. Has it been a hard day fighting the Northern tribes again?"

"Looks more like a hangover to me," one of the others chimed in. All five burst out laughing. There was a small collection of half heard sniggers from a few others in the main room too.

The rustling of chain mail was about all that could be heard as the old man turned around. Placing his elbows on the bar behind him, he stared at them. With a shaking hand he pinched the bridge of his nose. "Why is it that you five are in here every day making a nuisance of yourselves?"

"Hey now, we only come in for your tales of bravery from the olden days," replied the first man.

"Careful now, Serriman," muttered the innkeeper, standing behind the old knight. "I don't want any trouble." Serriman turned back to the bar, nodding in understanding. The innkeeper looked at him in concern and asked, "Now, what can I get for you?"

"So, old Sir knight," asked the first man, getting to his feet, "don't you have any tall tales of your well renowned bravery for us today?"

"Go away, Farraj. I'm not in the mood," Serriman answered. He tried to growl but instead his voice sounded cracked and old.

One of the other men at the table put up an arm to pull the first speaker back into his chair. The whole gesture was done merely to mock the old knight further. "Careful now, Farraj, he'll slay you like a Nierhoth."

The speaker smirked again and snorted, "I don't see a sword. Did you lose it somewhere?"

Serriman turned back to look at him again. Ignoring the restraining hand from the innkeeper, he stepped forward. "I don't need a sword to deal with the likes of you, boy."

"Really?" the speaker replied as he drew a short sword from a scabbard on his belt and held it up. "I think you'll need it."

Uthan reached over to tap Diarus on the arm and found that the Daiharlon was already getting to his feet. No one else in the bar paid the beastman any attention as he silently stood, watching the situation.

Farraj took a few steps closer to Serriman. He spun his sword in a few arcs, sending it from hand to hand in one continuous fluid movement. "So, have you ever seen moves like these, old man? I'm sure one of the desert tribes you've told stories about has used them on you. What defence did you use against them then, huh?"

He stepped closer again, tossing the sword up into the air a little. He was savouring the moment as the old man moved back, trying to avoid the blade.

The inn went deathly silent at the same time as one of Farraj's companions gaped, his mouth opening and closing like a fish, trying to say something to his friend.

"I think I could be a slayer of beastmen as well, wouldn't you say? I think I might go out and replace you as the great hero and get some beast kills to my name," Farraj said loudly, unaware of the heavy silence around him.

"That would be interesting to watch," Diarus said in a slow deliberate voice.

Farraj turned around, opening his mouth to tell the voice to mind his own business. He found himself looking into the huge chest of the

Daiharlon. Backing away a few paces, Farraj got a better grip on his sword.

"You'll need something much better than that bread knife against these," Diarus continued. His eyes sparkled menacingly as he drew his two falchions.

"It's still five against one," Farraj said, looking to his friends for help.

The Daiharlon chuckled lightly.

Still seated at the table, Gauduin watched in amusement. "Some people just can't understand when it's time to leave."

Another of the men stood up and raised his hands. Shaking his head fearfully at Farraj, he sidled past the Daiharlon. As soon as he had squeezed by, he fled through the door.

"I only count four," Diarus said. He cast a quick glance at the remaining men, all of them had paled to a ghostly white and stared at him with wide eyes. "That is unless you three would like to leave now as well."

Without waiting a heartbeat longer, they ran from the inn, knocking over their chairs in their haste to escape.

"That just leaves you and me," Diarus continued.

"Should we send for a healer now?" Serriman muttered from his place, propped up against the bar.

Farraj spun to face the old man. Shakily he asked, "What?"

Serriman threw a hard punch. His leather gloved right fist struck Farraj's jaw hard. The younger man was sent into a daze, twisting into a slump on the floor. Looking down at the unconscious form, the old man muttered, "Someone should have done that a long time ago. It might have taught you some respect."

Diarus turned and walked back over to his table, sheathing his weapons. Serriman followed, calling after him, "I didn't need your assistance there, friend, but I thank you for it anyway."

"Yes," Diarus answered, without even a hint of the sarcasm that would have been appropriate for the situation. "You appeared to have it all under control."

"I did," Serriman answered. He pulled a chair over and sat at the table with them. "But, by way of a thank you, let me buy you a drink. It won't be much but it's the best I can...." He trailed off as he looked at Uthan.

"Hello, granddad," Uthan said weakly.

"Uthan?" Serriman asked slowly. "What are you doing here?"

"You wouldn't believe me if I told you," he replied gloomily.

"And," Gauduin cut in, "this really isn't the place to be telling anyone either."

"What?" Serriman asked, looking at the dwarf as if seeing him for the first time. "Who are you?"

Diarus cast a slow searching stare over the inn's occupants. They were still engaged in hushed conversation. A few of them were casting nervous looks in their direction. "We're too visible," he said under his breath.

The serving girl brought a tray over, filled with mugs. Setting them down on the table in front of the travellers, she said, "Mister Kall says thank you for not killing Farraj. These are on him."

"Pass on my thanks to him please," Serriman replied brightly. Without looking at Uthan, he then asked, "Is your father here with you?" Taking the lad's shake of the head as no, he then asked, "Where is he?"

Uthan shrugged, "I don't know now. Kora-Tus was attacked by Black Flame Knights a few months ago."

Serriman sat bolt upright and his hand shook against the handle of his mug. With his lower lip trembling, he asked, "Is he..?"

"No, he's alive. So is mother. I'm sure of that. Many of us left the village early on as we got a warning when Lessa-Tus was raided and burned to the ground," Uthan replied. His eyes filled as he remembered the night.

His grandfather nodded in understanding. Draining his mug, he patted Diarus on the arm and said, "Come on, drink up. We'll go elsewhere and you can all tell me what's so important."

"We can't stray too far, we're meeting friends," Uthan said.

"More of you?" Serriman exclaimed then inclining his head to Diarus, he asked, "Like this one?" The Daiharlon snorted loudly, causing two drinkers on the nearest table to glance around nervously. "Sorry, I didn't mean any offence," Serriman added quickly. He patted Diarus on the arm again, "I'm just not used to seeing your kind this far south." Looking back at Uthan, he said, "So we can't stay here and talk and we can't stray too far. What do you suggest then?"

The merchant Varion Doo'ar Cherre led Medoran and Qwansien through the busy streets. Twice Medoran had to push people away from his horse as they tried to sell him something. The place they were taken to was a large wooden building. The roof was nearly forty feet from the ground and the walls were dark, weathered wood with no windows. A high wooden fence bordered an adjoining area of land at one end where men were hard at work loading several wagons. Four heavyset men wearing only chain mail vests and baggy green silk trousers stood at the large double doors on the opposite end of the building. They smiled and nodded in greeting to Varion and his guests as they approached. The largest of the four pushed one of the doors open.

"I'll have to look in the scrolls and see where the gryphons are at the moment. I could be wrong but I believe one of them should be back in a few hours. I've been hiring them out, you see," Varion explained as he was dismounting. Then handing the reins of his horse to a small boy, he walked away to a series of small huts set against one of the walls.

"You know," Qwan said slowly, "something isn't entirely right about this."

"What do you mean?" Medoran asked, looking around the inside of the vast building.

The elf shrugged, "If you were in his position, wouldn't you know for certain when your hired items were due to be returned?"

"I don't know," Medoran replied. "He's got to be a busy man, maybe he has someone dealing with it all."

Inside the hut, Varion leant against the wall. His servant stood nearby with another man. This one was tall with long red hair that was tied back at the nape of his neck. Three long, jagged scars flowed down the right side of his face, making his already thin beard look even more pathetic. Despite this, however, Searth still looked menacing. He peered through a small shuttered window at Qwan and Medoran as they waited on their horses.

"Is it them?" Varion asked impatiently. "If it isn't, I stand to make some money from them."

Searth snorted and grinned, showing a set of broken yellowed teeth. "Yes, Varion, I believe it is. The one with the eye patch is definitely Medoran."

"Cornak has a big bounty offered for him, does he not?" Varion asked.

The red headed man nodded, "You'll get your share, don't worry."

"I wasn't worried, Searth. I'm never worried about getting things that are owed to me," the merchant stated.

As if the merchant's stare had pierced a hole in Searth's back, the man turned to face Varion. "Are you implying something?"

"No," Varion answered, spreading his hands. "I don't believe I am."

"Good," Searth replied before he went back to the shutter and continued watching. "The capture of Medoran is one thing but Cornak wants the others as well."

"Others?"

"There's a group travelling with him," Searth answered. "A lad, a dwarf and two women."

The merchant shrugged, even though the gesture was unseen by Searth. "I'll send them on their way. If they're travelling with these others then they'll have to meet up in the city somewhere. Your men can capture them all in one swoop."

"Exactly what I was thinking, Varion," Searth replied.

"Do you think you can capture them?"

The red haired man laughed but the sound was empty of any real humour. "I think I can do it, yes. Sell them a gryphon. You'll have it returned to you soon enough and they won't be around to ask for their money back."

Varion emerged from his offices and gestured for Qwan and Med to follow him. He led them through a series of animal pens, many of which were empty, to a separate enclosure. The walls of this pen were wooden, reinforced with heavy steel bars. A pair of men waiting outside the enclosure hastily pulled a set of double barn doors open. As the men finished their task, Qwan and Medoran both heard the strange keening calls of a gryphon.

"This is the last gryphon I have right now. Unfortunately it is also very young. We've not been able to tell the sex of it as yet," the merchant announced, leading them inside the enclosure.

Qwan saw the creature first. For a moment he held his breath. It sat majestically on a heavy slab of dark granite, staring calmly at the strangers. Two large wings were folded behind its back, giving only the slightest impression of how big they would be when outstretched. Its tongue, however, lolling from the side of its beaked mouth spoilt its regal pose. The elf leaned against the bars of the cage and he slowly put his hand out while he lowered himself to his knees. The gryphon watched him intently.

"I can't really say whether this one will be of much use to you," Varion said, quietly. "As you can see, it doesn't appear to share the intelligence these creatures are usually blessed with."

The gryphon stood up, showing its size to be no larger than a very small pony. Its sleek, feline body rippled in the light as it cautiously climbed down off the slab. All the time, Qwan was being studied by the gryphon's strange eagle eyes. They saw the glimmer of claws emerge as the creature moved onto the straw that covered the floor of its cage.

"I'll go and get you a collar and leash if you like," the merchant muttered.

Qwan still did not answer the man. Instead he remained perfectly still, holding out his hand for the gryphon to inspect. Gradually it came to the bars and sniffed Qwan's outstretched palm. Finding nothing threatening about the elf, the gryphon sat down heavily again and licked the elf's hand with a long, sticky tongue before letting out a soft purring sound.

"I think that means we'll take him," Medoran said, unable to take his eyes off the creature.

Chapter Sixteen

"You know we're being followed?" Qwan said as he and Medoran rode along calmly through the busy streets. The gryphon walked beside the elf, curiously looking at everything around it.

Medoran nodded, "They've been following right from when we left the merchant."

"Any guesses why?" Qwan asked.

"Not one," came the answer.

The elf grinned, "I guess we'll find out soon enough."

Ever since leaving the building belonging to the merchant, two men on horseback had been behind them, keeping a careful distance.

"Do we try to lose them?" Medoran asked.

Qwan shook his head, "I can't imagine we'll be able to having a gryphon with us. Let's find out what they're after first."

They turned a corner and reached a busy square. In the centre there was a large fountain and at one end a huge statue. It stood on one of the rooftops and looked out over the scene. Medoran patted Qwan on the arm and gestured to the steps of one of the buildings. Demien and Cassmed walked down them, escorted by a short portly man. Their horses were brought around from a tunnel to the building's west side. Demien and the man shook hands, then embraced. Cassmed tapped Demien on the arm and nodded in the men's direction. Seeing Demien look over, Medoran waved.

"Behind me," Medoran said quietly as Demien and Cass walked over, "are two men. They've followed us for a short while now."

"Usually that wouldn't be a concern for you," Demien responded quietly, keeping her head still as she focused on the two men with only her eyes.

Qwan nodded, "Me neither, but these are entirely different circumstances."

"What do you want to do?" Demien asked.

"Mount up," Medoran muttered. The two girls did as he said, knowing the one-eyed rebel was already formulating a plan.

Cass risked a quick peek over Medoran's shoulder at the two men. "Med, there's more than two there and they're signalling to someone."

Both Qwan and Medoran turned in their saddles to see more riders appearing in the street entrance. There was a small group now.

"Okay, I'm guessing they're not friendly," Demien said slowly. She turned to Med and grinned, joking, "Who'd you piss off this time?"

"What's the plan?" Qwan asked as the riders, seemingly impatient, began edging into the square.

Medoran grinned like a madman suddenly. He pulled on his reins, turning his horse around to face the riders and kicked his heels hard. The horse charged forward, galloping towards the riders. Caught up in the excitement of the moment, the gryphon took to the air, soaring only a few feet above the ground, quickly zipping around Qwan and the others to fly straight at the pursuers. Behind Medoran the three others charged forwards.

The mounts belonging to the other men reared and panicked. Some were thrown from their saddles. Only a few were able to bring their screaming horses back under control quickly enough to race after the quartet. Medoran pulled hard again on the reins, urging his horse around a tight corner, followed closely by the flying gryphon. Hooves skittered on the flagstones of the street, trying to find a purchase on the hard surface. Demien was next, Kainan taking the corner sure-footedly. Both Qwan and Cass had to slow their horses in order to avoid slipping on the flagstones.

The street they rode into was empty save for shadows caused by the sunlight being blocked out by the high buildings. Ahead they saw Medoran pull his horse to a halt as more riders, all brandishing swords waited patiently for them.

"How'd they know we'd come this way?" Cass asked quietly.

Demien looked back in the direction they had come from. Riders slowly trotted in from the other street, coming from both directions. Flatly, she answered, "Because they didn't give us any other choice."

"Get out of there now!" Dionis's voice rang in the back of Uthan's mind, vibrating inside his skull.

The young mage sat up suddenly, looking first to Gauduin, then to Diarus and, speaking in a quiet, deliberate voice, he said, "We have to leave here now."

"What? Why?" Serriman asked. He looked around the bar frantically, "What's wrong?"

Both Gauduin and Diarus shot questioning looks at Uthan. He just shrugged and answered, "I don't know why. I only know we have to leave here now."

Gauduin nodded and rose from his seat, "That's good enough for me."

Diarus moved to the door, mostly ignored by the patrons of the inn. An arrow thudded into the wooden doorframe, scant inches from his hand. The Daiharlon stepped quickly back inside. "I guess we know why," he said bluntly.

"Those youngsters are pushing their luck now," Serriman said. He started towards the door before Diarus placed a huge hand against his chest. In comparison, the old man's body was minuscule.

"Don't go out that way, there're too many of them," Dionis said in Uthan's mind and then the young mage relayed the message.

"There were only five of them, Uthan. Your friends and I can take care of five!" Serriman exclaimed.

"It's not who you think it is," Uthan replied.

"I see at least six, all with bows," Gauduin said, peering out from behind a table.

"There are more just along the street," Uthan said.

By now, all the drinkers were watching them. The innkeeper had stopped wiping down the table he was at and was staring horrified at the arrow sticking into his doorframe.

The dwarf looked over to him and asked, "Is there another way we can leave?"

The innkeeper nodded dumbly and pointed to the stairs. Serriman grabbed his grandson by the arm, dragging him in that direction.

"Follow me," he called," I'll show you the way."

They fled upstairs and across the gallery on the second floor to a small door. Serriman pushed it open and took them down the corridor beyond. It was brightly lit, with sunlight streaming in through windows on one side and polished wooden doors running along the other. At the far end there was an outer door that Serriman pushed open revealing a staircase beyond leading to the roof.

"We're going up?" Gauduin asked incredulously. "Where are we supposed to go from there?"

"It has to be better than taking our chances with those archers," Diarus replied.

Dionis appeared, floating on the stairs. Serriman almost jumped out of his skin, stumbling back into Diarus. The bat's disembodied voice was concerned as he said, "Be careful, they have some archers on the roof opposite too. They just went up."

"What is that?" Serriman asked, regaining a small amount of his composure.

"A friend of sorts," Gauduin answered. He turned to Dionis again and asked, "How many exactly?"

"Four at the moment."

"Four archers, they could pick us off too quickly," Gauduin replied.

"No, they're watching the doors below. If you're careful about how you open this one you could get out there without them knowing," Dionis suggested. "You need to move now though. Others have just entered downstairs."

Angry shouts filtered up to them from the main room below. Diarus pushed the others on and up the last flight of stairs. Gauduin pulled the door to the roof open a few inches. Dionis appeared beside it, floating in the air with his wings outstretched. As cautiously as possible, Gauduin peered around the doorframe. Almost instantly he came back inside, his face pale.

"They've got a siege bow up there," he said slowly.

"A siege bow?" Serriman asked. He pushed Gauduin aside, going to look for himself. A moment later he pulled back inside the stairwell, "They have as well."

"It'll be to take the Daiharlon down," Dionis stated. "They're not taking any chances."

"Should I feel honoured?" Diarus asked, just as flatly.

"They're looking away now," Dionis said.

Serriman slipped out of the stairwell, moving out of sight behind a small wall on the edge of the roof, just in front of them. Uthan followed close behind. The dwarf was next; stopping behind the stairwell he flattened himself against its wall as Diarus charged out. Suddenly there came several shouts from the archers. These were followed by a small swarm of crossbow bolts that flew overhead as they tried to hit the Daiharlon. He dropped to one knee, rolling onto his left shoulder. Twisting and flipping back to his feet, Diarus changed direction and moved off to his left. Now he was facing the archers as they hastily prepared their large siege crossbow. The string was released before the six-foot long solid steel arrow could be loaded properly, sending it off target.

Diarus snatched out with his hands, grabbing the arrow as it speared past him. The momentum of its flight sent him spinning. Almost at the same time, one of their pursuers emerged from the stairwell. The Daiharlon thrust out with the arrow, lancing it into the chest of the man. He let the arrow go and charged at the siege crossbow. Clearing the jump effortlessly, he collided with two of the men, knocking them from their feet and breaking both their necks on impact.

Before the other two were able to react, Diarus was up again. He unsheathed his falchions and lashed out. The closest man received a deep gouging wound in his stomach, emptying his intestines on the floor. The second falchion bit deep into the forehead of the other man, removing his scalp with a cloud of dark crimson. The Daiharlon wound the handles on the siege crossbow quickly and slammed another of the steel arrows in position. A moment later two more of the men appeared from the stairwell, holding their short swords ready. Diarus pulled the lever hard, releasing the heavy bowstring with a loud leathery crack. One of the men fell backwards, screaming as the arrow speared through his shoulder, nearly ripping his arm away. The second man looked over to see Diarus hurriedly trying to reload.

Gauduin ran from behind the stairway towards the enemy. Grabbing his arm, the dwarf spun him around before driving his sword up into the man's groin. With a sharp twist, Gauduin pulled his sword clear again. The man toppled to his knees, a distant pain filled look on his face, before Gauduin's sword struck a finishing blow.

"Come on if you're coming!" Gauduin roared to Diarus. "There're more of them!"

Landing a hard boot to the thick pedestal supporting it, Diarus toppled the crossbow over, breaking the handle in the process. He took another run up and leapt back across to the roof of the inn again, just as more archers came into view. Both Daiharlon and dwarf got to safety behind the wall with Serriman and Uthan, as more arrows burst out through the doorway.

Seizing the moment when he knew they would be reloading, Serriman ran across the rooftop, halting at the edge. An open alleyway, spanning nearly eight feet in width, loomed in front of him. Before the old man knew what was happening, Gauduin ran past him, clearing the alley in one leap and continuing on. Suddenly, Serriman was grabbed and hoisted onto Diarus's shoulder. The Daiharlon took a running jump, landing right behind the fleeing dwarf. Uthan was last; he ran up and leapt off, sailing through the air over the alleyway. He felt himself dropping, falling short of reaching the opposite roof. However, before he could react, invisible hands grabbed his arms and feet, pushing him on further. He landed softly on the rooftop, unsure of what had just happened.

"Where'd you get them?" Dionis asked, flying beside Uthan as he sprinted across the roof behind Diarus.

"Get who?" Uthan asked in between breaths.

"The Air Elemental that just carried you across there."

"Oh him," Uthan replied, "the Oracle."

"Impressive."

To which Uthan could only nod in reply as there were more shouts from behind followed by three bowstrings that thumped loudly.

One arrow went sailing wildly overhead, the second passed through the spirit form of Dionis. The bat turned in the air and glared at the bowmen. "I'd yell at him," he said with a low growl, "if he could actually hear me." Beside him, Uthan tumbled to the ground crying out in pain. Dionis looked down. The third arrow was lodged in the back of his thigh. "Uthan!" Diarus yelled, seeing the young mage fall.

The Daiharlon ran back and pulled Uthan to safety behind a large roughly carved gargoyle. Taking the arrow in one hand he snapped the shaft, throwing away the largest portion of the wood. He looked up at the spirit bat hanging in the air nearby. "We need to get him down from here and to a healer."

"They will only follow you there," Dionis replied flatly.

Serriman and Gauduin appeared beside them and the old man knelt next to his grandson and looked at the arrow. From inside his breastplate he produced a small roll of bandage. "We can stop the bleeding for now but it looks deep," he said, examining the wound.

"Not here though," Diarus insisted, "they'll be coming after us."

Uthan pulled on the Daiharlon's shoulder. Wincing in pain, he said, "Help me stand. I'll get rid of them."

"How do you plan on doing that?" Serriman added sternly.

With a faint flicker of a smile, Uthan answered, "You'll see."

Diarus placed his hands under Uthan's arms, standing him up

effortlessly. With the Daiharlon behind him for support Uthan limped out into the open. There were five of the archers coming towards them. Three held longbows, arrows notched and ready. Seeing Uthan and Diarus standing in the open, they slowed down cautiously scanning the area for the others. One of them dropped to one knee and, with his bow, aimed directly for Uthan's chest. The bowstring snapped from his fingers, sending the arrow flying.

Uthan raised his left hand the palm facing the man, and then he muttered a few words under his breath. A jet of searing flame whooshed from around his fingers. The arrow shaft was incinerated completely before it could reach its target. The ferocity of the flames knocked the iron arrowhead aside. The bowman screamed in agony for just a second as the fire engulfed him completely. The remaining four men tried to turn and run. They lived only a couple of seconds longer than their comrade had. Four blackened corpses pitched from the rooftop, thick foul smelling smoke pouring out from holes in their flesh where the fire had erupted.

"Okay," Uthan said, dropping his arm back to his side. Thin tendrils of white smoke curled up from his fingers. "I don't think there's anymore."

Qwan nonchalantly loaded his crossbow while the gryphon stood defiantly in front of him, glaring at the enemy. As one man began to edge his horse closer, the gryphon hissed loudly.

"We're not getting out of this without a fight, are we," Cass muttered, unsheathing her sword.

Qwan's crossbow bolt was fired, taking the first man through the chest. In reply, the others raced towards them. Unsheathing his sword and hooking his bow on the saddle again, Qwan answered, "No."

The gryphon leapt at the closest rider, taking him from the saddle. His horse reared in panic, blocking the path to the other horses. With beak and claws, the gryphon savaged the man, cutting his screams dead. It looked up from its kill to hiss again at the other riders. With the rearing horse and the murderous gryphon in front of them, they held back.

Riders from the opposite end brought longbows up, arrows trained on the companions. Before they could fire, Medoran urged his horse into a charge. Three archers let their arrows loose, all missing Medoran completely. The others threw down their bows and drew swords before the one-eyed swordsman was amongst them.

"Qwan, Cass, you two hold this end!" Demien shouted, racing across to help Medoran.

Cass glanced between the two groups. Medoran had already killed two men so a pair of riderless horses had trotted away, trying to escape the commotion around them. Kainan galloped in, shouldering two more of the enemy aside while Demien stabbed out, dispatching one of the riders. The second attempted to catch her with a vicious backhand slash. She easily deflected the blow, sliding her sword off the blade and opening the man's throat. The gryphon held the other riders back, slowly stalking its way towards them. They had clearly not expected the creature to fight and were totally unprepared. Their horses whinnied and shied away, pushing into each other to escape the gryphon's fury.

Qwan switched to his crossbow again and took aim at a rider trying to get around behind Medoran. The bolt pierced his cheekbone and as he cried out in pain, Medoran turned to see him. Quickly, the swordsman swept his blade out, the tip slicing open the man's throat and silencing the screams. Cass followed Qwan's example. She grabbed her bow and notched an arrow to the string. She took aim at one of the riders being held back by the gryphon and fired. The arrow caught the man in the chest causing the other riders to shout in panic. One grabbed a bow of his own and took aim at Cass but a bolt from Qwan's crossbow pierced his eye socket.

Another rider closed in on Demien. He slashed and stabbed, keeping the warrior woman on the defensive so she did not see the enemy moving behind her. Quickly, Medoran jumped from his saddle. He grabbed the rider, knocking him from his horse and the two men crashed into a wooden trapdoor at the side of the street. The wood shattered into brittle fragments around the two men as they disappeared into the darkness below. Demien leant closer and finished her opponent with a slash to the chest. She leapt from her horse and moved to the broken trapdoor.

"Med! Are you okay?"

From the darkness below she could hear groaning. The voice was not Medoran's. Calling to Cass, she then waved before dropping in through the opening.

Cass tapped Qwan on the arm and gestured to the broken doorway. "I think we're leaving."

Qwan nodded and quickly whistled to the gryphon, pointing to the sky as it turned to him. Without knowing fully if it understood the signal, Qwan leapt from his horse and followed Cass through the trapdoor, leaving the riders to try and get around the gryphon.

"Get after them!" one of the riders yelled. "Searth'll have our skins if they get away!"

Half carrying the young mage, Diarus lead him back to behind the gargoyle where Gauduin and his grandfather waited. Serriman stood, wide-eyed and in shock at the sight he had just witnessed. Uthan was lowered to the rooftop again while Diarus looked around at their surroundings.

"There's a trapdoor over there," Gauduin said absently. He too was staring in surprise at Uthan. "How long have you been able to do that?"

Flashing another weak smile, Uthan said, "It wasn't entirely me."

"But... but," Serriman stammered.

"I was given some help," Uthan answered. "Right now I can't explain it in depth. My leg hurts too much."

Diarus found the trapdoor that the dwarf had mentioned. He knelt beside it, pushing down on it but the weathered wood would not budge.

"I already tried it," Serriman said. "It's locked from the inside."

The Daiharlon asked, "What is this place?"

"Some church or another, I think," Serriman replied, "although it could as easily be a brothel."

"Well, we'll soon find out," Diarus replied then punched the wood hard. It shattered with a loud cracking sound beneath the impact of his fist.

The building was a disused temple. With Uthan clinging to his back, Diarus climbed down a ladder onto a wooden walkway. This was situated two floors above ground and gave them a good view of the temple. A large, black, stone altar sat at one end of the room, adorned with two statues. One was a snake, coiled with its head back ready to strike at the other. The second statue was an armoured figure, probably human judging by its build. In one hand it held a shield between it and the snake; in the other, a stone longsword was ready to cleave the serpent in two.

"Followers of Sen Goddarm," Serriman said, his voice was respectfully quiet as he gazed down at the statues.

"Who?" Diarus asked, never having heard the name.

Gauduin answered, "Sen Goddarm. He was a knight two thousand years ago. They called him the God Arm."

"He is one of the most revered knights ever," Serriman continued.

The Daiharlon nodded, "Killed a lot of snakes, did he?"

Oblivious to the sarcasm in Diarus's voice, Serriman answered, "The snake is supposed to represent the demon, Arrkainel, who appeared to Sen in the form of a mighty serpent."

"This is a place of worship to him?" Diarus asked.

Serriman nodded, "There were many places like this in older times. When being a knight really meant something. Not like now when a street thug can wear black armour and call himself a knight."

"It's a temple alright," Gauduin said. He headed off along the walkway, leading towards a rickety looking staircase at the end. As he walked, he continued explaining that Sen Goddarm had been an inspirational figure. Knights had sought out one of the statues put up in his honour when they had lost courage or discipline. Eventually people had begun erecting temples dedicated to his name.

As Diarus followed with the injured Uthan, Gauduin continued, "The Royal Knights were disbanded after the last king died and the monarchy was replaced with an Emperor. In honour of the Royal Knights the Imperial Knights were founded. It was okay for a while, like nothing had changed." He reached the stairs and tested them to check they would take his weight. The wood creaked slightly as he started walking down. Waiting for Diarus to reach the floor as well, Gauduin took up the story again. "After the beast wars, the number of knights had dropped quite badly. Many of them had been in the frontlines of violent battles. In order to try and restore his forces, the Emperor gave every remaining knight a squire. Many of these squires were inducted into the ranks without any real tests. More and more were brought in this way so the numbers were built up again. But, with all but a small portion of original knights, they were nothing more than glorified soldiers. Honour became a trait to mock. The final nail in the coffin of the knighthood was the Black Flame army. General Cornak was an Imperial Knight; then he just gathered together a collection of thugs, bandits and murderers and called them knights."

The floor of the temple was clad with large rough cut, granite flagstones. Many were cracked or chipped, rocking slightly as the group walked on them. Half melted candles sat in stands and others littered the floor. There were blobs of yellow wax that had long ago melted and sealed them to the flags. Fumbling with a small flint and steel, Serriman lit several of the candles near the altar. Diarus lay Uthan down on the dusty floor. The young mage had paled considerably.

"He's lost a fair bit of blood," Gauduin observed.

Serriman handed the bandage to the dwarf, who then slid the tip of his sword along the leg of Uthan's trousers, tearing the cloth to get at the wound. The broken shaft of the arrow stuck up at a right angle to his leg. Blood was already congealing around the wound. Taking the splintered shaft between his fingers and thumb, Gauduin muttered, "This is going to hurt, Uthan, a lot."

With a sickening sound and a sharp intake of breath from the mage, the arrowhead was wrenched free from his leg. Gauduin handed it immediately to Diarus before wrapping the bandage around the open wound.

"We still need to get him to a healer," the dwarf said, securing the bandage.

Serriman looked to the large double doors at the far end of the room, "What about those men?"

The Daiharlon snorted, "They won't be chasing anyone. They're all dead."

The room Medoran had landed in was exceptionally dark, almost as if it was night. The man with him lay on the floor, groaning in pain. After the brittle door had shattered, they had rolled down a flight of stone steps. Luckily the rider had taken the brunt of the fall. At the very last step, Medoran had heard the snap. Now the man lay unmoving, having broken his neck, yet still not dead. Feeling a pang of pity for the man, Medoran drove his sword through his heart, killing him outright. Above him he heard Demien call his name. She almost fell on top of him, practically diving down the stairs to find him. His one eye had got used to the dark quickly and at the opposite end of the room he saw a door, partially hidden by a stack of wine barrels. Grabbing Demien's hand he led her across the floor.

The weak light from the doorway was blocked out again as Cass followed by Qwan fled down the stairs. The elf did not need to wait for his eyes to become accustomed to the dark and he saw Medoran at the other door, trying to pry it open. He grasped Cassmed by the wrist and hurried across the floor to help.

Beyond the solid wooden door was another cellar-like room with stone pillars that held the ceiling in place. Two torches gave off a faint orange glow from the distant wall. Outside there were raised voices. Qwan flipped a bolt into his crossbow and fired at the open trapdoor. A pain filled grunt followed by a thud signalled the death of another of the pursuing force.

"That should give us a few more seconds," Qwan muttered, reloading his crossbow.

"Don't waste them," Demien hissed, pushing Medoran and Cass into the other cellar. She glanced back over her shoulder at Qwan and said, "We need to find another way out."

"Well find it quick," the elf's reply was curt, "I can't keep them back forever."

Medoran was over in a shadowed corner. On the floor around him, he could smell stale beer and wine. He prodded a section of wall with his boot. "Cass?" he called. "Hand me one of those torches."

The girl carried a torch across to him and gasped. She turned to Demien and said, "I think we have a way out."

Medoran got down on all fours and thrust his boot against a large metal grille. One of the corners moved sending a shower of mortar dust to the floor. A second twang of a bowstring followed by a scream told them another of the enemy had fallen to Qwan's accuracy. Medoran kicked out again, a little harder. This time the grille fell away completely. It landed with a small splashing sound.

"Oh great," he said, wrinkling his nose at the overpowering stench. "Sewers."

He moved gingerly through, trying to find out how big a drop there was on the other side of the hole. A moment later he disappeared. There was another splash followed by Medoran saying, "Damn it!"

Demien appeared at the hole, sliding herself through. Looking at her lover in concern, she asked, "What's wrong?"

"I'm covered in shit," he replied.

From above, Cass's legs appeared. Demien reached up and grabbed her feet, helping her down slowly. They stood in a foot of vile, black water. The stench of sewage filled their nostrils, making their stomachs churn. Oily black slicks stained the walls, coming up to waist height, signalling the highest point the foul waters reached.

"Where's Qwan?" Medoran asked, moving a little way away into the darkness.

Tossing the torch down through the opening to Demien, the elf answered, "Right here." He splashed down into the water, ignoring the stench that floated up form the water.

"What about the horses?" Medoran asked, looking around at the walls and ceiling of the sewer tunnel. The torch flames flickered and dance wildly, casting long sinister shadow versions of the friends.

Demien answered, "Kainan will keep them together. They should still be there. We just need to find a way back to them."

"That shouldn't be too hard," Medoran answered. "Once we find a way out of the sewers that doesn't lead us back to those riders."

"Who were they?" Cass asked, glancing from Medoran to Qwansien.

"Black Flame?" Demien asked.

"Looked like mercenaries to me," Medoran replied.

Qwan agreed, "They could be working with Cornak. If he doesn't have knights in the city he has to have some kind of presence here. Maybe that's how he's been keeping an eye on the Imperial Knights."

"And keeping an eye on who comes into the city," Demien muttered.

From above them, they heard the sounds of muffled cautious voices as the mercenaries entered the second cellar. Demien quickly dipped the torch into the murky waters, extinguishing its light immediately. The gloom of the tunnel swarmed over them and mingled with the foul odour from the water; the darkness felt overpowering. Cass found herself trembling. There was the taste of greasy tin in her mouth and her mind was racing. She was unsure if it was the aftermath of the battle or the impenetrable darkness in the sewer where anything could be living. She was unable to see even her comrades, not to mention anything else. The elf took her hand and led her on, moving as quietly as was possible through the water.

His voice came from only a few inches away from her ear as he said, "Are you alright?"

"I'll be fine when my heart slows down," she mumbled in reply.

Even in the pitch-black, she knew the elf was grinning. "It's just an adrenalin surge, we all get it."

Cass knew differently. She could still feel the blood racing through her veins and a sound inside her skull, like waves crashing against rocky beaches. It was the same feeling she had been experiencing since she had ridden to the temple with Demien.

"But there has to be others, right? Why are they chasing you?" Serriman asked, pacing back and forth across the stone floor. "Who were they?"

Gauduin exchanged a glance with Diarus; they were both clearly thinking the same thing. Uthan wiped sweat from his forehead and tried to sit up.

"Black Flame followers?" Gauduin suggested.

Diarus shrugged, "If what you've said is true then I don't see any other choices."

"What about the others?" Uthan asked taking huge gulps of air.

Appearing for a moment beside Uthan, Dionis said, "I'll go and find them and make sure they're safe." He disappeared again, leaving behind a faint blue afterglow.

"And what is that?" Serriman blurted out. He looked like a man desperately hanging onto one last thread of sanity.

Diarus, Gauduin and Uthan looked at each other. The dwarf shook his head slowly.

"We're heading into the Demonic Realm to rescue someone's soul," Uthan said slowly. "These people must think we're out to try and kill the Black Flame himself."

"And are you?" Serriman pushed.

The dwarf flashed Uthan a dark look as the mage said, "If we get a chance to, we will."

"And that bat thing? He's helping you?"

"Yes," Gauduin answered.

"Okay," Serriman said finally. He stood looking at the statue of Sen Goddarm and the snake demon for a moment before asking, "Do you need another sword?"

Before anyone could answer, they heard voices from somewhere along the east side wall. They were muffled, as if heard from behind a screen. In the flickering candlelight, they could see the wall was covered with a thick purple curtain. When it billowed a little Diarus and Gauduin were instantly on their feet, weapons drawn. Then a faint but unmistakable odour filled the air. Gauduin's face split into a wide grin as the heavy curtains were pushed aside and Qwan led the others into the temple.

"They found you too then?" the elf said. Water dripped from his clothes, forming puddles on the floor. He sat down, letting the dust stick to his trousers, and took his boots off. More foul smelling water was emptied onto the flagstones. "We could hear you talking down there so you might want to lower your voices."

"You smell like a sewer," Uthan said, wrinkling his nose as Demien sat on the floor next to him.

"Probably because we've been down in one," she replied, emptying water from her boots.

Gauduin sat next to Qwan, wrinkled his nose at the smell before moving himself a little way away and said, "We need to be going. If Cornak doesn't already know we're here, then he soon will."

"Cornak won't come into Dacenheim though. He'd be a fool to do it," Serriman said quickly.

Qwan looked up, seeing the old man for the first time. Without taking his eyes off him, the elf asked, "Who's this?"

"My grandfather," Uthan replied.

Serriman bowed his head in greeting, saying, "Sir Serriman Camarr, offering my services to you in this time of need."

"Sir?" Medoran asked.

"Yes. Formerly a Royal Knight," Serriman replied proudly.

Medoran nodded. He sat on his haunches, rocking back and forth in thought. "There is something you can do for us."

The old knight opened his arms in an enquiring gesture, "Anything that is within my power."

"Our horses. We had to leave them," Medoran said. "Can you get them for us?"

Serriman thought about this for a moment, then slowly he said, "You're asking me to run and fetch your horses?"

"Have they seen what you look like?" Demien asked.

"No but..." Serriman started.

Demien cut him off, saying, "In which case you'll be able to at least get to them. It's doubtful they'll be guarded."

Sullenly, the old knight turned and headed towards the great doors of the temple. A thin shard of sunlight fell across the floor as the door was opened just enough for Serriman to exit.

"He didn't give me chance to tell him where they were," Medoran said flatly.

"I'll find them for him," Dionis said, reappearing yet again next to Uthan.

"Good," Gauduin said, "I'll go and get ours. In the meantime you four need to do something before they find us by the stench alone!"

"Charming!" Qwan replied with a smirk.

Searth sat at the large window watching the horses. He had seen the group led by Medoran race into the alley and had gone into the inn to watch the fight. The mercenary leader had sat patiently ever since his men had followed the group into the cellar. Now an ageing man had wandered into view, heading towards the horses.

"That's him!" whispered another man in the room with Searth.

"The one with the boy?"

"Yeah," the man replied.

Searth grinned in triumph. "See?" he said. "I told you they wouldn't let a horse like that go."

"You want him followed?"

The mercenary leader looked across to the man and nodded. "Take the rooftops. Don't let him know you're following him."

Serriman pushed the door to the God Arm's temple open and led the horses inside. Diarus was on his feet instantly, both falchions flashing into view as the old knight entered. While they had waited patiently for Serriman to return, Qwan, Med, Cass and Demien had cleaned up the best they could.

"I found them," the knight called cheerily.

Demien rushed across to Kainan. The horse snorted and nuzzled her, clearly happy to be back with his rider again.

"Any sign of them?" Gauduin asked. He had only returned a few minutes before.

"Not a glimpse," Serriman replied.

"Me neither," Gauduin replied.

Uthan winced as he tried to stand, "Do we take that as a good omen then?"

The dwarf shrugged.

"I also found this," Serriman said proudly. He gestured to the gryphon that padded cautiously into the temple, looking downcast. It slowly wandered over to Qwan, lowering its head. "It was waiting with the horses, so I assumed it was yours. It seemed quite enamoured with the big white one."

"You found one then?" Gauduin said, looking at the creature.

Qwan stroked the creature's feathered head, talking to it in gentle, soothing tones. It sat down in front of him and began nuzzling its head into the elf's chest playfully. Looking up at the dwarf he nodded, "Right before that merchant sent people to chase us down. Remind me to have words with Boron when I see him next."

Gauduin could not take his eyes off the creature as it rolled over onto its back allowing Qwan to stroke its belly. "And this is going to help us kill a dragon?"

"Uthan, are you able to ride?" Qwan asked, ignoring Gauduin's dismissive words. The lad nodded. Qwan turned back to Gauduin and said, "I don't like the idea of those men being out there hunting us so we'd be better off leaving here soon."

"It'll be a hard ride to Skull Gate, Uthan. Do you think you're up to it?" Gauduin asked again.

"When I get my strength back more, I can heal it myself," Uthan nodded. He was still pale. The bandaging on his wound was dyed with a small circle of his blood.

"You can't do it now?" Serriman asked slowly.

Turning to look at the old man, Uthan shook his head sadly. "I've tried. I can't do anything. It's not like I'm tired. I just can't cast."

"Gauduin?" Qwan asked slowly, listening to Uthan's words. The dwarf looked over. "When you removed the arrowhead, what did you do with it?"

"It's on the floor somewhere," Gauduin answered, "Why?"

"Let me see it."

Uthan held the arrowhead in his hand, "Here it is. I thought I'd keep it."

Qwan smirked, "A memento of the first time you were shot, huh?"

He took the arrowhead from Uthan and held it up to the candlelight. The head was nearly flat but the edges running from the point were razor sharp. They flowed back into two slightly curved tips. One of those tips, however, had snapped away. The break was completely clean, as if the arrow had been crafted that way. "Uthan, I think you may have a piece of the arrow still in there," Qwan said finally. Catching the questioning glance from Gauduin, he tossed the arrowhead to him. "Mage killers. Take a look at the points at the back. One's been broken away."

"How did I not see this?" Gauduin asked, more to himself.

"That's why you can't cast, Uthan. This arrow was created just for you. It's made from the right mix of iron and copper so it'll break inside you. The shards of iron left behind render your magic ability close to useless. It'll slowly poison your blood so you won't be able to cast effectively, or at all, until we get that splinter out of your leg." Qwan explained.

"So we need to get him to a surgeon," Serriman cut in, coming to sit next to his grandson.

"No," Uthan said, so quickly everyone looked at him. "There's no time. We'll think of something else on the road."

"Are you sure, Uthan? That might not feel as bad now, but it'll hurt like hell after a few hours in the saddle," Demien asked.

"We don't have the time to spare. There's another army advancing." Uthan looked at her imploringly. Everyone in the group felt a chill pass over them as Uthan continued, "An invasion force is coming here from the Demonic Realm. We have to stop it all."

"Yes," Gauduin said slowly, as a memory came back to him, "Hedrial did say something about that."

"Meligonn," Medoran said slowly.

Qwan looked over his shoulder at the swordsman, "You know him?"

With a shrug, Medoran said, "I know of him. I've heard the name many times in the past and I've heard many stories."

"You can bet they're all true as well," Qwan answered.

"His reputation isn't cute and cuddly then?" Demien asked lightly.

"Far from it," Medoran answered, "he's worse than Cornak."

"The longer we stay here, the closer he gets," Uthan said again, reminding them all. "We have to go."

Serriman stood up and started towards the door, "I'll go and fetch a horse."

"Grandfather, no," Uthan said, stopping the old knight in his tracks. As the old man turned to look at him, Uthan continued, "I need you to stay here. Make sure the Emperor knows about Meligonn."

"And you think he'll listen to me? A broken down relic of a knight?" replied Serriman. He appeared to sink inside himself, appearing much more like an old man.

His grandson nodded, "You have to try."

"If we don't reach the Flame before Meligonn gets here, thousands of people will be depending on that warning," Qwansien said.

"Don't try and appeal to my sense of the heroic!" Serriman snapped. He paced away, heading towards the door, before turning back and looking at his grandson. "Do you know how long it'll be until they arrive?"

Uthan shook his head, "I only know they're coming."

"You realise the Emperor will question where I got this notion from?"

The young mage remained silent for a while, wondering how he was to explain.

"Well?" Serriman prompted.

"I went to see an Oracle in Barache. He showed me," Uthan said slowly.

Serriman fell silent letting the answer sink in, "You've seen Meligonn?"

"In my mind, yes," Uthan said with a nod. "I don't know for certain if that's how he looks though."

"Describe him," Serriman pressed.

Uthan closed his eyes, letting the sight of the huge armoured warrior flow into his mind again. Watching the image of General Meligonn leading a horde of armoured creatures as they swept through a small village in flames, Uthan said, "He stands taller than Diarus here, twice as wide. He wears full plate steel armour that hides everything except for his eyes. All I could see of those were two points of furious red light. It was like he could see through the visor. His armour was a green grey colour and behind him were more like him, just not as tall. Meligonn himself was unbelievably huge."

Behind Uthan, Qwan said, "That's Meligonn."

The ageing knight sighed and leant against a pillar. He pinched the bridge of his nose. Speaking from behind his hand, he muttered, "I think I'm sobering up too much. I'll pass the message on and try to get the Emperor to call back all legions."

"Tell him he should send soldiers to Skull Gate," Gauduin said.

Serriman nodded and wandered over to the door of the temple and grabbed hold of the heavy door handle. Leaning his weight on it, he said, "You had better get going now. The sooner you leave the sooner you get there, right?"

They climbed into their saddles, each protesting silently at the prospect of more heavy riding. Thanking Serriman, they each walked their horses from the temple. Uthan extended his hand to his grandfather, pausing on the way out.

"Take care, lad," Serriman said quietly. "I wish I was going with you."

"You'll make sure they're ready for them, won't you?" Uthan asked, concerned.

His grandfather nodded and smiled, "Listen to you. Anyone would think we'd swapped places or something."

Uthan rode out into the sunlight, blinking and shielding his eyes with his hand. Behind him, Diarus paused by Serriman who asked, "Take care of him, won't you."

"I will." Diarus answered. The Daiharlon followed the others outside.

Serriman left the temple, closing the heavy door behind him. It thudded with a loud clunk. He stopped to watch them ride off down the street for a few moments until they were out of sight. Turning, he nearly walked into Searth and almost jumped out of his skin. The redheaded mercenary was standing patiently, leaning against the wall. He stared intently at Serriman, as if waiting for the old man to say something.

"Oh," Serriman muttered putting his hand to his chest to calm his heartbeat down, "it's you."

Chapter Seventeen

Carved almost a century before by demon hands, Skull Gate remained a looming and ominous place. It was a large human skull crafted from the wall of the mountainside itself. It served as a terrifying symbol of the deadly inhabitants of the land that lay beyond. From their vantage point, the travellers on the road could half-see the gate through the morning mist above the trees. They had stopped on the crest of a hill to rest a moment. Gauduin had chosen this spot in order to give Uthan, Cass and Diarus all a chance to see Skull Gate.

"It's unbelievable," Cass muttered.

Uthan, still as pale as he had been since leaving Dacenheim, grinned suddenly. "So why do they call it Skull Gate?"

Closer to, Skull Gate was yet more eerie and chilling. They walked their horses through the thinning trees until they stood at the base of a large set of steps cut into the rock. They snaked up the mountainside, stopping around fifty feet above the ground. A plateau lay between the top of the steps and the gate, completely empty save for one miserable looking tree.

The skull itself was nearly a hundred feet tall. The rock had been smoothed away, making a stark contrast to the rougher areas surrounding it. Two hollow eye sockets glared out at the Empire, brimming over with malevolence. Between its great stone jaws, it held the actual gates, two tall doors of black wood and iron.

"Do we have to go through there?" Cass asked with a distinct shiver.

Medoran answered, "There's no other way."

"There're no other gates anywhere else?" Cass asked, not quite believing it. She looked at the others silently hoping one of them knew of an alternative route.

"Legends tell of a pass made through here by the Lord of Demons. He was given a glimpse of the Empire in a vision and sought it out. There was a terrible battle in which he was beaten back. The jungles of the Demonic Realm fuelled his powers and without them to call upon on this side of the gate he was no longer indestructible. But at the same time he did not want others of his kind to rule here so he built this gate to keep them in and as a way to keep the Empire out. Any other passes were destroyed as he wanted to make sure few would dare to enter his world," Demien explained the story.

"And we're joining those few now," Cass muttered to herself.

"Not standing here, we're not," Gauduin said gruffly. "Look, the elf and I have been in there often enough. It's a dangerous place if you don't know where you're going. That's all."

"I don't know where I'm going though," the girl replied, the words erupting in a hail of nervous energy.

"No," Gauduin nodded in reply, "but you're with people who do. And you're letting this talk of legends worry you. Aren't you supposed to be a fighter or something? Let's see a little more fire in you." He quickly fell silent as Cass's worried expression became full of anger. He glanced away and muttered, "Something like that would be just as good, I suppose."

"We're not going to let anything happen to you," Uthan said slowly. "I'm not going to let anything happen."

The girl turned on him, "And how are you likely to stop it? You can't cast!"

Demien took her young friend's arm and pulled her away. Looking the girl straight in the eyes, she said, "You need to calm down, Cass."

"Everyone get it together. We're burning daylight here," Qwan said suddenly. Everyone turned to look him, responding more to his commanding tone of voice than his words. He ignored the raised eyebrows from Demien and Diarus and the tilt of Gauduin's head. "Now, Med and I are going to call the gatekeepers. The rest of you wait down here. Including you," Qwan said, adding the last words as he pointed to the gryphon.

Medoran handed his reins to Demien and wandered slowly up the steps. Behind him, Qwan followed, crossbow loaded and held ready. Lower down, Gauduin drew his sword, stepping a few paces away from his horse. The rebel swordsman paced confidently across the plateau, marching over to an ancient-looking wooden framework. A thick rope, so rotten it could have fallen apart at any moment, hung from the frame. Medoran reached out, taking a firm hold of the rope and pulled. A bell tolled loudly, causing a large flock of birds to fly into the air. From somewhere in the gatehouse, the sound of cogwheels turning sounded. Then, slowly, the gates opened inwards to a low, grinding sound of steel and stone.

A look of shock spread rapidly across Medoran's face and, behind him, Qwan drew his crossbow up quickly to take aim. Catching the movement from their vantage point on the lower ground, the others looked at the open gate in horror. Demien sprinted up the steps, trying to reach Medoran before the black armoured General Cornak. He strode out from the gates, flanked by a pair of blue skinned giants who were pushing them open. Both giants wore heavy manacles around their ankles with chains as thick as a man's arm, which disappeared into a cave beyond. The giants had cloth hoods tied down over their heads, blinding them. Suddenly, both of them stopped their work to sniff the air as the bolt was launched from Qwan's bow. It whooshed past Cornak's shoulder and disappeared behind him.

Medoran grabbed his sword, wrenching it clear from the sheath hanging on his belt and moved forward. Cornak, already holding his sword in his right hand, walked out to meet the rebel swordsman. He brought his sword up over his shoulder and struck down hard. Medoran jumped back, avoiding the general's blade. All around Cornak, Black Flame Knights charged out from the gateway.

Amongst them were two large warriors who appeared to be nothing more than suits of heavy plate armour. The dull green of their protective coat was a stark contrast to the shining black of the smaller human knights around them. They carried huge maces in equally huge hands.

The elf dropped his crossbow and, sword in hand, charged to meet the knights. He thrust his blade forward, stabbing one in the eye socket. Jerking his sword arm back, he brought the blade clear before twisting and slashing into the back of another knight's knees. Even before the man had fallen properly, Qwan cut another knight with an upward slash that opened his jaw and throat. More and more of them came forward, many running past the elf to attack those on the ground below.

The gryphon raced out from cover to help his master. He snapped and flailed with beak and claws as several knights fought to encircle him. His tail curled around ankles, flipping knights onto their backs. He beat his wings hard, causing small clouds of loose dirt to float into the air.

One of the larger warriors strode across, mace raised high to break the gryphon's back. As it was brought down it struck only the hard packed ground. The creature sprang back, hissing and snarling at the new threat. From the corner of his eye, the gryphon saw the second warrior moving closer. He leapt into the air, wings beating hard to take him up and away from the heavy maces. Making a quick cry, the gryphon circled the battle as if looking for an opening where it could help.

Gauduin was the first on the lower ground to meet the foe. He slammed the flat of his sword against the head of the closest, sending the man into a daze. The knight stumbled into the path of two others, sending the three of them tripping to the ground. Demien then leapt in amongst another pair. Her blade opened a deep line of red in the face of one knight. He twisted to the ground, screaming. The second was impaled through the stomach. Behind her, Cassmed was firing arrows into the enemy, aiming for the less armoured faces with amazing accuracy.

Kainan reared, clubbing his hooves into the head of another knight. First, his helmet was tipped away. Then the second kick connected with his head and the large hooves broke his skull before he tumbled into the path of one of his comrades. Cassmed sent an arrow into the cheek of the next man. It pierced his face right below the eye. He cried out in pain, his hands scrabbling for the arrow shaft to pull it free. Cass fired again and this next arrow found its target, burying itself deep in a man's throat. He pitched forward, landing on his screaming companion. The extra weight dropping down forced the arrow deeper into the man's skull, piercing his brain. Almost instantly the screaming stopped.

Cornak and Medoran fought on the plateau, ignoring the activity around them. The general thrust his sword point out, aiming for a swordsman's unprotected stomach. Medoran stepped to the side and pushed the blade away. In answer, he lashed out at head height savagely. Cornak quickly grabbed the shoulder of the closest of his men, pulling the knight into the path of Medoran's sword. The slash opened the knight's throat. Blood sprayed into the air, gushing from the open wound. The general put his boot into the small of the dying man's back and pushed him into Medoran. The swordsman sidestepped again, letting the knight tumble by. Then Cornak darted forward, sweeping out with his blade at chest height. Medoran dropped to one knee, dodging the attack. His sword arm snaked out, attempting to pierce through a gap in the general's armour. Cornak batted the thrust aside and punched Medoran in the jaw. The punch knocked Med off balance; he tumbled backwards, scrabbling on the ground to hurry to his feet again.

Cornak jumped at him. Landing right beside his fallen opponent, the general slammed his sword down, intent on cleaving his sworn enemy's head open. Medoran rolled to the side and spun on his back. His legs swept around, slamming into the sides of Cornak's calf muscles. The general pitched to the side, his shoulder armour striking the rock floor loudly. Getting back to his feet again, Medoran dodged an overhead attack from a nearby knight. He sidestepped the blow and turned, bringing his weapon around and up biting into the knight's fingers. His sword clattered to the ground as the knight held his bleeding hand. He looked up at Medoran in a mixture of pain and shock, a heartbeat before the swordsman swung around again and sliced his throat open.

On the ground below, Cassmed had discarded her bow and was deflecting blow after blow from two knights at once. The pair lanced and slashed out again and again, almost in complete unison. She had no time to reply or to launch an attack, only barely having the chance to block. From behind her a third knight ran over; she heard him but did not dare take her eyes off the duo attacking her.

Diarus appeared, both falchions cutting through air and knight alike. Both blades sunk down into the shoulders of the third one. Beneath the sheer strength of the impact, the heavy shoulder plates were dented in and the knight cried out in pain. One of the falchion blades cut through the chain mail protecting the areas between the joints in the knight's abdomen. With one arm, Diarus hefted the knight up on his blade while to the girl, he roared, "Cass! Down!"

Without fully knowing why, Cass threw herself flat on the ground. She gasped painfully as the wind was knocked out of her. There was a loud clatter followed by grunts and cries. Glancing to where her opponents had been, she saw them lying under the corpse of the third man. A shadow fell over her. Instinctively Cass rolled onto her back, ready to pierce the owner of the shadow in the groin or belly.

From above, Diarus held down a hand and pulled her to her feet. "Are you okay?"

She nodded; drawing in harsh ragged gulps of air. In her chest she felt a stabbing pain, a white hot agony with each breath she drew.

Seeing the girl wincing, Diarus pushed her behind him, "Rest a moment or two. I'll keep them back."

Cassmed did not answer. She had seen the look in Diarus's eyes as he had helped her stand. Giving in to the blood lust that his race was known for, the Daiharlon threw himself into a small group of knights; they all hit the ground hard. Three of the them were suddenly motionless, broken necks and smashed skulls killing them from the collision. All too quickly, Diarus was on his feet again. He lashed out with his swords, spinning on his heels in a dance of death. Two more knights were decapitated. A third fell screaming, a deep gaping wound in his barely protected stomach.

Then a shadow fell over him. Diarus turned in time to see the thick steel mace of one of the larger armoured warriors swinging towards him. It struck him hard under the jaw, knocking him over. Sluggishly, Diarus pushed back up to his feet again. The armoured warrior stood mere inches taller than his Daiharlon opponent. The second warrior advanced quickly, slamming a shoulder into Diarus's chest, knocking him flat again. As the Daiharlon struggled to get up, a heavy boot struck him full in the face. For the briefest of moments, Diarus saw two pairs of large hands reached down for him. Then the world spun into darkness.

Standing in the tree line near the horses, Uthan was trying desperately to cast. In his mind, images of fireballs and flying ice spears flashed. He could see them clearly as he tried to pull his energy together but each time the spell died on his lips. Watching his friends slowly being overwhelmed, he crept over to the nearest of the horses. It was Medoran's. The longbow was still attached to the saddle. Uthan untied it and the arrows and then notched one. Pulling the string back and taking the best aim he could at the closest of the knights, his mind began to scream at him. It was reminding him that he had never fired a bow in his life. Trying to shut out the words of warning, Uthan let the string go. The arrow sank deep into the back of the knight's neck as he bowed his head a little, exposing the flesh. He fell dead immediately. Quickly, Uthan notched another arrow, as one of the other knights looked his way. The man started running toward the mage his sword raised high.

Uthan again let the string go. The arrow glanced off the man's helmet, merely stunning him a moment. Fumbling with the string, Uthan pulled it back a third time. Again the arrow bounced harmlessly from the knight's armour. Seeing he had done no damage with the bow, Uthan dropped it to the ground and drew the short sword from his belt. He could barely remember using a wooden sword when playing with the other children in the village. Again his mind was screaming at him, telling him he did not know the first thing about sword fighting but, instead of listening to the voice, he thrust forward. The blade's tip pinged from the knight's breastplate. As if he was swatting a fly, the knight backhanded Uthan in the jaw. Sparks of light flashed in front of his eyes as the gloved fist hit him again in the face. A third punch struck the boy in the cheek, sending him sprawling to the ground. Uthan tried to open his eyes, tried to get up but his left eye felt glued shut and the left side of his face hurt. His limbs felt leaden.

"Stay down," warned a harsh voice looming above him.

Ignoring it, Uthan tried to sit up. More flashes of colour exploded in front of his eyes. Then there was darkness.

There were still many of the knights swarming over them, like giant black beetles. Qwan and Gauduin were fighting back to back, their blades sweeping loudly through the air in front of them. All around them was a ring of knights, each trying to get past the blades and in for the kill.

Demien was fending off another four when a fifth ran in behind her and kicked the back of her legs. The swordswoman fell backwards, striking her head against the ground. The knights she had been fighting grabbed the unconscious woman by the arms, hauling her to her feet. Cass ran over and she skewered the knight holding Demien's left arm through the face. The other was dispatched just as quickly. Catching her before she fell to the ground, Cass half dragged the limp Demien to the horses.

"We have to get away from here!" she bellowed to Qwan and Gauduin.

The elf risked a glance over to the girl and saw Demien unconscious. He nodded in reply.

"We're leaving?" Gauduin asked, sending his sword into the belly of a knight before pulling it free to block a potentially decapitating attack from his left.

"Yeah, I'd say so," Qwan replied. "When I give the order you know what to do right?"

"Run like hell?" Gauduin answered.

"Exactly!" Qwan replied. He snaked his sword out, raking the tip of the elfish sword across the cheek of a knight. "Now! Go!"

Gauduin charged forward, holding his sword to the side. He dropped to his knees, sliding forward a few feet. The sword edge smashed into the shins of one knight. The man cried out in pain and fell. Without bothering to stop and finish him, Gauduin pushed himself up to his feet and ran to the horses. Holding his sword in two hands, Qwan spun on his heels. He slammed his blade down and into the gap between the shoulder armour and the helmet of one knight. Sliding it free again, Qwan dropped to one knee and twisted, sending the blade tip into the groin of another. To his left side there was a surge of knights as they all tried rushing forward to get the elf. With a half smile, Qwan waved and ran to the horses. He leapt into his saddle to find both Uthan and Demien unconscious and placed on theirs.

Standing in front of the horses with her sword held ready, Cass shouted, "We can't leave yet."

Medoran and Cornak were stuck in the middle of a large group of knights as the pair duelled back and forth. Not one of Cornak's men surrounding them attacked; they merely stayed where they were to stop Medoran escaping.

"What do we do?" she asked, almost pleading with the others.

"What we do best," Qwan said. He kicked his heels to his horse's flanks and charged into a closely-knit group of knights. His sword slashed down into the head of one of them and his helmet was sent sprawling from his head. Behind Qwan, Gauduin ran over and drove his sword blade into the back of the dazed knight's head, finishing him off.

No sooner had Qwan and Gauduin reached the foot of the steps than they were assaulted by more of the knights. Eight of them attacked at once, driving the pair back. A ninth man managed to get behind Gauduin. The dwarf was kicked in the back causing him to fall forward, winded. Rolling onto his back and trying to get up again, he looked up into the faces of four knights. Four sharp sword blades were placed at Gauduin's throat, a warning to stay down. Qwan slid from his saddle as another knight touched his blade to the back of the elf's neck, quietly saying, "Stop right there."

The elf spun on his heel and thrust his sword up, aiming for the knight's groin. The knight was waiting for the move however, and stepped back. Quickly, he slammed a heavy fist into Qwan's face. The elf was knocked flat on his back, stunned. More knights surrounded him, one pinning him down to tie his hands; others had poured down the steps and run over to pull a struggling Cass from her saddle.

High above them, the gryphon circled one more time. It cried out again, the sound was a strange mournful keening that spoke of the creature's despair. Seeing Qwan unconscious in the hands of an overwhelming enemy, the gryphon turned and fled Skull Gate. It sped through the mountains, disappearing towards the Demonic Realm.

Up on the plateau, Medoran had no idea his friends had all been captured. He and General Cornak battled back and forth, slashing and parrying and thrusting and dodging. Starting to breathe a little more heavily, Cornak barely dodged a sideways sweep. He twisted away, backhanding his sword out. The blade whooshed through the air viciously. Medoran leant back as the tip of the blade passed an inch from his nose. Before Medoran could regain his balance again, Cornak hit him with a vicious kick and Medoran was sent sprawling backwards to the ground. His sword bounced from his grasp, clattering on the rock several feet away.

Cornak ran forward, jumping at the swordsman who rolled to his left and the general landed heavily. His blade struck the rock, sending a burst of splinters across the ground. Medoran rolled up onto his shoulders and pushed to his feet. Cornak's blade danced out twice more, aiming to open Medoran's chest. The swordsman jumped back out of range then he struck out with a foot, catching Cornak on the right knee. The general's leg was pushed out from under him, knocking him off guard. Medoran seized the moment. He darted across the rock and picked his sword up. Behind him was another of the knights and Medoran turned and saw the man a moment too late. A hard right fist caught him under the jaw, lifting him from his feet. The knight quickly dashed over to the fallen swordsman and rained down a series of hard clubbing punches. Two ugly purple bruises formed on Medoran's cheekbone and temple. Blood dribbled from a split lip. With a satisfied smirk, the knight stood up again.

Cornak came over to stand beside the man. He glared down at Medoran. "Did I need help?"

"No, General," the knight said hurriedly.

With a nod Cornak said, "Good, as long as you all remember that. Get him up."

The general turned away as a pair of his men lifted Medoran by the arms and legs. He slid his sword back in the scabbard and took a step away. He sniffed back and spat a large glob of mucus onto the rock. "You know," he said slowly, "there's never been a clear victory between Medoran and myself. Each time we've fought there's been intervention."

"Yes, sir. I see," the knight said.

Cornak nodded, "It's not a question of killing the man or capturing him or whatever. It's a case of knowing who is better."

The general spun around with his right fist hooked and struck the knight squarely on the point of his jaw. His head smacked loudly against the rock, sending a dented helmet clattering away. An angry, red swelling began to cover the man's clean-shaven chin.

"You just robbed me of that knowledge," Cornak said. He moved to tower above the fallen man. Watching him struggle to rise, Cornak kicked him savagely in the ribs, then the head, then the ribs again. He knelt down at the man's side, watching patiently as he coughed, sending bubbles of blood from his lips.

"Next time, don't do it," Cornak growled.

He stood up again and looked at the rest of his men. They all watched him nervously. "Get the prisoners into the wagon and bring their weapons and horses. We're taking them back to Dessendor."

"What about him?" asked one of the knights, indicating the man at Cornak's feet.

The general stared down at him, "Bring him with us and patch him up. I'm sure he's learned his lesson."

Seated in the corner of the prison wagon, Uthan looked around him. His companions, with the exception of Demien, were all awake. Medoran sat opposite Uthan with his back to the bars. His jaw and right cheek were bruised. In his lap, he held Demien's head, stroking her hair gently. Cass sat close by, her knees brought up against her body, her arms wrapped tightly around them. She watched Demien like a hawk over the top of her kneecaps. Diarus, Qwan and Gauduin lined the left wall of the wagon. All three had been chained up, hands behind their backs and their feet chained together. Large cast-iron locks held the chains in place and all six carried the air of defeat about them.

Watching them sit and do nothing but seemingly accept this turn of events filled Uthan with frustration. He felt his blood surging. The need to shift around and do something became too great for him. Feeling the cold bars of the cage against his back, Uthan closed his eyes and tried clearing his mind. The pain in his leg gnawed at his concentration. He opened his eyes again, feeling the wagon stopping.

The sky had darkened. Hues of red, orange and purple painted the sky as the sun dipped away.

"They're making camp," Qwan muttered.

"You have a plan?" Medoran asked, his voice dry and cracked.

The elf shook his head, "I don't see a way out of this one yet."

"So what happens now then?" Cass asked hotly. "Do we just sit here and let them kill us?"

Qwan turned on her suddenly and snarled, "I notice you're not chained to the bars here, girl. Why don't you think of something?"

"There is no way out at the moment. We just have to sit back and wait for an opening," Medoran said slowly.

"Not as if we have the luxury of time though," Gauduin said with a shrug.

"What about you, big man?" Medoran asked, looking at Diarus. The Daiharlon had been sitting motionless the whole time his head was bowed. "Do you think you could break those chains?"

"I've tried," Diarus answered.

"Try again," Qwan muttered.

Diarus strained his shoulders, trying to pull his wrists apart. The chains clinked together as the links tightened as much as they could. After a few tense seconds, he let out a loud breath and shook his head.

"I'd really love to know what these are made from," he said, relaxing again.

"I'm sure they'd tell you if you asked them nicely," Qwan answered sarcastically.

"You are not helping here, Qwan," Gauduin growled.

"Quieten down," Medoran said suddenly. Catching the looks from Gauduin and Qwan, he added, "now."

Voices reached them; six of the knights walked coolly over to the cage. Four of them carried poles with nooses on one end, the fifth held a long iron key. The last man held a loaded crossbow, the bolt aimed at Diarus's forehead. Carefully, the key holder opened the door. The prisoners did not move.

"Beastman, get out slowly," ordered the bowman. "And if anyone tries anything, the first bolt goes through his brain."

Two of the noose men moved forward. They rammed their spears through the open cage door, slipping the nooses over the Daiharlon's head. They pulled his head back, stretching his neck uncomfortably while the key holder unlocked the chains that held Diarus to the cage bars. Using all their strength, they hauled him through the open door and down to the ground with a hard thump. The other two noose men got into position. When all four nooses were tight around Diarus's neck the cage door was locked again. All the time the bowman did not take his aim away from Diarus.

Once they had left, Cass looked at Medoran and asked, "Why'd they take him?"

The swordsman shrugged.

Diarus was half dragged to a small clearing, fighting against the four men holding the ropes around his thick neck all the way. He ignored the threats from the bowman, believing that, had the man wanted to shoot him, he would have done so before. The Daiharlon's wrists were tied to a length of thick chain, the other end of which was tossed up to a knight in the branches of a great oak tree. Three more knights pulled on the chain, keeping Diarus upright. The Daiharlon looked around him. A metal brazier sat to one side, hot coals burning in a warm, orange fire. Close by was a low wooden table. Three daggers, an iron arrow and a branding iron all lay on it, like surgeon's tools.

"It's all about the sound of a scream," Cornak said, emerging from the shadows like a ghost. He stood by the brazier, letting the fire glow play across his face. Holding his eyes on the Daiharlon, he continued, "I don't know exactly what it is about it. But the sound of a scream of agony or fear... well it really gets inside me. I like that feeling."

"What are you talking about?" Diarus asked, impatiently.

"Before I joined the Imperial legions I found my wife in bed with another man. I killed him there and then. My wife screamed her lungs out, scared for her own life. She begged for a long time. The sounds of her screams found their way inside my skull and stayed there," Cornak explained.

"I see," Diarus answered with a mocking nod. "So you killed her and her screams still haunt you, right?"

Cornak, picking up on the mockery, replied, "Not at all. It started something inside me. All the screams of those who are about to die are like wine."

"You brought me out here just to tell me all this? I'm honoured," Diarus said coolly.

The general smirked malevolently as he reached onto the table for one of the daggers. Holding the blade in the flames for a few moments, he said, "You know I've made a great many people scream in terror and pain. For example, humans, a few dwarves and elves, but never once have I made a Daiharlon scream."

"We don't scream," Diarus replied, but the mockery had gone from his voice.

"So I've been told," Cornak replied. He pulled the dagger from the coals and looked closely at the tip. It glowed faintly with the heat. "I'm interested in finding out for myself though."

"I don't hear any screams," Cassmed said slowly. She was watching the direction Diarus had been taken in. A cluster of the small canvas tents cut off her view. "How can you be sure he's not talking to Cornak?"

"What can he tell Cornak? The bastard already has us here," Medoran replied.

The frantic sound of a horse galloping came from somewhere in the darkness. Camp guards came forward with bows. The horse galloped into view, foaming around its mouth and nostrils. The camp guards lowered their bows, seeing the rider was clad in the familiar black plate. He charged in and leapt from his saddle. Breathing heavily, he said, "I need to speak to General Cornak now."

"He's busy," answered one of the guards.

"This is important," the rider breathed. "Green Ghosts have been attacking Dessendor."

One of the guards ran off through the tents like a hare. He returned moments later with the general in tow.

The rider saluted stiffly, standing up straight, "Sir, it's the Green Ghosts."

"They're attacking my fortress?" Cornak growled.

"They know the main force is away, General. And there are more of them than we believed," the rider continued.

"More?"

"They've been joined by refugees from some village we left in ruins," the rider answered.

Cornak smiled, "An army of villagers out for my blood? Do they have pitchforks?"

"There's a lot of them, sir," the rider continued.

"How many is a lot exactly?"

"A few hundred at the last count. But the number has been growing by the day, sir. Someone is rallying them together," the rider answered.

"Another rebel leader," Cornak said. "Well, in the morning I ride back to Dessendor with the last rebel leader as a prisoner. Let's see how the nerves of these farmers will hold when they see one of their rebel kind hung from the flagpole without his skin."

He looked around to the camp guards and ordered, "Put the beastman back with his friends. We move early in the morning."

"Do you want me to ride with you to Dessendor, sir?" the rider asked.

"No," Cornak replied. "Take a fresh horse and ride back now. I want you to meet the army there tomorrow. Scout the surrounding area. I want to know where the enemy is in hiding for us."

The rider saluted again and disappeared to get a replacement horse.

Cornak wandered over to the prison wagon and stared at Medoran. "It seems you've been an inspiration to a bunch of farmhands."

"You're going to slaughter an entire mob?" Medoran asked with a sneer. "Good luck."

"I won't need it. Your rotting carcass hanging from the fortress flagpole will be another symbol of this realm's defeat. That should beat the enthusiasm out of them," Cornak replied. The general turned away, cutting Medoran off from responding.

"I'm going to enjoy killing him," Medoran said slowly.

"If you get a chance," Qwan answered. "If the Ghosts get him there won't be much more than a puddle of blood left to soak into the grass."

"You're certain these Ghosts are that good?" Med replied.

Qwan grinned, "They'd better be. I trained them."

"As good as they are, Qwan, they'll be fighting an army," Gauduin replied.

"They'll hold their ground," the elf answered.

"They'll have to," Medoran said. "Otherwise those farmers are dead."

"You think a handful of archers can protect them?" Cass blurted out, startled by the realisation.

"If Boron is this new rebel leader as I'd suspect he is, he'll have told them all the risks from the beginning," Qwan replied.

The girl looked at him and shook her head, not willing to accept his words. "That doesn't make it right, Qwan. Those few hundred people will be slaughtered."

"They have nothing left to lose. That makes a man more dangerous," Qwan replied.

Even as he spoke the words, he knew Cass was right. After all his small band of outlaws had just bolstered their numbers with untrained, unskilled men and women, and, in doing so, had condemned them all to die.

Chapter Eighteen

Dessendor loomed on the horizon, nestling between the forests and the small foothills. The column of Black Flame Knights rode as carefully as an army could, through the trees. Cornak was at the front, seemingly unfazed by the potential threat against his adopted fortress. They emerged into the clear grasslands that surrounded Dessendor as thin wisps of early morning mist, left over from the dawn, curled across the ground. Cornak sat in his saddle, searching the tree line that ran in a rough semi-circle around the field.

"Scouts report nothing, sir," stated a knight, riding up from the rear of the column. Cornak just grunted. "Do you think they've moved on, sir?"

"No," Cornak turned to look at the man, "they're in hiding if they were ever here to begin with. We continue on, draw them out if they're still here."

The general raised his hand, signalling to his troops, before riding out across the exposed grassland.

From the north, a rider charged out of the trees, racing across to the gates of Dessendor. He saw the knights and angled his horse, going to meet them. The column moved into position, waiting for the threat to emerge from the trees.

"General Cornak, sir, they're coming!" the rider shouted, gulping down air.

Cornak drew his sword, "How many?" he shouted back.

"There must be nearly two thousand of them now. There are Imperial troops with them too, sir," the rider said as he reined his horse in next to Cornak's.

The general turned to look at the trees, "How far behind you were they?"

"Only a few minutes, sir. My patrol walked right into them," the rider said.

"All dead?" Cornak asked.

The rider nodded, "We never stood a chance. They had men in the trees above us and others just appeared as if up from the ground. They were everywhere."

Turning away from the breathless rider, Cornak called, "The enemy is headed this way after all. I want them slaughtered. Not one man or woman is to remain amongst them. No prisoners."

"Sir?" the rider started carefully. Cornak looked round at him, raising an eyebrow for him to continue. "The prisoners. Wouldn't it be a good idea to get them inside?"

"Why?" asked another knight nearby.

The general flashed an angry stare at the interruption before gesturing for the rider to continue.

"If the mage gets free and is able to cast then he could easily kill hundreds in one go," the rider answered.

"These are nothing more than farmers and a handful of outlaws," the other knight retorted. "I think we can handle them."

"The scout is right," Cornak said so suddenly the second knight closed his mouth immediately. "Besides, the boy is to be delivered alive."

"They have archers, some of the best I've seen," the rider continued. "It's almost a shame really."

"A shame?" Cornak asked, raising an eyebrow.

Gulping under the full effect of Cornak's anger-filled stare, the rider said, "A shame they have to be killed. Marksmen like that are hard to find."

"You and six others are to get this prison wagon through those gates. I want archers on the battlements, ready to take care of those marksmen," Cornak growled.

The rider saluted as the six other men were quickly chosen. The wagon was driven forward with the traveller's horses in tow. A volley of arrows flew from the trees, stabbing into the ground near to the wagon. The prison escort paused a moment, checking where the arrows had been shot from. The original rider pointed to a large tree a few yards inside the forest.

"There!" he yelled, pointing at a dark shape in amongst the branches.

Cornak spurred his mount forward, charging at the tree. Behind the general, his men surged after him. The sound of crossbow strings being pulled back was audible over the sounds of the hooves.

Inside the prison wagon, Qwan watched, wide-eyed and stunned. He could see the shape in the tree, motionless and seemingly waiting.

A volley of bolts flew up from the crossbows of the charging knights. The elf saw many of them hit the archer and he yelled, "No!"

In front of them the heavy gates of Dessendor ground open. The wagon was escorted safely inside the walls and the gates closed. The knights climbed down from their saddles and started to the battlements, yelling for archers. An arrow suddenly whistled down, taking one of them through the eye. As he fell, the other five looked around them. The men at the gates were not Black Flame Knights; they wore brown and green cloaks.

Two of the braver knights unsheathed their swords and ran forward. Arrows pierced their skulls before they had taken their third step. The other three tried to run away but the original rider cut one down before riding after another. The last clearly knew he was captured and threw his sword to the ground. Raising his hands in the air, he turned to look around. From under the battlements, a larger man wearing the now familiar brown and green cloak strode over. He wrapped one thick arm around the knight's chin, pulling his head back. A dagger appeared in his other hand, becoming a blur of shining steel as it slit the knight's throat. He let the body go and turned to look at the prison wagon. A large smile split his bearded face as he saw the stunned look on the faces of the prisoners.

Moving over to stand before the chained elf, he said, "Nice prison break, huh?"

"Boron, I love you!" Qwan yelled, laughing loudly.

"Steady on, Qwan," Boron replied, removing his huge battleaxe from his back. "I know it's been a while but that sort of thing hasn't changed."

The giant slammed the edge of his axe against the lock on the wagon door and the iron smashed under his weapon, the door swinging open.

From outside there were loud angry shouts that made Boron smile even more. "It looks like they found the second part of the plan then."

"That poor archer," Cass said, climbing out of the wagon.

"Oh, I wouldn't worry about him," Boron said casually, helping the others out of their chains. "He was dead long before we put him up there."

The Black Flame rider dismounted and wandered over. He removed the helm and tossed it to the floor, grinning at Qwan all the time. Seeing him without the helm, Qwan grinned even more,

257

"Harhn, I can't believe you fools pulled this off."

"I thought you'd have recognised me back out there, Qwan. You're losing your edge," the man replied, laughing.

Gauduin interrupted quickly, looking pointedly at Boron. "What do you mean he was dead long before?"

"Amazing, huh?" Boron replied. "The archer is just one of their own dead. We tied him into the tree last night."

"So there is no angry mob of farmers out there?" the dwarf asked.

"Nope," the man called Harhn replied, "that was just amazing acting on my part."

"Bloody good performance," Gauduin said. "You had me believing it."

"More to the point," Medoran cut in, "it had Cornak believing it."

More angry shouts sounded from the trees.

"Well, it did," Boron replied. "I think he's found the others now."

"Others?" Qwan asked.

"The bodies of the other knights. You don't think he left this place totally unguarded, do you?" Harhn said.

"You took this place by force?" Medoran asked. He looked around him at the people gathered in the yard. Nodding and smiling to some he recognised from the last village he had been in, he added, "I'm impressed."

"You must be Medoran," Boron said, extending a massive hand in friendship to the swordsman.

Taking the hand, Medoran nodded.

"There are a lot of people here from Karaka-Tus. Cornak himself attacked the place shortly after you left. They all speak highly of you," Boron replied.

"He's coming over," shouted a voice from the battlements.

Boron gestured to the battlements and grinned at Qwan, "After you?"

They wandered up the steps and onto the wooden walkway. Along the wall men turned and greeted Qwan, many of them from his own Green Ghosts group. Boron led him on and stopped next to an old man wearing the armour of the Royal Knights. The elf had to look twice as Serriman Camarr, Uthan's grandfather, greeted him with a huge beaming smile and an extended hand.

"How'd you get here?" the elf asked.

With a chuckle, Serriman pointed to an ugly blackened right eye and answered, "Much the same way as you did."

"Open the gates!" Cornak yelled up.

Serriman looked down at him, "General Cornak, I must tell you that Dessendor is no longer occupied by Black Flame scum."

"Who the hell are you, old man?" the general roared back.

"It doesn't matter who he is, Cornak," Boron roared back. "The prisoners are now inside, perfectly well and no longer your prisoners."

Cornak stared up full of hate, "Boron, I'll have your treacherous carcass for this!"

"Promises, promises, Cornak. Do you know, from up here you look like a beetle," Boron replied, casually.

The general signalled over his shoulder. Arrows were fired from crossbows, clearing the battlements and causing most of the fortress occupants to duck. He yelled back, "I'm going to make sure you live a long time, Boron. Your life is going to be filled with a new pain everyday. I promise you that."

Against a chorus of taunts and cheers from the men on the battlements, Cornak turned his horse away, leading his men back across the grasslands and out of bow range.

"We could have just killed him there," Qwan stated slowly.

"True," Boron answered. "Although that would still leave his army to fight us."

"There'll be another occasion," Serriman said. "They'll be camped out there for sometime I would imagine."

"An army just for us," Qwan laughed, suddenly seeing the irony in it all.

"Not quite," Boron replied quietly. "They didn't go to Skull Gate to capture you. They were there to catch the lad." He pointed to Uthan as the young man sat leaning against the wagon, holding his leg. "Cornak's been told to catch him at all costs and to be wary of him."

"Uthan gets an army after him. Typical. Someone of my talents is completely overlooked," Qwan said, shaking his head in mock disbelief.

"Yeah, Qwan, Uthan, the boy has power," Boron said, clearly not seeing the humour in the elf's words.

"I'd never have guessed," Qwan replied sarcastically. "I know he has power, I've seen it used."

"No, Qwan. He has real power. The kind of ability to kill an army," Boron continued. "Cornak was told to deliver him to the Black Flame."

"To the Flame? Wish we'd have thought about this sooner," Qwan said dryly. "We could have let them take us there and saved us some trouble."

"I get the distinct impression you're not taking this seriously, elf," Boron said levelly.

Qwan snapped; the word elf caused him to bridle. Hissing, he replied, "I've been in Dacenheim, hunted because I was with Uthan. I've had to travel here, there and almost every bloody where because of Uthan. I know he has real power. I know they want him specifically. I can only assume the Black Flame wants the pleasure of killing him personally. Or is there some other blatantly obvious point you want to share with me?"

"How do you know all this?" Gauduin asked, coming up the stairs behind them. He slipped in between them, putting an end to any more bickering.

With a shrug, Boron replied, "It isn't hard to learn things like that in a fortress held by the general."

"I have a question though, Qwan," Harhn said. He had unbuckled the black breastplate and arm armour. Underneath it he wore a dark green shirt. "If Uthan is as powerful as they're saying, why didn't he cast and get you out of there?"

"He has some pieces of an iron arrowhead in his leg. It's stopped him being able to cast," Qwan answered.

"I'll see if I can find someone skilled enough to sort it out for him," Harhn said with a nod.

"What the hell is that thing doing in there?" Boron said, looking suddenly at the prison wagon.

Qwan looked down to see Diarus pull himself through the door, helped by Demien and Medoran, "He's with us."

"I can see that, Qwan, but why?"

"He's a Daiharlon," Qwan replied, moving down the steps to help. "I'd rather have him with me than against me."

Boron called after him, "You can tell me the full story later. He looks like he needs patching up too."

He turned to one of the men on the battlements next to him and muttered, "Doesn't look that impressive really."

"Oh, he is," Serriman said, moving past on his way down, "he really is."

The old man wandered down the stairs, coming to a stop next to Diarus and his grandson.

"Granddad?" Uthan asked, confused. "What are you doing here?"

"I came here the same way you did just about. Remember those men who chased us?" Uthan nodded. "Well, they caught me immediately after you had escaped Dacenheim," Serriman explained. Medoran and Gauduin wandered over. Serriman looked up at them, concern filling his eyes. "That Boron is a dangerous man. Something about him doesn't ring true with me."

The dwarf studied Serriman for a moment or two, as if gauging the old man's concerns. Finally he said, "You'd better come somewhere quiet with us. And tell me the whole story."

Demien looked up at Medoran. She was busily tending to the burns and cuts covering Diarus's body. With a nod, she said, "Go with them, I'll catch up later."

Gauduin turned to her and muttered, "Tell Qwan to come over and find us as soon as possible, okay?"

The three of them turned and walked off, finding a quiet spot under the battlements. Keeping his voice low, Serriman began recounting his story.

"Once I left the temple in Dacenheim, I ran into someone I had believed was a friend. As it turns out, he began working for the general out there. I think he was in charge of those men who chased us. Anyway, I was incapacitated and so couldn't deliver that message.

"When I woke up I was right outside the gates in a small donkey-drawn cart. Your friend, Boron, came over to Searth; he was dressed in black armour. They talked for a very short while like they knew each other before Boron slashed Searth's throat. He just killed him outright, no emotion at all. He told me I was to act as his prisoner, and believe me, from the look in his eyes, I didn't fancy arguing. Next thing, we were in through the gates. He waited until nightfall, then opened them up and all these people flooded in. Half of the remaining knights were dead before the alarm was raised. I don't know what he's doing exactly, but he's dangerous, Gauduin. I'd watch your backs if I were you."

"We will be," the dwarf answered.

Medoran watched the old knight as he had unfolded his side of the events. Leading Gauduin away from him again, he muttered, "Interesting tale."

"You don't believe it?" Gauduin asked.

"I don't know what to believe," Medoran said. "There's a gut feeling about all this though. It's like Cornak has been one step ahead of us all the time. Someone somewhere has given him information."

The dwarf grinned a little, "Ever the suspicious leader, huh?"

"It's kept me alive so far."

"Well, I for one think we should be keeping an eye on Boron. He may have got us out of that cage but look where we ended up," Gauduin said. "It's the frying pan into the fire."

"So what's the big deal?" It was Qwan. He came over with a water skin.

Gauduin answered, "The boy's grandad just gave us a warning."

"Oh?" Qwan asked, raising the skin to his lips to drink.

"Yeah, seems your friend Boron is quite the killer," Gauduin continued.

"This I know. He's not someone you turn your back on when you've pissed him off," the elf chuckled dryly. He grew serious a moment, looking at Gauduin. "You still don't trust him?"

"No, Qwan, I don't," Gauduin answered.

"Well, keep it to yourself," the elf replied sharply. "I've known you as long as any of my friends. Keep an eye on him. If he is a plant I'll deal with it."

Chapter Nineteen

Around General Cornak there was activity as he had given orders to build a camp. The wind was gathering strength with every passing moment and whipped around their tents, threatening to rip them from the ground. Thunderclouds loomed in the near distance, carrying a storm of furious proportions. Cornak, already furious that he had to lay siege to his own fortress, had ordered his men to cut down trees in order to make a more sturdy camp. He stood at the edge of a shallow foundation ditch, watching the activity on the battlements fade. The lieutenant he had called for earlier arrived and Cornak glared at him silently. The man had removed his breastplate. His dark shirt was covered in dirt from digging as he wearily saluted.

"I'm told you know Dessendor inside and out, lieutenant," Cornak said evenly.

"I think I do, sir," the lieutenant replied.

Cornak turned his gaze back to Dessendor again, "I need someone who knows, not thinks they know."

"Yes, sir."

"Well? Do you know Dessendor?" Cornak persisted.

The lieutenant quickly answered, "Yes, sir, I do."

"In that case, lieutenant, you are excused from camp building. I want plans of that fortress drawn up immediately. I want to know where every stone is in that place," Cornak said.

A chill rolled down the lieutenant's back. He could not be sure whether it was the calm even tone of voice his general was using or just the sudden cold of the approaching storm. Saluting again, he turned and left hastily.

Uthan and Diarus had been taken to a long, low-roofed building that was being used as an infirmary. The rows of bunk beds along one wall marked it out as having previously been a barracks. Qwan and Medoran held the Daiharlon up, his great arms draped over them. They struggled under his weight as they moved him into the room.

Behind them people watched, warily. No one had wanted to get too close to the beastman, each believing in the ancient tales of violence and savagery. Diarus himself had drifted into unconsciousness again. Not once during the torture had he given in. Not one sound had escaped his mouth. It was this stubborn silence that had driven Cornak on and on, nearly killing the beastman in the process.

Harhn had found a healer amongst the villagers. The man was short, skinny and it seemed completely hairless. He had begun fussing over the wound in Uthan's leg immediately. When asked about Diarus, the man had merely glanced over and muttered about not knowing anything concerning the Daiharlon race. Qwan had hotly told him to think of Diarus as a really big man and that had appeared to be enough.

"A really big man?" laughed a voice from the doorway. "He's a savage from the north. He doesn't belong here."

The group turned, almost as one, to see a man leaning against the doorframe. Medoran was the first to approach the individual. Putting out a hand in front of him, he said, "Kaiss, whatever your problem is, now is not the time."

Kaiss just glared at Medoran. From between scarred lips, he said, "So you've sided with the beastmen now."

Qwan stepped forward smartly, pointing a loaded crossbow right into Kaiss's face. "My friend here has a lot more patience than I do," the elf said deliberately. "I'd just bury this in your face. Do you understand what I'm saying to you?" As Kaiss nodded, Qwan continued, "Good, so go now and let us tend to our friends in peace."

As the bow was lowered, Kaiss got a little of his bravado back. Pointing at Medoran, he said, "This isn't over."

"Out of everyone Cornak's men could have killed, they had to leave that sack of dung alive," Demien said, shaking her head.

Boron entered the room, blocking the light from the door for a moment. He looked over at the motionless Daiharlon with a concerned look on his face. "He only expresses a concern we all share."

"And what would that be, Boron?" demanded Qwan, his patience almost at an end.

"You travel with a beastman. Many are saying they don't know whose side you're on now," Boron replied.

As the elf looked up sharply, Boron fell silent. He understood the problems of trust all too well.

Medoran sank down onto a bed and relayed to the giant warrior the idea of attacking the Black Flame to put an end to it all. As he spoke, his voice betrayed his exhaustion. He said he had not believed Cornak would have attacked so soon. Boron's face was impassive, not a muscle twitched as he suggested everyone in the fortress should be told this.

Medoran stalked outside, closely followed by Demien, then Qwan. He marched into the centre of the courtyard and looked around. People were gathered along the wall, watching the Black Flame army and in the courtyard going about small tasks Boron had set them to. A few turned and saw the swordsman standing calmly, as if about to say something. Those few nudged others who turned their attention to Medoran. Soon the majority of Dessendor's occupants, Green Ghosts and refugees alike, watched the rebel leader. Seeing he now had everyone's attention, he explained his reasons for leaving Karaka-tus that night. The fortress's occupants began looking at their feet sheepishly as he revealed their plans. His words appeared to hold the assembled crowd in thrall, wiping away the suspicious expressions and replacing them with ones of respect or, in some places, guilt.

From behind him, Qwan stepped up. He quickly filled in the gaps left out of Medoran's speech, making a point of showing his disdain for anyone who doubted them and those who marked the Daiharlon out as just a savage beast. He quickly reminded the Green Ghosts amongst them that they were still considered outlaws in the Empire. Leaving those words ringing throughout the courtyard, Qwan waited patiently, looking from face to face. Some he recognised, others he did not. Slowly a murmur of approval washed through the crowd.

Harhn was the first to answer, "I never for one moment questioned which side you were on. But when I saw that Daiharlon pulled out of there, I did question your sanity, Qwan. But if you say he's okay then it's good enough for me."

"Good. Now it just leaves us to make sure this place is totally impregnable," the elf replied, stalking off to the battlements.

Cornak's men had built a wooden wall around their camp, protecting it from the wind and oncoming rain. Hundreds of tiny campfires were dotted around the area. "They're getting settled in nicely, huh?" Demien said with as much irony as she felt she could muster.

Leading the two of them away, Gauduin muttered, "We can't stay here too long, not if we're going to get through Skull Gate before Meligonn."

"I don't see how we're going to get past that army, Gauduin," Qwan answered quickly. He called down to the courtyard, "Harhn? Did anyone get a message to the Emperor?"

There was a snort from one of the men on the walkway that answered the question perfectly.

"Aside from running out there and fighting them man to man, there's no other way out right now. And they outnumber us too greatly, so it's not advisable," Harhn said, coming up behind them.

"We don't have time to wait this out either," Qwan muttered, more to himself than anyone else. Catching the raised eyebrow from Harhn, the elf explained quickly their reasons for needing to leave the fortress as soon as they could, swearing the outlaw to a vow of secrecy.

The colour drained from Harhn's face as Qwan told him of Meligonn. The outlaw clearly knew what Qwan would ask long before he had heard the request. He was to lead the refugees to the safety of Dacenhiem's walls as soon as the siege was broken. The elf did not hold back with his words either as he described how important it was for the rest of the fortress not to know about Meligonn yet. He had reasoned that many would rather put themselves to the sword than fight on against a seemingly hopeless situation. After a moment's argument from Harhn, the outlaw agreed to the oath. He understood that every death inside the fortress would drain hope from the others.

For a while longer they stood watching the activity in the camp. The sun touched the distant, mist shrouded mountains to the west. Heavy looking rain clouds masked its fading light even further. The sky to the east was fast becoming a deep shade of blue and stars could be seen in the few gaps between the clouds.

"Put three on watch tonight," Qwan said.

"What if they attack? Three men aren't going to be enough to raise the alarm and organise the defence," Harhn replied.

"They won't attack. Now, the sun's behind us and those rain clouds are coming this way." Qwan was adamant as he continued, " It'll chuck it down tonight so by the morning all this stone will be slick. He'll have the morning sun behind him, in our eyes, and he'll be hoping these walls are going to be as slippery as ice. My guess is, if they attack, they'll do it in the morning." Having explained his theories on when the attack would happen, he questioned Harhn about the various defences at their disposal.

As if he had been asked many times already, Harhn ran through the list of resources. There was a pair of siege crossbows, but very few of the thick solid steel bolts to fire from them. Offhandedly, he mentioned the surplus of armour and weapons left by the Black Flame Knights. There was an apprentice blacksmith amongst the refugees who could craft new bolts from that metal. With a broad smile, he also mentioned several barrels of miner's blasting powder had been found and enough food, water and fuel to last a couple of months at least.

Qwan nodded, listening intently to the items listed. He made no comment until Harhn was finished. After questioning the Green Ghost on the abilities of those gathered within Dessendor's walls, Qwan outlined his plan to defend the fortress and maybe hit back at the Black Flame Knights. His subtle smirk assured them all of his belief in the plan. It was enough to inspire confidence in everyone around him.

Finally, with everyone nodding in approval, he said, "Get this blacksmith working. He's got the whole night to make as many siege bolts as he can. Make sure he has a few people to help him. We'll need those powder kegs brought out as well. If we can't get them accurately, then we'll try to take them out in numbers. We need everyone ready by morning."

"In that case," Demien interrupted, "I need to see this smith now. I need replacement armour."

"I see nothing wrong with what you're wearing if you'll pardon my stares," Harhn said mischievously.

Demien shrugged, "I'm giving this to Cass to wear. She needs it more than I do."

"Why not just have more made for her?" Qwan questioned.

"This is what you might call an heirloom," Demien said, "It gets passed from teacher to pupil and it's about time Cass took it and I had more made. It won't be much extra work for him and he'll need to fix armour for others here."

The elf nodded.

Harhn, with a broad grin, said, "In that case I'd like to suggest leather."

"Come on," Qwan said, leading Harhn away as he caught the glare

Demien directed at his friend, "There's too much to do without your shameless flirting."

Outside, the rain poured down. The night watchmen huddled behind the wall, taking as much shelter from the wind and rain as they could. Waxed leather cloaks were pulled tightly around them, hoods drawn up over their heads. It had become impossible to see too far ahead through the downpour. The three watchmen, knowing that there would be no attack during the rain, sought instead to stay as warm and dry as possible.

They did not see the black cloaked figure climbing the stairs and moving across the wooden walkway. It made no sound on the sodden wood. The featureless shape merged with the darkness almost perfectly, becoming invisible in the night. The face beneath the hood looked out across the grasslands to where it knew Cornak's camp to be. A short bow was drawn from inside the folds of the cloak. An arrow was notched and fired out into the night sky, landing somewhere unseen in the field. The bow was placed back inside the cloak again then the figure turned and looked around at the fortress. There was no sign of movement, no sound other than the rain and the wind. No one had seen anything.

Moving just as silently, the figure went along the walkway, coming to an area of wall, hidden by an old tower that had long since fallen into disrepair. From inside the cloak, it produced a coil of dark rope. One end was fixed to an exposed beam within the stonework of the tower and the other was tossed over the side. After another check to make sure no one had seen it, the figure left the walkway and returned to the shadows of Dessendor.

Uthan reluctantly opened his eyes, expecting to be blinded by sunlight. Instead he was greeted by a dull dawn. The morning sky beyond the infirmary window was painted shades of white and grey that reflected the coldness outside. His leg was numb and through the strange, foggy sensation in his mind, he remembered the arrow shards trapped in his leg. Carefully, he tried to sit up. A tidal wave of dizziness engulfed him. Dropping back to the bed, he bit back the almost overwhelming need to vomit, screwing his eyes closed with the effort. Every nerve ending screamed at him, sending mixed signals to his brain. He was numb while at the same time able to feel the pain, he was cold but burning up. Then, finally, the dizziness passed. Uthan opened his eyes a second time and sucked in a deep gasp of air. With very careful, slow movements, he rolled onto his side.

That was when he saw Diarus. The sight of the huge Daiharlon lying beaten, bruised and bloodied on the bed next to him, made Uthan forget about his own pain. He placed his hand, palm flat against the bandaged wound on his thigh. From the fingertips he could feel warmth growing. It passed into his leg, corroding away at the numbness, the pain and the cold. His flesh glowed with a soft golden light and beneath the bandages; he could feel the wound closing, knitting itself back together again.

"You're awake," Cass said, coming into the infirmary.

Uthan took his hand away from the wound and nodded. A faint dizzy sensation swept over him again, forcing him to grip the bed tightly.

"I saw the light your casting caused from outside," Cass continued. "How do you feel?"

"Tired," Uthan replied before asking, "is Diarus going to be okay?"

Cass could not answer for a moment. Finally, she shrugged and said, "The healer doesn't think so. He said he's done all he can."

"He's going to die?"

"They've not said that, no one's dared to yet. But they're all thinking it," Cass said. She sat down on the bed next to Uthan. Seeing the tired rings under his eyes, she continued, "You should go back to sleep. We need you rested and well."

Uthan stood up and crossed to Diarus's side, swaying a little. He placed his hands on the Daiharlon, one on his chest, the other on his forehead. Closing his eyes and chanting softly under his breath, Uthan began trying to heal Diarus.

The glow started from Uthan's heart, pulsing through his skin. Soft, yellow gold light travelled through his veins, up into his shoulders and along his arms to where it emerged from his fingertips. Lying motionless on the bed, Diarus was bathed in the aura. From her place on Uthan's bed, Cass could feel the heat emanating from him. There was a wet sounding crackle from the Daiharlon's body. Very slowly, Cass stood and crossed to stand behind Uthan. Her eyes widened a little as she watched the various cuts and stab wounds first being emptied of vile, yellow pus before closing themselves up. Both light and heat grew in intensity. Looking at Uthan, she saw beads of sweat breaking out over his face. He swayed more and more, threatening to topple over at any moment. Cass reached over to support him, only to pull her hands back sharply from the heat. The sounds of Diarus's flesh pulling itself together ceased and a heavy silence fell over the room. Just as suddenly, the light stopped. Uthan, barely conscious, toppled backwards, right into the waiting arms of Cass.

Qwan came in just as Uthan fell. He darted over, taking the young mage's weight from Cass and putting him back to bed.

"Is he okay?" she asked quietly.

"He's just exhausted. He'll be fine," the elf replied. He looked closely at the girl. There were slight, purple rings forming under her eyes, a telltale sign of her lack of recent sleep. Not unkindly, he said, "You should go and see Demien. She was coming over for you just now. Then try to get some rest yourself."

Cass entered the room she shared with Demien. The warrior woman stood holding up her new armour, looking at it critically in the sunlight. The top resembled a dress upon first inspection. Thick dark leather had been moulded to form an ample chest and the waist seemed all too constricting. A short skirt was connected to it, made from strips of the same material. She already wore a pair of equally thick leather trousers. More of the similar leather strips had been woven together along the sides of her legs. Seeing Cass's shadow in the doorway, Demien turned to her friend. Inclining her head to the new armour, she said, "You really can tell this was made by a man, can't you!"

Nodding, Cass entered the room fully, closing the door behind her. She sat down heavily on the foot of her bed. Demien pulled her shirt over her head, tossing it one side. With more than a little struggling, she pulled the armour on, fixing it in place. Reaching behind her, she felt for the buckles that pulled the leather tighter around her torso. She looked down and noticed her chest a tanned cleavage bulged over the top of the dress.

"Yeah," Cass said with a smile, "definitely made by a man."

Sighing and shaking her head in disbelief, Demien loosened the straps behind her. Instantly, she could breath more comfortably again. The cleavage had almost disappeared entirely.

"Is this what you wanted to show me?" Cass asked, grinning. "That you have cleavage as well?"

Demien fixed her young friend with a long stare. "I have something for you. But make more comments like that and I'll not bother with it."

She moved over to Cass's bed. For the first time since entering the room, Cass noticed the sheet covering a small collection of bumps and mounds. Demien grasped the sheet, pulling it away in one movement. Beneath was her old plate armour. The girl picked the shining breastplate up, holding it almost as if it were a baby instead of crafted steel. She barely heard Demien's comments about trying it on as she gazed at the gift. Gently taking the breastplate from Cass's fingers, Demien began to help the girl into her armour.

There was a cry from outside and they all heard the words clearly. Someone had shouted Cornak's name.

Sword in hand once more, Medoran sprinted out from the infirmary and into the morning light. Standing between him and the large gates of Dessendor, flanked by a pair of his black armoured knights was General Cornak. The two knights held crossbows, aimed at Medoran while Cornak grinned hungrily, seeing his adversary. Kaiss was on one knee in front of the general. Cornak's gloved fingers grasped a tight handful of the man's hair, pulling his head back and exposing his throat. The refugee's eyes were wide with terror and his mouth gaped open and closed, too afraid to make a sound.

"Someone here was kind enough to throw a rope over the wall for me and my men. So thoughtful, although I know you won't agree," Cornak sneered.

"If he dies, you follow!" Medoran returned hotly.

"Really?" Cornak asked.

In his left hand he held a short dagger. Slowly, emphasising the movement, he brought the dagger up to Kaiss's throat. Behind Medoran, Qwan moved to the side, letting his comrade hold the general's attention. His bowstring thumped loudly and the bolt whistled through the air towards Cornak's arm. One of the general's men stepped forward, taking the arrow to his right shoulder. Only barely registering the hit, he turned to Qwan and fired in reply. His arrow sailed past Qwan's right thigh by mere inches.

"And chaos ensues," Demien muttered starting to run forward. Her newly made leather armour allowed her to move with a tremendous increase in speed.

Seeing the warrior woman running straight towards him, Cornak drew his dagger across Kaiss's throat before pushing the man to one side. He cast the dagger to the floor and drew his sword. Demien ran into him, feinting to the left then thrusting in to his right side. Cornak twisted, moving around behind her. Before the warrior woman could turn, Cornak backhanded his fist into the base of her skull, knocking her flat to the floor.

There was a yell from behind the general. He half turned, just in time to see Medoran charging at him, sword spinning in a fury of shining arcs. Their two swords clashed noisily, filling the courtyard with the angry sound of steel on steel. Neither Cornak nor Medoran said one word as the weapons came together time and time again. Beneath the sudden berserker style rage of Medoran, Cornak was gradually driven back. Their blades flashed back and forth. Each attack was blocked and returned, which, in turn was blocked again. Medoran's fury subsided a little. The swordsman now lashed out with carefully timed attacks, trying to pry a way through the general's defences rather than batter them down. Cornak had almost recovered from the first furious onslaught though he was still breathing hard and his limbs felt weary.

Medoran backed away a few paces, keeping his guard up. His lungs felt ready to burst, desperately seeking to take in more air than they could hold. Cornak did not follow him, did not attack. For a few brief moments they rested, glaring at each other, annoyed that the other was skilled enough to have made the fight last as long. Despite this though, there was clearly a grudging respect between the two, as they watched one another, without uttering a sound. Feeling new raw energy flow with his blood, Medoran surged forward again. He brought his sword in an upward sweep, intent on inflicting a killing wound upon his opponent.

The general sidestepped the move and calmly brought his own blade down, clashing against Medoran's sword. The sound of metal sliding against metal rang in their ears as Medoran twisted and forced his blade up, moving his opponent back a step. In answer, Cornak spun on his heel and fired out a hard, scything kick. Medoran leant back, causing the kick to miss him by a fraction of an inch. Before the general could bring his foot down again, Medoran smashed his own boot into the side of Cornak's other knee.

The general dropped to the ground, having just enough sense left to roll out of the way of Medoran's sword tip as it skewered the dirt where his head had been. While the swordsman jerked back on his weapon, pulling it free from the ground, Cornak kicked him in the small of the back. As Medoran stumbled forward, the general got slowly to his feet, feeling the fiery protests in his muscles. He sent out an angry thrust, followed by a sideways slash, back and forth. Medoran blocked each attack and in response, the swordsman backhanded his sword hilt into Cornak's face. The general blundered back, a thin trickle of blood coming from an open cut on his lip. He licked at it, tasting his own blood and smiled a little, exposing bloodied teeth.

Medoran stepped in again, this time going for a thrust to the general's stomach. Cornak stepped away and caught Med's arm, twisting it back painfully. As the swordsman cried out in pain, Cornak muttered, "You're tiring. Maybe you're not as good as you once were."

He pushed his opponent away again and stepped back a pace, watching him in amusement. Pain flared in the nerves around Medoran's right shoulder. His sword arm, already feeling weary and leaden, began to grow numb. He switched hands for a moment, flexing the fingers in his right hand to get the feeling back. The hand felt as if it was no longer a part of his body at all. Ignoring the cumbersome feel to his sword in his left hand, Medoran burst forward again, sending out a series of thrusts and slashes.

Cornak ducked a slash and turned his back on Medoran, allowing him to get in close. He jammed his elbow into Medoran's chest, winding him. The swordsman tumbled to the ground, feeling the air explode from his lungs painfully. His sword was flung from his grasp, clattering against a wall. The general stood up straight, looked from Medoran to the sword then back again.

Through his malevolent grin, he said, "It looks like it's over at last. You're beaten and so are your pitiful freedom fighters."

Medoran waited for him to get closer, allowing the general to believe the elbow to his ribcage had stunned him. As soon as he was close enough, the swordsman forced himself upright as quick as he could, hitting Cornak with a hard left uppercut. The punch struck the general under the jaw, causing him to stumble. Seizing the opportunity, Medoran dashed across and retrieved his sword. He ducked just in time as Cornak's blade swooped over his head. From the corner of his eye, he saw the general's other hand come into view, holding an ornate dagger. Another explosion of white hot pain flared in his ribs as the blade was driven between them. All his energy seemed suddenly drained. He felt his knees weaken, unable to hold him a moment longer. He looked down to see the dagger hilt sticking out of his chest. A harsh painful coughing fit overcame him. He could taste the iron tang of blood in his mouth as it came up from his lungs. Feeling the warmth dribble from his lips and down his chin, he looked back at Cornak. The general was smiling triumphantly. He raised his sword, ready to decapitate the fatally wounded swordsman's head.

Sneering, he said, "I win."

A sudden fire filled Medoran once more. The rage coursed through his veins, giving him one more burst of unnatural strength. He ducked out of the way of the life ending attack and answered with a side slash of his own. The edge of his sword opened the general's throat, causing a cascade of red to fall onto the ground. Cornak stumbled back a few paces, dropping his sword and clutching at the wound. His mouth gaped and eyes widened. Medoran shuffled backwards a few steps before falling against the wall. Landing in a sitting position he could only watch as Cornak's body weakened and pitched to the side. The last thing Medoran's one eye saw before it glazed over, was the lifeless corpse of his most hated enemy. The Black Flame General, traitor to the Empire was dead. As Med died, he smiled one last time in victory.

Chapter Twenty

Demien stiffened suddenly. Deep within her she was filled with a heavy feeling of dread. She looked to where she had last seen Cornak and Medoran battling. They had disappeared around the side of one building and the sound of fighting had ceased. The uneasy feeling filled her stomach. Without realising what she was doing, Demien sprinted across the yard and, turning the corner, she saw Cornak lying on the ground. The pool of blood around his head and neck was already congealing. The corners of her mouth flickered a little; it meant that her lover had proven himself to be the better swordsman. As she continued walking towards Cornak's body, she saw Medoran sitting slumped against the wall. She wanted to smile but a voice inside her screamed, telling her something was wrong. Carefully, she moved closer.

"Med?" she asked, uncertain if he could hear her. When he did not even stir at her voice, Demien suddenly sprinted the last few yards. Dropping to her knees beside him, she saw the dagger in his ribs. She placed her fingers under his jaw, gently lifting his head so she could look into his eye.

It stared out, lifelessly from his bruised face.

Tears stung her eyes as they ran down her cheeks. She cradled his head in both hands, leaning forward to kiss his forehead. Placing it gently back against the wall and closing his one eye with her fingers, she muttered, "It shouldn't have ended like this."

Cassmed jogged around the corner, stopping sharply as she saw Demien crouched by Medoran's body. She could feel Demien's grief so she backed away, feeling tears welling inside her. Rounding the corner again, she found Diarus, Boron, Gauduin and Qwan.

"What is it?" Boron asked, seeing the tears.

"Med," was all she could say in reply.

"Cornak?" Qwan asked quickly.

Cass nodded, "He's dead." The elf started forward but Cass put a restraining hand on his chest, keeping him back. "Give her a few moments please. They need to be alone," she was unable to keep her voice from choking.

"The other knights?" Boron started.

"Uthan woke up and killed two," Cass replied. "Harhn is searching the fortress now to make sure there aren't others hiding."

"Diarus and I killed about six or seven," Boron said with a satisfied nod.

"One small victory," Diarus added.

Cass looked up to him, clearly wanting to say something. Looking away again, she muttered, "I'll go and check on her."

Demien just stared, through a mist of tears at Medoran's face. His mouth was curled slightly, a smile of triumph. She reached out and stroked his cheek.

"He did it then," Cass said quietly.

"Yes. He did."

The girl placed a hand on her friend's shoulder, "I'm sorry, Demy. I really am."

Demien placed a hand over Cass's and looked up. For the first time since they had met, Cass looked back and saw her best friend broken. The usually strong jaw trembled; the unnervingly beautiful eyes were red from crying. Slowly she stood up and looked to the skies, unable to focus on anything else.

"We should get him inside," Cass said softly. "You too."

Diarus came from behind them. As gently as the Daiharlon could manage, he scooped Medoran's body up in his arms and carried him away. Cass led Demien behind them, holding onto her friend's arm.

Medoran lay on an infirmary bed. His face was peaceful, a faint smile fixed firmly across his lips. He wore a clean shirt of bold blue, open at the neck. His hands rested on his chest. To anyone who did not know the truth, they would swear he was merely sleeping.

Uthan stood calmly at the foot of the bed, staring at his travelling companion with misty eyes. In his hands he held the dagger that had slain Medoran. There had been a buzzing in his head when he had brushed his fingers over the hilt. The symbols etched along the blade had burned in his mind when he had seen them and the scrollwork on the hilt seemed to glow with a blue tint. Cornak had slain Medoran with the very dagger Uthan had had to retrieve. He could have laughed at the irony had it not claimed the life of his friend.

"You have the dagger," the Oracle said, his voice buzzing inside

Uthan's mind. It was not a question.

"Yes."

"Your destiny awaits you Uthan," the Oracle continued, "he knows you are coming now. The Black Flame must be stopped."

Not taking his eyes from the still form of Medoran, Uthan clenched his jaw and replied, "He will be."

Demien sat in a large common room. There were only a few others in the room with her, each of them keeping a distance from the warrior woman. She was half huddled on the table, her head resting in one hand as her arm was propped against the wood. Her eyes idly stared into the flames of a roaring fire to her right side. In front of her sat a large clay tankard of wine. In the flames she saw Medoran fighting in his berserk style. A style that was completely opposite to what she had expected of him the first time they had met. In her mind's eye, his sword flashed, dancing in a flamboyant display of deadly patterns. Each time it fell, so did an opponent. His image stopped fighting a moment and flashed a quick toothy smile.

She gripped the tankard so tightly her knuckles whitened. Deep inside her she could feel rage boiling in the pit of her stomach. Sitting upright on the bench again, she drained the tankard in one gulp, then stood up and paced around the table pausing to look once more into the flames. Without a sound, Demien hurled the tankard into the fireplace, scattering the embers. Ignoring the looks cast her way by the rest of the people in the room, Demien strode outside.

People scattered quickly, moving out of her path as she stalked across the yard to the gates. Cassmed stood in the doorway to the forge. Seeing her friend's direct movements towards the gates sent a chill rolling down the girl's spine. She shouted, racing across the courtyard to try and stop Demien as the warrior woman roughly shoved a refugee to one side and began to lift one of the huge bars on the gates. Qwan and Boron hurried out of the forge after Cassmed. The elf was the quickest of all three and caught up with Demien first. As he reached out to take her arm, she spun round, striking him hard on the jaw with her fist.

Boron was next to catch Demien. He saw the mask of white hot fury etched over her normally calm features. He stepped forward to try and grasp her when Cassmed pulled him back.

"No!" she hissed, watching her friend in horror, "she'll kill you."

"What the hell is she thinking?" Boron demanded. He tried to shrug free of Cassmed's grip as he watched Demien toss the heavy wooden beam to one side effortlessly.

"That's the problem," Cass answered, trying to step around Boron and carefully approach the warrior woman, "she isn't thinking."

"We need to stop her now," Boron said. He was about to add the words "before she opens the gates" but Demien was already pulling the left side gate open. Instead he shouted to Demien, "What are you doing?"

"She won't answer," Cass replied on Demien's behalf.

The girl started making her way calmly towards Demien. Trying to keep her voice soothing, she spoke, trying to calm her friend again. The warrior woman flashed a quick glance in her direction. The fury visible in her eyes was enough to halt Cassmed in her steps. From outside, they could already hear the shouts of Black Flame Knights seeing that the gates were opening.

Turning back to look at Boron, Cass answered his earlier question, "She wants a fight."

"She needs to rest," Uthan announced, striding past both Boron and Cassmed and right up behind Demien. He reached out a hand to tap her on the shoulder. Savagely she spun round and lashed out with a right hook that should have knocked Uthan's head from his shoulders. He merely leant back as if he had seen the punch coming. Demien's other hand quickly came up to try another blow. Uthan caught her wrist and pulled her effortlessly closer to him. She cast him a glare that would have turned many men to quivering wrecks but Uthan just stared calmly back.

As their eyes locked onto each other in a silent battle of wills, Uthan declared, "Sleep!"

As if all her energy had been drained, Demien dropped to her knees unconscious. Uthan caught her under the arms, stopping her from toppling completely to the ground.

"What did you do?" Cass demanded hotly, running over to take her friend from Uthan.

The mage did not answer; instead he raised a hand to the gates, palm outstretched. A barely seen ripple passed through the air, causing the gates to slam closed with a loud boom. Turning to Boron, he said, "We should bar these gates for now."

Having checked Demien was okay, Cass glared at Uthan. "When will she wake up?"

"Soon," Uthan answered. His face was blank and emotionless for a few moments. Slowly, the expression melted away, his concern shone through. "She'll be fine. I just put her to sleep for a few hours. Hopefully the rest will do her some good."

Boron laid a hand on his shoulder. A similar look of concern was evident on his face even as he congratulated Uthan.

Cass nodded, calming down a bit and said, "You're lucky she didn't kill you."

Uthan shrugged, trying to appear as nonchalant as he could. The pure animalistic fury in Demien's face haunted him however. He knew she could have easily killed him. Trying to put the image from his mind, he said, "I've split up many bar fights with a simple Sleep spell."

"Now, Cass, we put her to bed and you can explain exactly what happened here," Boron said. The tone of his voice suggested arguing was unwise. "And we need to know if something like this is going to happen again anytime soon."

"When she wakes up, she's going to be really mad," Cass said, as Uthan helped her carry Demien into the infirmary so the healer could make sure she was fine.

"Maybe," Uthan said quickly.

"No maybe about it, Uthan, she will be," Cass answered. "You don't go Primal then fall asleep and forget about it."

"Speaking of which," Boron said, entering the infirmary, "what the hell went on with her out there?"

Cass shrugged and sat on the bed next to Demien. "I can only tell you some of it."

"Then you'd better start talking, girl," Boron said quickly.

She stared at him coolly, then began, "When one of us suffers a severe traumatic experience we can go into a rage. That's the Primal state. We don't recognise anyone as friend or foe, just something that is there to be killed."

"Pure bloodlust," Uthan said with a nod.

Boron glanced at the mage, then back at Cass, "What do you mean by 'we'?"

"That I can't tell you," Cass said.

"Can't or won't?" Boron asked.

"Both." The giant exhaled deeply but Cass put a hand up, stopping him from saying anything else. "Just let's leave it like that."

"That isn't much of an explanation," he said gruffly.

"No," Cass replied, "but it'll have to be enough."

"Will she continue this Primal thing when she wakes up?"

With a rueful smile, Cass answered, "More than likely. It's not something you can just put aside."

"So what do we do with her?" Boron asked.

"One thing is for certain," Cass said, her voice now grave and serious. She gestured to another bed across the room. The healer stood over it, tending to an injured man. "You really shouldn't leave him in the same room with Demy."

The man was Kaiss and upon seeing him, Boron's mouth opened in disgust, "What is he doing here?"

"He's still alive," the healer said, looking up. "Cornak didn't cut him deeply enough to kill him."

"If he let Cornak in then he should have died," Boron hissed his reply.

There was a snort from Cassmed, "He let him in alright and if Demy knows he's in here, she'll slaughter him."

"There's nowhere else to put either of them," Boron explained. "These two are currently the most unpopular people here. They hate him and are scared shitless of Demien."

"I'll put a guard in here and make sure we keep them separated," the healer said.

"Oh that's good, she'll kill the guard just to get at him," Cass fired back.

"No, she won't," Uthan said suddenly. "I'll keep my eye on them."

Uthan sat studying the leather bound spell book of Hedrial's. He had sat close by the sleeping form of Demien for a few hours now. From the edge of his vision he saw the blue light shimmer into existence.

Dionis on appearing asked, "Are you feeling better?"

"A lot," Uthan answered.

"You woke up and slew a pair of knights who came in here to kill you," Dionis continued, "I saw the spell you used."

"I didn't even realise I knew it," Uthan said, "I was barely awake and then the images were in my mind."

"Do you think you could cast it again?" Dionis asked.

"I've been searching the book to find it," Uthan replied, "but it doesn't seem to be here."

"It isn't," Dionis said, "Hedrial didn't know it."

"Then how would I?"

"That," Dionis said carefully, "is something I'd like to know the answer to myself. You shouldn't know it; the mage who created it was very jealous of his work. No one has ever learned how it was done. Leave it with me and I'll be back soon."

He faded into the air again, restoring the room to its natural light once more. No sooner had the blue light faded from the room than explosions of brilliant colour erupted in front of Uthan's eyes. He felt the sharp cracking blow against the back of his skull moments before he crumpled forward to the floor.

Behind him stood Demien. In her right hand she held a thick white candle. She watched Uthan fall with a blank emotionless look before striding across the infirmary to stand over her prey. "Kaiss?" she said, gently.

He opened his eyes but seeing Demien standing over him, he paled.

"Is it true? Did you really let Cornak in?" she asked. One hand casually brushed a few hairs from his forehead. "No, it's okay. I understand I know you did."

Kaiss's eyes widened a little, making him appear like an animal caught in a trap. He opened his mouth to say something but his wound prevented him from speaking.

"It's okay, I know you feel bad. It's only right that you should do so." The warrior woman suddenly leaned closer to him until her face was mere inches away. The hateful fires rekindled in her eyes again as she hissed, "You brought about Medoran's death today. As far as I'm concerned you have as much guilt resting on your shoulders as Cornak did."

Kaiss now understood he was looking into the eyes of his killer. He tried to push Demien away but the cut to his throat had robbed him of his strength. Kaiss could not have moved a tiny kitten, much less the Primal warrior woman in front of him. Demien moved away, straightening up again.

"You make me sick, Kaiss. We protected you for so long and this is how you repay us."

The aromas of warm, meaty broth and freshly baked bread assaulted Cass's nostrils as she shifted her weight in the chair again. She sat at a long table, idly dipping a spoon into a bowl of broth in front of her. Her appetite had eluded her completely. Her companions sat with her around the table discussing how to break the siege but their words were nothing more than a droning to Cass. All she could think about was her grief at Medoran's death. Each time she thought about him though, her mind wandered to the one who had let General Cornak into Dessendor. He was still alive and lying in a bed close to Demien. Suddenly she sat bolt upright on her chair, everyone looking at her sharply.

"What is it?" Qwan asked quickly, reaching out a hand to steady the girl, fearing she was about to fall.

"It's Demien," Cass said. "She's awake!"

Before they could register the words, Cass kicked her chair away and sprinted out of the room, heading to the infirmary.

A slanting beam of afternoon sunlight cut through the window, picking out the polished steel of the healer's knife as Demien looked along its flawless edge. She turned her gaze back across to Kaiss, who was in return, watching with wide terrified eyes. Demien arched an eyebrow, "You're sorry, is that it?"

Kaiss nodded, closing his eyes for a moment, tears streaming down his cheeks.

"Oh! I suppose that makes it okay then. I guess that means you're forgiven," Demien ranted. She paced back across the room while holding the knife tightly in her left hand, "Make sure you apologise to Medoran."

"Demy! No!" Cass yelled, running into the room.

"Get out, Cass," Demy said, coldly. She did not look at her friend; instead she raised the knife to Kaiss's throat. The tip of the blade pressed against his flesh, drawing a small pinprick of blood.

A moment later, she felt hands pressed against her neck as someone jumped up onto her back. Then legs wrapped around her waist, stopping her from dislodging her assailant. The knife was involuntarily dropped from her grasp as she brought both hands up to try and pull her attacker away.

Uthan brought his head in close to her ear, "You need to sleep."

The soft comforting feel of sleep sapped at Demien's resistance. She struggled in Uthan's grip, gradually growing weaker and finally, she dropped to one knee. All the time, Kaiss watched from his bed, unable to comprehend what was happening.

A heartbeat before Demien submitted to the drowsy feelings, Uthan whispered, "When you wake you will feel no more pain. I will hold it for you."

Flashes of bright white light filled the room, causing Cass and Kaiss to both instantly close their eyes. Diarus ran into the room, holding his arms in front of his face to shield it from the blinding light. Sunlight began to cast strange shadows in the dull afterglow as Uthan let go of Demien's head again. He stumbled back a few paces before landing heavily on his backside. He rubbed at his eyes, fighting the sudden overwhelming urge to cry; he could feel the tears building up. He shook uncontrollably, clenching and unclenching his fists. Panting like an animal, he muttered, "I've taken her pain away. She'll sleep easier this time, I hope."

"You did what?" Cass asked incredulously.

"Her pain and grief at losing Medoran, it's all in me now," Uthan replied, struggling to rise. Staggering and swaying, he left the infirmary and headed into the main courtyard.

Chapter Twenty-One

Uthan sat on the catwalk staring down at the funeral pyre. A dull rhythmic pounding drummed on in his head, as a reminder of the blow he had taken earlier in the day. The headache had sapped at his concentration all afternoon, making it difficult to cast. The chill in the air had only taken away the bite, turning it from a stabbing, mind-numbing pain to a dull echo. He had spent the last hour looking out of Dessendor, turning to magic to fine-tune his sight. He had watched the Black Flame Knights construct crude siege ladders and a battering ram.

Down below him in the courtyard, people were gathering. Everyone stood around the pyre to pay his or her respects to Medoran. Some stood close to Demien, placing a consoling hand on her shoulder as they passed. Since taking her pain from her earlier in the day, Uthan had seen Demien lose her berserker fury and become calm again. She still mourned the loss of her lover but now she was not attempting to kill those who came too close.

Seeing the swordsman's body given up to the flames of the pyre brought pangs of grief to Uthan. He fought back the tears, trying to remember that, even though he mourned the loss of a friend, the grief he was feeling was Demien's. It was the pain of a lost love, not a comrade killed in battle.

"So this is where you are," said Cassmed quietly. Her voice pulled him from his thoughts sharply, almost causing him to start.

He settled back against the stone again, calming himself. At first he showed no reaction as the girl came closer and sat immediately beside him. Cocking his head slightly away, he looked at her. Her face in the torchlight was stunning, the eyes especially so. They were a deep brown on the surface and seemed so innocent, yet he could see the fear and pain grown from everything she had seen in her life.

Cass turned her gaze away from the burning funeral pyre and spoke in a hushed voice, "You've been up here all afternoon."

Uthan just shrugged in reply before Cassmed smiled weakly and, looking him in the eyes, continued. "I've seen Medoran kill so many men over the past year. There've been times when he's fought and hasn't even broken a sweat. I started to believe he was immortal." A cloud of sadness crossed her face, forcing her to look away at the pyre again. "Now I know he's not. It's a scary thing to have the illusions you build of someone shattered in such a way. Does that make sense?"

"Yeah," Uthan nodded as Cass grew silent, too choked up to say any more. Then he said gently, "Maybe you should settle down somewhere safe when this siege is over. Get away from the fighting."

Cassmed shook her head slowly, "I wish it could be that simple, Uthan. I honestly do." She looked into his questioning glance and continued, "Demien and I were told to help you. And she won't abandon this quest or any of you now. There's no way she'll do anything else until she has her revenge for Med's death."

"What about when she does? What will happen then?" Uthan asked after a moment's pause.

"She and Med were going to go to Draseus. She thought Med was going to settle down on a farm or open some kind of surgery. They had talked a lot about marriage before he lost his eye," she said slowly.

"Things changed after the torture then?"

At first Cass only nodded. Then, as if the following silence was compelling her to continue, she explained the history between Medoran and his most hated adversary. She explained how Cornak had raided the village, then captured and tortured Medoran. Ending the story, she added, "Med had carried that hate with him for a long time. He'd spent his life since then finding ways to hurt Cornak. He was trying to lead small villages into uniting to rebel against the Black Flame Knights. He wanted to mould them into a new version of the People's army, the type of army he had fought in alongside the Royal Knights during the beast wars. He was doing this when we met him. Demien and I were travelling at the time."

Cass then went on with the tale and explained how they had come upon a small group of houses, not even a village, and had been attacked by Black Flame Knights. This had been close to the beginning of her training so she had been no use to Demien. The experienced warrior woman had not been able to drop Cass off somewhere and hope that she would remain safe. So they had ridden hard across some hills as the knights had chased them for a couple of hours. One of Medoran's men had seen the chase and sent out a message for aid. By the time they had reached the next village, there had been about fifty men waiting for the knights. It had been a slaughter not a battle.

Uthan said slowly, "Medoran's fight is over now though. He can find peace."

"He can," Cass agreed, "but Demy can't. She loved him so much she wants to finish this and train me so she can die and be with him. In her mind she is ready to die, she wants to, she just can't right now. She has to stay alive for only the gods know how long because she has a job to do."

After a few moments reflection, Uthan laughed once. Cassmed looked at him, eyebrows raised in an unspoken request for him to explain the joke to her.

"Ever since we met up I've been wondering why you're here with us. If I didn't know you, I wouldn't have thought of you as a fighter, and it's only recently I've seen that side of you really come out. Everyone else kind of has a personal reason that I can see. But you, it's almost as if you came along for the ride."

"In a way I did," Cassmed replied, her voice carrying a seemingly infinite weight of sadness. "By nature I don't think I really am a warrior. I know I'm not ready for all of this." She waved a hand around her at the fortress.

"You are really good with a bow though," Uthan started, trying to sound positive.

"One of the best Demy has seen," Cass said. Her tone suggested she did not quite believe it herself.

"You're one of the best I've seen," Uthan said.

"And how many archers have you really paid attention to?" Cass asked, raising an eyebrow. As Uthan shrugged, she continued, "Anyway, I had nowhere else to go. There's nowhere safe enough in Demy's eyes except at her side. And I no longer have a family."

"Dead?"

"No, they're alive. They just pretty much disowned me," Cass replied.

"They disowned you because of this?" Uthan asked, shocked.

Cassmed nodded and continued, "Demien was told my whereabouts by the High Priest of the order. I couldn't believe it at the time. All my life my mother had always shown a great pride and love of my younger sister. I had never once heard her say she was proud of me. So when Demien came with the news about me I couldn't wait to tell my parents. They had to be proud of me then, right? Wrong. That night around the dinner table I told them about it. But my mother wasn't really interested. She was too busy telling me how my sister's riding was coming along. At one point that night she actually stopped me in the middle of what I was saying and told me she was sick of hearing about it."

Uthan felt sudden pangs of hurt, remembering his parents and how they had been when he had been chosen. He forced his mind back to where he was now, listening to Cassmed instead, believing that Demien's pain would just make the memories feel worse.

"For most of my life at home, my mother had always treated my sister as if she was the only child there. I hadn't been born to them, or I was an inconvenience. Demien gave me a way out of that. My mother was constantly trying to tell me I wasn't good enough for it in the week before I went. I wasn't fit enough, or strong enough or clever enough. I felt I wasn't welcome in their home again. She didn't say the words but that was what was implied. I can never go back there," Cassmed explained.

She went back to watching the funeral pyre burn steadily. Beside it stood Demien, half cloaked in shadow, half in orange firelight. Even though the warrior woman was standing amongst people, she seemed solitary, lost in her mourning.

"Thank you for taking her pain away," Cass said suddenly. "I wish there was something I could do for you in return."

"It's nothing," Uthan said. He could feel his neck and cheeks reddening a little.

She got to her feet and looked out between the merlons at the camp. Between the wooden windshield walls she could see the lights from the campfires. Even with the darkness of night shrouding them, she could make out the tiny shapes of men working on siege towers. Three tall ones, reaching nearly fifty feet in height had been built over the course of the day. There was also a small catapult.

"We think they'll attack tomorrow sometime. They're building towers and making their final preparations now," she said.

"They've been building them all afternoon," Uthan said. He remained seated on the catwalk, watching the pyre burn away. "Ladders and a battering ram too."

"You don't sound too bothered by any of this, Uthan," Cass said. "Do you know something we don't?"

"We could all be dead this time tomorrow," he answered slowly.

"That sounds hopeful," Cass replied with just a hint of sarcasm.

Uthan shrugged and returned her gaze while standing up. Stretching, he sighed and said, "I don't know anything about tactics. I just know there's a lot more of them than there is of us. The only thing I can see in our favour is we're in here and they're out there."

Cassmed felt a chill run down her spine. Instinctively she hugged herself to keep the cold at bay. Keeping her gaze locked on Uthan's eyes she asked, "Uthan, have you ever been in love before?"

He turned back to look at her. He shook his head and answered, "No. Not really." Again he looked out at the campfires, this time with an immense look of loss in his eyes. "Now it looks as if I'll never get a chance."

Feeling Cassmed move to stand closer beside him, he turned around. She was staring directly into his eyes. Something deep inside made him want to step closer. Then he did so. The kiss that followed seemed to take forever to come as they moved their heads together so slowly.

Then, that something that had made him yield to the kiss stirred. The hair on his forearms and neck stood on end. Carefully he moved his arms around to embrace Cassmed. Tingling rippled throughout his entire being as he felt her arms wrap themselves around his waist. She pulled him closer, crushing their bodies together so he could feel the warmth of her skin through their clothing. He felt her tongue slide forward, softly tracing the lines of his lips. Inside his head, Uthan felt himself growing dizzy. Fireworks exploded on the inside of his closed eyelids and a shudder passed through him. Blood began to heat up in the region of his chest; next it raced throughout the network of arteries inside his body. A heavy drumming sound caught in his ears, threatening to explode at any time.

Trembling he pulled away from the kiss, his breathing had become harder. Uthan could actually feel his pulse as if the rushing of hot blood would burst his veins. He had known his first real kiss would be memorable, but the soft embrace and warm touch of Cassmed's lips had gone beyond any expectation he might have had. The fire still burned throughout him, making him subconsciously wonder if he would not burn up completely. Cassmed's eyes bored into him, a sense of wonder and enjoyment betrayed by their glow. The cloak of loss and despair still hung within, but now merely a background to the other new feelings. She moved her arms away from his waist, pulling herself free from his embrace as she did so. Uthan had begun to consider something might have been wrong when she reached forward and took his hand.

Her touch was warm and soft and squeezing his fingers tenderly she whispered, "Come with me."

Once more Uthan obeyed the instinct that told him to go. Their hands were clasped so firmly together Uthan secretly wondered what it would take to tear them apart at that moment in time. They moved along the catwalk and down the stairs silently. Cassmed's eyes had focused on the doorway to the room she had been sleeping in. She led him towards it, moving through the shadowy courtyard quietly. She did not appear to notice the knowing gazes coming from Qwansien, Gauduin and Boron, or the faint but genuinely warm smile from Demien. As they moved into the gloom beyond, Uthan wondered if any of them heard the bolts slide home as Cassmed closed and locked the door behind them.

The frantic shouts rose Uthan, bringing him back from his peaceful slumber. He opened his eyes, feeling the lids sticking together a little, and turned his head.

Cassmed's head lay on the pillow next to his. Her long brown hair partially covered her face, showing only a hint of the sensual lips and one closed eye. Without moving, she groaned.

"What are they yelling?" she asked, sleepily.

Uthan sat bolt upright, making out words in the shouts. Throwing the covers from him, he quickly dressed and started towards the door.

Then Cassmed heard it too. Her eyes flashed open and sitting up, she asked, "This is it, isn't it."

Uthan nodded to her and ran out of the room. Outside, the battlements were alive with people, running to carry out orders barked at them by Boron and Qwansien. As he jogged up onto the catwalk to stand with them, the elf turned to him.

"Don't worry, we asked them to wait till you two were finished," he joked.

Uthan flushed a deep shade of red, forcing a smile under the knowing stares of Qwan and the others. To regain his composure he looked out across the fields. Not far behind him, Cass followed, buckling the straps of Demien's old armour.

The Black Flame camp had been torn down. The logs from the walls had been used to make barricades. Poles had been inserted into the barricades to allow them to be lifted and carried across the battlefield. Three tall siege towers were being moved in a circle to surround Dessendor, keeping just out of bow range. The small catapult that had been constructed stood between two of the barricades, guarded by a team of men.

"They're keeping the towers far enough back," Harhn said, coming over to the others on the battlements.

Boron nodded, stroking his beard, "They will. I should think they'll create some diversion here," he said, pointing a finger to a quickly sketched map of the fortress. "That'll draw our attention away from those towers so they can get them close to the walls. That, I guess will be their plan anyway."

"Uthan," Qwan asked, "can you cast some kind of Fire spell on those towers?"

A loud crack sounded from across the field and all eyes turned to the catapult. Those quick enough could see the small black barrel sailing through the air toward them. Many on the ramparts ducked hurriedly. Keeping his eyes fixed on the barrel, Uthan raised a hand and high overhead, the barrel exploded in a cloud of black sulphurous smoke. Wooden splinters rained down from the sky, mere yards away from the solid gates of Dessendor.

"Blasting powder!" Gauduin muttered, cramming closer to the wall to see.

Qwan squinted through the smoke, across to where the remnants of the Black Flame camp was situated, "Where are they storing it?" he asked, almost to himself.

Off to the elf's left, Boron ordered their archers to open fire. A cascade of piercing death was sent out, raining down on the closest ranks of the enemy soldiers. A dozen of them fell under the arrows. Across the battlements of Dessendor, Boron watched his archers firing at will. The Ghosts were picking off targets easily but the village refugees were not as accurate.

"Take a second to aim and pick your targets carefully," Boron said loudly.

One man shouted and pointed out to the field. Qwan raced across to look at where the man was indicating. Six wide ladders were being dragged across the grassland. Beside each one was a large siege crossbow with thick, slick looking rope tied to the end of the grappling hooks. At the opposite end of the wall, six more ladders were hauled into position. Knights, with heavy hammers, slammed the firing pins of the crossbows. Bowstrings thumped loudly, firing the solid iron grappling hooks over the walls. From the periphery of his vision, Qwan saw one puncture the chest of a Ghost archer, killing the man outright. The ladders were quickly in upright positions, having been hauled up by horses. Knights ran at the ladder bases, beginning their frantic climbing before they had even been secured.

Gauduin unsheathed his sword and swung at one of the ropes. His blade bit hard into the slimy looking sisal, cutting it half away. The ladder rocked badly, unsteady the now weakened rope. Several of the village archers dropped their bows and took up their swords instead, following the dwarf's lead.

Qwan brought his crossbow up, touched the bolt tip to a flaming brazier and fired on the nearest of the ropes. The bolt head slammed home, cutting the rope deeply. The flames however, were immediately extinguished. He looked round to another pair of Ghosts who had chosen to copy him. Qwan just shook his head and called to them, "Don't bother. The ropes have been soaked. Flames are useless this time."

Another loud explosion sounded near the gates.

"More powder casks," hissed Qwansien, looking over to Gauduin.

"Uthan, if you've got some big spell to use, now would be a good time!" Gauduin yelled, taking a swing at a knight as the man's head appeared at the top of a ladder.

The young mage was behind him, kneeling on the battlements. Sweat beaded on his forehead as he fought for concentration amongst the chaos of the attack.

Another ladder slammed against the merlons to his left. Immediately a rope loop was hooked over the wall, holding the ladder in place. A Ghost archer fired at the first knight to appear over the top. Receiving an arrow to his throat, the man fell back, knocking the next four men beneath him from the rungs.

Quickly, Demien ran across, knife in hand. She sliced through the rope loop and called a pair of men to her. One of them grabbed hold of the ladder's top and strained but the warrior woman put a hand on his shoulder. Shaking her head, she said, "Push it to the side. Their weight won't let it fall away. But to the side, well maybe we can take a few of the others with it as well."

The men nodded in agreement and, with a broad smile, the first man grabbed two thick handfuls of the broken rope and jerked it back hard. From the other side, the second man and Demien pushed the ladder. The timbers groaned in loud protest as the weight of the armoured knights sent it toppling to the side. It smashed against a second, then a third and a fourth, taking them to the ground with it and sending yet more of the attacking force screaming to their deaths. Boron ran over, his bowstring pulled taut and he leaned out over the wall and fired. Pulling the string tight, he fired repeatedly at the knights below. Three more ladders were sent crashing to the ground along the other side of the wall. Screams went up from below as knights were crushed under the weight of the timbers and their comrades. Bodies bounced from the ground like rag dolls. Everywhere a ladder crashed, Ghost archers ran to the walls and fired down, making sure there were no survivors.

A third explosion sounded, sending tremors through the stonework as a cask of blasting powder erupted against the wall. Defenders close by were thrown from their feet.

"Someone deal with that catapult!" bellowed Boron, taking aim at a pair of knights trying to reach one of the surviving ladders.

Uthan stood up suddenly and turning to Boron said, "Fire an arrow into the air."

Boron reacted immediately, then looked back at Uthan. The mage's eyes flashed bright blue. Raising a hand with two fingers extended, he gestured to the arrow. The sky above them darkened with thick black storm clouds. Men not already committed to fighting looked to the heavens and many offered a silent prayer. The arrow exploded in the sky, becoming hundreds more. As they began to rain down over the battlefield they caught fire. More arrows appeared to shoot down through the clouds, diving into the field. As if they were liquid, the flames splashed over enemy soldiers, horses and barricades, burning them all. Knights and their mounts ran in all directions, screaming in panic and agony as flames torched their bodies. The smell of burning flesh and hair caught on the wind and reached the defenders, turning their stomachs.

Gauduin pointed to the catapult and chuckled. The wood was covered in flames. One of the fire arrows had struck a powder cask loaded onto the catapult. The resulting explosion had scattered blazing debris everywhere. The team of knights whose job it had been to guard and use the weapon were lying on the scorched grass, dead, smoke curling up from their blackened bodies.

"The towers!" someone yelled from the western wall.

Qwan, Demien and Serriman all turned to look. Fiery arrows were still raining from the sky, mingling with those fired by the archers on the walls. The three tall wooden siege towers were shrouded in flames and the knights were desperately trying to put the fires out.

There were shouts from another section of the walls where the enemy was climbing into the fortress. Instantly, Demien and Qwan were running, bounding across the battlements' walkway. Demien punched an attacking knight in the face as he pulled himself over the merlons from a ladder. On his way past, Qwan grabbed the top upright of the ladder and pulled it with him. Next, Demien jumped in amongst a trio of attacking knights, immediately ducking into a crouch and cleaving the legs from the first two.

Hearing more shouts of alarm, Boron looked around to see a cluster of knights spilling over another section of wall. Harhn and a pair of Ghosts were being driven back, allowing more of the enemy to enter Dessendor. Boron gestured with his sword at the enemy and yelled, "We've got a breach!"

"We're on it," Gauduin called, running past Boron with Cassmed hot on his heels.

Two knights had clambered through a gap in the merlons and had quickly slaughtered four of the defenders on the wall. Sprinting for them, Cass easily overtook the dwarf. The girl had dropped her bow and was now surging across the wooden walkway, sword firmly in hand. The first of the knights saw her coming a moment too late. Cass skidded to a halt at his left side before thrusting the tip of her sword up under his jaw. The blade had been driven in with enough force that it jammed against the top of his helm. Not wasting time on retrieving her weapon, Cass instead took the dead knight's sword from his hand, before pushing the body to one side. She twisted sideways, allowing a pool of slick blood on the wooden planks to work to her advantage.

The remaining knight brought his sword down with a heavy chopping motion that could have cleaved the girl in two. But lashing out with an armoured boot, Cass struck him in the stomach. The blow did nothing more than knock her opponent off balance. Then as he moved back to try a second swing, Gauduin collided with him. For a moment both dwarf and knight pitched into the wall. The knight tripped and fell, trying in vain to grab a firm hold as he went back into the gap between merlons. Cass grasped Gauduin's shoulder, pulling him back from a possible fall. At the same time, she leant against the dwarf, using him to propel her into the air. Both of her boots were driven into the off balance knight, sending him over the wall and to his death.

Looking at the girl and impressed, Gauduin paused long enough to say, "You're getting good at this, girl."

On the west wall, Qwan heard Boron's warning and turned to see the knights advancing. He patted Demien on the shoulder and said, "You take care of this, I'm going to help over there."

Serriman nodded, too out of breath to answer with words. Demien pushed Qwan's hand away before whirling in amongst another small cluster of the enemy. Slicing the head from the first and stabbing the second through the stomach plate, she turned to Serriman and yelled, "We need to clear this wall now!"

With a loud cry of exertion, Diarus ran over. In his hands he held a huge block of granite, taken from the stone wall of Dessendor itself. He carried it over to the ladder and just dropped it. From below there were screams of agony and the sounds of breaking wood as the granite block smashed its way through the rungs. The Daiharlon then reached out and using only one hand picked up a knight by the throat and hurled him over the side.

Meanwhile, Qwan ran across the ramparts to meet his chosen opponents. Jumping up onto one of the merlons and running along the edge of the wall itself, the elf kicked at a ladder. It swayed violently, causing one of the climbers to lose his grip and tumble to the ground. A volley of arrows sailed overhead as Black Flame archers sought to take the elf out. Ignoring them, he leapt down in amongst the invaders on the battlement walkway, swinging his sword and spinning on his heels in a whirling dance. Skewering one knight through the face then spinning away to cleave open the jaw of another, Qwan dispatched the enemy with relative ease. He spun his blade into a dagger grip and thrust it under his arm and up, lancing into the underside of another knight's jaw. Sliding the blade free again and dumping the man's body over the side, he looked around. The walls were nearly clear and as he looked at the field outside, he realised Uthan's Fire Arrow spell had dwindled away It had left only thick, black smoke curling up from scorched areas of ground and the towers had become flaming ruins.

He caught movement to east and shouted, "Archers on the move!"

A group of forty riders raced off to the eastern woods, heading into the tree line.

"They're skirting around us," hissed Boron.

From the western wall, Harhn shouted, "Archers to the west!"

Following his outstretched arm, they saw another group of riders separating from the main army. In front of them, more archers crept forward, moving to kneel behind the barricades again. Demien glanced at the mage who was kneeling on the ramparts a few feet away.

"Uthan," she called waiting for him to acknowledge her before she continued, "do you have anything else ready to throw at them?"

"I'm working on it," he breathed.

Agonised screams came from the east wall. They turned to see a group of archers, mainly refugee villagers, tumble from the ramparts, arrows protruding from their bodies. Screams and shouts followed as the few remaining defenders tried to return fire. More arrows whistled overhead from the west as the archers there charged out from the trees. Pulling Qwan and Demien with him, Gauduin ducked behind the wall, waiting as the arrows sailed past.

Qwan rose to his feet quickly and fired an arrow of his own. From the ground he heard the scream of a horse as the steel arrowhead struck its flank. Sitting back behind the stone again, he muttered, "Whatever Uthan has coming, I wish he'd hurry up."

"Heaven's fire took a lot of magical energy," Demien said. "I've only ever seen it once before and the mage casting it had to rest for hours afterwards."

A huge roar went up from the north end of the field, where the main bulk of the Black Flame army had been waiting, unscathed by Uthan's earlier spell.

"From the sound of that we don't have hours," Qwan answered as he moved at a half crouching height along the walkway. Passing Ghost archers, he tried to fire upon the enemy until he reached the north wall. There he peered out between two merlons and cursed.

With shields surrounding them, so making an impregnable box of steel, a group of men charged between the smoking barricades across the field. Around them, archers sent a hail of steel tipped missiles, keeping the defenders from the wall as much as possible. As the phalanx got closer to Dessendor, the men threw off their shields, revealing a long heavy battering ram.

"They're going for the gates!" yelled one of the defenders.

As if to silence him, an arrow pierced his upper chest. The momentum carried him back, sending him plummeting to the courtyard below. In his place, three Ghost archers swarmed to the wall, bowstrings thumping. Below them, the gates shuddered loudly as the ram crew slammed against them. Showers of mortar dust rained down from between the blocks, shaken loose by the impact.

"Those gates have stood for two centuries," Serriman said proudly. "It'll take more than a Black Flame ram to break them down. At least, I hope it will."

The ram struck the gates a second, then a third time. On the third strike, the distinctive sound of cracking wood was audible. A look of horror passed across the faces of those directly above the gates as they heard the unmistakable sound.

Qwan heard it too. He patted Serriman on the shoulder and said, "Hope just ran out."

To their right side, Boron yelled to his archers, "Will someone please shoot that ram crew!"

There was no need for a second order. Seven archers stood up and fired down on them, ignoring the hail of covering arrows that came in return from the Black Flame barricades. Two more of the Ghosts fell back, clutching arrows to their chests. Qwan stood up quickly and fired down into the top of one knight's head. The tip punched a hole through the man's helmet and into his skull. As he fell, another knight quickly ran over to take his place at the battering ram.

"We can't shoot the entire army, Qwan," Boron called across to the elf, "and they're breaking those gates."

"Uthan!" Qwan yelled, "Do you have that spell ready yet?"

"A Trap spell on the gates is about all I have the energy to do right now," he replied, moving to sit next to the elf.

Qwan twisted to his feet, fired again and dropped back to his previous sitting position again as more black arrows sailed overhead. He ordered, "Do it then."

"It won't last for long though and it won't take them all out," Uthan tried to explain.

The gates boomed again and the cracking sound was louder this time. Taking the steps two at a time, Uthan ran to the gates. The sight in front of him made his blood freeze. Thick, splintered cracks had formed in the wood. Three of the seven bars locking the gates had snapped. He dashed across to kneel in front of the huge entranceway as they boomed again. The cracks widened as the centre sections were pushed inwards. He heard the screams of men in agony as arrows from above found their targets. A moment later Diarus was next to the mage, both falchions drawn and ready in case the battering ram was to break through.

"The moment they shatter the gates, a hail of black glass fragments will rain down and shred those around the gates and wall," Uthan told his friend. "We need to clear the wall."

"Retreat from the walls!" Diarus bellowed suddenly. Another loud cracking sounded now a large section of the gates were nearly in splinters. With a lot more urgency in his voice, Diarus added, "Now!"

"What's going on down there?" Boron asked, coming over to Qwan as the elf fired again.

"Uthan is placing a Trap spell on the gates. It'll do a lot of damage to this wall, if it's triggered."

"If it's triggered?" Boron replied with a laugh.

"What do we do from down there? Wait and fight them as they come through?" asked one of the closest of the Ghosts in horror.

The elf shrugged. "I guess so, unless someone else has a bright plan."

"Actually I do," Serriman said with grin. As all eyes fell on him, he grinned again and asked, "Not afraid of the dark, are you?"

Down in the courtyard, Diarus watched as the battlements began to empty of defenders. They ran down the steps and flooded away from the wall, going into the buildings and ushering the fearful occupants out to follow them. Meanwhile Gauduin trotted over to the gates and told Diarus of Serriman's plan.

"Go on," the Daiharlon said without looking away. "I'll bring Uthan in a moment."

Gauduin glanced at the breaking gates as they boomed once more. A small cluster of arrows cascaded over the wall, killing one of the village refugees as he emerged from the doorway of a building. The man did not scream, merely pitched forward to the ground. In his dying arms a small child, no more than three years old, pushed herself from him and ran, crying in horror. She quickly joined the collection of women and children who emerged from doorways and were being led away. Beside the victim, a Green Ghost archer fired an arrow back over the walls, leaving it to pure chance that he had actually hit anything other than the ground.

A heartbeat later, Uthan was on his feet again and running from the gates while screaming to Diarus, "It's ready."

Serriman led them all into a small stone building set against the southernmost walls. At first sight, it appeared to be nothing more than a small area for guards to take shelter from the rain. Many did not see the old knight push a small stone behind the lip of the entrance. A section of the stone floor dropped down, forming steps that led into a pitch-black stairwell. Lighting a torch, Serriman led them all down the steps and into a vast underground room. The torchlight added an unsettling element. Using a voice filled with awe, Serriman dropped to one knee, and then, offering a salute he said, "The Hall of the Dead."

The gasps coming from the defenders as they entered the hall for the first time echoed in the great space. In the small circle of light around them, they could see row upon row of stone caskets lined the floor. On the lids, stone figures had been crafted, representing the brave or mighty Royal Knight sealed within. The air was musty and had an oppressive feel to it. They could all tell that the tomb went on a lot further into the darkness ahead but the heavy atmosphere had quickly quenched any thirst for exploration. Dust showers fell from the ceiling as the steady rhythmic pounding on the gates continued. Fearful eyes all looked upwards, as if they could see through the stone separating them from the courtyard. Serriman ushered the last few remaining defenders in through the doorway and pushed on another stone. Behind the door, the stone steps rose up to the roof again, sealing off the entrance.

"Is there another way out of here?" Demien asked, wandering across to the closest wall.

"No, only one way in," Serriman answered her. "It's a tomb, remember."

"So we're trapped down here?" She snapped her head round to glare at the old knight before she moved across to one of the caskets and sat on the stone lid. Ignoring the wincing from Serriman, she asked, "So, if we hide here long enough they'll go away? Is that your plan?"

The pounding from above grew in intensity. Even through the sound was dulled by the rock, they could hear the telltale cracking sounds as the gate gave way. One child whimpered and a woman began sobbing uncontrollably. Then, as if from the heavens, they all heard the sharp cracking thunder. Wind whistled down, carrying with it the sound of something else. At first it sounded like rain or hail, then, as it came closer, it was like the sound of millions of arrows whooshing past. Things struck against the courtyard floor with a chorus of sharp pinging. Quietly at first, this wave of sound was punctuated by the wet screams of men being torn to shreds and the harsh scraping of metal being ripped apart.

Qwan looked at Uthan, "That's it triggered then?"

As the young mage nodded, Qwan asked, "So what do we do now?"

"We stay here and hide obviously," Demien answered sarcastically.

The background noise signalling the death of many above subsided. Qwansien quickly stepped forward. Nodding to Serriman, he asked, "Is there any chance they can find their way down here to us?" Serriman replied that there was not.

"Good," the elf responded before he asked, "Uthan, can you cast again?"

"Not at the moment," Uthan replied. He sat down heavily against a casket, dropping his head to his hands.

"How long until you can?"

"I don't know. I couldn't do either of those spells before today," he slurred, as if he was fighting sleep.

"Okay, as soon as you can tell me," Qwansien continued. He moved onto Boron. "Casualties?"

The giant looked at him, lines of weariness were etched on his face. Sweat and black dust streaked his forehead. His eyes were dull and lifeless as he spoke, "I counted thirty-two. Eleven were Ghosts."

The news hit the elf like a rock. He sat down heavily, stunned by the count. "That's nearly a third of the people we had here."

"We can't make a full assault out there. Many of these survivors are women and children," Boron said.

Hearing the report, Uthan's heart sank. The nerves in his legs trembled as blood coursed through them, bereft of the adrenalin that had only moments ago carried him on. He closed his eyes. Projected onto the inside of his eyelids he saw a shape. A magic symbol in gleaming white light was almost tattooed there. Sitting next to him on the floor was Hedrial's old spell book. With no recollection of how it had got there, Uthan placed it in front of him and rapidly thumbed through the pages. Words in almost every language imaginable seemed to blend in with strange magical symbols, many of which Uthan could not remember seeing. The page turning quickened as the image of the symbol burned itself into his mind's eye. He found it blazoned across the top of a page. Written in Hedrial's neat handwriting next to it were the words, 'Blood frenzy'.

His finger followed the words underneath. At first he could not read them, then, slowly tracing them back again, Uthan found himself understanding. Moving his lips silently, he began chanting.

Above him he could hear the sounds of Black Flame Knights entering Dessendor. There were angry shouts and orders. Heavy thudding sounds shook the ceiling of the Hall of the Dead as blocks of heavy stonework were moved aside.

"It sounds like the walls have come down," exclaimed Gauduin.

"They'll tear this place apart till they find us," Cassmed stated with a startling calmness.

"No, they won't," Uthan replied suddenly. As all eyes fell on the young mage, he explained, "They'll be too busy killing each other to remember we're here."

A loud booming sounded, shaking the hall and sending dust raining down on them. Steel on steel rang out, mixing with the cries and shouts of knights. Three high-pitched screams were cut short.

Demien looked sharply at Uthan and demanded, "What did you cast?"

"Blood frenzy."

"Never heard of it," Gauduin said in a hushed voice as Qwan shrugged in agreement with the dwarf.

"I have," Demien said. "It was used to give small armies that little bit extra. The mage would fill their minds with it and give them images of the enemy. The infected warriors would then just slaughter until nothing was left to kill."

"All I did was feed them an image of themselves," Uthan replied. "Now we let them kill each other and wait."

"Remind me never to annoy you," Boron said.

For nearly an hour the fighting continued, never once calming down. In the Hall of the Dead, young children whimpered, too afraid to cry. The nerves of those who were not accustomed to battle were fraying. People openly shook with fear. Gradually the volume lowered, as there were less and less Black Flame Knights alive to fight.

"Put out some of the torches," Qwan said, getting to his feet. He slotted an arrow into his crossbow.

"What?" Cassmed said hurriedly.

"We're leaving," Qwan said, with his usual mischievous smile.

Gauduin nodded and stood up. He stretched his arms behind his back before unsheathing his sword. Behind them, Demien, Diarus and Boron followed, all brandishing their weapons, eager to get out of the stuffy darkness around them. Gesturing to Serriman, the elf said, "Open the door for us, please."

The block was pushed in. In the heavy, near silence of the hall, the grating of stone on stone was loud. The wall section dropped away forming steps again. Qwan peered cautiously up the stairwell.

"It's all clear," he whispered, beginning to climb cautiously.

They crept outside into the sunlight again, unnoticed by Black Flame Knights. What was left of the attacking army now stood in a rough circle, facing each other. Armoured corpses littered the fortress alleyways.

"I count twenty," Qwan muttered as Gauduin joined him behind a wall.

"We can take out twenty of them between us easily," Gauduin muttered with a grin, "What's going to be left for the others to fight?"

Serriman moved over to the wall and slid past Gauduin. Leaning closer to Qwan he said, "Give me some covering fire, will you?"

Before either the elf or the dwarf could retort, Serriman charged out into the open, sword raised high. Yelling like a madman, he drove into the circle, cleaving the head from the shoulders of the nearest, and first knight to react. Blood misted up into the air as the man's head spun to the floor. Keeping his sword moving, Serriman lanced the tip into the throat of another man. Then the rest of the knights reacted, knowing they had a new enemy in their midst. They swarmed at the old Royal Knight, weapons ready to hack him to pieces.

Qwan and Gauduin ran from behind the wall. The elf shot a bolt quickly, piercing one in the eye socket. Without wasting time to reload the crossbow, Qwan dropped it to the ground and removed his sword from its scabbard. The dwarf was already amongst the Black Flame Knights. He swung his wide bladed sword in an arc, keeping several knights at bay and cutting deep into the legs of one. Then the others came flooding out. Demien, Boron and Diarus all picked opponents and attacked. In only a few seconds, the entire circle of knights had been slaughtered.

"Is that all of them?" Gauduin shouted.

The answer was a series of nods from the others and raising his axe in triumph, Boron yelled, "The knights of the Black Flame are no more! We hold Dessendor!"

Chapter Twenty-Two

A pall of thick, greasy black smoke hung over what was once Dessendor. Some of the Black Flame corpses had been dumped unceremoniously into the large furnace to get rid of them. Carrion birds had already begun to circle overhead, watching anxiously for the opportunity to feast on the dead.

The piles of remaining corpses were too high to be cremated in the furnace. Instead, three large pyres had been constructed outside, using the remnants of the timber from the siege towers, ladders and barricades. Flames now ate hungrily at the bodies. The air was full of the stench of the burning dead. Broken and twisted sections of the gates lay amongst the wreckage of the northern wall and huge chunks of stone were strewn across the courtyard. Shards of shining black glass in all sizes were scattered across the ground and embedded in the stonework that was, until recently, the north wall, serving as a reminder of Uthan's devastating magic.

Separate, more respectful funeral pyres were built for the fallen amongst the defenders. Around them stood various family members or Green ghost comrades, honouring their memories and to the west, the sun was on its steady descent.

Uthan sat, perched on the splintered remnants of the northern wall battlements, looking over the fortress. He twirled a piece of obsidian between his fingers, idly scratching into the wood at his feet. After seeing the devastation the hail had caused, Uthan had been driven to find a piece of the volcanic glass and keep it, hoping it would remind him to never use that spell unless it was with good reason. He looked at the great piles of burning corpses outside the fortress. The smoke towering above them made the field almost invisible. The sight brought a strange feeling to Uthan. It was not guilt; he knew that, these men had sought to kill him. But the idea that he had the power to destroy an army had unsettled him. He had tried reassuring himself, telling himself he had known it for a long time but the feel of the now cold glass in his hand only served to reinforce his emotions.

The other companions were close by with the horses. They had spent the past hour discussing their new strategy. Harhn was to lead the refugees to Dacenheim as planned. However, there were several casualties amongst them who were not ready to be moved. Demien had volunteered Cass, Serriman and Boron to stay with the wounded and take them to Dacenheim when they were able to make the journey. Cass had argued against it, furious at being left behind. Serriman had finally been the one to placate her by requesting her help. He had suggested Medoran have a memorial in the burial hall under Dessendor.

"Only take what we absolutely need," Qwan said, tearing Uthan from his thoughts, "we have to travel light."

"Do we take the horses?" Gauduin asked. "The jungle heat is not going to go well with them."

The elf nodded and said, "Uthan has a low level energy spell to help them adjust to the heat. We'll be taking a spare one as well, in case we're able to bring Hedrial's body back." He caught the raised eyebrows and expressions and continued, "I'm just providing us with an option. Besides, who knows, we may end up needing another horse to carry any extra weight."

"You mean the dragon scale," Gauduin said gruffly.

"Secondly yes," Qwan answered, "but first I mean Hedrial's body."

Harhn walked over, once again wearing the green and brown cloak of the Green Ghosts. With a broad smile, he extended a hand to Qwan. "The caravan is ready to go now. We'll be leaving soon."

"Us too," Qwan replied. "Be careful out there."

"I'm to be careful? I'm not the one riding into hell," Harhn said. "Make sure you get back alive."

The elf nodded, "I don't plan on dying on this trip!"

"You'd better not be. Who's going to come and get me out of that Dacenheim jail when they throw me in it," Harhn countered, only half joking.

"They won't throw you in a cell, Harhn. You're a war hero now."

"I hope someone's told them that," Harhn laughed. He nodded to the rest of the companions. "I hope to raise a drink with you all in the future."

He climbed up into the saddle of a chestnut mare and walked her through what was once the gate. Various shouts and calls went out, as people got their horses and carts moving. People called to the group as they passed, thanking them for the protection and waving goodbye. After a few moments, the caravan had left Dessendor, leaving behind nothing more than a collection of deep wheel tracks and the distant sound of riders.

"Our turn now," Qwan muttered. He pulled himself into his saddle, patting his horse's neck as it protested quietly.

"Take care, Qwansien. It has been an honour fighting alongside you," Serriman said, extending a hand to the elf.

Qwan accepted the hand and replied, "You too, Sir Serriman."

"Take care of my grandson, won't you," the ageing knight added, keeping his voice to a whisper.

"You have my word on it."

Kainan pawed at the ground, anxious to go as Demien climbed into her saddle. The huge white horse snorted in anticipation, shaking his head. Checking all her weapons were in place, Demien looked round to see Cass giving Uthan a kiss on the cheek. "Come on, Cass," she said loudly. "The poor boy is going to be gone for the gods only know how long. You could at least kiss him properly."

"I was going to tell you to make sure she comes back in one piece," Cass replied, glaring at Demien while directing the words to Uthan. "But I'm beginning to change my mind."

Then she reached up and grabbed hold of his black tunic, pulling him closer to her. Kissing Uthan full on the lips for what felt, to the two, like an age, Cass ignored the clapping from her friend. Demien reached down and put a hand on the younger woman's shoulder, gently prying her away.

With a broad smile, she said, "As much as this moment was purely timeless, we have to go now."

Cass's eyes filled a little, only enough for Demien to notice. Speaking in a hushed voice that sounded as if it would crack at any moment, she said, "Get back here soon, Demy."

"I will." Demien nodded.

An anxious whinnying from Gauduin's horse made them all look round. Gauduin held tightly to the reins, watching the beast's head shake frantically.

"Can we go now, please?" Qwan said loudly. "Gauduin's horse is impatient."

The comment brought chuckles from the others. Qwan's horse started off toward the ruined gates, followed closely by the others in single file. After they had left the fortress and rode out around the still smouldering corpse piles, Gauduin spurred his horse on to ride beside Qwan.

At the tattered gates of Dessendor, the three remaining companions watched their friends travel east. To the northwest, the caravan looked no bigger than ants as it wound its way over the hills. Without saying anything, Boron laid his hands on the shoulders of both Cass and Serriman, carefully leading them away from the sight of their disappearing friends.

Carrion's bone shod boots clicked against the flagstones as the necromancer entered the large chamber. The room was almost completely in darkness, the only source of light being that coming in through a small open window. Aside from a large throne crafted from obsidian, sitting against the far wall, the chamber was empty. The throne itself was only half visible in the shadows of the room.

Carrion strode across the floor, arms locked behind his back in an impassive gesture. The necromancer wore a robe made of bleached bones and black, greasy looking feathers. Two large animal skulls sat on his shoulders, the morbid cloak flowing down from them and out behind him. His own face resembled the skull of a large bird with lank, greasy hair that was tied in a topknot. The stench of death and decay hung around Carrion like a bodyguard. The dark hollow eyes in his face regarded the throne before him as he knelt on one knee, clicking the bone of his cloak loudly against the flagstone.

"You bring bad news," a voice said from the shadowy region of the throne.

"You know what I'm about to say then?" Carrion asked, looking at the flagstones in front of him. "The Spirit Mage is free. General Cornak and his knights are slain and naturally he has lost the dagger. I have communed with the general's spirit."

"You have assured him of the price of his failure," the voice seethed.

Carrion nodded, "He was most unhappy with the decision."

"Then he shouldn't have failed me."

"Do you really wish me to remove the bond?" Carrion asked, only now daring to risk a glance at the throne.

"I have made my decision, Carrion. Do not have me repeat myself. General Cornak's soul is not to be restored to life again," answered the voice. The words were laced with menace, causing Carrion to flinch visibly. "You will commune with General Meligonn now. He is to go forth into their miserable Empire and tear it to pieces. I want that boy here and that dagger destroyed. You will also remind him of Cornak's failure and what it has cost him."

Chapter Twenty-Three

The stone steps of Skull Gate still held the carnage left from the battle that had led the group to Dessendor. Carrion birds and scavenger animals had taken only a few of the carcasses, leaving the rest to the flies and decay. The air was thick with the stench of putrid decaying flesh. Broken swords and armour littered the bloodstained rock.

"They leave a foul taste in the mouths of the animals too, I see," Demien said.

A large raven perched on the chest of one corpse. It looked up from the hole it had been opening in the throat, watching them warily. It flapped its wings threateningly, cawing at them.

"This smell is turning my stomach," Gauduin announced.

"That's good news. We won't need to stop while you eat," Qwan replied dryly.

"Very amusing," Gauduin answered. "After this stench, the sulphur in that ravine will be like roses."

"Glad you feel that way, Gauduin," Qwan said. He slotted a bolt into his crossbow then continued, "because you can go up there and open the gates."

"What? Do it yourself!" Gauduin replied.

"Gauduin, it's simple to understand. You go up and open the gates while we stand back here with our bows ready." Qwan shrugged and leant forward, resting his arms on the pommel of his saddle.

"And being so short it'll be easier to shoot around you," Diarus added.

Casting a dark look at the Daiharlon, Gauduin climbed down from his saddle and jogged up the steps. He unsheathed his sword from his back and propped it against the stone jaws of the skull. There was a low rumble from inside the stone as Gauduin pulled hard on the ancient rope, all the time keeping his eyes on the gateway. The smell of sulphur wafted out past his nostrils as the gates swung inward. Instinctively, Gauduin reached for his sword, sweeping it up in a wide arc. He peered through the gap, and then signalled to the others before going back over to the rope and pulling again. As the gates swung all the way open, Diarus suddenly let an arrow fly into the orange light. Gauduin spun on his heels, taking his sword up again. Seeing nothing, he glared at the Daiharlon.

"There was a spider," Diarus replied.

"You nearly scared me out of my skin," Gauduin replied. "For a spider!"

"I hate spiders," Diarus shrugged.

"Well, I think you killed it," Qwan said, "so it's not going to be bothering us anymore."

Diarus snorted and urged his horse on up the steps. The hoof beats echoed out across the dead silence of Skull Gate. The horses wanted to shy away from the heat and smoke coming from the gates. As they entered, they all began to sweat due to the increase in temperature. For what looked like an hour's ride in front of them stretched a long tunnel. Black volcanic dust carpeted the floor, masking the sound of the horses' hooves. The walls glowed with red and orange light, reflecting from the end of the tunnel. Sounds of bubbling lava could be heard, dulled down by the echoing from the rock walls. Riding in single file, with Gauduin at the front, the group was silent, feeling the tedium of the claustrophobic tunnel set in.

Ahead of them, the pathway opened out onto a ledge, wide enough for six horses. A wall of searing heat blasted into them, causing their skin to prickle. The ledge led them down along the side of the cavern wall. Far below them was a river of magma. Heat and dark, foul-smelling smoke rose up from it, forming a haze that made the other side nearly impossible to see. At the bottom of the ledge there was a platform, carved from hard white stone. The volcanic lava merely lapped harmlessly at the base. On two pillars hundreds of magical runes had been carved and they glowed with a soft blue light, blurring in the air slightly. A large brass bell hung from one of the pillars.

"That's to call the ferryman over," Qwan explained, nodding in the direction of the bell.

"Should we use it?" Uthan asked.

Qwan looked at him and in a monotone voice, he repeated, "That's to call the ferryman over."

Diarus reached out and pulled on the bell rope. The peels rang out across the cavern, echoing back to them from the distance. Over the bubbling sounds, they became aware of something moving towards them. A white stone longboat, covered in more of the glowing blue carvings pushed through the lava. Two oars dipped into the magma, as if it was nothing more than warm water.

"Gauduin," Qwan called. As the dwarf turned to look at his companion, the elf continued, "Let me do the talking here. We don't need a repeat of last time."

The boat turned and pulled alongside the jetty. The sight of the creature seated aft brought a look of disdain to Gauduin's face. A sheen of sweat covered its partially clad, green-skinned body. Two small, pink eyes regarded them as the boat was brought into position. The goblin's thinning black hair was tied in a greasy topknot and scrawny looking muscles rippled under his skin as he docked the boat.

"Can you take us across?" Qwan asked stiffly.

The goblin thought about it for a moment, looking at the Daiharlon warily, "Just four?"

"Five," Qwansien corrected.

"Yes, five," the goblin repeated carefully. He did not take his eyes off the huge beastman. "Fifty gold."

"Fifty?" roared Gauduin, outraged. "I could get a barge and get across there for less."

"Dwarf would row it? Dwarf don't know how," the goblin replied.

Qwan put a hand out to stop Gauduin from saying another word. Looking straight at the goblin, he said, "You'll get forty."

"Forty gold. Now," the goblin said with a shrug. Qwan reached into his saddlebag and pulled a small pouch free. As the purse was tossed to the deck of the longboat, the goblin waved them aboard. Gesturing to a rail at the front, he said, "Tie horses there."

He waited for them to settle into the seats before taking the longboat away from the jetty again. The oars dipped into the lava with a hiss. All around the boat, thick black smoke curled up in pillars from the molten river passing around them. Rowing tirelessly through the thick lava, the goblin looked from companion to companion.

"What bring you to Demonic Realm?" he asked finally.

"Our business is our own," Gauduin growled gruffly.

The goblin shrugged, clearly not getting the malice behind the dwarf's words. "Not many people travel this way anymore."

"Boiling hot river of lava and choking smoke-filled air. Why ever not?" Qwan replied sarcastically.

"Last human was wizard. Very old man," the goblin continued, not listening. "Not seen him come back though."

The mention of the wizard made Uthan look up sharply. He glanced sideways at Qwan, noticing the elf feigning disinterest.

"There's a lot of unrest back in the Empire," Qwan replied. "Wizard, you say?"

The goblin nodded and smiled, revealing stained teeth. "Talk of war, talk of death."

"So, the wizard didn't come back then?" Qwan pressed, trying to hold onto the mask of innocent curiosity.

Looking at the elf, the goblin boatman answered, "No. He be dead now."

"What makes you say that?"

"General Meligonn has army. Huge army of beastmen and Nierhoth. Meligonn hates humans," the goblin answered. He spoke as if he had been waiting years to tell someone. Looking at them again, he asked, "So, why you travel this way?"

"We have business," Qwan replied airily.

"Nothing you or your master needs to know," Gauduin spat suddenly, starting to his feet.

Quickly, Qwan put another restraining hand on the dwarf, pushing him back into his seat. The goblin laughed. The sound was as if his throat was blocked with thick fluid. Uthan's stomach turned at the sound.

"Boatmen have no master, but Baymothesis."

"Baymothesis is a boatman?" Uthan asked. "I thought it was a dragon."

The goblin arched his brow at the mage, "Baymothesis is master."

"Your master is a dragon?" Uthan pressed.

Cackling wildly, the goblin answered, "Yes. Dragon is master."

"Well, you'd be a fool to disobey him," Demien muttered.

"Are you wizard?" the goblin asked, looking right at Uthan.

Before Uthan could answer, Qwan interrupted. "No, he isn't."

"Sure?" The goblin pressed, "He look wizardy. So, why you travel to Demonic Realm?"

"You've asked that already," Qwan replied. His manner was continuously calm but his companions could see his jaw clenching as his patience wore thin.

"Asked yes, answered no," the goblin replied.

Around them, the viciously hot magma bubbled loud in their ears. Everywhere a bubble burst, there was a tiny jet of flame licking at the stifling air. Clouds of thick, eye-stinging smoke shrouded both sides of the river from them. Somewhere to the side, they caught the echoing sound of rocks tumbling from the mountain walls, finding their way to join the molten river.

"We're mercenaries," Qwan said finally.

"Mercenaries?"

"Yes," the elf replied, gritting his teeth. "The wizard who came through here is a wanted man back in the Empire. We've been hired to bring him back."

The goblin nodded, eyes wide. With a conspiratorial edge in his voice, he said, "Wented away in hurry. He did."

"Well, it's not surprising. He knows we're after him," Qwan said, ignoring the disapproving looks from the dwarf. "Besides, if you had a Daiharlon after you, wouldn't you want to be somewhere else?"

The goblin did not reply. Instead his pink eyes flashed across onto Diarus, sitting the closest to him. As the Daiharlon stared back impassively, the goblin switched his gaze to something else.

"What is that for?" he asked, reaching out for the tip of the folded dragon lance, sitting in Diarus's pack.

The Daiharlon slapped the groping hand away quickly, "It's for killing things."

Again the goblin stared at Diarus, this time with a little irritation. "Only asking," he muttered under his breath. "Only being friend."

The sound of falling rocks came to their ears again. Thick splashing sounds could be heard as they tumbled into the magma not far away. The boatman cocked his head to the side, listening intently. The rockslide came from the left. As the sounds echoed in the chasm, it was as if the whole mountainside was collapsing. For a few moments, the goblin settled the longboat to a halt, waiting and listening to the rocks. With a whispered voice, he told the companions, "Very dangerous. Rock falls and maybe smash boat."

Finally the sound trailed off. The goblin dipped the oars back into the lava again and rowed off through the choking smoke clouds. It was only a few moments later when the boat was slowed down again. A bank of the thick smoke rolled away to reveal the carved stone jetty of the opposite bank. More, deeply carved runes glowed blue in the otherwise orange glow. A narrow ledge ran along from the jetty and up a short distance to enter in through a large tunnel.

"All here now," the goblin cackled.

"Thank the gods," Gauduin muttered. He pushed himself to his feet with a barely audible grunt.

Hearing the noise, Qwan turned to his friend and asked, "Getting old then?"

They led the horses off the long boat and onto the stable rock. Starting towards the ledge, they were halted by the goblin that held out a hand to Qwan.

"Good luck," he said, smiling as best he could.

Reluctantly, Qwan accepted the hand as a gesture of friendship, "We'll be seeing you again soon, I expect."

"Maybe, maybe," the goblin said. "Demonic Realm dangerous. Death waits everywhere."

"Very poetic," Gauduin muttered under his breath.

"Considering goblins are usually about killing and eating, yeah," Demien said, leading Kainan up the ledge.

With a flicker of a smile, Diarus added, "Actually they usually just whimper around me."

Qwan looked up at the tunnel entrance. At the far end he could see a large gate, bigger than Skull Gate. An outline of sunlight could be seen around the barrier. Moving away from the gate tunnel, he scanned the rock wall, trying to look through the clouds of smoke. Finding what he was looking for, he nudged the dwarf, "Let's go."

They began their climb up the ledge. Behind them followed the goblin, giggling and clasping the bag of coins to his chest. He darted in between them, working his way to the front before running up the rest of the way. A thick plume of smoke wafted across towards them, hiding the goblin from view for a moment. Once it faded away behind them again, he had vanished.

Stopping beside the main gate tunnel, Qwan called a halt. He searched the mountain wall, looking for something. Finally, with a triumphant smile on his face, he led them further up the ledge. Behind him, Demien, Uthan and Diarus all stood in confusion. Gauduin, half following the elf, cleared his throat noisily. As Qwan turned to look, the dwarf gestured to the tunnel.

"I know," Qwan said, "but we're not going through that way."

"And where exactly are we going?" the dwarf demanded.

"We're following the goblin. He disappeared into another tunnel."

"Oh well, that's okay then," Gauduin muttered, "let's follow the little idiot who could probably just serve us up to Meligonn."

"He won't betray us," Qwan replied with a shrug of his shoulders.

"And why won't he?" Gauduin asked. "Some lost sense of honour that goblins seem to have forgotten over the centuries?"

"Not quite," Qwan replied. "He won't see us. There's an entire maze of tunnels up here. Some of them lead out on to the side of the mountain. Well, at least I hope they do."

They entered a large chamber, partially hidden amongst the rocky mountain wall. Stalagmites, some bigger than Diarus, shot up from the floor, many of them stopping inches away from the points of opposing stalactites. The effect was like stepping into the mouth of a giant beast with thousands of teeth. Keeping behind a row of the stone fangs, they watched the goblin disappear down one smaller side tunnel.

Qwan nodded further up the cavern, indicating a slightly larger cave off to their left. "We take that one. It'll take us an hour or so longer but we'll be higher up when we exit."

Leading the horses over a floor that was covered in the volcanic black dust, the group kept to the far side of the cavern, hidden by the shadows. Leaving the orange glow of the lava behind them, they slipped unseen into the rocky corridor. As they travelled further along the tunnel, the air took on a heavier, oppressive feel. The dry choking heat was replaced by energy sapping humidity. The dull, orange light faded away, leaving them in darkness. They turned bend after bend, listening as the bubble of the lava flow died away and was replaced by a distant cacophony of bird and animal calls.

"Be careful, there's a scouting party just before you exit this tunnel," Dionis said, so suddenly they all jumped out of their skins.

"You need to stop doing that," Qwan hissed through gritted teeth.

"Do you want me to wear a bell?" Dionis answered.

"It might help," Qwan replied.

"What was this about a scouting party?" Demien said, trying to gain some order.

Dionis looked at her and answered, "There are six of them: three Nierhoth and three beastmen. I'm surprised the beastmen haven't scented you already."

"We can take six," Gauduin said, unsheathing his sword with a gentle hiss.

After taking another couple of bends, the tunnel joined into a wider cave opening. Brilliant golden sunlight lit up the otherwise dull grey rock of the outer cave. Outside, in the distance was a wall of green and brown, the heavy jungles of the Demonic Realm. The myriad calls of birds and animals filtered up to them. Here and there was a splash of colour from flowers or one of the many exotic creatures. It was here they saw the scouting party.

Three Nierhoth tribesmen squatted at a wall just inside the cave mouth, looking out over the jungle with slanted black eyes. They wore loincloths, knee-high boots and vests, all made from roughly cut animal skins. Dirt, smeared with sweat, covered their exposed hairy arms and legs. Their lank hair, greasy with sweat, hung unkempt around their thick necks and shoulders. Serrated scimitars protruded from cracked leather belts around their waists.

Standing at the very edge of the cave mouth was a tall, solidly built beastman. His face was dog-like, with a heavy muzzle and ears on the top of his head. Two, thick, tusk-like fangs came down from his top lip, giving him a permanent snarl. Dark brown fur, stained blue in places, covered his bare upper body, arms and head.

The remaining two beastmen stood near the back of the cavern, only a few feet away from Qwan. Their attentions were drawn away from the tunnel at their exposed backs, instead staring intently at the jungle sky. Both were Lizardmen, who looked like crocodiles walking on their hind legs. A row of dark green scales extended from their spines, giving both a fearsome appearance. Thick tails, almost as long as the Lizardmen were tall, curled across the floor. One tail tip was a mere inch from Qwan's foot.

Qwan gestured to Gauduin a few feet behind him, out of sight of the scouts. Two fingers, then an open flat hand, palm facing in, three fingers, followed by a sweeping motion, then one finger that pointed out along the length of his arm. The dwarf nodded, taking the gestures to mean the positions of the enemy. Qwan held up one finger, then held up his crossbow and moved a few inches closer. The elf took a careful aim, between the heads of the burly Lizardmen, levelling the bolt tip with the back of the Sniffer's head. Time seemed to slow as the bolt was released. It whistled past the heads of the Lizardmen, causing them to whirl round and face their attackers. The bolt continued to sail on, piercing the back of the Sniffer's head and sticking out of his eye socket. Before he had pitched out of the cave dead, the two Lizardmen surged forwards to attack Qwan.

As the elf stepped aside and drew his sword, Gauduin ran out from behind him, sword held high above his head. He flicked the weapon out, batting away the club of one beastman but driving the tip of his sword into the chest of the second.

Diarus appeared from the tunnel suddenly, Demien hot on his heels. Both charged into the Nierhoth as they made to escape and raise the alarm. With his two falchions whirling, Diarus decapitated one of the tribesmen and drove down into the shoulder of a second. The third and final tribesman received the point of Demien's sword to his face. Instantly he crumpled.

The last of the Lizardmen ducked around Gauduin's hard overhead swing and flicked with an attack of his own. Qwan stepped in quickly, shoving Gauduin to the side to avoid the clubbing blow, before severing the Lizardman's arm below the elbow. As it opened its long jaws to scream in pain, Qwan quickly thrust his sword into its mouth, piercing its brain.

"I told you we could take six," said Gauduin, watching the elf pull his weapon free.

"We didn't even break a sweat," Demien muttered, moving closer to the cave mouth. As she looked out, she could not prevent the gasp from escaping her lips.

Qwan came over to look. The mountainside sloped sharply down. Their vantage point was a few hundred feet above the ground. Razor edged chunks of grey stone made it look treacherous to cross. At the base of the mountain was semi-flat ground that was cracked and dried out from the sweltering heat. The grass was sparse, bleached yellow from the sun. The open land was swallowed after nearly a hundred feet by lush, thick jungle. Trees and bushes rose up like an impenetrable wall of green, as if challenging the mountains themselves. What made it worse was the ground below them was also littered with beastmen and tribesmen. They waited around huge campfires that sent thick plumes of white smoke into the air.

"How do we get through that lot?" Uthan asked, coming to stand behind them.

Demien just shook her head, "With great difficulty I would think."

"We'll need to move soon," Qwan said. "These beasts are bound to be missed."

They watched a group of around twenty heavily armoured warriors disappear through the gates. Diarus was the first to voice their thoughts, "The invasion is starting."

With a glimmer of a smile, Qwan said, "It means there are less of them for us to have to worry about in the meantime."

"Unless they come in here from behind us," Demien reminded him.

"I can't see how they will."

"That goblin might talk," Gauduin said. "Simple deduction will tell them where we are."

"And how do you propose we get out of here then?" Qwan replied calmly, even though his jaw was clenching as a sign of his growing irritation.

The dwarf shrugged and threw his hands in the air in desperation. "I don't know, Qwan. Why don't you just ride out there and attack them?"

Instantly the dwarf appeared to regret his words as a thoughtful glimmer appeared in the elf's eyes. A slow smile broke out across his angular face as Qwan replied, "That's not so stupid an idea, Gauduin."

"No, Qwan, attacking an army is a really stupid idea," Gauduin stressed quickly. He raised his hands defensively as the others glared at him.

Qwan stood up again and wandered across to where they had left the horses standing. "I'm not going to attack the army," he said finally.

"Good." The dwarf shook his head, relieved.

"I'm going to attack some of it."

"Qwan, no, this is a really bad plan. I didn't mean it," Gauduin said.

The elf looked over his shoulder at them all and shrugged. "No, it's a good plan. I'll ride in amongst them and whip up some chaos. You use the distraction and get out of here and into the jungle."

"And in the meantime you get killed?" Demien put in.

Qwan just shrugged again. To Gauduin he said, "You lead them to Mount Drakkar. If I survive this I'll meet you there."

"You had better stay alive," Gauduin replied.

"I plan on it. I'll have a dragon hide to sell later on and then I can retire a rich and very fat elf," Qwan answered with a broad grin.

He vaulted up into his saddle, looking at the terrain outside the cave mouth. It sloped steeply down to the ground, carpeted in chunks of broken rock, looking somehow more treacherous than before. Here and there large boulders offered potential hiding positions, as did the few trees that managed to claw a space between the solid, mountain debris.

"This is just suicide, Qwan. No matter how you look at it," Demien said slowly.

The elf just glared back this time. Grabbing a firm hold of the reins, he asked, "Are we done here?"

"If you won't listen to reason, then yes. We're done," Gauduin replied.

"Good," Qwan answered. "Now saddle up because you won't have a lot of time. See you at Drakkar."

Jabbing his heels into the sides of his horse, Qwan almost flew out of the cave mouth. Clouds of dust and loose rock chippings kicked up behind him, obscuring the sight of him as his horse sped down the slope.

The closest ranks of the army looked up, seeing the horse charging their way. There were several Nierhoth, all lazily camped around a large cooking fire. At the back of the circle, a tall, dog-faced soldier, dressed in chain mail, roared and thrust his fist in Qwan's direction. In answer, the circle of tribesmen leapt to their feet and surged up the slope to meet the elf.

In the cave, the remaining travellers were already mounted. Within moments the horses leapt from the cave, galloping down the slope at an almost impossible speed. Trying to keep his eye on the ground ahead to prevent his horse tripping and breaking both its neck and every bone in his own body, Gauduin risked a glance in Qwan's direction.

The elf had his sword in his hand. The sun caught the blade, making it seem as if it was on fire as Qwan swept out and down, cleaving through the shoulder and neck of one Nierhoth. Two more ran in to take the dead tribesman's place. Qwan's horse grew skittish on the uneven ground and slid a few feet down the slope. For a moment the Nierhoth stopped in their tracks, unsure whether to attack or not. Flicking out his sword, Qwan carved through the throat of one, sending a cloud of bloody mist up into the air. There was a roar from further in the camp, which alerted more and more of the waiting army to Qwan. Offering a small, mocking salute to one incredibly large creature, clad head to toe in thick green plate armour, Qwan pulled on his reins and turned his horse into the jungle. The last thing Gauduin saw of his lifelong friend was the elf's dark horse leaping a fern and disappearing into the tree line, closely pursued by a group of Nierhoth on foot.

"I'll kill him if he survives this, I swear," Gauduin muttered. Then he cursed himself, silently, for not paying attention to where he was going. Nearly jumping out of his skin as suddenly trees and bushes raced past him, he too entered the jungle of the Demonic Realm.

Chapter Twenty-Four

Warriors, clad in thick plate mail armour, strode through the tunnel from the Demonic Realm jungle, oblivious to the blast of dry heat that washed over them. They marched along the ledge to the bank where the longboat was still tied in place. Wordlessly, they stood and waited for the boatman to return.

"Did you kill them?" the goblin cackled excitedly, bounding down the ledge towards the warriors.

They all looked directly at him, making him shrink away immediately. One of them took a step closer to him, forcing a whimper from the goblin's lips.

"Them?" came a harsh grating voice from deep within the black spike helm.

A little more bravado returned to the goblin as he nodded and answered, "Yes. Travellers."

The warrior turned to one of his comrades and spoke to him, speaking a language the goblin could not comprehend. The sound was dark and hinted at an ancient evil. The second warrior turned and disappeared through the tunnel.

A moment later, the first warrior turned back to the goblin and asked, "How many?"

"Five," the goblin answered, holding up five fingers. He opened his mouth to say something further but it closed shut involuntarily as he saw the warriors all turn to look at the gate tunnel.

Standing a head taller than the rest, General Meligonn walked out onto the ledge. The general was clad head to toe in solid plate armour, stained a dark green. His massive gauntleted hand rested on the pommel of a heavy looking sword that was almost as big as the goblin. Two great horns came out from the sides of his helm, sweeping out then forward like a Daiharlon. A thin slit at the level of his eyes appeared to be the only potential weak point in the general's armour. Behind the slit were only pitch darkness and two red pinpoints of glowing light.

He stared down at the ferryman and said, "You had travellers come through this way. I only know of one."

"No. Five came across," the goblin answered.

Focusing his red glowing eyes on the goblin, Meligonn asked, "Then where are the others?"

The voice seemed to shake the goblin to his very core. It had sounded like a large block of stone being dragged across wet gravel and echoed in the goblin's ears.

"Don't know. They were here together," the goblin answered, trying not to look Meligonn in the eyes. "Didn't see them leave."

"One of them rode into the outlying flanks of my army. There were no others," Meligonn returned. He turned to his warriors and said, "They must have sacrificed the one as a distraction to get into the jungle unseen."

"Said they were hunting wizard," the goblin added helpfully.

Meligonn's eyes flared brightly. He focused the full force of his gaze on the cowering goblin, "Was there a younger one with them?"

The goblin nodded.

"Tell Baymothesis I will personally guarantee him a treasure pile bigger than even he can imagine if he kills them," Meligonn said. "With the exception of the boy, however. He is to be taken to the Flame."

Uthan had not known exactly what he had expected from the Demonic Realm. He had understood about the heat, yet now, carefully walking his horse through the tightly packed rainforest, he felt the full force of its energy sapping humidity. They had ridden for only a few hours, eager to put as much distance between them and the vast army as possible, yet Uthan felt as if he had not stopped moving for weeks. Quick glances at his companions told him, that they were victims to the heat too. He found himself growing increasingly grateful of the charm he had placed on the horses. Even so, they had to move them on slowly.

The ground was thick with plant life, rising and dipping sharply in banks and valleys and hills. Anywhere, Gauduin had warned, could be a venomous snake or spider waiting to spring. They felt the eyes of hundreds of animals on them as they progressed. The path they were forced to take seemed to wind endlessly, taking them at least three times as long as it would have done if they had travelled in a straight line. At several points along the path, they saw the remains of half eaten animals. In a few cases, the skeletons were more humanoid, but not actually human. The rain fell without any real warning in thick droves, soaking them to the skin in mere moments. It turned the ground slick beneath the horses' hooves, making the going even more treacherous.

In the canopy high above them, birdcalls rang out, warnings to others about the travellers invading their territory. The chattering of monkeys and buzzing insects joined in the symphony. Branches high above them crackled and broke as unseen creatures surged through the trees, seemingly stalking the travellers. Thorn-covered vines and creepers hung down from the treetops in an immense web of greens, yellows and browns. There were splashes of almost violently bright colours here and there as flowers dotted the jungle around them, trying to get their share of the moisture before it evaporated again. Gauduin had also warned them not to stop and risk inhaling the sweet perfumes. Uthan was left to guess as to whether it was due to potentially dangerous insects waiting in the flowers or that the pollen had some poisonous effect. Neither idea put him at ease with the jungle.

Shards of hazy sunlight filtered down through the few gaps in the treetops, obscuring vision in places. The travellers became the targets for a veritable army of insects. Anything that crawled or flew found its way to them, taking tiny bites into their skin. On at least three occasions, Uthan had looked up into the shelter of the canopy and glimpsed shapes struggling against silvery white spider threads. He quickly realised that everywhere in this jungle, danger lurked.

From somewhere to the north, they could hear the dull roaring of water. Gauduin had told them there was a river there but pointed out that it was better to go nowhere near it if possible. Carnivorous fish and birds lived in and around the water, locked in a constant battle to feed on the other. The dwarf had said that if he was going to go, it wasn't going to be by a fish or a bird!

The rest of their journey that day had been made in near silence as Gauduin listened to the cacophony of calls, making sure they were not out of the ordinary. They stopped to camp for the night, only when the rainforest had become too dark to travel in, and, even then, only when Gauduin had chosen them a safe enough place to rest. That evening the dwarf made them check each other for bites and cuts, anything that would seep blood and give infection a chance to take hold.

During the night a large snake of over twenty feet in length had stalked them. It wound its way down around the thick trunk of a tree, making for the horses as they stamped the ground nervously. Diarus had been the first to see it. The Daiharlon leapt to his feet and ran to the horses, almost nothing more than a shadow in the darkness himself. One of the mounts screamed in panic. The next moment they heard the telltale hiss of a sword being drawn followed by a loud thump as the blade's edge had bitten into wood. Diarus reappeared a moment or two later, cleaning his falchion on a piece of cloth before sheathing it. His left forearm had two large punctures that bled only a little. A faint buzz suggested that the insects had already scented the Daiharlon's blood. Uthan had quickly cast a healing spell on the bite mark, watching as the thin clear venom flowed out from the wound. The following morning, nothing remained of the snake. The night denizens of the jungle had reclaimed the carcass.

"That's the way it is here," Gauduin said, his voice full of weariness. "Everything is reclaimed, nothing is wasted."

They continued on, ignoring the cascading rain that was thrown from the sky rather than falling. It always stopped as suddenly as it had started; the deafening sound of water hitting the leaves and branches above them was replaced by the calls and hoots of birds and monkeys. Then the stifling heat quickly took a firmer hold again, turning the moisture on the ground to steam that rose in clouds.

"How much further?" Demien asked after they had been travelling half the next day.

Gauduin reined his horse in and pointed to the north. "Another few hours in that direction and the jungle will thin out. You'll be able to see Drakkar from there on."

Skull Gate opened, vomiting a horde of Nierhoth tribesmen into the Empire. They poured down the steps and flowed in amongst the trees, tearing the forest apart recklessly as they did so.

Behind them, General Meligonn followed. His armour clanked noisily as he strode down the steps, watching his army pouring around him like a sea of monstrosity. The general was filled with a sense of disdain. Apart from the forty or so heavily armoured warriors, the rest of the army was nothing more than a rabble. They were, however, the best he could find. Most of his army had been rounded up and slain after the beast wars. Of those, only a hundred remained, most of which had been taken by the Black Flame himself and stationed in the Flame's fortress.

A small toad-like creature scampered over to the general. Standing next to him, the creature was dwarfed, barely coming up to Meligonn's waist. A forked tongue flicked out of the green jaws, tasting the air around its flattened face. Two bulbous eyes swivelled left and right, taking in the carnage being waged on the Empire's forestlands.

"Where do you want us to start, General?"

Meligonn scanned the area, watching four Nierhoth and a large, grey, troll-like creature pulling a small tree from the ground. He spared the toad the slightest of glances, and yet caught its look of excited anticipation. Speaking loud enough for many of his horde to hear, Meligonn answered, "Bring this realm to its knees! Kill everyone you can find. Destroy their homes and lives. This Empire is ours for the taking!"

Uthan looked straight ahead. The jungle immediately in front of him was just as suffocating and dense as it had always been; yet he could sense it thinning out ahead. The almost constant feeling of being watched seemed to be easing off. They had had to walk their horses for the last few hours as the ground had become increasingly dangerous, rising and dipping everywhere. Of the delves, many had been hidden by thick undergrowth, the horses breaking a leg or bites from hidden animals. Steam had curled up from the ground as the stifling heat had increased again. The air had become increasingly heavy with the musty smell of damp soil, dead leaves and other jungle debris. Now, ahead of them, Gauduin cleaved through a net of creepers hanging across their path like a curtain. In the resulting gap, they could see spots of brown in the middle distance. The jungle was almost at an end.

With renewed strength they moved forward, picking up their pace. Almost as if it had been cut away, the jungle abruptly ended. Across the open plain the rocky spire that was Mount Drakkar came into view. Gauduin held up a hand to bring the group to a halt, a short distance inside the tree line. He let go of his horse's reins, allowing them to trail on the ground; safe in the knowledge his horse was not going anywhere.

Sitting down on a fallen tree, he said, "We'll rest here for a while."

"What about Qwan?" Uthan asked with concern in his voice.

"I'll go and watch for him," Demien answered.

She moved swiftly through the remaining jungle; her movements were impossibly silent as she ran. Selecting a tree in mid-run, she launched herself into the air and caught hold of a lower branch before allowing her momentum to swing her around and into the tree. Considering the weapons Demien carried, her movements were agile and catlike. The muscles in her legs and arms bunched and flexed, revealing the strength required for powering her way up the tree. Her leather armour creaked with the movement, mirroring similar sounds made by the tree itself as she climbed. Perched in amongst the branches and creepers nearly thirty feet from the ground, Demien settled down to watch over the plains.

The others sat a short distance away, trying to regain as much of their energy as possible. They ate a meal of salted meat and dried fruit even though none of them felt hungry. All around them the sounds of the jungle continued, blissfully ignoring their presence. From her place in the tree, Demien whistled. The sound, so different from the bird and monkey calls they had grown used to hearing over the past week, made them look up. The warrior woman gestured out across the plain.

Immediately Gauduin was on his feet, charging across the jungle floor to drop flat amongst the half exposed roots of the tree. For a few moments he remained absolutely still, watching the plains. Then, ever so slowly, a grin broke out across his face. "Well, I'll be damned," he muttered, "the fool actually made it."

He stood up and whistled to his horse. It trotted over calmly, ignoring the undergrowth that crackled loudly under its hooves. The dwarf hurried into his saddle and urged his horse on, riding fast across the plains. Uthan and Diarus reached the tree line just as Demien dropped softly to the ground. All three looked out from the jungle as Gauduin rode out to meet the other rider. Smiles of disbelief were plastered over their faces as they saw who it was.

"Keep your ears open," Demien said, vaulting into Kainan's saddle and speeding out to follow Gauduin.

"What for?" Uthan asked.

"The calls of the jungle," Diarus answered. "If they stop we're in trouble."

"How do you do it?" Gauduin called across the space between him and Qwansien.

The elf slid down from his saddle, landing lightly on the ground, "Do what?"

"Stay alive?"

With one of his trademark smiles, Qwan shrugged and replied, "Pure talent."

He waved to the others as they rode up. "After that chase," he said, overemphasising how tired he felt, "I can't wait to get home. I think I'll have a peaceful life as soon as this is over."

"No, you won't," Demien said, clapping a hand on his shoulder.

"No, you're right. I'll go back to causing trouble somewhere," Qwan joked.

"Personally," Gauduin said, "when I get through with all of this I'm going home and I'll be locking my doors. Next time an old friend comes by and asks me to babysit his apprentice for a bit, I'm going to pretend I'm not home." The dwarf grinned, splitting his beard from ear to ear and showing his brilliant white teeth.

"Look who I found," Qwan said. Close by him was the gryphon he had bought from Dacenheim. It lay patiently on the ground, watching everyone with a look of bemusement. The creature had grown a few more feet in length since it had flown away. The silky feathers on its golden yellow wings shone, as did the fur on its feline body. Clearly life in the jungles of the Demonic Realm had been good to it.

"I found myself face to face with a large and not very nice spider. The gryphon found me somehow and all but tore the thing to shreds."

"Well, well!" Gauduin almost whispered. Then, turning to Mount Drakkar he said, "Now, let's get up this mountain and get inside before we're seen."

The ground rose a little, becoming broken and torn, as if Mount Drakkar had punched up through the earth many centuries ago. Lumps of twisted rock littered the area around them, providing very little in the way of cover should they need it. The grass became sparse and was faded yellow, struggling to survive. Just ahead of them was the foot of a large set of steps. Carved from the rock of the mountain itself, they wound their way around and up, disappearing into the distance. A thick archway, also carved from the mountainside, framed the foot of the stairs.

"Do you know where it is you're going?" Gauduin asked the young mage.

Uthan shrugged, "I don't fully remember from the vision, but it's like I'm not in control anyway."

"Okay, you lead on and we'll follow," the dwarf said, gently pushing him forward.

"I think you should all know," Diarus started suddenly. They turned to him, expectantly as he jerked a thumb over his shoulder to the jungle behind them. "It's gone dead back there."

"Oh shit," Qwan cursed then he drew his sword and swung it a few times, testing his balance.

Gauduin moved across, looking out at the tree line. The jungle had fallen silent and unmoving. The creatures within the trees were hiding. The whole rainforest itself was afraid. The hairs on the back of his neck bristled. Just as much to reassure himself as the others, he muttered, "It doesn't mean anything really."

In answer, they all heard the screech that sounded like nails dragged along stone. It set the nerves in their teeth on edge. A flock of birds swarmed up from the trees, fleeing for their lives. The gryphon stood up, opened its beak and let out a long drawn out hiss, while looking around with sharp eyes.

"But that does," Qwan answered grimly. All of their earlier joking had faded. The elf pushed Gauduin back, putting his arm in front of the dwarf's chest, "Get back and make sure Uthan does what he needs to do."

"What?" Gauduin said, fixing an incredulous stare on his friend.

Qwan scanned the sky above the jungle. Without turning his attention from the search, he said, "You heard me. See that he gets there safely."

"Yes, I heard you. I was waiting for the part where you added you were joking," Gauduin said.

From high above them, the leathery thump of dragon wings beating against the air filtered down to their ears. They both craned their necks, trying to see through the mists above them. A dark shadowy shape slipped across the sky menacingly.

Again, Qwan pushed Gauduin back. "There's no time to argue," he shouted, "go on. I have the gryphon here with me to help." Looking at Diarus as the Daiharlon was watching the sky anxiously, he called, "And you can go as well. There's no telling what lies inside there. Uthan has to be protected more than I do."

"And of course this has nothing to do with you wanting to take all the credit for killing a dragon," Diarus muttered.

"Of course it does!" Qwan replied.

Diarus shook his head and jogged a few steps over, retrieved the folded lance from his saddle pack and tossed it to Qwan. "You'll need this," he shouted.

Looking at the lance as it dropped to the ground at his feet, Qwan smiled and mouthed his thanks, before gesturing that they leave.

Running up the steps, ignoring the protests from his weary leg muscles and heaving lungs, Uthan caught a glimpse of the dragon as it speared out of the mists past him. On the ground below, he heard the thump of a bowstring, followed by Qwan shouting angrily. Baymothesis circled in the air, looking first to the group on the stairs then down to the elf. The long red and brown, scaled body rolled in the air, tail twisting out behind it like a corkscrew. From the tip of the fanged snout to the tip of the long tail, Baymothesis was a hundred feet. The wingspan was almost the same. A rainbow of colours was picked out in the oils on the wing membranes as the sunlight caught them.

Meanwhile Qwan had locked another crossbow bolt into his weapon and was taking aim. The dragon flew directly overhead, bellowing its fury at their trespassing. Falling backwards, Qwan let loose the bolt. It whistled straight up, piercing a hole in Baymothesis's softer underbelly. The elf fluidly rolled over his head and up onto his feet again. Casting the crossbow to one side, he ran to his horse, stooping to pick up the lance on his way. He vaulted into the saddle and patted the horse's neck as it snorted loudly, annoyed at him jumping onto its back, but at the same time concerned with the dragon. He pulled back on his reins, bringing the horse out onto the plain again.

The earth shook as Baymothesis dropped to the ground. Huge talons, the length of Qwan himself, raked at the ground as the immense bulk of the dragon shifted from wings and air sacs to legs. The gryphon snarled viciously and moved to stand between the monster and Qwansien. It locked stares with Baymothesis, clearly unafraid of the dragon despite being greatly dwarfed by it. It pawed at the ground, its claws tearing slender gashes in the dirt.

Baymothesis gave its long body a good shake, rattling its scales noisily. It watched the gryphon for a few moments. Long jaws opened in a big yawn, revealing the rows of razor sharp teeth and the tongue that was twice the length of Qwan's horse.

"Are we keeping you awake?" Qwan yelled across the plain. Inwardly he laughed at the comment. He unfolded the lance, driving the sections into place with firm deliberate clicks.

The dragon unfurled its wings, beating them experimentally, causing a slight breeze. Small clouds of dust whirled lazily into the air around its body. Fixing the elf with its yellow eyes, Baymothesis drew in a deep breath, filling its air sacs that would take the dragon back up into the air. The muscles in its powerful rear legs bunched together for an instant before it propelled itself forward. Its wings beat faster, thumping against the air with a hard leathery crack. Qwan kicked his heels to his horse, sending the animal into a charge towards the oncoming dragon. All he could hear was the heavy breathing of his horse and the thundering of hooves on the dirt. Ahead of him, he locked eyes with the dragon. Baymothesis, flying with its claws only a few feet from the ground, opened its massive jaws wide and bellowed in fury.

Before the mounted elf could clash with the dragon, the gryphon drove itself hard into Baymothesis's shoulder. In a furious storm of slashing claws and beak, the gryphon tore into its opponent, opening deep gouging wounds that caused the dragon to writhe in pain. Qwan pulled his horse to a stop to watch as the golden yellow blur caused Baymothesis to land again.

Qwan's horse snorted loudly in reply and the elf muttered, "My thoughts exactly."

Snaking his long serpentine neck round, Baymothesis clamped his jaws onto the back of the gryphon and tore it away. It was almost in disgust that the dragon tossed the smaller creature to one side. It watched for a few moments as the gryphon bounced on the ground and rolled a couple of times before stopping. With his tail, Baymothesis prodded it. When it did not move, the dragon turned back to the elf.

Again the dragon swelled itself up and drove forward. Qwan's horse, overwhelmed by bravado of its own, leapt into life, straining to meet the dragon on the field. At the very last moment, Baymothesis swept overhead again. This time, Qwan had expected the move. He brought the tip of the lance up into the air, holding on tight as it tore into the softer underbelly. Baymothesis twisted in the air, climbing higher to bring his body away from the lance. Seeing small dots of dark red on the tip of the lance, Qwan grinned.

Halfway up Mount Drakkar, Uthan stopped dead. He stared at the mountain wall itself, searching for something amongst the cracks. Demien and Diarus who were following a few steps behind him, stopped so suddenly that they nearly collided with the young mage.

"Why stop here?" Demien breathed, listening to Baymothesis's screeching in the air.

Uthan pressed a hand against the rock and muttered, "The doorway. It's here."

In the darkest parts of his mind, he heard a series of clicks. He looked more deeply into those parts and saw symbols. Without fully realising he was doing it, Uthan began tracing a finger along the rough rock where his mind was seeing the images. The clicks became steadier, as if workings inside the rock were falling into place.

Vaguely, he heard Gauduin bounding up the steps, boots slapping frantically against the rock and then the dwarf asked, "What's he doing?"

Demien quickly shushed him.

There was a harsh grating sound of stone on stone, setting Uthan's teeth on edge. He opened his eyes again, letting the glowing symbols fade into the back of his mind. In front of him a large doorway had opened. The thick, sickening stench of decay immediately came out to greet them, forcing Uthan to turn away.

"Do you think your friend is down there?" Demien asked, paling at the smell.

Gauduin moved past her to stand in the tunnel entrance. Peering into the darkness, he muttered, "I hope not."

In the sky above Qwan, Baymothesis circled, fixing the elf with a baleful stare. It roared again, sounding its hatred. Jaws opened and the head aimed down at Qwan. With a loud whoosh, Baymothesis coughed a fireball at the elf. White hot fire splashed down onto the ground in front of him. His horse reared suddenly, causing him to fight for control. Sparks reeled into the air past the elf's face. Calming his horse again, Qwan muttered to himself, "Well, I think that pissed him off."

Throwing its huge horned head back in a loud bellow, Baymothesis dived. Qwan spurred his horse into a gallop, attempting to reach a point beyond which the dragon could aim. Flecks of foam were thrown from his horse and beneath the flesh he could see the muscles moving in a fluid union. The dragon hurtled through the sky over Qwan's head. His reactions took over at that very same moment. The lance, almost as if it had chosen to do so by its own design, moved into a vertical position. Then Qwan threw it hard into the air, yelling loudly with the effort.

Baymothesis screamed. The lance had pierced its side causing a deep wound. A small fountain of blood spurted into the air, forced further by the air released from one of the air sacs. Clutching at the lance with its smaller front legs, Baymothesis pulled it free, snapping it into two sections. Casting another baleful glance at the elf, Baymothesis threw the broken lance to the ground. Beating its two wings again, the dragon hung in the sky, glaring down at the elf on horseback.

Sitting back calmly in his saddle, Qwan called, "Why bother with the dramatics? We both know what you're going to do!"

Opening his jaws again, Baymothesis sent a jet of flame towards the elf. Qwan pulled hard on the reins, turning the horse away quickly. Moving at a gallop, the elf spurred his horse on. Baymothesis swooped down, racing along behind him, chasing Qwan with the fire spray. Now all around Qwan was a searing heat that felt as if it could burn his flesh from his bones.

Hedged in on all sides by walls of fire, Qwan brought his horse to a halt. The animal reared, panicked by the heat of the fire and the smell of the smoke. Over the sound of the crackling fire, Qwan could hear the steady thump of Baymothesis flapping its wings. The heat and smoke served to distort the sound, making it impossible for Qwan to determine which direction it was coming from. A sudden roar to his left made Qwan roll sideways out of his saddle. As he fell, he kicked his horse on the flanks, making it bolt. A heartbeat later, the huge shadowy form of Baymothesis parted the smoke clouds. Seeing the horse running, it gave chase immediately, sliding back away through the flames again.

Qwan drew his sword quickly and pushed himself upright. He blinked hard, rubbing his stinging eyes to free them from smoke and tears. Putting his forearms up in front of his face, he ran and jumped through one of the walls of fire. His breath came in sharp painful wheezes. Fighting back a coughing fit, Qwan ran on, trying to get to somewhere with less fire. Rolling onto his knees, he scanned the flames. Over the top of the crackling, he heard his horse snort loudly only to be interrupted by a loud, wet snapping sound. Somewhere to his right he heard the other horses cry out in terror. He gripped his sword tightly in his hands, waiting to see the dark shadow fall over him again. Beads of sweat rolled from his face, dropping to the ground unchecked.

"Come on, you bastard," Qwan muttered, searching the flames, "where are you?"

To his left, the dragon walked calmly through the wall of fire. For a few moments Baymothesis paused, taking in the area in front of it, looking for the elf. Flames licked up around the dragon's scales, unnoticed by Baymothesis itself. Finding the elf only a short distance away, the dragon roared.

Gauduin took a few careful steps into the darkness, almost disappearing from sight entirely. He gestured to the mage, beckoning him to enter the tunnel, "Can you cast some light in here?"

The foul smell caused Uthan's stomach to lurch. Concentrating more on not vomiting, Uthan mouthed a single word and waved his right hand in a small arc over his head. Above him a small ball of glowing white light blinked into existence. It floated in the air, growing in intensity until the light was bright enough to see the tunnel in front of them. Almost immediately it veered left and down. Right away, they saw the source of the sickly sweet smell.

A row of corpses littered the far wall. Limbs had been twisted around each other in a gruesome, mocking embrace. Many of the bodies were little more than skeletons now, the flesh long since given way to the writhing mass of maggots that had fed on them. Feeling the need to be sick again, Uthan pointed a hand at the corpses and uttered another magical word. Tiny snakes of fire danced around his outstretched fingers for a moment before they leapt at the corpses. A pall of equally foul smelling smoke filled the tunnel as the magic fire quickly reduced the corpses and the maggot piles to nothing more than ash.

The light orb slowly drifted off into the midst of the smoke, casting strange dancing shadows on the walls around them. Jogging to keep up, the travellers followed the light as it led them through the ashes and smoke and down a set of roughly carved stone steps.

"More steps! I don't believe this," Gauduin panted, following Uthan closely. Turning to look at Demien over his shoulder, he said, "You know I have this belief about the ancients and stairs." The warrior woman arched an eyebrow. "I think they believed that if something wasn't at the end of numerous staircases then it wasn't worth finding after all."

"Sounds about right to me," Demien replied.

The stairs stopped, leading the group into another short tunnel. At the end of the tunnel was a large door. Made of solid iron bars that appeared to have been interwoven together into a barrier, the door looked as if it had stood in place for centuries. Demien walked calmly over and pressed a hand firmly against the metal. From behind Gauduin added his muscle power, but the door remained solidly where it was. Stroking his beard in one hand, Gauduin muttered, "It's stuck fast!"

With a snort and a half smile, Demien said, "Well, after the ancients have led us down all those steps it'd be pretty dumb of them to leave it unlocked, right?"

"A little courtesy on their part would have been good though," Gauduin replied, distractedly. He was peering closely at the bars of the door, his nose only an inch or so away. Finally, he walked off, throwing his arms up in the air. "Blasted thing would have to be iron as well, wouldn't it."

"Can't blast it open with magic then," Uthan said, more for his own benefit.

Gauduin turned to glare at him, then noticed he was talking to himself rather than the others.

"What about brute force?" Demien asked with a sly grin on her face.

"On that?" Gauduin asked, jerking a thumb in the door's direction. "It'll need to have some power behind it."

"Well, we do have a walking tool of destruction with us," Demien said, nodding at Diarus.

The Daiharlon looked from them to the door then back again. He shrugged and turned away, walking back in the direction of the stairs.

"Where are you going?" Gauduin called after him.

"He's getting a run-up," Uthan answered quietly. He looked up at them and added, "I think you should move back now."

They flattened themselves against the wall as the speeding form of Diarus raced past. At the very last moment, the Daiharlon pushed his heavy body into the air, turning his shoulder to the door. The iron hinges broke away from the wall on impact, the door flying into the room beyond. Diarus hit the ground hard, letting out a pained grunt as he rolled to his feet. On his upper right arm there was already a sore-looking purple bruise. He began kneading at the muscle with his fingers, trying to coax life back into the limb again.

Uthan, Gauduin and Demien slowly followed him into the room.

"Are you okay?" Gauduin asked, seeing the Daiharlon holding his arm. The dwarf then stopped dead in his tracks, taking in what the Daiharlon was staring at.

They were in a large cavernous room. All around the walls were enormous piles of bright jewels and coins. Ornate weapons and armour littered the floor, all trophies from previous battles that Baymothesis had won. High above them an opening in the wall let in small shafts of sunlight. The light bounced off the gold, lighting the entire room with a soft golden glow. Chains ran from the walls, ceiling and floor, fixed in spiked brackets. They all converged into the centre of the room, entwining themselves around the object of their attention. A large statue of a man made from shining steel.

The Forged One

Glaring across at an adversary it clearly had not counted on, Baymothesis slunk forward a few paces. Its right front leg came up, bringing a handful of razor-edged claws with it. Qwan rolled back and to his left, somersaulting to his feet as the claws raked the ground where he had only just knelt. As Baymothesis swept out again, Qwan was running towards him, leaping over the claws with ease. His sword flickered out as he passed, nicking into the scaly flesh. Rearing its head up high so it towered above the elf, Baymothesis sucked in a deep lungful of air, ready to blast gouts of flame.

Qwan prepared himself to dive to the side and to hope that the fire would miss him when a golden blur hammered into Baymothesis's side. The smaller creature attacked with a renewed fury, tearing into the dragon's flank. Baymothesis threw its head back and roared in anger. Qwan ran in, and drove his sword up into the fleshy belly of the dragon. It reared up on its hind legs, screaming and scrabbling at the blade. Qwan dropped to a crouch again and reached into his left boot for his dagger. Taking a few careful steps back, he threw it overarm into Baymothesis's neck.

At the same time the gryphon sank its razor-sharp claws in between the dragon's scales, clinging onto the beast while its beak tore entire chunks of flesh away. Screaming in agony, Baymothesis inhaled deeply, swelling itself up. Qwan recognised what was happening: the dragon was seeking to escape. He ran forward; ready to grab hold of his sword hilt as it protruded from the wound. Almost effortlessly, Baymothesis swept out a front arm. The limb struck Qwan firmly in the chest, sending him flying through the air to land hard against the scorched dirt. His breath exploded from his lungs in a pain-filled gasp. He struggled to rise again and resume his attack but agony speared through his side. The fall felt like it had broken several of his ribs, each breath caused him to wince. Looking over, he saw the gryphon had moved up Baymothesis's back and was tearing and raking at the dragon's shoulders and neck. The dragon's wings unfurled, catching the rising wind with a loud thump. Baymothesis screamed louder and giving its body a mighty shake to try and free itself from the sword, it leapt up into the air. With its wings beating and its air sacs swelling further, Baymothesis soared above the ground.

From his vantage point, Qwan watched as the dragon barrel rolled in the air, trying desperately to shake the gryphon free. Drops of blood fell from the fight. The viscous dark red blood of the dragon was mingled with a distinctly lighter shade of crimson. It was then Qwan glanced to where the gryphon had been tossed at the beginning; the ground was stained with a wide smear of red. He suddenly felt a pang of guilt. The gryphon was also heavily injured but was now up in the air battling the dragon while he could only sit on the ground in pain and watch.

High above him, the pair wheeled and rolled, dived and climbed. The gryphon's claws held it fast to Baymothesis's shoulders, refusing to let go. Then the dragon appeared to slow suddenly. Its neck straightened and its throat strained to screech but only a small belch of dull flame erupted from its jaws. Its whole body shivered violently, scales rattling in an unsettling chorus set against the rushing wind. Baymothesis's wings became limp, falling down to its sides, air rushed out from the sacs, erupting in a fountain of flame from its jaws.

With one last roll that nearly wrenched the gryphon from its back, Baymothesis turned to the ground and began the long, spiralling descent. Qwan watched, detached from the action as the dragon fell closer towards him. Almost before he realised it, Baymothesis's body crashed to earth, raising a large dust cloud that rippled out from the impact, blowing the remaining fires out. The shock waves jarred Qwan's body, bouncing him into the air. He cried out in pain as his already damaged ribs struck the hard packed dirt again.

For what felt like an eternity, Qwan lay as still as possible on the ground, listening to the sound of his own breathing as he fought to calm it and ignore the pain from his battered ribcage. From the periphery of his vision, he could see the now dead form of

Baymothesis. The impact had broken every bone in the dragon's otherwise tough body. The underbelly had split open from the impact and vast amounts of blood and gore had been flung across the field. The mixed smell of blood and soot hung heavily in the air around him.

Lying close by the broken dragon was the gryphon. Its head lay at a sickening angle to its body. Both wings were broken, the bone piercing flesh in a few places. Seeing the creature in such a pitiful state brought tears to Qwan's eyes. Despite the pain that came with each sob, the elf wept openly, mumbling an apology to the gryphon over and over again.

Chapter Twenty-Five

"So how do we move it?" Gauduin asked. He wandered around behind the Forged One, stepping over and under the taut chains. They were made from solid links each one being the size of Gauduin's fist.

Uthan ran a hand over one of the nearby chains. "They're made of iron," he muttered, "so I can't use magic."

"You have to hand it to whoever put him here," Demien said, wandering around to the statue. "You can't get in through the mountain without using magic but, as soon as you're in here, it's useless!"

Kneading the muscles in his shoulder, Diarus moved to one of the brackets holding the chain to the wall. Bracing his foot against the rock, he grasped firmly onto one of the links and pulled. The muscles in his arms and shoulders swelled up with the effort. Gritting his teeth and grunting, Diarus continued pulling with every ounce of strength he could summon. Finally letting his foot drop back to the floor again, he breathlessly said, "They don't give even a little."

"This just gets better," Gauduin muttered. "Can't break them, can't pull them out of the wall."

The dwarf turned away from the statue in frustration and wandered in amongst the riches stored around them. Diarus walked right up to the Forged One, staring at the shining steel surface. Ducking under and stepping over chains, he circled the statue, keeping his puzzled gaze fixed on the Forged One's head. He jumped back with a start as the eyes blinked once.

Demien and Uthan both looked up at the Daiharlon at the same time.

Raising a quizzical eyebrow, Demien asked, "What?"

"It's alive," Diarus replied in hushed tones. "It blinked."

Before Uthan or Demien could say anything, an exclamation from Gauduin caught their attention. Leaving Diarus to stare curiously at the Forged One itself, Uthan and Demien skirted around the piles of wealth littering the cave. They found the dwarf looking at a large, rusted metal box. A thick lever stuck upright from the top. Gauduin was trying to throw it but the rust held it fast.

"I think," he said through gritted teeth, "this mechanism may free the chains."

"Why do you think that?" Demien asked, watching the dwarf with a sense of amusement as he placed a foot against the box to get more leverage.

Red-faced with the exertion, Gauduin answered, "Call it an educated guess."

"And it could also very easily bring the mountain down on top of us," Demien countered.

She pointed up to the darkened ceiling. There was a web of chains there, criss-crossing each other. Heavy-looking gear wheels could only just be seen sticking out from gaps in the rock walls. Large ancient-looking weights hung from more chains, barely visible in the shadows.

As Gauduin and Uthan both looked up, she added, "Somehow I can't imagine it's as easy as throwing one lever."

"Then get ready to start digging a way out," Gauduin replied, puffing and panting as he continued to free the mechanism.

Almost feeling sorry for the dwarf, Uthan called Diarus over and gestured to the box. Gently, the Daiharlon pushed Gauduin to one side and grabbed hold of the lever.

Gauduin shook his head and between deep breaths, said, "It's no good. The thing is stuck fast there."

Diarus simply nodded and pulled hard. With the squeal of metal upon metal echoing through the cave, the lever moved. Deep within the rock there was the sound of gears stirring into action. The chains wrapped around the Forged One began to move, slithering away from him like they were somehow alive. A sudden tremor rocked the ground they stood on. Gauduin leapt back from the lever. Showers of dust rained down on the four friends from the ceiling. As the sound of the entire mountain vibrating subsided, Uthan turned in a complete circle, searching all around them.

"What was that?" he whispered.

Speaking in a hushed tone, Gauduin answered, "I have no idea."

"Gauduin," Demien began, very quietly, "I really think we should get out of here."

"I think you're right," Gauduin muttered.

High above them, sharp cracking sounds filtered down to them.

They could hear the desperate sound of rock groaning against rock. The last of the chains disappeared into holes in the walls and the mechanical sounds instantly stopped. No sooner was the chain free from the statue, than Demien was running to the door, dragging Uthan with her. A few paces away from the exit, he skidded to a halt and turned to watch. Gauduin was pushed through, almost thrown by Diarus, as the Daiharlon reached for a large kite shield. He held the shield over his head, protecting himself from the showers of dust and small pieces of rock that tumbled from above. Looking past the Daiharlon, Uthan saw the Forged One come alive.

The statue raised his arms and threw his head back. His mouth opened, releasing a silent scream, which Uthan still, somehow, managed to hear. Fire danced in his eyes, giving him a defiant look. Suddenly, everything went black as tons of rock fell from the cavern ceiling, burying the Forged One. Thick clouds of yellow grey dust billowed through the door and into the corridor around the four companions.

As the dust settled, Uthan stood up having shaken a thick layer of debris from his body. He paced back across to the doorway, staring at the rocks that now barricaded the entrance. Testing the rock wall, he asked, "Now how do we get it out?"

A steady pounding began to reach their ears, muffled as it found its way through the avalanche.

Getting to her feet, Demien muttered, "I don't think we need to. It's doing it itself."

"What?" Uthan asked, turning to look at her.

"I mean he's freeing himself," she replied. "We should get out of here now. There's no telling how safe the rest of this place is."

Finding new strength in the threat of being buried alive, the group ran up the winding stairs, taking them two or three at a time. They ignored the frantic pounding of their hearts and the burning pain of their protesting leg muscles. Behind and below, the pounding of the Forged One freeing itself from its tomb was nothing more than a series of distant vibrations in the rock. They found their way out of the tunnels and sprinted down the steps outside Mount Drakkar, blinking in the sunlight.

The broken body of Baymothesis was amongst the first things they saw upon reaching the ground. The smell of blood was thick in the air; several deep splits covered the dragon's body, exposing its insides. The ground was charred; here and there a tiny flame still ate away at the grass.

"I don't believe he did it," Gauduin muttered, walking towards the gigantic corpse. He walked around its head, grimacing at the trail of thick, dark blood that ran from the corner of its mouth, spilling out onto the blackened ground. As the dwarf took in the scene he found Qwan sitting on the ground with his face in his hands. "Qwan? Are you hurt?"

Letting out a shuddering breath, Qwansien looked at his friends. They could see the tracks on his face where tears had come unchecked.

"He caught me hard in the ribs. One or two may be broken."

Uthan knelt beside the elf and prodded his back. Qwan cried out loud. With a wry smile, Uthan said, "I'd say there are a few broken ones there alright."

"Can you fix them instead of poking me please?" Qwan muttered through a clenched jaw.

He grunted as Uthan pressed a hand against his side. A soft, yellow glow lit the mage's hand as if he was made of light. If Qwan had listened closely he would have heard the faint sound of his ribs snapping back into place. As it was he was too busy clenching the hilt of his sword in his fist to block out the pain. Gradually the light faded and Qwan released his grip and began to breathe more easily again.

"Can you stand?" Gauduin asked his friend. Demien offered her hand to the elf to help him.

"Only one way to find out," Qwan answered, taking the hand and letting Demien pull him to his feet.

He slipped his thumb under the lone glove he wore, peeling the leather away from the back of his hand. For the briefest of seconds he looked hopeful. Then, seeing what was under the glove, all sparks of that hope died.

"What's wrong?" Demien asked, noting his expression.

Qwan peeled the glove away, allowing them to see the back of his hand. An ugly symbol had been etched into his flesh. White scar tissue was drawn into a jagged circle with two lines running parallel through it.

"You're an outlaw to your own people?" Demien asked, knowing what the symbol meant.

Qwan nodded sadly. "This symbol is why I can never return to my own lands. And why I never speak of them. It was burned into my hand by the supposedly Holy fires of the Elfish Royalty. It can't be removed and it limits the use of my hand. A reminder from the Elfish Empire."

Gradually from the direction of Mount Drakkar, they began to hear the sound of hammering as metal pounded against rock. For a few moments they all looked at the mountain, waiting for the Forged One to explode into view.

"So, do we follow it or what?" Diarus asked quietly.

Uthan looked at Gauduin. "Is there anywhere else Hedrial would have been taken?"

The dwarf shrugged, "Anywhere really."

"Isn't it a safe bet that he would have been taken to the Flame?" Demien asked. In answer to the raised eyebrows and questioning glances, she continued. "It just seems to me that if the Flame knew he was here to unlock the Forged One then maybe he'd want to know how many others know about it as well."

"That's if he's not here somewhere," Gauduin replied, with a nod.

A shrug from Uthan was followed by, "He's not here. I can't feel him."

The pounding sounds grew louder, followed suddenly by the hard noise made by cracking rock. From where they waited, they could see a shining steel fist burst through the wall of Mount Drakkar. A heartbeat later the second fist came through. The Forged One tore chunks of rock away, tossing them aside as if they weighed nothing. Sunlight caught the shining body, making dazzling sparkles of light that made all five of them have to look away. White-hot fire seemed to burn deep within the Forged One's eyes as it looked out at the daylight for the first time in centuries.

Watching the Forged One start off at a steady walk to the north, Gauduin muttered, "We should mount up and follow it then since it knows where it's going."

"Good thing it's indestructible. It can take out anything before it gets to us," Demien said with a grin.

As they mounted up to follow the Forged One, Qwan looked over at the ruined corpse of Baymothesis. For a moment or two he felt proud of the victory, until he saw the gryphon again. This time, a lone tear rolled down his cheek. Bowing his head, Qwan uttered a silent prayer to the gods and turned away.

"I wish we had had some time to at least hide that dragon skin, you know," Qwan said as they rode along. "We could make a fortune back in Dacenheim with it. I would be able to retire quite comfortably."

With a snort, Gauduin answered, "That's if we survive this."

Qwan clapped his friend on the shoulder, "Gauduin, I have survived two armies and a dragon so far. What else is there to throw at me?"

"Tempting fate as always," Gauduin muttered.

The Forged One had walked ahead, carving a path through the jungle. The companions rode behind, allowing the horses to progress at a gentle walk in the close heat. Ahead, they could hear the thrashing sounds as the statue punched and swiped its way through the undergrowth. There was the occasional angry squawking of a bird or a fearful growl from a large cat disturbed by the metal man's progress. Up ahead they heard a steady roar where the stifling jungle before them was carved in two by a wide river. The sound of crashing water was deafening as they reached the bank which sloped down steeply. Four tall rocks pierced the white, foamy surface, resembling giant fingers. Reining the horses in along the top of the bank, Uthan looked around him, snapping his head this way and that.

"Where's it gone?" he asked, searching for the Forged One.

"It must have got across," Gauduin sounded fed up.

"Not yet it hasn't," Demien exclaimed as she pointed to the second rock.

Striding through the water, which seemed to have no effect on it at all, was the statue. The fast current pushed against it, slowing its progress while white foam crashed over its head, hiding it beneath the water for seconds at a time.

"If it gets across before we do, we lose it," Gauduin complained, "and I don't know where we're supposed to be going."

Diarus drew a length of chain from his saddle bag. "It's a good thing I brought this from Dessendor, isn't it."

While the others looked at him blankly, Gauduin was the one to voice the question, "What are you thinking?"

"If iron chains held it down back in that cave, then there's no real reason they wouldn't do it again," the Daiharlon answered. "I don't see why it wouldn't work here. Just loop one end over its head and stop it while we find a way across."

They nodded in thoughtful agreement, silently impressed. The

Daiharlon, using his huge strength, began knotting links of the chain together, forming a noose.

Demien nodded across the river, "Better hurry. It's nearly there."

Diarus followed her gaze. The statue was wading towards the bank. By now the water had fallen to its thighs, fizzing and bubbling as tiny carnivorous fish tried in vain to tear into its steel legs. Climbing down from his horse, Diarus walked closer to the bank. He swung the chain above his head, half aware of the steady whistling as air raced through the links. The loop sailed out from the Daiharlon's hands, leaving a long length of it to trail between his fingers; his aim could not have been better. The Forged One stopped dead in its tracks as the iron links dropped down around its neck. Caught in the middle of a huge, striding step, the statue, off balance, toppled backwards with a loud splash. Almost immediately, the water around it fizzled and roared into life as shoals of fish attacked the motionless steel man.

"Okay, so how do we get across?" Diarus asked, patiently.

"Follow the sunset for one mile," said a voice from behind them. They spun round to see a short creature watching them. His mottled, green-skinned body was naked except for a dark, ragged loincloth. Lank, greasy hair was tied in a topknot, falling to the back of his elongated head. He regarded them with bulbous, yellow eyes that had cat like pupils. Moving his horse carefully around to walk it along the bank, Gauduin nodded to the creature. The others led their horses away, following the dwarf through the barely visible trail. No one had said anything to the strange guide as they left him behind at the riverbank.

"What was that creature?" Uthan asked, unable to keep silent about it any longer.

The dwarf shrugged, "No one knows much about them."

"Once, they were slaves to a demon king, then something set them free," Demien said, riding behind Uthan.

"They live here, in the jungle?" The mage was intrigued.

"Apparently so," Gauduin replied. He kept looking up into the trees and to his left, largely ignoring the river to their right.

"So what set them free and why?" Uthan asked.

Behind him, Demien shrugged and shook her head. "No one knows for certain. There were legends about one of their own kind rising up. But that's all they were - just legends."

"No one's tried to find out?" Uthan pressed.

Gauduin looked around, "They don't talk to outsiders unless really necessary."

"Why?" He was not giving up.

"They just don't," Demien answered.

Uthan nodded, thinking to himself for a few moments. "So," he said finally, "having that one there point us to this track was unusual?"

"Pretty much," Gauduin answered.

"Which is why you don't trust it?" the young mage was to the point.

"What makes you think that?" Gauduin returned casually.

"You're looking up into the trees a lot more than usual," Uthan answered quietly.

The dwarf smiled, "It can't hurt to make sure we don't have any more surprises."

"Are they likely to attack then?" Uthan asked, becoming aware of the energy bolt he was beginning to form subconsciously.

Demien put a hand on his shoulder, having noticed the energy crackling around his left hand. "No, they won't, in fact they'll keep their distance."

"He was probably just fishing in the river and wanted us away from there," Gauduin said, also noticing the magic building up. "I just don't want to be caught out."

The rest of the trail was walked in near silence. The travellers breathing became more laboured and seemed to grow louder as they felt the oppressive jungle heat sapping their energy. In the canopy above, monkeys screeched down chattering warnings at the companions. From the undergrowth to their left, a large cat watched them pass, anticipating its chances of bringing one of them down.

The bridge they finally came to was little more than a thick tree. Long ago, some force had pushed against the trunk enough to tilt it over but not destroy it. The roots, many of which were visible, clung tenaciously to the soft brown dirt. The topside of the trunk had been worn away, only mere stumps remaining of the branches that had once sprouted from the heart of the tree. This had been worn flat in places, the thick bark stripped away to leave only dark wood beneath.

Leading his horse carefully up over one of the thicker roots and onto the makeshift bridge itself, Gauduin announced, "Well, it's one of the better bridges I've found in this place."

It was early evening when they had finally hacked a trail back through the undergrowth to the riverbank where the Forged One had attempted to cross. Qwan moved carefully down to water's edge and peered into the murky depths.

"Its still in there," he called back. "Surrounded by fish!"

"Slow learners," Gauduin muttered, standing a couple of feet away from the elf.

Sitting down heavily on the ground, Qwan asked, "So what are we going to do?"

"Set up camp here for the night," Demien said. "That thing isn't going anywhere and we won't make much more progress through all this undergrowth in darkness."

The evening meal came in the form of the carnivorous fish from the river. Diarus had spent nearly an hour catching enough for all of them, using an arrow to spear their sleek bodies. Gauduin had constructed a small fire, easily controllable and not too likely to send any telltale clouds of smoke into the sky. The ground around them was steadily cleared, creating enough space to allow them to sleep comfortably without having to worry about poisonous snakes or insects. Even so, Uthan cast a small illusion that made the group almost invisible to the jungle's nocturnal denizens.

He was the last to settle down for the night and lay awake, staring into the canopy high above him, listening to the night time sounds. Water rushed in its relentless race below him. Putting his head on the pillow of his bedroll, close to the soft dirt, he could hear things moving, burrowing under the earth. Eventually, the sounds of the jungle at night once again gently lulled the young mage into a deep sleep.

Chapter Twenty-Six

The sound of metal striking metal caused Uthan to open his eyes. He blinked rapidly, not just from the sudden light but also from sheer disbelief at the sight that confronted him. The jungle was no longer there. Instead, he stood on a flat plateau of a mountaintop that seemed to be thousands of feet above a scorched, dry rock and sand desert. In the centre of the plateau was a forge that shimmered with intense heat. Working away at it was a burly man. A black cloth was tied across his face, masking his nose and mouth from the fumes created by his forge. His bald scalp was sweating profusely and his eyes of pure blue stared into the white-hot flames in front of him. He pumped a large set of bellows, blowing air into the furnace and Uthan caught a faint smell of molten metal that he felt was familiar.

Standing away from the forge were eleven figures. Whilst they all wore different colours and styles of clothing, each figure seemed to radiate light from inside their flesh. Uthan knew who they were immediately. They were the First, the Gods. None of them paid any attention to the young mage; instead they stared out across a vast expanse of desert and the object of their focus was a volcano. Thick clouds of black, choking smoke hung in the air above it, the undersides glowing with an angry orange aura. As Uthan watched the smoke, he saw a malevolent face form and reform, time and time again as the clouds moved in the air. He did not need to second-guess as to what he was staring at.

The sound of chains brought his attention back to the forge. The blacksmith had tilted a large slab of rock onto its end with a set of slender looking chains. Dropping the end of the slab into a small dip in the plateau, the smith moved around his forge, collecting a heavy hammer. With a mighty swing, the hammer smashed into the slab. Shards of rock were sent reeling away and huge gaping cracks formed in the surface. From under the cracks, Uthan caught a glimmer of shining silver. Two more swings reduced the stone slab to mere pieces, balancing in place. The smith began tossing the chunks aside, revealing the gleaming, steel Forged One. Eleven radiant faces looked at their creation and smiled triumphantly upon seeing the perfectly cast features.

High above, Uthan heard a sudden screeching. Instinctively, he dropped to his knees and looked up to the skies. Circling the mountain was a dragon, larger than Baymothesis, yet less terrible to see. Gold and silver scales caught the fiery dawn sunlight. The creature soared through the sky effortlessly, gliding on translucent wings as it watched the scene unfolding below with patient interest.

The smith, standing inches away from the statue and scrutinising every inch of his work, turned to the Gods. "You are pleased, mighty ones?" he asked them.

"We are," one of the Gods answered. He was taller than the rest, dressed in white and grey robes. His face, while appearing youthful, carried a wisdom that only age can bring. He was Rastell, the father of the Gods and, as his sparkling blue eyes took in the sight of the Forged One, the smith bowed and backed away.

High above them all, the dragon screeched again. Rastell raised a hand, fingers outstretched to the dragon. With another screech, the magnificent creature stopped circling, hanging in the air, placing Rastell in an angled path between it and the Forged One. Its long jaws opened, directing a jet of searing flame down at Rastell. The fire impacted into the God's outstretched palm, burning away into small, flickering flames. Uthan watched in awe as the jet finished, leaving only the small ball of fire in Rastell's hand. The God then carried the flame across to the Forged One, placing it inside a hollow in its chest. Immediately, the smith came over, holding a plate of identical gleaming steel. He fixed it into place, covering the dragon flame completely.

"With fire and steel you are born here today," Rastell said. The Forged One's eyes opened, staring directly into the piercing blue of Rastell's stare. "One from our family has given himself to darkness. You shall stop his rise to evil in a way we cannot."

The statue nodded once, turned and walked to the edge of the plateau. As if the potentially lethal plummet held no danger, the Forged One stepped off the edge and began moving down the mountain.

Uthan darted across the plateau to watch. Reaching the edge, he was suddenly aware of where he was. Below him he could see a familiar set of steps, cut into the very stone of the mountain itself. He looked back at the distant volcano again. The statue's path would take it straight to the fiery mountain. As Uthan watched the clouds writhe and whirl, the face within them, despite being full of hate, smiled.

Uthan sat bolt upright. He was back in the jungle again, still in the dark of night. A horde of nocturnal insects made their chorus of sounds, a chittering harmony that Uthan found strangely comforting as his mind raced. On the edge of his hearing, he was aware of footsteps; something was moving next to the water's edge. He made his way closer to the bank, keeping at a half crouch, half crawl. It was the same creature that had pointed them towards the bridge earlier. He padded back and forth along the water's edge, looking into the murky depths then at a small net in his hands. It was hard to tell exactly, but the strange creature appeared confused or shocked.

"You should get away from there," Uthan said calmly.

The creature looked up, startled, "What is it doing there?"

"Its ours, we left it there," Uthan replied slowly.

"How will you get it out?" The peculiar individual was staring back into the waters at the Forged One. "The fish will eat you."

"We'll manage," the young man answered, "I know a few things."

"Magic? You need to know lots of magic."

"I know enough."

"Good. Good for you then," the creature replied. He crouched by the river, gingerly dipping his fingers into the cool water. "Is that why you are here?"

"We're here searching for a friend," Uthan answered quickly although he had a sudden aversion to trusting this strange being.

Stroking the water, the jungle dweller stated, "But this is not your friend."

"Our friend is elsewhere. We hope this thing might lead us to him."

"This one leads along a dangerous path. Your friend is dead if this one leads you to him."

"And what would you know of my friend?" Uthan felt himself flushing angrily. He rose up onto his knees, balling his fists.

"You should sleep," the creature said. He turned and looked directly at the young mage, his yellow eyes glazing over for a few moments.

Feeling his limbs go weak and heavy, Uthan moved back up the bank and settled down onto his bedroll. His eyelids grew heavier as he felt the pull of sleep. He laid his head down for a moment, snapping back awake again with a start. Glaring at the small being, he growled, "What are you doing?"

"Sleep," the creature persisted. Again Uthan felt himself drifting off.

Almost standing over him, the jungle dweller continued staring down with blank, mist-covered eyes until he was certain the young mage was asleep. Then he turned and moved back to the river's edge again. Focusing on the Forged One beneath the water, he sat down and crossed his legs. In a low, barely audible voice, he began chanting words in an ancient magical language that none of the companions would have understood.

From elsewhere in the river, a school of the carnivorous fish swam over to the statue and began nipping at the chain, pulling links this way and that. More and more fish appeared, joining in the frenzied action until the water was bubbling with the sudden activity. Then the Forged One sat up with a loud splash and finally, as water cascaded from the steel muscles, it stood up. Two, long, striding steps brought it out of the water and onto the bank, where it stopped a moment and stared down at the creature with eyes of blazing dragon fire.

Staring straight back, the creature said, "You must go away from here. You are dangerous."

He watched the Forged One turn away and begin its journey again. Turning back to the water, the creature watched the fish as they picked at the chain. There were only a few of them now, the majority having realised it had not been food after all. The creature watched calmly for a while before plunging his hand into the water, all the way to his shoulder. The fish swam warily just out of his reach as he grasped hold of the chain and withdrew it from the cold river again. For a short while he sat and scrutinised it, checking every link as if looking for something. Finally, he just dropped it on the grass next to him and curled up in a ball on the ground, drifting into sleep himself.

Uthan awoke the following morning, roused into life by Demien shaking him by the shoulder. Her voice was tense and urgent. Sitting up and rubbing his eyes, he sleepily asked, "What is it?"

"The Forged One, it's gone," she said.

Uthan's eyes snapped open and almost throwing himself onto his feet, he ran down to the river. Diarus was crouching at the water's edge, searching the dirty brown water. "Where is it?" Uthan asked.

The Daiharlon shook his head and shrugged. "What about the chain? It stopped it moving," Uthan said.

In answer, Gauduin held the length of chain up for inspection, "Not any more, it isn't."

Uthan sat down heavily on the ground, dropping his head into his hands.

"I sent the metal man away," said a voice from the trees. Uthan's unwelcome guest from the night before walked out of the jungle towards the riverbank, carrying a large bird over his shoulder. Looking back at the mage, he added, "Being here was dangerous. For you and for him."

Putting a restraining hand on Uthan's shoulder, Demien asked, "Why dangerous?"

The creature sat on the edge of the river and began plucking the bird's feathers out in handfuls, casting them into the water. Glancing over at them, he said, "Make some fire."

"You won't get anymore out of him right now," Qwan said suddenly. The creature had begun chanting in some arcane language with his head bowed. All around the feathers that had been tossed into the rushing water, they could see fish swarming. The others looked back towards Qwan as the elf began making a small fire. Without looking at them, he explained, "He's praying."

Dropping down to sit opposite, Gauduin asked, "You know what he's saying?"

"Sort of," Qwan answered, with a shrug. "I've heard the words before. They lose something in translation but it basically means 'Forgive me for this life I take. It is done to keep me alive so I may serve.' It's Kaelish."

Uthan wandered over, "What's Kaelish? I've never heard of it."

"You wouldn't have," Gauduin answered. "No one uses it, the language belongs to Kael, The Monastery City."

The creature ceased his prayer and brought the bird over to the fire. Fixing it onto a makeshift spit and placing it into the flames, he did not look at them as he said, "Your friend was the wizard?" As Gauduin nodded, he sadly continued, "He went to the dead place."

"Then that's where we're going," the dwarf answered quickly.

Shaking his head, the creature said, "No. You must not go there. The dead place is dangerous. The wizard will be dead now. Bad things live there."

"We're going," Gauduin said flatly, staring directly into the big yellow eyes in front of him.

The creature nodded then looked at Uthan calmly, "Then I must show you. Keep you alive." He watched the fire darken the meat before tearing a chunk off and going to sit by the river. The companions watched him settle down and eat, occasionally tossing a piece into the water.

"At one with the forest, isn't he," Demien muttered.

"My question is, do we trust him or not?" Gauduin said.

Demien reached into the fire with a dagger, carving a small sliver of meat from the cooking carcass. The scent filled all their nostrils, reminding them all that they were hungry. Chewing on the meat, Demien said, "I don't see that we have a choice. We need to get to this city and he's the only one who can guide us."

"Do you have a name?" Gauduin called down to the creature.

He craned his neck a little and paused. "Targy."

"How far is it to Kael?" Gauduin asked.

Targy took another bite of the meat before tossing the chewed bone into the water. "Three days travel maybe. No more."

Gauduin swallowed the mouthful he had been chewing on, "What do you mean 'maybe'?"

"Travelled there many times. But not for many days now," Targy replied. "Bad things live in Kael. Best not to go there." Qwan commented on how he had killed a dragon already and flashed one of his infamous grins. "Demons," Targy answered. He moved closer to the fire, looking straight into Qwansien's eyes. "Worse than Baymothesis. They feed on souls. Left to agony and fear."

"What about the Forged One?" Diarus asked.

Targy stared into the flames, "Sent him away. If the dark man knows Baymothesis is dead, he knows that metal man is set free. He will send men to find him."

"I'd be surprised if there's anyone left to rampage through here," Qwan said.

"Always more waiting," Targy warned.

Pushing himself to his feet, Gauduin slung his sword scabbard over his shoulder and began kicking dirt onto the fire. The rest of the group broke camp quickly, as Targy scuttled around the site, obliterating all traces of them ever having been there. He led them along a heavily overgrown path, allowing them to only cut a small area at a time. Looking behind them, they could see why the path was virtually unchanged by their passing; even the scrutinising eyes of

Qwansien could not see a great difference.

The only break in scenery came at nearly noon on the second day. For an hour before, they could hear the heavy rumble and crashing of water. Emerging from the trees, they found themselves standing at the tall, sloping banks of a river. To the west, a great, rock wall towered up above the trees. Cutting a deep wedge into the top of wall was a white, foamy waterfall, crashing down into the river below. The whole area smelled fresh, like an early morning in spring.

Targy pointed to a cluster of broken, stone blocks littering the river, "Once there was a bridge."

The water crashed around them wildly, which made crossing, seem impossible. Gauduin was the first to ask, "So how do we cross?"

Targy's gaze went to the mist rising from the base of the waterfall. A path led around the top of the bank they stood on, disappearing behind the crashing water.

"Where does it come out?" Gauduin had to shout over the sound of the waterfall.

"Goes under the river. Comes out in the jungle," Targy replied, gesturing to the trees lining the rock wall. He began walking along the path, not bothering to check if they were following or not. The noise was deafening as they made their way forward, the rushing of the water and the sound of the horses' hooves echoed in a crescendo from the rock.

Two days later the jungle had begun to thin and was becoming much less suffocating. The further through the undergrowth they travelled, the quieter it became. There were now very few animals in the trees or on the ground, only a couple of the bright feathered birds called out. The only sound of life was the monotonous buzz of flies around them.

"Even the spiders are bright enough not to come here," Demien complained, swatting at a fly by her right ear.

Here and there, a broken pillar of dark grey stone jutted up from the undergrowth. Many of them were carpeted in thick, green moss and twists of tangling vines. Bringing up the rear of the line, Diarus stepped on something with a loud crack. Above him, five or six birds abandoned their perches with a noisy fluttering of wings. Each of the travellers, including Targy, had stopped in their tracks.

Gauduin looked at the Daiharlon's feet, hidden amongst ferns and thick grass. "I hope," he said deliberately, "that was a very brittle twig."

Diarus said nothing. Reaching down, he withdrew something coloured a dull, yellow white from the grass. Shards of bone fell away as he brushed the grass off the object. The Daiharlon shook his head and tossed the jawbone over, into the waiting hands of the dwarf.

"So this, I take it," Demien said, nodding to the grey stone pillars around them, both standing and fallen, "is Kael."

"No," Targy answered. He walked several steps further and hopped up onto a stone block. Pointing to the north, he turned to look at them and said, "That is."

Chapter Twenty-Seven

"Everyone stay alert," Gauduin urged, stepping around the ruins of a solid, grey stone wall.

Qwan, standing behind his friend with his sword in his hand, muttered, "No danger of falling asleep here."

"You're joking, aren't you?" Gauduin replied, with a broad grin. "You could fall asleep on a battlefield."

In front of them was a wide stone arch. Three, roughly-cut blocks lay across the open archway, surrounded by a scattering of stone chips. The earth under their feet was dead, nothing but dirt and stone and the jungle died away nearly fifty feet from the wall. The boundary itself stretched for nearly a mile in either direction and at its tallest, it was twenty feet high. In several places, the stone had either crumbled or had been ruined, broken away by something or someone. More pieces of the identical rough, grey stone littered the ground.

Qwan swatted a fly away from his face. "Is there any chance we can get moving?"

Gauduin held up a hand to silence him. Taking great care to tread carefully on the broken stonework, he moved through the archway, darting across a few feet of open ground. He ducked behind a pillar, broken away at his head height. The gravel-like ground behind him gave away the positions of Qwan and Diarus as they slipped through the arch and sprinted across to hide behind a small wall.

"Uthan and Demien?" Gauduin whispered to which Qwan gestured back to the arch, "And Targy?"

Demien appeared at the dwarf's right. "He stayed in the jungle."

Gauduin nearly jumped out of his skin at the sudden sound of her voice. Looking round at her, he hissed, "There are demons here. Big, nasty ones. You don't sneak up on people when there are big, nasty demons around!"

With the sound of light crunching footsteps, Uthan crept over. He ducked down between Diarus and Qwan, muttering, "Targy pretty much asked us to reconsider coming in here."

Qwan gave a wry smile and said, "Looking at the place I could be forgiven for thinking he has the right idea."

Uthan peered over the dust-ridden wall to get his first glimpse of Kael. The ground was shaped into uneven steps for what seemed like miles. He could see at least one roughly cut staircase, carved into the ground itself, leading between the broken terraces. Everywhere there were remains of walls and pillars forming a skeleton of what once must have been a magnificent city. Here and there, he saw a large crater, torn from the very earth, almost as if something had burst up from underneath long ago. Now only thick, black smoke churned up from within, piped into the air in great plumes, to touch the sky.

"They say even the rain that falls here is a killer," Qwan said in a hushed voice.

Uthan was not listening though. His attention had been grabbed by something much more horrifying. On a pillar, roughly twenty to thirty feet from him, was a human corpse. The legs however were nowhere to be seen. It appeared to sprout from the stone of the pillar itself and had arms that hung from its twisted shoulders with hands and fingers outstretched. The eyes were sunken and its mouth hung open in a constant, silent scream. Another similar corpse hung from the other side of the pillar. Looking around the area, Uthan saw more and more, most hung from pillars and walls. A few however, had sprouted from the ground itself, arms pushing against the rock around their waists. Until now, he had mistaken them for statues or rubble piles.

Following Uthan's gaze, Qwan remarked, "They must be the souls."

"There are hundreds of them," Uthan whispered in shock.

"Probably closer to thousands," Qwan said, nodding in agreement.

Demien asked, "So how are we going to find your friend?"

"I can't see them clearly enough to be certain, but most of these bodies look like they've been here some time," Qwan said. "We just need to find the ones that have been trapped more recently."

"Are you saying Hedrial is one of those now?" Uthan asked, wide-eyed.

Qwan shrugged, peering over the wall, "He must be."

"Uthan," Gauduin said, getting the mage's attention. "Can you talk to Dionis?" As Uthan shrugged in reply, the ghostly bat appeared over his shoulder. "Have you been waiting all this time?" Gauduin asked.

"Pretty much," Dionis replied, flatly. "So you think Hedrial's here?"

"We've been told he was brought here," Gauduin answered.

The spirit looked out over Kael, "Do you want me to try and find him?" Gauduin nodded. "I'll do what I can," Dionis replied, "but this really isn't good if he is here."

"You're telling us," Gauduin muttered, as Dionis faded into a subtle afterglow.

Qwan moved out from behind the wall, holding his sword tightly in both hands. Scanning the ground in front, he leant closer to Gauduin and said, "We'd better get moving we're not going to find him hiding back here."

Nodding, Gauduin hauled himself onto his feet again and followed the elf. Standing in the open, he took up position a few feet to Qwan's left. Behind him was Demien, then Diarus, with Uthan bringing up the rear. The dwarf ushered them into position, in a line, with enough space between them to swing a sword. Moving to stand between Diarus and Demien, Uthan felt faint trickles of power flowing through his arms as he prepared energy bolts. Diarus had both falchions held ready, one held in a dagger grip. Passing one of the larger craters, Uthan peered over the edge. The stench was foul, reminding him strongly of rotten eggs. The heat was worse than the smell however. It stung Uthan's eyes and boiled the breath in his lungs, forcing him to turn away. From somewhere to their left, they heard the clatter of falling rocks, clearly audible despite the constant bubbling from the craters. Demien flashed a look at Gauduin and Qwan, the elf nodded in reply. Moving like a ghost, she slipped off to the left, ducking between a pair of ruined walls.

Dionis glided in between the towering smoke plumes, keeping at a good height above Kael. He had heard about the demons and, even though he was already dead, the stories worried him. Below raced a glowing map of slender lava flows but the smoke that was billowing up partly obscured his view of Kael, granting him only brief glimpses at any one time. The corpses he could see all looked ancient and identical when seen from such a height. Yet still Dionis was not comfortable about flying at ground level because amongst the ruins were the Haunters of The Dead City. He was hoping he would be able to sense Hedrial when he was closer to him.

Qwan, Diarus and Gauduin crept through the ruins of Kael, moving in single file. Staying a few paces behind them was Uthan. Each glance at the twisted corpses sent a shudder through his body and he was sure that the images he saw would haunt his nightmares forever. Looking at the others, he could see their anxiety mounting as well. Qwan constantly switched grips on his sword, changing it from hand to hand. Gauduin held his great sword in two hands, occasionally flexing his finger while his eyes darted this way and that. Diarus's head swivelled around, scanning the terrain around him at every sound, whether imagined or not.

The smoke around them grew steadily denser as they found themselves wandering between lava-filled craters and trenches. Through the smoke, shapes loomed menacingly, only to be discovered as more corpses left to decay. Using his keen sight, Qwan picked a path through the ruins, carefully staying clear of the bodies. Ahead of them, blurred in the hazy, foul air, they saw a faint blue glow coming towards them before the familiar form of Dionis took shape.

"Have you found Hedrial?" Gauduin asked, rubbing tears from his stinging eyes. Dionis nodded, solemnly.

"Okay," Gauduin said, "then take us there."

"If only it was that simple," sighed the bat.

"Why isn't it that simple?" Gauduin asked as his soot-streaked face darkened.

"There's a small group of those Haunters around him."

As Diarus asked how many, the spirit glanced back over his shoulders into the gloom and replied, "I counted eleven."

Demien lay between the rubble of a broken pillar and wall, perfectly still even though the broken stonework dug into her skin. The earth beneath her was composed of black soot and grey volcanic dust. In the gloom, all around lay broken buildings and archways. Clouds of the thick, choking smoke rose up between ruined walls and piles of broken blocks, casting shapes that loomed into vision in the half-light. Her sword was in the soot and dust before her. A thin veil of smoke drifted across, concealing her position but the very same smoke also prevented her from seeing very far. Somewhere in front, she could hear the sound of rocks falling, something was moving across the ground just beyond the black haze ahead of her. The footsteps made hollow, crunching sounds. Slowly, Demien eased her body forward, sliding out from behind the rubble. To her left she was suddenly aware of a sniffing sound. She froze instantly, listening intently as her hand crept across the ground to the sword hilt in front of her. Behind her were footsteps, another creature. Demien snatched the sword up, showering dirt in a trail behind it. The warrior woman was on her feet and turned just in time to see the demon a short distance away.

The humanoid body was muscular, without a single ounce of fat, and it stood over seven feet tall. What flesh there was, looked as if it had been flayed or burnt from its body. Dried blood plastered the chest, neck and arms, as if painted on and the creature's legs were bound in leather straps, many of which dangled from the sides. A scarred, fleshless face turned in Demien's direction. It slowly tilted its torso backwards, nostrils flaring as it sniffed at the air. A strip of bloodied leather was bound tightly across the eyes, blinding the creature.

"I go to all the trouble of hiding and they can't see," Demien muttered to herself as the demon stalked towards her. Swinging her sword in front of her, Demien leapt to her right, vaulting over the rubble to land lightly on the dirt again. The other Haunters began picking their way around the debris, circling the warrior woman. Then they advanced, one from the right, the other from behind. Holding her sword out in front of her, Demien jumped forward, aiming to strike the first creature in the head as it stepped over part of the wall. It sidestepped the blow easily, slapping out with a cruel, taloned hand to knock her down. Demien twisted in the air, landing on her feet. She slashed out at leg height, aiming to cleave through the demon's knees. It leapt high into the air, clearing the sword blade with ease.

Propelling herself up into the air again, Demien spun and kicked out, driving her booted right heel into the leather-bound face of the demon with a sickening snap. She watched the Haunter stumble back for a few brief seconds only to advance on her again, seemingly unaffected. Demien suddenly sprinted away, making for a long, low wall, the demons quickened their own pace, desperate to catch her.

The warrior woman leapt the wall easily, sending a puff of grey dust up into the air as she hit the ground that immediately dropped away into a long, wide trench. Unable to stop her momentum, she allowed herself to drop down into the trench, changing direction to run along its path. Behind her, the demons followed, easily keeping the same pace. To her right she could see the shadowy bulk of the jungle through the smoky air, ahead of her was a stretch of open ground. Heading through a cluster of pillars and their grotesque trophies, Demien raced as fast as she could. The demons spilled through an archway behind her. One let out a harsh, braying sound, like a cord being pulled through a taut drum skin. Five sets of footsteps slammed against the ground as they all continued their chase.

Then, listening to the footsteps tirelessly gaining on her, Demien was aware of something else. She risked a glance over to her right only to see a sudden flare of green light explode from the jungle. The demons stopped, seemingly sensing the afterglow. Demien saw a small campfire with a figure, partially lit from the firelight, seated behind it. With a flick of its wrist, the figure dropped something else into the fire. Bright blue flames fizzled up suddenly, illuminating the entire area. Instantly, Demien saw the identity of the figure.

It was Targy. He sat across from the fire, calmly watching the Haunters in the distance as they stood sniffing the air apprehensively. They remained rooted to the spot as if unsure of what they were facing. Demien paused for a few moments, getting her breath back before her pursuers poured out from the ruins. They cascaded down a sharp drop, kicking up clouds of dark grey dust under their skidding feet. Forgetting about Demien, they advanced on Targy's campfire instead.

Feeling her nerves shouting at her to move, Demien's eyes went back to the creature. He merely sat calmly by his fire. The demons were almost on him. Yet he remained completely still as they stalked him, creeping slowly forward like cats hunting. Before she could yell a warning, another flash of brilliant green light exploded from the fire. Four of the demons were hurled back, striking the ground with bone-shattering force. The others stumbled around or dropped to their knees, holding their heads. Demien did not wait to see more, she propelled herself into a mad dash to leave the area. Behind her, orbs of glowing green light burst up into the air from Targy's fire, exploding in a brilliant blast of sparks.

With Qwan and Dionis at the front, the companions crept forward through the smoke. Over his right shoulder, Qwan saw a faint green light in the sky, dulled somewhat by the haze.

Gauduin followed his gaze and, seeing the light explode, he asked, "What was that?"

"I don't know," Qwan replied, distractedly. "I don't think it's anything we need to worry about just now though."

"What about Demien?" Uthan asked. "What if it's her?"

Dionis suggested going to look and began floating up higher as Qwan nodded and carefully continued forward. Through the thick smoke they could see dull shapes gathered in a group. They were hunched over something, clawing and tearing at it. "Looks like it's still feeding time," Qwan said with a wry smile.

Diarus moved to crouch next to the elf and unsheathed his falchions. Testing the edges, he asked, "Time to break up the feast?"

Another of the glowing orbs, this one much more intense, shot up into the air. The explosion of green sparks was infinitely more visible. The demons all turned towards the light for a moment, obviously able to sense the power as it burst into a brilliant shower of sparks. Quickly they pushed up onto their feet and loped off in the direction of Targy.

With a shrug and another glance at the sky where the light had been, Qwan muttered, "I don't think we need to."

"I'm liking this less and less by the minute," Gauduin said, watching the demons fade into the smoke.

"Is it clear?" Uthan asked, pushing forward a little.

Gauduin pushed him back down again, "Settle down. We don't know yet."

"It looks clear to me," Uthan said.

"The impetuosity of youth," Qwan said to his dwarfish friend. "Don't you just miss it?"

"No," Gauduin replied bluntly, "it's what got Suman killed."

Flashing a toothy grin at Gauduin, Qwan replied, "Actually I heard it was a big sword that killed him."

"I think if we're going to move," Diarus said, pushing himself into a position ready to run, "then now would be the best time."

The Daiharlon straightened up quickly and started jogging through the smoke. Eager not to lose the beastman, Gauduin and Qwan hurried after him with Uthan in tow. On the ground in front of them, where the demons had gathered, was a large greenish grey skinned corpse. Its chest muscles had been ripped and torn away, exposing a broken ribcage underneath. Deep, gouging claw marks were raked across the stomach and face. The arms and legs lay twisted and broken, caught forever in mid-struggle.

"One less Orc in the world to worry about," Gauduin commented.

"I can feel him," Uthan announced suddenly, staring with wide-open eyes into the smoke at a group of hazy, black shapes.

"Please tell me you mean Hedrial," Gauduin said, shifting his grip on his sword ever so slightly.

Uthan turned to look at them, he sounded distracted as he asked, "Can't you feel it?"

Standing up again, Qwan shrugged, shaking his head, he replied, "Feel what?"

"The pain," Uthan said calmly, "it's all around us."

They followed Uthan in amongst the collection of pillars; not one of them could contain the shudder that wracked each of them at the sight before their eyes. On each of the damaged faces was etched an expression of pure terror and agony. Bones were exposed, piercing through ragged flesh and tattered clothing, others had been flayed, leaving only a mockery of a human corpse. Those on pillars had had their lower bodies removed, the torsos appeared to be fused to the stone, the flesh pulled taut from shoulders, necks and backs. Others seemed to grow out from the dirt itself like macabre plants. Uthan led the way through the gruesome forest of bodies, instinct telling him not to get too close to any of them. He came to a stop finally, standing in front of yet another of the columns. Although it was no different to all the others, they found themselves staring open-mouthed in horror at the corpse hanging in front of them. Both Gauduin and Qwansien knew him instantly but both immediately wished otherwise.

Hedrial's flesh around his exposed chest and face was blackened from the intense flames and heat he had been subjected to. The skin of his face had been all but burnt completely, leaving semi-human features behind. The hair that had once adorned his head and face was almost entirely gone. Only a few singed whiskers sprouted from blistered muscle. The flesh was burned away from his fingertips, turning them into thin claws that were outstretched in front of him. His back and shoulders were twisted at awkward angles, as if his spine had been shattered. Torn pieces of cloth, that had been the last few scraps of Hedrial's robe, had been fused into place by the same fire.

Qwan had to turn away, paling considerably. He fought the urge to vomit, sucking in deep breaths of the putrid air. Gauduin dropped to his knees. The dwarf's eyes were red with tears that ran down his face, washing away grey ash in streaks. Uthan closed his eyes, screwing them tight, trying to shut out the image that would surely haunt him forever. Bowing his head, he felt himself shaking violently; unable to stop the quiet sobbing that slowly overwhelmed him.

"So what do we do with him?" Diarus asked. He had given them all a moment or two to come to terms with the sight. The Daiharlon himself had been stoic, not taking his eyes from the demonic trophy.

Gauduin just turned away, walking over to a stone block and slumping into a sitting position on it. Qwan had moved a few paces away in the opposite direction, standing with his back to the pillar.

"We have to bury him at least," Uthan said, trying to keep calm.

Diarus gestured to one of his falchions, silently offering to cut the corpse down. Both Gauduin and Uthan nodded. The Daiharlon stepped closer to the pillar, his blade held high. With a vicious hissing, the corpse burst into life, reaching out to grasp hold of Diarus. Bone fingertips raked out, clawing at the Daiharlon's face. Caught by surprise, Diarus jumped back and drew his second weapon. All around them, the corpses hissed and spat, suddenly full of malevolent life.

"Are they supposed to do that?" Diarus asked, visibly shaken.

"As a rule... no," Qwan replied.

From deep within the smoke drifts they heard the disembodied sound of running feet stamping against the hard packed dust. The sound seemed to echo from all around, as it grew closer. Turning this way and that, they looked past the writhing bodies and tried to see through the smoke.

"Over there," Uthan said, pointing to a soft blue glow approaching them. His fingers crackled with energy as he tried to focus, willing an energy blast into place.

"Hold it!" called Dionis, emerging from the smoky clouds, "I've found Demien."

"We've found Hedrial," Uthan replied in almost a whisper.

The spirit stopped, hovering in the air. He watched the corpses, flailing and writhing angrily. Flatly, he replied, "So I see."

"You're a ghost. What do we do, Dionis?" Qwan asked urgently. He flinched as a clawed hand swept past him.

Diarus leant back and twisted away on his right heel as another arm lashed out at him. With a loud angry snort, the Daiharlon forgot himself and retaliated. His left falchion hacked into the forearm of the corpse, cleaving it away.

"Stop!" called another displaced voice from the smoke. Targy came jogging out, followed by Demien. The small creature looked sadly around at the thrashing corpses.

"These things are trying to kill us and you want us to stand back and take it?" Gauduin bellowed, sweeping out his blade. The cut opened a deep, gouging wound in the chest of a grounded corpse. Still the thing continued its desperate attempt to grasp hold of the dwarf's legs.

Targy looked at the dwarf as if seeing him for the first time. Speaking slowly he said, "I did not speak to you." He looked again around him at the corpses and shouted, "Stop this now!" One nearby body hissed and spat a globule of venomous saliva at the creature. Targy stepped calmly back, letting the spittle splash on the ground. He moved a few paces away and sat down, all the time watched by the curious companions; even Dionis was intrigued. From a concealed bundle on his back, Targy quickly made a cone of twigs. He looked up at Uthan and pointed to the cone. "Fire?"

Uthan ducked instinctively as a corpse slashed at the air a foot away from him. He looked at Gauduin and Qwan for support. The elf shrugged helplessly and Gauduin raised his eyebrows, inclining his head towards Targy. Taking care to avoid the flailing arms, Uthan moved over and sat opposite the strange creature. He opened his palm and spoke a few words under his breath. A small flame grew in the air above his hand. Moving carefully to avoid extinguishing the tiny flame, Uthan placed it onto the twigs; within a few moments they all succumbed to the crackling fire.

Targy opened a small pouch at his side, withdrawing a handful of fine red powder that had a faint, pungent odour, he tossed it into the fire. The resulting sound was like huge waves crashing against rock cliffs. The smell intensified, bringing a rolling bout of queasiness with it and, so briefly that only Uthan saw it, the flames in the campfire blazed with an angry, magma red. Curls of dark black smoke, tinged with redness, drifted up from the fire, twisting out into the air like slender snakes. They floated above the heads of the travellers, winding their way through the pillars and ruins around the group, as if searching for something. Here and there they touched a thrashing limb that drew back instantly, recoiling in pain or fear.

Targy reached into the pouch for another handful of sand, again he tossed it into the flames. More tendrils of the smoke drifted out around the corpses.

"What is this?" Uthan asked.

Targy looked up at the young mage and put a long finger to his lipless mouth. A third handful of sand was added to the fire and more tendrils appeared within the smoke, which wrapped themselves around the pillars and their gruesome captives.

"It's a net of some kind," Dionis exclaimed quietly, secretly impressed.

With a nod, Targy said, "Yes, a net for souls."

The stench of burning flesh and hair intensified. It stung their eyes and made their stomachs roll violently. To keep herself from falling over, Demien sat down dizzily on the ground. Knotting themselves together, the smoke tentacles formed a loose grid, winding around the corpses. Targy held his hands above the fire, palms flat and facing down. His fingers flexed slightly and he closed his eyes and let his head fall back. A murmured low chanting escaped his mouth, barely heard at first but gradually it grew louder and louder. Its droning echoed in the ears of the companions. Shivers spilled down Uthan's spine, goosebumps broke out over his skin and the hair on the back of his neck stood on end. He felt a surge of power coursing through his veins as the nerves in his legs shuddered. His breathing became heavier and a soft sheen of moisture appeared on his brow, despite the chill that gnawed at his bones. Peering upwards, he saw the net tighten. Wails and screams came from the corpses as the soul net tightened around them. They cried out and flailed in one last desperate attempt to be free.

Then, one by one, their struggles stopped. Faint blue and green wisps of foggy light soared up, escaping the corpses through the eye sockets. All eyes apart from Targy's turned to Hedrial's thrashing corpse. A noose tightened around the broken neck, until green, misty light soared out of the burned face. Gauduin wiped tears from his eyes as he looked up at the spirit form of Hedrial, slowly taking shape as it floated higher into the air. He sniffed loudly, and then looked at the others to see similar reactions from them.

"I'm sure he'd thank you all if he could," Dionis said. The spirit familiar's voice was barely above a whisper, full of awe.

Uthan, believing he saw Hedrial's ghost looking down on him and smiling, nodded meekly. He got to his feet and carefully walked across to the corpse that now hung limply from the pillar. "Targy, can we bury him now?"

The creature did not answer.

Uthan turned, ready to ask again but Targy was no longer there. The small fire was dwindling away, leaving only a few curls of natural white smoke. All around the group, the corpses hung limply from their pillars or slumped on the ground where they lay. But Targy could not be seen; he had left them alone to bury their friend.

Chapter Twenty-Eight

It seemed almost symbolic that as soon as the hideous corpses had been dealt with, the heavy blanket of smoke and fog had begun to lift. A thin veil still hung over the ruined city but visibility was improving. The strange disembodied howls of the Haunters could still be heard, but now more faintly. To the north, the sky was mottled with thick, black clouds, the source of which was the volcanic mountain situated beneath them. Uthan sat by Hedrial's tombstone, silently staring out across the wasted land to the volcano.

The group had buried the remains of their friend. Diarus had once again displayed his immense strength by moving the heavy stone block into place, covering the grave to protect it from scavengers. The burial had been done more with relief than sadness at finally putting Hedrial to rest. Qwan had reminded them all that there would be time to grieve later. For now, Gauduin and the elf knelt by the grave, heads bowed in silent prayer. Diarus and Demien waited a little way away with the horses, giving them the time they needed to lay their friend to rest properly.

Uthan stood up, moving to stand near Diarus and Demien.

"It's a pity he disappeared. We could have used him against the Black Flame," Diarus said, nodding at Uthan to acknowledge him being there.

"Used who?" he asked.

"Targy," Demien replied. "He just called those demons to him back there. I think he destroyed them."

"I could have killed them too," Uthan said quietly. "If I knew what I was doing."

"I'd say he knows where to find the Black Flame too," Diarus said, not hearing Uthan.

The young mage looked up, pointed to the volcano and said, "That's where the Flame is."

Demien and Diarus both stared at the angry-looking clouds that seethed with a ferocious red underglow.

"How do you know?" Qwansien asked; both he and Gauduin had finished their prayers and were also looking out at the volcano.

Uthan did not reply, he took the reins of his horse and started to lead it away towards the volcano.

The throne room was silent. Even though Carrion knelt before the throne itself, he could barely see the dark figure seated there. The long shadows fell around the Black Flame like curtains.

"So," the Flame said, after what had seemed like an eternity to the necromancer, "neither the dragon, nor your precious Haunters have been able to stop the boy."

"He does not travel alone, my Lord," Carrion tried excusing his failure. "The Haunters say their feeding ground has been denied them."

"That is not my concern, necromancer," the Flame hissed.

The emphasis on that final word brought Carrion up sharply. He risked a look up to the darkened throne, instantly looking away again as he felt the eyes of his master boring through him, then replied, "No, of course not, my Lord."

"So, the precious toy created by my family has been released and is making its way here as we speak," the Flame seethed.

"I have spoken with General Meligonn, my Lord," Carrion began. He paused a moment or two before continuing, "He is bringing his horde back through the jungle. They will capture the boy and his companions. They will also make sure the Forged One is no longer a problem."

"Will he really?" the Flame growled. "Or will he too fail to bring me this boy's head? Am I to hide here in these walls and hope my minions actually have it in them to deal with the tasks I set them? No, I don't think so; no doubt the boy will come here to me. If so, I will have the pleasure of killing him and all those he travels with myself. I, necromancer, will deal with this if I have to. Let them come to me and I will show the rest of the Gods why they were right to fear me."

Carrion shrank back as the Flame stood up. Even through the darkness, the necromancer could see the fallen God's malevolent rage building. He could feel the ripples of power echoing through the vast throne room. Clearing his throat to try and hide the worry he felt at his Lord's anger, Carrion asked, "What do you wish of General Meligonn in that case, my lord?"

"My wish? My wish is for the general to achieve that which I ask of him. Kill the boy if he manages to find him and destroy the Forged One," answered the Flame in a cold voice. "Remind him of the fate of those others who have failed me so far. Remind him that I can be very unforgiving and assure him he should pray I don't have to kill the boy myself."

"It doesn't matter what we've fought until now, it can only get worse from here on in," Qwan announced. He sat calmly in his saddle, staring directly ahead at the volcanic mountain.

"Looking forward to it," Demien said calmly.

In amongst the thick, sulphurous clouds being belched out by the volcano, they saw a great slab of rock floating on the smoke. Sitting on top of the rock was a castle, made of jet black obsidian.

"When they live in a floating castle," Gauduin said slowly, "it usually doesn't bode well for the people attacking it."

"It must take some power to hold it up there," Diarus agreed.

"It's going to come down with a really loud bang then," Uthan commented, pushing his horse on forward past his companions.

"Seriously," Qwan pointed out, "if something moves in there, chances are it's going to try and kill us."

"So, kill it first," Diarus muttered.

"How exactly do we get up there?" Demien asked.

Uthan turned to them all and, with a broad grin, answered, "Close your eyes."

As they did so, Uthan closed his eyes too. When he opened them again they flickered with sparkles of brilliant, ice blue energy. "No matter what you feel or hear, it'll be better for you if you try and keep your eyes closed," Uthan explained as he arranged the other four on the dusty ground in a rough circle facing outwards. The young mage knelt in the centre, with one hand against the ground and his fingers pushed into the dirt. His eyes, staring at the soil in front of him, flashed with raw magic, then the ground around them shifted until cracks appeared, widening into a circle around them until they sat on a small island of dirt.

"What's happening, Uthan?" Gauduin asked nervously.

"Yeah," Qwan added, "I'm starting to feel a little silly just sitting here."

"We're going up!" Uthan answered, throwing his head back and staring into the sky. His voice echoed with power, sounding as if it was five voices in unison. Before anyone could answer him, the island had pulled free and moved up into the air, trailing showers of powdery soil behind it.

Feeling his stomach lurch, Gauduin exclaimed, "I'm not sure I like this. A dwarf's feet should stay on the ground."

"They are on the ground," Uthan said.

"Oh, by the Gods! That was what I was afraid of," Gauduin answered.

Leaving the dusty ruins of Kael behind, the travellers soared up into the sky. As they drew closer to the fortress, the air itself became more difficult to breath. The thick, choking odour of sulphur filled every breath they took. They finally risked opening their eyes to see they were flying towards the huge, floating rock rather than the fortress itself. Getting closer, the travellers could see a series of caves that burrowed into the sides of the structure. Building up a little more speed, Uthan steered them towards one.

Despite trying to concentrate on his spell, Uthan could not help admiring the landscape sprawled out below him. Behind lay a blanket of thick, lush green that was the jungle. It stretched out seemingly for hundreds of miles, right up to the distant, grey mist-shrouded mountains. Directly under him, in a circle so immense it was impossible to see clearly, was scorched brown land, painted here and there with greys and blacks. Then, thick clouds obscured the view as the dirt island flew over the lake of magma, rising gradually on the super-heated air. In front of them, the obsidian fortress was waiting, almost daring them to issue a challenge.

Gauduin nodded to their left side. At the edge of the volcano, five small dragons with riders were attacking something on the ground, circling above it before making swooping attacks.

"As long as they don't see us, it's all fine," Qwansien called, raising his voice above the noise of the rushing wind and bubbling lava.

"And if they do?" Gauduin asked, seated next to his old friend.

Facing forward, so the dwarf would not see his mischievous smile, Qwan answered, "We hope for the best."

Moments later, the threat of being seen by the distant dragons was gone. The travellers shot inside one of the many tunnel entrances that pockmarked the surface of the floating rock. The sudden change in pressure caused their ears to pop uncomfortably. Dark rock whizzed by them as Uthan steered the dirt island through a series of turns, dips and climbs along the corridor with little or no effort. Finally they entered a huge chamber in the centre of the rock with a large plateau at one end. Landing on the roughly carved floor, they jumped from the dirt island and watched as it crumbled completely into a pile of soil.

Uthan walked a few paces away, breathing heavily. He rolled his shoulders, trying to ease the tension in them, but every muscle in his body seemed to twitch at once. A distant thumping pain rolled around inside his head. His friends watched him carefully while he tried to regain his composure. He was only vaguely aware of them, until eventually Demien asked if he was okay. He looked over at her and nodded, before saying, "I wonder if the Forged One is close by."

"Better hope so," Qwan muttered, "it'll be a short fight otherwise."

Ignoring the burst of flame that loosened yet more pebbles around its fingers, the Forged One continued to climb the side of the volcano. Above him, five small dragons wheeled in the air. One would occasionally break away from the group to dive at it, either attempting to jolt it loose from the mountainside or to send a jet of flame towards it. Yet still, the steel man clung tenaciously to the rock, steadily moving upwards. Each time a blast of the dragon's fire came close, it twisted and moved out of the way.

Dragging itself over onto the relatively flat top ridge, the Forged One stood up. Faced with a lake of molten rock, it stopped and looked around. From behind, a dragon swooped in, its front claws outstretched. The Forged One was sent tumbling forwards, rolling to the edge of the lake as the dragon slammed into its shoulders. Rolling back onto its knees, the Forged One searched for the enemy. A blast of flame hit the ground at its feet, exploding into the rock. Large cracks spread out from the blast, making its footing more treacherous. To the left, a dragon was landed by its rider and another dropped to the right, both watching the steel man like a cat watching a mouse. The dragon to its left soared into the air again, moving backwards and up but the Forged One did not flinch. The dragon to its right, forced by its rider, leapt at the shining statue, gliding a few feet above the ground. Its wing slapped hard against the Forged One's head, sending the metal statue into a spin. Reaching out quickly, it grasped hold of the dragon's wing, pulling it down along with itself as they tumbled over the edge of the volcano and down into the lava below.

The dragon's rider leapt off just in time, his shoulder striking the rock surface with a hard crack, he bellowed in pain, scrabbling clear of the edge. From the volcano, he heard his dragon screaming in fear and pain. He lowered his eyes for a moment, grieving for his long-time companion, before getting to his feet. Moving further from the edge he signalled to his comrades, circling above him. One of them landed close by, allowing him to climb up on the saddle behind the rider. A moment later, the dragon lifted off again, soaring over the bubbling lava. They each looked down, straining to see through the thickening black clouds. There was no sign of the dragon or the Forged One.

The companions wandered through tunnels that had been carved into the great rock, not fully knowing where they were going. Every branching corridor looked identical to those they had already travelled. Only Uthan appeared to know where he was, leading them round bend after bend, turning off into other tunnels seemingly at random. When asked if he knew, Uthan would only shrug and explain that it felt like he was being guided. He led them through several larger chambers, each one being empty.

They came to a long, bare stretch of corridor. Roughly carved doorways led off from it making it appear like some kind of living area. Uthan carried on straight past the doors, not bothering to look inside at the smaller rooms. They were nothing more than cells, it seemed, with small palette beds in the corners and bundles of rags and sackcloth as makeshift mattresses. There was an eye-watering stench of stale sweat and urine that drifted out into the corridor.

"And yet no one is home to challenge us," Qwan spoke thoughtfully as he poked his head through one of the open doorways.

"I'm thinking," Demien replied, "all his army is elsewhere."

"Yes," Gauduin answered, stalking past them and continuing along the corridor, "they're all back in the Empire tearing it to shreds. Now let's get a move on here."

"Doesn't anyone else think this is too easy?" Qwan asked, moving up to walk behind Gauduin. "Surely there should be guards or servants at least."

"I'm trying not to think about that," Gauduin muttered his reply.

The corridor led to a large room that was dimly lit by a pair of flaming torches. A long rectangular table was in the middle of the room, filthy plates of half-eaten food cluttering its wooden surface. A few half heard squeaks and the soft scraping of rats signalled the only life inside the room. Against one wall was a rickety looking weapons rack that seemed barely able to hold the three, rusty halberds that were propped up in it. The rock floor was carpeted with dusty straw that gave off a thick, musty odour. Prodding a half-chewed bone with the tip of her sword blade, Demien commented, "I'm assuming there aren't even any servants down here."

"There's something not right," Uthan muttered, staring into another wide corridor that led away from the chamber.

He began walking through the doorway when a sudden yellow flash stunned them all. For the briefest of moments, they could all see a symbol that hung in the air in brilliant, blue light. This was accompanied by a definite, faint metallic taste. There was a high-pitched buzz, just on the edge of hearing, before the ceiling of the tunnel came down around Uthan with a deafening rumble. Diarus grabbed Gauduin by the collar and yanked him backwards away from the heavy chunks of rock as they bounced into the living chamber. Clouds of thick, grey brown dust billowed up, causing them to shield their eyes.

Chapter Twenty-Nine

Kneeling on the cold, stone floor of the throne room, Carrion stared calmly at the darkened figure in front of him. The necromancer was more at ease as he said, "They're within the palace, my Lord. The boy has triggered a Ward spell."

"And?" the Flame demanded as he sat forward in his throne and stared down at Carrion.

"One of the corridors has suffered a cave-in. I believe they may have been caught in it."

"You believe they may have been caught in it," the Flame said, in a slow deliberate tone. "I would suggest you go and be absolutely certain they have been caught in it. I will not tell you one more time, necromancer. I will deal with the survivors myself this time." With a long dramatic sigh he added, "And there will be survivors, won't there?"

As the dust clouds settled, the companions saw the tunnel entrance that Uthan had disappeared into was almost completely blocked off. Qwan raced across and began scrabbling at the smaller rocks, trying to squeeze past the cave-in.

"Did he escape it?" Gauduin demanded, following the elf as close as he dared. Sidling carefully over a large piece of rock, he called out for Uthan.

"He has to be under all this," Qwan said, shaking his head.

The dwarf shot him a look. "Then," he started, ignoring the dust that caught in his throat, "we have to dig him out." He grasped at a boulder, easily as big as his torso and started to pull. Diarus placed a hand on his shoulder, gently pulling him back away from the rockfall. "We can't let him just stay buried under there," Gauduin protested weakly. He sat down heavily, as if all his energy had suddenly been taken from him and just stared at the rocks.

"We're not going to," Diarus said calmly. He walked back over to the rubble and grabbed a large lump of rock. The muscles in his shoulders and arms strained, bulging against his tanned skin as he pulled the rock away from the pile. Rivers of dust poured down from where the rock had been.

Demien reached in, moving smaller chunks of stone from the resulting hole. Leaning closer to Diarus so only he could hear her, she muttered, "You really think he'll still be alive under all this?"

The Daiharlon shook his head and let out a deep sigh, before pulling another great boulder free from the pile. He carried it into the tunnel, dropped it and moved back to the pile. Placing his great horned head into the gap he had made, he muttered, "No. But we can't leave him here either way."

He rolled a third boulder away, letting it fall from the rest. Grabbing another huge lump of rock, he started suddenly. The sound of rocks falling from behind the slide made them all jump. Demien was first to react, reaching for her longbow. Drawing back the string, she gingerly moved around the rocks, picking her way as carefully as possible without taking her eyes from where the arrow was aimed. Uthan was sitting in the corridor, with his back to them, staring into space. Lowering her bow, Demien walked across to him, slipping and sliding occasionally on loose rocks. Reaching his side, she gently put out a hand, touching the young man's shoulder, "Are you hurt?"

He cocked his head to the side, looking at her. His eyes were blank, almost as if he had never seen her before. A tiny trickle of blood from his scalp ran down his temple as he slowly shook his head.

"Good," she replied with a nod then offered him a hand up.

Uthan pushed himself upright, using the wall for support instead of taking Demien's offered hand. He swayed on his feet for a moment or two, having to put out a hand to the wall behind him for support once again. Demien called back to the others, letting them know Uthan was okay. They clambered around the rockslide to get to him, all showing their concern.

"I should have known a bunch of rocks couldn't hurt you," Qwan said with a grin. When Uthan didn't reply, he asked, "Or did they?"

"Are you okay to continue?" Gauduin asked, coming to stand right in front of the young mage. Uthan just nodded and gestured along the corridor that was now clouded with thick dust.

"I really wish he'd shut up and let one of us get a word in," Qwan said, sarcastically as Uthan started walking.

"At least we won't get more questions for a while," Demien replied, starting to follow Uthan.

"Just keep an eye open for any more damned Ward spells," Gauduin grumbled striding past them.

They moved through the tunnels without any further incident. Uthan walked several paces in front of them, moving as if he was in a trance. He only turned to his companions when indicating which passage or doorway to take whenever there was a choice. He led them through carved tunnel after tunnel and into what looked like a hallway. The roughly hewn rock gave way into brick worked walls. Steps of considerably smoother stone ran up to a large hole in the roof. With Uthan in front again, they quickly moved up the stairs and out onto the top of the great rock. Here they found themselves staring straight at the dark malevolent structure of the Black Flame's fortress.

Thick clouds of black, choking smoke wafted all around them as the group stood in front of the great doors. The orange light from the lava below reflected off the gleaming obsidian walls. Diarus pressed his hands against the black steel gates, straining to push them open. They groaned inwards, metal squealing against stone. Flanked by Demien and Gauduin on one side, and Qwan and Uthan on the other, the Daiharlon walked in through the immense doorway. Inside, they were faced with a wide hall, stretching into the fortress itself; at the far end there was a pair of studded wooden doors. Thick pillars of smooth stone lined either wall, interspersed between them were tall statues, each one more grotesque than the last.

"Why do these evil ones never have normal statues?" Qwan pondered as he flexed his fingers around the hilt of his sword while stalking forward.

With her gaze flicking back and forth, taking every inch of the hallway in, Demien replied, "Don't worry about the statues. Where are the guards?"

"My guess?" Qwan replied. "They'll be waiting for us somewhere around here."

"Is anyone wondering how he knows where we're going?" Demien asked, watching the mage's back as he moved to the doors with purposeful striding steps.

Barely talking above a whisper, Gauduin replied, "I'm trying not to think about it."

"It feels like a trap," Demien said anxiously.

"Of course it is," Qwan answered, far too cheerfully for Demien's liking.

"Let's hope he snaps out of it before it's sprung on us," she replied, nodding at Uthan as he led them through into another shorter corridor.

There was a heavy, black door waiting for them at the end. A grinning, demonic face cast in iron on the door itself, taunted them. Uthan pushed the door, letting it swing open into an impossibly large chamber beyond. Without waiting for the others to follow, the young mage strode calmly inside. Qwan and Gauduin had their swords already out of the scabbards as they jogged in behind him. The only light to enter the chamber came from the open windows that lined the walls. The floor was empty apart from a large, obsidian throne set against the wall to the right of the door. Above them, the ceiling was shrouded in shadow from which distant clicking sounds filtered down to the companions.

"So this is the group that has evaded both my armies," a voice sneered from deep in the shadows.

Apart from Uthan, who had stood facing the throne from the moment he had entered the chamber, the others snapped round to see a dark clad figure emerge from the semidarkness.

The slender body, standing just over six feet tall, was clad in tight fitting leather clothing, mostly made up of straps. The skin of his face and hands were ghostly pale. His black hair stood on end and it writhed in the slight breeze from the window while his jet black eyes appeared to flicker. He stepped closer to them, coming out of the shadows completely. As he did so, the companions realised his hair and eyes were actually black flames. "You killed a centuries old dragon and escaped the clutches of demons. I really was expecting more of you," he said darkly.

The clicking from the ceiling grew louder. Looking up, Gauduin saw dark shapes detaching themselves from the shadows and start moving down the walls. From the far end of the chamber more shapes skittered across the floor. Strange creatures with long, spindly limbs knuckled their way towards the travellers. Their flesh gleamed with an oily sheen, obscuring their features. Only their malevolent, glowing green eyes were visible through the viscous oil.

"Yeah," Qwan said flatly, "it's a trap."

Uthan suddenly ran at the Black Flame. Gauduin and Qwan both tried to stop him, reaching out to grab him as he passed. "Uthan, no!" Gauduin shouted.

A dark smile crossed the face of the Flame's evil face, "He's not trying to attack me, you fools!" All three companions had the same sinking feeling as they saw Uthan stop at the Black Flame's side. With a malicious grin, the Flame said, "He's just returning to his master."

Chapter Thirty

"So you all came here without the artefact and only a small hope of killing me," the Flame said. He flopped back down on his black throne, draping a leg over one of the arms. "And now with the boy gone, how exactly do you intend on doing any of this?"

"Gone?" Qwan muttered. He, like the others, had been unable to tear his eyes away from Uthan who stood near the throne, waiting patiently.

"Yes," the Flame replied, wearily as he looked harder at the trio. "You've not realised it yet, have you." Seeing their puzzled looks, the Flame gestured to Uthan and said, "Show them."

Uthan with a malicious grin, turned to the four companions, then the air around him shimmered brightly. His skin darkened and changed form. Under the gaze of everyone in the room, Uthan became Carrion, the Black Flame's necromancer.

Flashing a worried stare to Gauduin and Qwansien, Demien said, "We left Uthan..."

"Buried under those rocks," the Black Flame mocked. "That just leaves you four."

"Was this why the other Gods kicked you out?" Qwan asked. "Because you just go on and on?"

"Qwan? Do you really have to annoy a God?" Demien spoke sharply as she looked around at the oily creatures that were surrounding them.

"The elf is just trying to buy you some time," the Flame replied casually. "It hasn't really worked though."

The door was opened again and a column of black and silver helmed soldiers marched in. Their leather scale armour was slashed and ragged and, in some cases, pieces were torn away completely. Sallow flesh, the colour of putty, hung in loose folds from their exposed faces. They lined up in front of the Black Flame and his necromancer, their red-rimmed eyes staring balefully at the companions.

"So that's where the guards were all this time," Diarus muttered.

"This is the part where someone yells 'Get them' and they all rush at us, right?" Gauduin said, the tiniest flicker of a smile touching the corner of his mouth.

Dryly, Carrion ordered, "Get them."

As the soldiers started forward, Gauduin flashed a toothy smile to Qwan and said, "Told you."

Targy sat by his fire patiently staring into the flames. He took a sip of water from his cup and sighed. Then, closing his eyes, he rolled his head back a moment. The muscles in his neck were limp, letting the head roll in a circle till it dropped to the front again, his chin resting on his chest. His chanting was almost inaudible when it started. Words were spoken so fast they blended into one another, making it sound like nothing more than a long stream of gibberish. As the chanting became louder, Targy's semi-limp body rocked back and forth. His head slowly rose again. When his eyes opened, they were glazed over, looking directly forward but without seeing anything.

In the caves below the Black Flame's fortress, the air around the rockslide became hazy and the floor shook. Showers of dust cascaded from the broken ceiling and the clatter of rocks echoed in the tunnels as the cave-in fell apart. From one side, the rocks at the bottom began moving. They pushed their way out from under the pile, sending more and more of the debris above toppling down. From beneath the rubble there was an eruption and rocks were hurled along the corridor. Clad in ornate black armour, trimmed with red, a figure stood up. From deep inside the grilled visor, orange yellow fire gleamed angrily.

Qwan stepped back, just in time to avoid the sword that was thrust towards him. He parried the blade, pushing his foe away. Around them was a wide circle of the enemy's guard, both human and the grotesque oily creatures. They waited idly, attacking the group from random directions. However, as quickly as they killed the guards, Carrion passed his hands through the air, bringing them to stand and fight once more. The elf glanced over to his friends. Both Demien and Gauduin were tiring visibly. The warrior woman was being methodical in parrying, careful not to waste precious energy on ripostes. Gauduin meanwhile swept his sword back and forth warily, keeping the larger, spindly creatures at bay. Diarus, however, seemed to have an incredible abundance of energy, striking out time and time again with hard cleaving attacks. The flagstones around him were already slick with the blood of his kills.

Targy stood up, moving back from the fire. Kicking dust and dirt over it, he scattered the ashes, killing the flames. With a deep breath, he said, "That is all I can do."

"Which was?" asked Dionis. The spirit hung from a low tree branch with his large, round eyes focused on the Black Flame's floating fortress. He had been unable to get inside the giant floating rock or the fortress itself. All he had had was his faith that Uthan could overcome the odds inside, until he had found the strange jungle dweller seated in front of a low campfire.

Turning to glance over his shoulder at the spirit, Targy replied, "I woke him up."

"He was unconscious?" asked the bat.

With a nod, the creature replied, "Yes. Rocks fell from above."

"A cave-in?" Targy nodded again. "Is he okay now?" Dionis continued anxiously. "What about the others?"

"Not under rock with him. There were only the spirit men. He walks with them now," Targy answered.

"At least there's that then," Dionis replied.

Targy shook his head sadly, "The boy should not be there. He is not ready. I have had to enter his mind and help him today."

"Enter his mind?" Dionis asked, raising as much of an eyebrow as he could.

Targy nodded wisely, "And now I think he is more ready. He must be there with the metal man."

Dionis shrugged, "The Forged One was dumped into the lava though. I'm sure I saw it."

Targy smiled cunningly, "It will get there. My people have their ways."

"Your people have confused the hell out of all of us, Targy," Dionis muttered. "You should have stopped the Flame long ago when you had the chance."

"I know," Targy answered sadly, "but things were different in those times. My people were weaker."

"Than you are now? There's only you left," Dionis replied coolly.

The creature looked at Dionis. "My people live on in the jungle spirits. This way we are stronger."

"Just not strong enough to keep the Flame back here," Dionis said. This time, he was more sympathetic.

Targy's shoulders slumped and he nodded. "That is why I must help the boy now. To make sure my people do not die again."

Fire entered the great hallway of the fortress first, brandishing his burning blade. The Elemental Warrior strode in confidently, followed by equally confident Water, Air and Earth. In front of them, the hallway was empty as Uthan entered, holding his short sword firmly in two hands. He looked around and then nodding at the doors at the end of the hallway, he asked the Elementals, "Is that the way?"

Standing beside him, Fire nodded silently.

"So what is this?" Gauduin muttered swinging his sword in front of a slender black limb covered in barbed hooks. "They just wear us down till we can't fight?"

Qwan speared a soldier through the chest and watched him fall only to get back up again. "Looks like it. Entertainment for a God."

"So what do we do?" Gauduin asked.

The elf backhanded the edge of his sword into the soldier's neck, knocking him down again completely. The soldier staggered back, his head sagging to one side uselessly just as two others filled the gap in the line, pressing in towards Qwansien. "Same thing we've done all along," he replied, taking a few experimental stabs at his newer opponents, "give them one hell of a fight till we think of something better."

Gauduin twisted on his heel, driving his sword hard into the exposed face of one of the oily creatures. The black skull was smashed under the weight. It screeched wildly, scrabbling at its face with two long front arms. Gauduin drove the point of his sword deep into the creature's exposed chest. Pulling his sword free again, Gauduin watched it fall to the floor dead. Other creatures close by looked on in curiosity, one reached out with a spindly leg, tapping the side of the dead one's shell.

Suddenly the door to the chamber was ripped from its hinges causing all eyes to turn to the open entrance as Fire calmly strode in.

Carrion pointed to the Elemental. Then, staring at his horde of reanimated soldiers, he yelled, "Kill him!"

A group of them marched over to block the path of the Elemental Warrior as Water, Air and Earth entered, bringing Uthan with them.

The Black Flame's expression was a mixture of anger and surprise, "Kill the mage!" he roared.

More of his soldiers joined the second attack. Fire leant back, avoiding the clumsy sword swipe from one before driving his own fiery sword deep into the man's chest. Earth and Air both stormed forward, cleaving through the soldiers as if they were nothing. Carrion raised his hands, trying to get his men to rise and fight again. But those slain by the Elementals remained motionless.

His voice showed his fear as he muttered, "Spirit warriors?"

"Elementals!" The Flame cursed loudly.

"Now we're getting somewhere," Qwan said, his usual cocky, half smile back in place.

The sound of stone shattering made everyone turn to its source. Part of the wall between the windows was dented in heavily, as if something had smashed into the outside. The Black Flame's angry expression changed, showing more than a little fear.

Carrion, facing the dented wall, stepped back, shaking his head. "What is that?"

"Your death," Uthan said, standing beside the necromancer. As Carrion snapped his skull-like head around, Uthan punched the air between them, sending a blast of invisible energy that struck the necromancer in the stomach. Carrion bounced against the hard stone wall with several bone crunching sounds.

"Parlour tricks, boy," the Black Flame growled, standing a foot away. Uthan inclined his head. The Black Flame's right hand came up, striking the young man under the jaw and sending him flipping through the air. Uthan's belongings were scattered across the floor as his pack was torn from his shoulders. The large book that had been Hedrial's flew open, the thick bound cover receiving a battering in the process. Sliding to a stop near to the book was a dagger wrapped in cloth.

A shining steel fist punched through the wall. The arm bent up at the elbow, pressing the palm flat against the stone before pulling a whole section away. Through the resulting hole, they could all see the carved, steel face of the Forged One. The eyes burned with a fury born of centuries of imprisonment. The Flame took a few steps back, muttering something.

"You're only delaying the inevitable," Uthan said calmly. He pushed himself upright again and stepped back across the flagstones to the Flame.

The Flame glared at him as he growled, "You think this is how it's supposed to end, boy? Think again."

Complete stone blocks fell away from the hole in the wall as the Forged One smashed his way through, kicking debris to the sides. Soldiers rushed forward to stop him, only to be hurled away.

From the dark of the ceiling above them, there came a deep-throated growl that shook the entire room; then leather rustled against leather. There was another sound, like glass clinking against glass and a cloud of dark smoke billowed down, engulfing them all.

Looking back at Uthan, the Flame said, "You really believe I wouldn't be prepared for this?"

Something moved in the darkness above. Fragments of stone tumbled from the ceiling as the growl turned into a loud roar. A flash of flame from up high lit up the chamber. For a few seconds, they could all see the enormous black and red scaled head of a dragon hanging from the stone beams. The beast glared at the room below, teeth bared in a vicious snarl. The shadows returned again, leaving only an image of the gigantic beast burned into their memories. A deathly quiet had fallen over the room, letting the hissing of the dragon's breath become the most dominant noise. With each exhale, they could all smell the strong stench of rotten eggs.

"In dragon's fire it was born," the Flame stated theatrically, "and in dragon's fire it shall perish!"

The Forged One merely inclined his head up to the ceiling, watching coolly as the dragon slowly climbed down the far wall. The soldiers in the room had all stepped back, moving closer to the spirit warriors instead. Qwansien, Demien, Gauduin and Diarus all turned to face the grotesque creatures behind them. They were trying to back away from the immense dragon too.

"It's a big one," Qwan said, impressed.

"Never seen a beast like it," Gauduin muttered. He quickly snapped his head round to look at his elf friend who was grinning broadly. With a chuckle, he asked, "Want to fight it?"

The dragon almost filled the opposite end of the chamber. Malevolent, green yellow eyes took in everything facing it. Claws, that were the length of an average man, clicked loudly on the rough flagstones. An impossibly long tail moved from side to side, scales scraping the floor. Puffs of grey smoke billowed out from the nostrils that were tall enough for any of the travellers to stand inside. Enormous muscles bunched and flowed under a scaly hide that looked impossible to pierce. The beast was double the size of Baymothesis and twice as fearsome.

Uthan moved back to stand near the Elemental Warriors. Fire and Water automatically took up defensive positions in front of the young mage, ignoring the remaining soldiers nearby.

"In fire," the Flame muttered, "it shall burn."

The dragon swelled itself up, shoulders hunching together. Uthan flashed a look at Fire. The Elemental Warrior nodded in understanding and started forwards, running to stand in front of the Forged One. Earth dropped to one knee and placed a gloved hand to the floor, the stones beneath him rippled like water at the touch.

Qwan jumped back a step, open-mouthed in surprise as a section of the floor rose in front of them, blocking them from the dragon's sight. He peered around the barrier only to pull his head back immediately as a large burst of flame erupted from the dragon's mouth. It shot around the wall, missing the companions as they instinctively threw themselves closer to the flagstones. The flesh was burned away from the remaining soldiers, leaving smoking corpses amongst the fire. High-pitched screaming came from the strange gangling creatures as more than a few were torched. A pair tried escaping the carnage, skittering back up the walls.

The Fire Elemental stood in front of the Forged One, arms raised. As the dragon fire rolled across the chamber toward them, Fire manipulated it, directing the flames away from the statue. In the bright yellow light, the Forged One seemed to glow with a new intensity. Uthan and the other Elementals stood and watched as the dragon fire completely engulfed the room. Unable to see his friends, he could only hope they survived the searing heat of the inferno. He watched the flames sweep around the throne; for a moment they hid the Black Flame from sight.

With a grin that could only be described as insane, the Fallen God stepped through the fire, staring directly at Uthan. "And now without the statue here to help you, how are you going to stop me?"

As suddenly as it had started, the inferno ceased. The dragon waited at the opposite end of the room, watching its handiwork. Small, flickering flames danced on the smouldering corpses that were now fused to the floor. Curiosity flashed through the beast's mind, showing in its glare, as to how the young human, his armoured bodyguards and the Black Flame were not only still standing alive, but completely untouched by its fire.

The Black Flame continued advancing on Uthan. His steps slowed though as slowly he turned his head. The Forged One was standing close by, staring at him. Pointing to the shining statue, the Flame yelled at the dragon, "Get rid of it now!"

From the Forged One's left side, the dragon swatted him with a huge clawed foot. The walls seemed to tremble as the statue was thrown against them. As he bounced off the stone, the dragon swatted him again, sending him into the opposite wall. The dragon's head shot closer to the Forged One, knocking it flat again as it tried to stand.

Uthan turned to Fire and whispered, "Try and get it out of there."

The Forged One ducked around the dragon and began taking long, striding steps back to the Black Flame. Sucking in another great lungful of air, the dragon released more flame directly at the statue. Fire ran forward, raising his hands to manipulate the inferno but the Black Flame released a fireball of his own, striking the Elemental in the back. For a moment, it distracted Fire giving the dragon the time it needed to cover the Forged One in searing heat. From the periphery of his vision, Uthan saw the Black Flame clasp his hands together gleefully. The Fallen God glanced sideways at the mage and sneered, "In dragon's fire it shall burn!"

Once more the flames subsided leaving only charred smoking flagstones. In the centre of the blast area was the Forged One. Face down, the statue smoked, glowing red in places. All around it were small pools of molten metal, giving off faint wisps of smoke. From their vantage point, Gauduin and the others could clearly see the fallen artefact. Its face was contorted beyond recognition as the fire had melted the detailed muscle structure, turning the warrior into little more than a shapeless chunk of metal.

Towering above the Forged One's remains, the dragon swivelled its mighty head, taking in the rest of the chamber with a renewed air of rage. Scales rattled against each other noisily as it shook its head. The claws of one foot clicked loudly on the blackened stone floor as it took a step closer to the gathered combatants.

With an evil half smile, the Flame said, "You can leave us now."

The dragon bared its sharp, yellowed teeth in a snarl, glaring at the Fallen God, breath hissing between them, filling the chamber with a rotten sulphurous stench. Then its nostrils flared as the beast took in another deep breath. Demien took her chance. Notching an arrow to her bowstring, she stepped back out from her hiding place and took aim at the dragon. The beast glanced at her momentarily before fading into nothing. Almost on instinct, she let the arrow fly. It whistled through air, passing through where the dragon's eye had only just been.

"Now," the Flame said, clapping his hands twice, "to deal with the rest of you."

All sound returned to the chamber again. The shiny black bodies of the strange, grotesque creatures shone in the afterglow of the remaining dragon fire as they surged towards the companions again. Tightening his grip on his sword hilt again, Qwan sighed and muttered, "If it's not one thing."

Uthan sank to his knees, his head swimming with despair and tears blurring his vision. He could not take his eyes off the Forged One as it lay motionless. Only vaguely aware of his surroundings, he glanced at Gauduin, hearing the dwarf call his name as if from a great distance.

In one hand Gauduin held a shining dagger up high so that Uthan could see it clearly. At his feet lay the torn cloth shroud that had hidden the weapon. His face was split in a grin that was half desperate, half triumphant. He tossed the dagger across the open floor, shouting one word. "Catch!" As the others looked at the dwarf, he shrugged and added, "According to Hedrial, it was dragon steel that would kill the bastard. Maybe the dagger will work since it's dragon steel."

"A dragon steel dagger?" Qwan demanded, exasperated. "And you just forgot to mention this?"

"Well, we were fighting for our lives," the dwarf countered.

"Those are usually the times when a powerful dagger would be needed more, wouldn't you say!"

"Well, with you nearly getting yourself killed every day it slipped my mind!" Gauduin boomed.

Demien cut in between the two as they stood glaring at each other. "Can we argue about this another time? Please?"

Meanwhile Uthan had pushed himself to his feet and run a few steps forward, reaching out with his right hand. In his mind he formed the image of the dagger sailing into his palm, fingers wrapping around the hilt with ease into a grip that felt so natural. With a gentle flick of his wrist, he caught the dagger and spun to face the Black Flame. For a moment the Fallen God was grinning. Then, slowly as he felt the presence of more dragon steel, his jaw dropped open in horror. Uthan ran the few paces between them and drove the blade deep into the Fallen God's chest, twisting it savagely as he did.

Jolts of invisible energy snaked along the blade, through the hilt and up into Uthan, throwing him into a series of violent seizures. As the Black Flame dropped to his knees, so did Uthan who was unable to let go of the weapon. His eyes rolled back in their sockets. Low-pitched wailing sounds filled the chamber as half seen, ghostly images rushed in a circle around Uthan and the Flame.

Shouldering one of the larger grotesque creatures aside, Diarus ran over to the young mage. He had got within a few feet when the raw, magical energy threw him back hard. Sitting up again, he looked at the violent display of power in front of him.

The Black Flame had disappeared completely while Uthan was on his knees, holding the dagger in an outstretched arm. His convulsions gradually stopped but blood was flowing from his nose and ears. Without the jolts of power holding him up, Uthan dropped forward as everything in the dark chamber went deathly silent. The loud clatter of the dagger blade on stone echoed off the walls.

Gauduin, Qwansien and Demien rushed across the floor helping Diarus up before moving over to check on Uthan. Gauduin pressed his stubby fingers to the young man's neck, checking for a pulse. His head dropped sadly and slowly he shook his head, unable to speak.

"He can't be," Qwan whispered.

"Whatever went through the dagger was too much," Gauduin said, choking back tears.

To herself, Demien muttered, "He will give us all freedom and in return take only death."

A sudden cracking sound from above made everyone look up while at the same time behind them, a piece of wall fell over, crashing into the middle of the floor in a cloud of dust. The entire fortress lurched, nearly throwing them from their feet.

Turning to his companions, Gauduin quietly said, "I think we should be leaving now."

He reached down for Uthan's body but felt nothing. Looking down he saw only the charred floor. Demien tapped him on the shoulder, pointing to one of the windows. The Four Elementals stood calmly waiting; Air held Uthan's limp body in his arms. Earth had his hand pressed against the wall, pushing a large chunk away and then watched it fall. A pillar swung down, broken at the base far below. The top hit something high above them, lodging against it and trapping the column at exactly the right place. It formed a makeshift path, running parallel to the outer wall. Nodding to Demien, the Elementals stepped out through the hole and dropped the few feet onto the makeshift walkway. The sky outside was thick with choking black smoke that curled up from the volcano below, while the stench of sulphur was carried on the wind.

Reaching for Gauduin's shoulder, she hauled him to his feet and half dragged him after the spirit warriors, gesturing for Diarus to follow. Qwan hurried after them, pausing only to retrieve the dragon steel dagger. At the inquisitive stares from the others, he shrugged and said, "We'd be really stupid to leave it here, wouldn't we."

Behind them, they did not see the charred necromancer, Carrion, getting to his feet and waving his hands at a few of the reincarnated soldiers.

Uthan's eyes snapped open. He was kneeling on dull grey stone, and a heavy mist hung in the air. Uthan looked around him but could see nothing other than the thick shroud of fog. He remembered the intense pain of the powerful magic surging through him, burning him from the inside out, then his mind was a blank. He looked down at his palms to see both carried burn marks and yet there was no longer any pain.

"You truly are a surprise," a voice said, distorted through the fog. Uthan flicked his head this way and that, trying to find the source of the voice. The mist hid the owner too well. Slowly a shape appeared which resolved itself into a dark figure walking towards him. A familiar voice said, "I thought destroying the plaything of my siblings would put an end to this."

Uthan pushed himself to his feet and asked, "Are we dead?"

The Black Flame laughed. "Gods do not die, you fool."

"So where are we?"

The laughter faded and the Flame glared at Uthan in disdain, "Between worlds. Not dead yet not alive."

"So I killed you after all," Uthan said, unable to hold a grin back.

The Flame surged forward and struck Uthan hard across the face. The young mage was sent sprawling to the cold stone floor again. Hissing, the Flame repeated, "Gods do not die!"

While Uthan struggled to his feet again, the Flame lashed out with a vicious kick. Uthan was flung high into the air before he crashed down again onto the stone. Pain flared in his ribs. Ignoring it, he stood up again and turned to face the Flame, except the Fallen God was not there. An overpowering sensation of fear stole over him but, keeping it in check, he declared, "So I'm trapped here then? And you're stuck here with me."

"If nothing else I can make your existence miserable," the Flame hissed, hidden within the mist again. "However, I really don't think I'll be requiring your presence for an hour much less eternity."

"And so you're going to try killing me here," Uthan muttered, more to himself than anyone else. He turned in a full circle, slowly, trying to pinpoint the direction of his enemy.

"Do you know what happens to a ghost when it is killed?" The Flame asked, conversationally. Uthan replied, saying that he did not. The Flame stalked out of the mists, almost running at Uthan. "They are sent into oblivion!"

"Then go there!" Uthan replied. He sidestepped the Flame and struck out with a punch. The air around his hand rippled with energy, dispersing the mist for a moment. The Flame was hit hard in the chest by the blast of unseen energy. He sprawled to the floor, sliding a few feet.

"So you've learned some tricks of your own quite quickly," the Flame said. The Fallen God rose to his feet and flicked out with both hands. Streamers of black energy were thrown from his fingertips, crackling against the mist. Uthan twisted away from one, only to be caught in the small of the back by another. As he hit the stone floor again, the Flame moved to stand over him, with a sneer he said, "And you're the same child who sent me here in the first place. Pathetic!"

More streams of the powerful black magic flayed into the young mage's body, causing him to cry out in pain. Uthan managed to roll onto his back. Gritting his teeth against the searing agony that threatened to overcome him, Uthan clutched at the Flame's ankle. The streams ceased as the Flame watched the mage with merciless eyes of black fire.

He reached down with one hand and grabbed Uthan round the throat. Holding the mage a foot above the ground, he sneered, "You were supposed to be the real Forged One. Did you know that? You, the Spirit Mage, were created by the Gods to rid their world of me."

"And I have done so," Uthan said, coughing and choking.

"No, all you've managed to do is lock me away for a while," the

Flame said, hurling Uthan away through the mist. When he next spoke, his words echoed, "And while you were at it you managed to annoy me."

In front of him, Uthan could see the mist swirling suddenly, as if a miniature tornado had started. Sparks of green crackled in the air around the swirl. The deafening silence was gone, replaced by the thunderous sounds of stone striking against stone and a constant thick bubbling sound. On the edge of his hearing he thought he could hear voices. They were so faint however that he could not make out any words or even whom the voices belonged to.

"Seems I won't be trapped here for long after all!" the Flame said, appearing suddenly behind Uthan. He drove a fist into the small of Uthan's back, moving past the mage as he dropped to his knees.

Something boiled deep in Uthan's body. He brought a hand up and grabbed the Flame's ankle. The Flame kicked the hand away in disgust and carried on walking for a few more steps before stopping and turning to look back at Uthan.

"I won't let you back there," Uthan growled.

"Is that so?" the Flame sneered. He stepped closer and brought his foot up in a hard kick. Uthan leant back, dodging the foot that would have hit him under the jaw. He stood up and punched the air again, sending an unseen energy bolt at the Flame. The Fallen God sidestepped the energy and grinned, "I think I can afford a few more moments to send you to oblivion first."

Uthan dodged under a flailing fist and ran towards the swirl. For a moment the Flame was stunned motionless. Then, as he realised what was happening, his face contorted into a snarl. He surged forwards, striking Uthan hard in the back. The blow was just enough to send the young mage sprawling into the swirling mist. With an anguished cry, the Flame snatched out a hand, grasping hold of the cloth of Uthan's tunic, trying desperately to follow.

Wind whipped up through a slender gap between the black stone pillar and the outside wall. It blew around the legs of the companions, threatening to send them plummeting to the hard rock below as the four clambered down the makeshift slope of a half fallen pillar. The sulphurous smell stung at their eyes, filling them with tears. Deep cracks formed in the pillar itself at their feet. Above them, the obsidian fortress was breaking apart. Great pieces of wall fell away from above, smashing to smaller pieces on the rock plateau below.

Every so often, they found they had to press themselves in as tight to the wall as they could to avoid being hit by falling rubble. It made their escape from the fortress take so much longer.

Twice during the descent, they had felt the pillar lurch violently, nearly throwing them off. On one of the lurches, Qwan had noticed it had not just been the column that moved but the great rock, holding the fortress in the air, had tilted. The Black Flame was dead and without his magic, his fortress was collapsing into the volcanic pit miles beneath.

They reached the base of the pillar and leapt down to the rock floor. Large cracks that looked like a drunken spider's web had formed at the base of it. Similar cracks ran across the walls, reaching up high enough to become almost invisible against the black stone. From above them they felt the falling of dust. Looking up, Qwan saw a large piece of wall break away, falling straight for them. He pushed them on several paces, stumbling on the trembling floor. Behind them, the wall crashed into the pillar base, breaking both into fragments and throwing up thick clouds of brown and grey dust. More pieces of stone rained down around them. Loud crashing sounds vibrated in the air, fighting with the bubbling of the lava for dominance. They looked around the rock for the Elementals, but the spirit warriors were no longer anywhere to be seen.

Dodging the falling rubble, Demien led them across the rough rock surface away from the building. As they reached the edge a blast of white-hot air knocked her back, making her eyes water, at the same time the rock tilted again. At the last possible second, Gauduin fell backwards, pulling the warrior woman with him. He wedged his heels against the rock, digging in to keep them from falling into the lava. The sickening smell of sulphur was even stronger in the clouds, making all four want to retch. It was as if their stomachs were being left behind as the rock dropped out of the air. Thick globules of viscous lava were flung skywards, landing around them, as the rock sank into the molten depths.

Further behind, six soldiers appeared from the wreckage of the palace alongside Carrion. Their crunching footsteps were barely heard over the heavy churning of the volcano below. Diarus was the first to see them and drew his falchions as he bellowed a challenge. The soldiers picked their way across the lurching rock, showing uncanny balance.

Turning to the others, Diarus said, "Find a way down quickly,

I'll take care of these things."

Before they could reply, he had bounded across to the soulless soldiers and began trading attacks with them. The sound of rock breaking brought Demien's attention to the ground in front of her. Cracks were widening throughout the rock, effectively cutting off the area they stood on from the rest. She looked around in a hurry as the rest of it began to fall away leaving their small area almost floating in the air. She yelled for Diarus.

The Daiharlon looked around to see a tide of lava beginning to wash over what was until now the floating rock. He hammered a large right hand into the closest of the soldiers and turned away. Another of the men took the chance to plunge his blade into Diarus's back. In response, the Daiharlon whipped round and smashed his forearm into the soldier's chest. The man crumpled into a heap. He reached back for the sword and pulled it free with a loud gasp of pain. Almost immediately he dropped to one knee, unable to stand. In the periphery of his vision he saw another of the soldiers loom over him, sword held high for the killing blow.

A flash of metal made Diarus turn to his left sluggishly. Qwan stood there, his sword held in an outstretched hand, piercing the throat of the soldier. Ripping the blade clear again, the elf looked down at Diarus and offered his hand while saying, "I think we have someone helping us!"

With Qwan on one side and Gauduin on the other, Diarus was aided towards the floating island. The main rock sank further into the volcano, forcing rivers of burning magma over the sides and down to the lands below. The soldiers continued their march towards the companions, intent on slaying them rather than escape the lava. A heavy tremor shook the rock, knocking them from their feet. One end began to sink further, turning the whole rock on its side. Without making a sound, the soldiers slid across the surface and into the molten lava. From the relative safety of their own floating island, the companions watched the Black Flame's palace disappearing once and for all.

Chapter Thirty-One

The companions were not surprised when their floating island had begun its descent to the ground. Looking over the edge, they had caught sight of a group of figures waiting for them. One appeared to be kneeling on the ground, looking up towards them. Tears stung their eyes from the smoky air they had left behind, making it hard for them to make out any details. It was only when they were close to the ground they could see who the figures were.

Air stood patiently, hands outstretched to them, using his power to lower the floating rock carefully to the ground. Close by stood Fire, Water and Earth, in a triangular pattern, guarding the kneeling figure. The sight of him brought gasps of shock from the four. Demien leapt nimbly from the rock and ran the last few paces to grasp Uthan in a powerful embrace.

"We thought you were dead," she laughed.

For a moment the young mage's features seemed to flow across his face like liquid. As Demien looked at him, she felt momentarily queasy, seeing the shift of his face. Gradually his own features seemed to fully assert themselves again and once more he was the Uthan they knew. Gulping down deep breaths, he simply replied, "I was."

"Well you look healthy for a dead man," Qwan laughed loudly. "That was a timely and impressive rescue. Thank you."

With a grin, Uthan answered, "Well you missed much of the journey going up. I thought you should at least get to see it coming down."

Turning to look back at the volcano, Gauduin said, "We did it, didn't we. We actually killed the Fallen God."

"Good for you," said a sneering voice inside Uthan's mind.

The mage started, looking around hurriedly. His friends noticed the sudden movement. He shrugged off Demien's enquiry saying,

"I just thought I heard something."

"*Oh it's much more ironic than that, boy,*" the Black Flame said. "*I'm inside you.*"

With robes that still smouldered from a multitude of lava burns, Carrion made his way across the dusty plains. He had not stopped to witness his last few remaining soldiers being engulfed by the volcano, but the thunderous churning sound of the ruined palace being swallowed by lava was still ringing in his ears. His escape had been far luckier than he wanted to believe. As the immense rock had lurched violently, he had been thrown into the air. One of the small dragons had swooped in close and inadvertently plucked him to safety. Using a minor mind spell, the necromancer had been able to control the beast, enabling him to escape the volcano. He had been dropped a short distance away from Kael before the dragon had just soared away, screaming its displeasure at being used instead of enjoying a meal of the necromancer.

His lungs felt as if they were on fire when he reached the first smoky ruins on the outskirts of Kael. He came to a stop, leaning against the dark, dust covered stone. Through the smoke clouds, he caught sight of several shapes moving carefully between the walls and pillars. He slid down the stone, hoping the Haunters had not scented him and knowing he had very little strength left even if they did. With an almost exaggerated sense of caution, Carrion moved away from the pillar and crept across the ground. He was grateful for the thick carpet of grey and brown dust since it dulled his crunching footfalls while the thick clouds of grey and black smoke that belched from Kael's broken ground hid him perfectly.

Suddenly aware of movement close behind him, Carrion broke out into a run, dodging behind collapsed walls and under ancient archways. He ducked through a tunnel made from two sections of wall that had long ago fallen into each other. Crouching in the darkness, he waited, trying to summon up enough stamina to cast some magic. From outside, the sound of movement was everywhere. Letting the surge of raw magic power build up inside him, Carrion walked out into the open. Tendrils of black and red energy crawled over him, in and out of his robes, spilling out from inside his dark hollow eyes and mouth.

Almost immediately, a huge gauntleted hand snatched out, metal-clad fingers closing around the necromancer's throat. Pulling Carrion in close to a large helm that was stained a dull green colour, Meligonn thundered, "Where are they?"

The companions rode on towards Kael in high spirits. Demien, Diarus, Gauduin and Qwansien chatted heartily, despite the fatigue in their limbs. Riding at the back of the group was Uthan. Rather than the jubilation expressed by his friends, he was wrapped in a dull sensation of despair. He rode with his head bowed low, staring distantly at the pommel of his saddle rather than the plains in front of him. The sensations of power he felt inside were daunting and overwhelming while at the same time there was a faint feeling of ecstasy.

"Enjoy the power while you have it," The Flame seethed. The Fallen God imprisoned in his head had been far from silent.

Uthan did not answer. He wondered briefly if it was possible to ignore the voice whose words bounced around inside his mind. He had heard enough of the Flame's curses, threats and promises by now.

"They're talking to you, boy!" the Flame announced, cutting through the veil of thoughts in his mind.

The mage glanced up to see his four companions sitting in the saddle, looking at him. Having got Uthan's attention, Qwan asked, "Do you want to cut right through Kael or take the long way round?"

"I just want to get home," Uthan answered grimly. He looked at the shadowy ruins before them. A shudder rolled through him at the memory of the macabre trophies of the Haunters. For a brief moment he considered changing his mind and taking the longer route but the taunting from the Fallen God had put a decisive end to those thoughts.

The horses shied away from the heavy cover of sulphurous cloud at first and the ground underfoot was treacherous. The carpet of volcanic dust hid numerous holes and pieces of sharp stone. The companions dismounted, choosing to lead their horses through rather than risk a fall. They had not gone far when the sounds of movement surrounded them.

"Haunters?" Demien asked, remembering with a shiver the last time she had met the demons.

"Oh far from it," the Flame said. Uthan imagined the words to be accompanied by an insane grin. *"General Meligonn is here with his horde. Let's see you escape this time, boy."*

From the smoke-filled shadows of a cluster of broken walls, a pair of large, armoured warriors surged forwards. Qwan met them head-on, firing a crossbow bolt into the visor of the first. While that one toppled to the ground, the second ducked his head. From Qwan's right, Diarus ran in, falchions coming down onto the back of the armoured neck. The sheer force of the blow rang out loudly, echoing through the ruins as the warrior fell flat to the dust, groggily trying to rise again. With both hands on the hilt of his wide bladed sword, Gauduin drove the tip of the weapon clean through the heavy armour.

"Definitely not Haunters," Demien said, dryly.

Uthan rocked on his heels, suddenly giving in to dizziness. He placed two fingers to his top lip, withdrawing them again to see a dark red stain. His head swam and his stomach rolled, then with a barely suppressed moan he pitched over backwards into the dirt.

Running to the mage's side, Gauduin quickly checked for a pulse. The others took up a defensive position around them, watching for more of Meligonn's hoard. Catching sight of shadows flitting through the smoke clouds close by, Qwan muttered, "This really is not a good time, Uthan."

"I don't think he can hear us," Gauduin said, his concern etched on his face.

"Really not a good time," Qwan repeated with more emphasis.

Uthan's eyes opened to see the Flame standing before him; both of them were surrounded by nothing but mist and grey stone.

"Back here again!" the Flame said, with a broad grin as streams of black fire shot from the Fallen God's palms, wrapping themselves around Uthan's body. The mage cried out as the magical fire burned his flesh. "You didn't honestly think I could just sit back and ride as a passenger throughout your mundane existence, did you?"

"So what are you going to do?" Uthan said through gritted teeth.

"I'm going to kill you," the Flame answered. The black fire in his eyes seemed to grow darker with his anger, "You really don't need to be a prophet to have seen that coming."

"The beastmen have left," Targy announced, emerging from behind a fallen archway. They all turned to him as he approached and then sat cross-legged beside Uthan's prone form. "The iron warriors remain."

"Why did the others go?" Demien asked, squinting through the smoke, trying to see the enemy.

Targy shrugged, "Haunters still dwell here. The beastmen fear the Haunters. They have learned the dark man has gone from the world and so they choose to abandon the iron warriors."

"You're certain?" Qwan asked. The elf was passing his sword hilt from hand to hand, anxiously waiting for an opponent.

"Saw them go," Targy said with a nod. He looked down at Uthan, and then, laying two fingers on the mage's forehead, he said, "Defend us. I will help the Forged One."

"The Forged One?" Gauduin asked as his confusion was mirrored on the other faces around him. "What are you talking about?"

"The boy has been Forged by destiny. He is the true Forged One." Targy replied. As Gauduin was about to ask something else, the jungle dweller placed a finger to his lips and said, "More iron warriors come this way. Defend us."

There was no chance for any of them to reply as the huge, hulking forms of Meligonn's armoured warriors loomed out from the fog. Almost to himself, Qwan muttered, "It never ends."

"Save your breath for the fight," Gauduin said. The dwarf shifted his weight from foot to foot, testing his balance while he glanced from opponent to opponent, sizing them up and thinking of the best way to attack. A sideways glance at Qwan told him the elf was doing the same.

The bulky warriors were emerging from the smoke all around them; their thick steel plate was dull grey green in colour. Spots of rust and decay were visible here and there. These tarnished areas seemed to be the only way to make out individual warriors. Each held a great double-headed axe in huge hands that looked like they could crush a head easily. They moved forward slowly, knowing they had their prey trapped and were obviously in no rush to end it.

"If anyone sees a good way out of this I'd like to hear it," Demien said, looking straight into the pinpoints of red that shone from behind the slit of the warriors' visors.

"Isn't it obvious?" Qwan answered, without his usual mirth. "We fight!"

"And most likely die," Gauduin added.

"No one should want to live forever," Qwan replied simply.

Demien snorted, "I'm not dying today."

"Then shut up and fight!" Diarus roared suddenly. He sprang forward with one falchion raised high. The blade clashed hard against the side of an armoured head, the metal ringing like a bell. As the warrior stumbled back, stunned from the blow, others flooded in to take his place in the circle.

Uthan hung in the air, held by strands of black fire that were wrapped around him, squeezing and burning him. He felt a strange buzzing sensation inside his skull that became overpowering, causing him to struggle for breath. The Flame stood before him, watching him with a distant curiosity, like he was dissecting an insect.

"I would have thought the Gods would have made you a lot tougher," the Flame said detachedly.

"He beat you and trapped you here," a voice said from behind them. The Flame spun round, snarling in rage. Over his shoulder, Uthan saw the owner of the voice was Targy.

"I might have known you'd turn up!" The Flame retorted. "Have you come to finish what your kind started all those years ago?"

Targy's eyes reflected the sadness of his words as he said, "Years ago you made my kind slaves. You killed us. You drove us into the jungles."

"And still you return here to make my ears bleed with your self-pity," the Flame replied. He began stalking towards Targy in a slow circle but the small jungle creature remained still, merely watching the Fallen God who hissed at him, "You shouldn't have crawled out from amongst your precious trees."

The strands of magic around Uthan loosened. Focusing all his concentration on them, the mage made them fade and become insubstantial, one by one. He looked at his arms. The flesh was seared and blackened causing a stench that was overpowering. Uthan felt his stomach churn at the smell and fought to control himself. As if he knew the mage was free, the Flame looked over his shoulder.

"Uthan, if you lose here, you lose everywhere," Targy said simply.

The Flame put a finger to his lips mockingly, "Don't tell him. It'll spoil the surprise."

"What do you mean if I lose here?" Uthan asked, watching the Flame while talking to Targy.

"He means," interrupted the Flame, "if I kill you here, I win after all and have a new body."

"Then I have to make sure that doesn't happen," Uthan replied.

"Now, it's about time you showed me what you're made of," the Flame said as if issuing a challenge.

He threw his arms forward, sending more streams of black fire to engulf Uthan. The young mage stood still as they wrapped themselves around him again, lifting him into the air. Uthan closed his eyes and clenched his jaw muscles as the streams tightened around his chest and stomach, crushing him. He let out a long deep breath and snapped his eyes open. The Flame took a step back involuntarily, looking straight into Uthan's eyes, which were now glowing a brilliant, ice blue. The air around him crackled and buzzed with power. The Flame glanced from Uthan to Targy, the jungle dweller's eyes were the same glowing blue. The black streams around Uthan disintegrated and the mage hung, statue still in the air.

The Flame snorted derisively and said, "More parlour tricks? I'm disappointed."

In response, Uthan's hands came up. Crackling with sparks of shimmering, blue energy, he unleashed magical streams of his own at the Flame. The Fallen God easily moved to one side, letting the energy sail harmlessly by. But as he opened his mouth to make a sneering comment, the energy swirled back round and caught him. The Flame struggled violently, trying to break free of the bright blue that snaked around him. Uthan's voice rumbled with tremendous power as he said, "Your brothers and sisters decided long ago you were to be removed from the circle. Your destructive path could not be tolerated, so they created me."

"And you're going to try and kill me now?" the Flame roared, his rage boiling over. "You're to send me into oblivion?"

"No," Uthan replied, his voice resonating as he continued, "the Gods do not want that."

"Then that will be their undoing," the Flame sneered. "I will escape your mind, boy! I will be reborn!"

"Not for many years at least," Uthan replied as he lowered himself to the stone floor and paced across to stand before his enemy. Standing toe to toe with the writhing Black Flame, Uthan, who now towered over the Fallen God having grown in stature, stared down at him, with eyes that held infinite power. He reached out with both hands, clasping the sides of the Flame's pale head. As the Fallen God howled in his fury, Uthan said, "For now you will simply lie dormant."

The Flame faded into the blue energy, dissolving until all that was left was Uthan's magic that he absorbed back into himself, soaking it up through his hands as the blue glow in his eyes faded and they returned to normal. Staring in front of him distantly, he asked Targy what had happened.

"You must wake and destroy the iron warriors," the jungle dweller said gently, standing before Uthan. "You have defeated the Black Flame."

The circle of armoured warriors slowly tightened around the companions. The travellers drew back together, standing over Uthan and Targy. A few of them had been dispatched, but the thick armour was almost impossible to penetrate so more had been merely stunned rather than slain. Diarus was bleeding from a deep gash across his back and blood poured from Qwan's forehead, running down into his eyes. He kept wiping a forearm across his head, trying to clear the blood away. Luckily Gauduin and Demien had managed to escape with only a few minor cuts between them but all four were weary. Their movements were becoming sluggish as they fought a second battle fatigue.

"So this is it?" Gauduin asked, through deep ragged breaths.

"Just like we always thought it would be," Qwan replied. "We die fighting."

"Shame really," the dwarf answered, "I was getting used to the idea that we were winning this."

"Charge on three?" Qwan asked.

"Don't see why not."

"Let's just get it over with," Demien snapped, looking from warrior to warrior.

The three of them glanced at Diarus; the giant Daiharlon flexed and rolled his shoulders, loosening the muscles. Cracking his neck, he growled, "This will be my glory; the time to join my ancestor."

As one, the armoured warriors silently brought their axes up, ready to deal the deathblows. But then there was movement from inside the companion's defensive circle; Uthan and Targy both stood up. Staring into the distance, the mage announced, "Get ready to run."

"Which way?" Gauduin asked, shooting a puzzled glance around him. "We're surrounded."

With a dark smile, Uthan replied, "Not for long."

Behind the armoured warriors there was more movement. Shadowy figures loomed up from the dust and out from behind the ruins. As they came closer to the iron warriors, the companions could see the hideous, flayed bodies covered in torn leather straps and plastered with dried crimson stains.

"Oh, just great," Demien muttered, "as if we didn't have enough to deal with."

Uthan continued to stare into space as the armoured warriors turned to look at the Haunters appearing around them. For a few moments, the warriors stared curiously at the blinded and bound faces, unsure why the demons had arrived. Then, in one fluid wave of raw, blood smeared flesh, the demons surged at the warriors. They tore at the armour plates, ripping and twisting the steel. They knocked iron warriors from their feet, raining blow after blow down onto the thick steel armour. Talons gouged and teeth bit. A few of the warriors, who were quicker than their comrades, were able to defend themselves. A heavy axe bit deeply into the leather clad chest of one Haunter, while another of the demons had his head lopped off. As the scene descended into chaotic slaughter, the companions turned to Uthan, who with a definite nod, turned on his heel and fled through the smoke.

They stopped at the edge of Kael, pausing within the trees to catch their breath. Qwan clapped Uthan on the shoulder and grinned, "Now that was the kind of timing that will earn you a place in legends for centuries to come."

Diarus took a couple of steps back towards Kael. He stared calmly through the swirling clouds of thick, grey smoke as a gentle breeze travelled through the ruins. With a loud roar, another of the heavyset warriors leapt from the shadows of a broken wall. Diarus sidestepped, letting the great axe slam into the ground instead of his head. The Daiharlon drove his arm into the back of the warrior's helm, knocking him off balance. While the iron warrior blundered forward, Diarus leapt on his back and drove him to the ground. Jamming his fingertips into the visor, Diarus pulled the large, helmed head back. The sound of bones cracking echoed as the warrior's thick neck was effortlessly broken. Releasing a deep breath, Diarus stood up again, threw his head back and let out a loud triumphant bellow.

A wicked-looking sword blade burst through his chest, turning

Diarus's triumphant expression to one of shock, then gradually into pain. He looked down at the steel protruding from his ribs, then a huge, metal clad hand clamped over his shoulder. There was a distinct, wet sucking sound as the blade was pulled free before the Daiharlon dropped to his knees, staring in bewilderment at the blood pooling before him. General Meligonn stood coolly holding his heavy sword in one huge hand, the tip now pointing at the ground. Placing his other hand casually against the side of Diarus's head, Meligonn pushed the dying beastman aside. Diarus stared blankly ahead, his life fading away before his head hit the ground. The companions were stunned into silence.

Then, bellowing a loud roar of anger, Gauduin stormed forward. He brought his sword up, ready to cleave through the heavily armoured general. Meligonn easily sidestepped the attack and allowed Gauduin to move past but Qwan had been right on the dwarf's heels. The elf lunged forward with the tip of his sword ready to drive through the general's visor. Meligonn's large blade swept up, leaving a trail of Diarus's blood behind it. The clang of steel on steel rang out as the skewering attack was easily blocked. An armoured boot came up, the sole slamming into Qwan's chest and the winded elf was thrown to the ground.

"And he chooses now to strike," the Flame's voice sneered from deep inside Uthan's mind. *"Just typical really."*

The words were accompanied by a strange buzzing feeling in the back of the mage's skull. He shook his head furiously, trying to clear the fog that overwhelmed him. Using the inner voice of his mind, Uthan replied, "I thought you'd gone."

"Oh, I'll always be here, boy," the Flame replied, *"you can't get rid of me. You're my prison."*

Demien had run at Meligonn. The two sparred as she desperately sought to find a way through the general's guard. Each thrust, slash or chop from the swordswoman was blocked by Meligonn's great sword or repelled by the thick steel plate. With one gigantic arm, Meligonn sent Demien sprawling.

"I guess we'll have to deal with him," the Flame said.

"We?" Uthan replied.

"Yes, we," the Flame answered. *"I may as well play along for the*

time being since I am trapped here. If you die, it could be the end of me!"

Meligonn stepped over the prone form of Demien, picking his way towards Uthan. He held his sword out in front of him, the point of the large blade directed right at the young mage's face. Uthan raised his arms, showing the general he was unarmed. There was a deep, metallic sounding snort from inside Meligonn's helmet. He brought his weapon up over his shoulder, about to deliver a deathblow. With a quick grin, Uthan brought up a hand, palm out. An unseen energy hammered into the general's armoured chest and the solid breastplate crumpled under the force. Meligonn was hurled from his feet, rolling backwards, head over heels. Uthan calmly strode over, closing the distance between himself and the general. He made a clutching gesture in the air and Meligonn was plucked from the ground by unseen hands and hurled far into the ruins of Kael.

"Now we destroy the Dead City," the Flame said.

"How?" Uthan asked.

He felt he could sense the Flame grinning maliciously as the voice said, *"Like this."*

"And I'm just to go along with your plan?" Uthan demanded.

"The spell is called Godsfire; Kael will be cleansed in flames. I find the whole idea vaguely ironic really," the Flame answered.

Uthan glanced at Targy, the jungle dweller, who nodded his approval before moving over to help Gauduin, Qwansien and Demien further into the trees. Uthan listened to the words of power being spoken inside his head. Several of them were whispered, only half heard but they caused his skull to begin to feel heavy. Deep inside him, Uthan felt rather than heard the words as he repeated them, many of which he did not even understand. He felt their power resonating in every fibre of his body.

Pillars of searing white flames, intermixed with blue, red, purple and black dropped from the sky above. They slammed down into Kael with terrifying force. Choking clouds of the thick, grey dust billowed high into the air. The smoke from the exposed lava pits was blown away and for the briefest of moments, Uthan could see the ruins of Kael in their entirety. The fire splashed over the ruins as if it was liquid, burning the gruesome trophies of the Haunters instantly, the stench of burnt flesh was caught in the air. The ground was like a giant drum, being pounded over and over by the magical fires. Uthan caught sight of a pair of Meligonn's armoured soldiers making their way over to where he had seen the general come to rest. A pillar of flame landed directly on them, driving them both into the dust. Mere moments later, the thick clouds that had gathered above Kael dissipated and the Godsfire spell ceased.

Uthan looked out at the ruins; there was very little left standing. Tendrils of greasy, black smoke curled up from the remnants of stone pillars and walls. Many of the larger stone blocks had melted completely, the resulting molten rock feeding the lava pools that had grown in size while massive craters pockmarked the ground. There was no movement in the ruined city and speaking to himself, Uthan asked, "Is that it now? Is it all over?"

"For now it is," the Flame muttered.

Epilogue

Uthan sat in his makeshift room staring at the shining dagger of dragon steel he had used to kill the Black Flame. Qwansien had told him it was his trophy and should be kept to represent one of the greatest victories for the Empire. He wanted to keep it, but knew he could not because he could feel tiny pinpricks in the palm of his hand as he had reached out for the hilt. Touching the dagger hurt the Black Flame inside him; as a result, Uthan felt the pain too.

He had sat earlier at a large table in the ramshackle room that had been made into a serviceable common room at Dessendor, mostly thanks to Boron. Cass had sat next to him, her arm around his shoulders as Demien, Qwansien, Gauduin, Boron and Serriman had joined them. All the wounded had healed enough a while back to leave for Dacenhiem, but Cass had insisted the others stayed behind to wait for their friends. However they had still been stunned the day that the four of them had walked their horses through the ruined gateway of Dessendor. The grief of Diarus's death despite being shared, was still too raw for all of them; the journey back and the joy at the defeat of the Black Flame had been marred by their loss.

Uthan's head still swam with the buzz of their conversation. Gauduin intended on returning to his woodland cottage and get some much needed peace. The others had all decided on travelling to Dacenheim for their own various reasons. Serriman's hope was to return Dessendor to its former glory. He planned on recruiting as many builders as he could. Uthan had been the only one not to talk about his future plans. He had thought about where he would go or what he would do now. In both their eyes and words, Uthan could tell he was expected to go with them to Dacenheim. The lure of the capital city was strong after the sweltering jungles, the searing plains and the choking volcanic dust. The bustle of civilised Dacenheim was indeed tempting.

A familiar blue glow filled Uthan's room slowly. Dionis hung in the air, watching the young mage in admiration. "So you're the true

Forged One. I didn't think to ever see a prophecy fulfilled."

"And to think I was a mere apprentice patching people up after tavern brawls only a year ago," Uthan replied with a nod.

"And now you're possibly the most powerful mage in the Empire," Dionis replied, then paused before asking, "What's it like?"

"Having him in here?" Uthan asked, tapping the side of his head.

As Dionis nodded, Uthan explained, "It's strange, I can feel the constant buzzing of magic in me but it feels like the power itself is just out of my reach. I can hear him talking to me and that in itself is unnerving."

"Do the others know?"

Uthan shook his head, "I'm not sure how they'll react to me and what's inside me. I'm not sure how I am reacting to it really. I just don't want to see them being disappointed with me."

"You're their friend," Dionis said calmly. "They'll understand."

"Maybe," was all Uthan could say. He stood up and reached for his pack. For a moment his gaze fell longingly on the dagger. Sadly, he shook his head and turned away from the weapon, starting toward the door.

"Where will you go?"

"The Black Flame will try to escape. At least, I can't imagine a Fallen God intending to stay imprisoned forever. I need to be prepared for when he tries to," Uthan explained.

"You're going to look for Targy?" Dionis asked. Catching the look in Uthan's eye, he added, "Take care, you know the Demonic Realm isn't easily travelled!"

Uthan smiled again before walking out into the courtyard where the evening air was cool against his face.

"*So touching,*" the Flame mocked from the dark recesses of Uthan's mind. "*I thought for a second I might actually start crying there.*"

Ignoring the voice, Uthan slipped through the broken gates of Dessendor and out into the night.

"*Not going east?*" the Flame asked, noting the direction Uthan had taken.

"Not right away, I have to go and pay my respects to the people of a good friend."

"*The Daiharlon?*"

"His name was Diarus Huhrn," Uthan answered. The moon shone down on the field around him. Not too far from where he stood, a rabbit lazily hopped across the grass. He stopped to watch it; then, glancing back at the sleeping fortress, he had a momentary pang of regret at leaving.

"You know the bat is going to tell them the truth, don't you?" the Flame muttered casually.

"I know," sighed Uthan.

To the Memory of David Gemmell

The greatest of storytellers, may the inspiration you created bring many more along this path

Printed in the United Kingdom
by Lightning Source UK Ltd.
120438UK00001B/37-57